THE EXPERIENCING OF
MUSICAL SOUND

MUSICOLOGY SERIES
Edited by F. Joseph Smith

Other volumes in preparation

Also by F. Joseph Smith

In Search of Musical Method
Phenomenology in Perspective
Facets of Eros (with E. Eng)
A Commentary on the Speculum Musicae,
    In-the-World and On-the-Earth (3 vols)

THE EXPERIENCING OF MUSICAL SOUND

Prelude to a Phenomenology of Music

F. Joseph Smith

GORDON AND BREACH

New York   London   Paris

Copyright © 1979 Gordon and Breach Science Publishers, Inc.

Gordon and Breach Science Publishers, Inc.
One Park Avenue
New York, NY 10016

Gordon and Breach Science Publishers Ltd.
42 William IV Street
London WC2 4DF

Gordon & Breach
7-9 rue Emile Dubois
Paris 75014

Library of Congress Cataloging in Publication Data

Smith, F. Joseph.
    The experiencing of musical sound.

    1.   Music — Acoustics and physics. I.   Title.
ML3805.S58   781'.22   77-18591
ISBN 0—677—04430—5

Printed in Great Britain by offset lithography by
Billing & Sons Ltd, Guildford, London and Worcester

Library of Congress catalog number 77—18591. ISBN 0 677 04430 5.

CONTENTS

In Memory of Our Son
IAN EDWARD
1976

INTRODUCTION

This book represents the work done by its author to begin to lay the ground musically and philosophically for enormous tasks that still remain to be done and may require a team of researchers in various fields relating to experiential phenomena. Coming from a background of musicological studies as well as active musical performance, the author's orientation is different from that of the professional philosopher as such, who is apt to understand sound phenomena in more generalized manner rather than addressing himself to specifics in music and music theory. These essays trace the path taken by the author in the last years and are studies that were a necessary prelude to a systematic work on the philosophy of musical sound, a work that is in preparation.

Most important has been the attempt to show the qualitative steps taken from Helmholtz through German and French phenomenology to the beginnings of a dialectic of musical sound. To understand the author, this trajectory should prove helpful. Carl Stumpf is revealed in this process as crucial to both musicology and philosophy. The laying bare of the experiential stratum beneath the categorial is essential to phenomenology, but the continuation of the reductive process in a more convincing dialectic is also envisioned. Implications for music education and seminars in sound is traced in detail, and the relevance of music to general society is underscored.

The fact that a phenomenological approach to experience, while an obvious improvement over a flat categorial or scholastic bias, is still caught transitionally in a kind of subjective idealism, serves to underline the provisional nature of the process we are all in, when it comes to western

THE EXPERIENCING OF MUSICAL SOUND   viii

thought. To deny that we are indeed in process to a more
realistic philosophy, a dialectic that takes in more than the
individual subject and even his intersubjective consciousness,
is not to see what has been happening. For the musician this
process must bring with it the emergence of a genuine social
consciousness in which music serves a crucial role. The
musician is more than an entertainer or one who merely
exults in his own experience of musical sound. The social
impulse within us must also gain expression in musical works
that get beyond the narrow ego base of careerism or indivi-
dualism. The world that is offstage is a real one, a hard one to
work and live in within its present limitations. The social
consciousness of the muser and the music-maker experiences
this materiality as well as the "spirituality" of his art. He
needs a philosophy that does more than observe or analyze
the world. These essays indicate many a tentative step taken
to open up the situation, philosophically and musically. But
they also clearly delineate the author's false probings, as well
as worthwhile leads he may have begun to develop. That is
the chief reason for calling these studies a prelude or prolegomenon to a philosophy of musical sound. Hence the need for
an opening onto dialectical thought, initiated by Sartre. But
even Sartre projects society from the individuality of the
subject, and his dialectic falters precisely to that extent. A
true and down-to-earth intersubjectivity will have to overcome phenomenology itself as represented even in some of its
best socially-minded authors. That this is implied, but barely
begun in these pages, will be obvious to the reader. After the
prelude must come the work itself, and this is in fact the
current preoccupation of this writer; but it must be a work
carefully thought out.

Finally, this text ought to be useful in seminars, as it
was for my many students and myself, in both philosophy
and music. As a background text for live existential work-
shops in sound, these essays can abet the effort to address
ourselves to musical experience as such, thus entering more
surely into music itself, rather than into abstract thought
about music. That musicology must show the way toward

musical experience, as well as history, is clearly pointed out. But music can never be allowed to lead away from life, and is in fact a crucial part of our present life struggle.

F. Joseph Smith
Chicago

Chapter 1

PRELUDE TO A PHENOMONOLOGY OF MUSIC

The scholarly world of today is beginning to see the need of getting away from over-specialization, and this is also true of the field of both philosophy and of musicology. It is in a spirit of openness that the author submits the following philosophical critique of musicology. As serious musicians and scholars we ought to be open to the horizons that lie beyond the historical dimension and current musicological method — beyond what Husserl would have called a "material ontology" — however important all of this may have been in the past.

We might be tempted to agree to a great extent with Carroll C. Pratt, who in *Musicology and Related Disciplines* states.† 1

The wide influence which philosophy has always had in the history of human thought and culture justifies a more important place than of late it has enjoyed in the American scheme of instruction. It may be owing to the current neglect of philosophy that musicologists have been far more historical than philosophical in the way they have approached their special studies.

Musicologists, in particular, if they are to fulfill their role as teachers of a great liberal art to a generation of students who have picked up on the run a formidable acquaintance with music of all kinds and descriptions, need in the classroom the wisdom of philosophy more than the facts of specialized research, however important these latter may be in their proper place.

What Pratt is talking about, of course, is in no sense a neglect of rigorous scientific training in musicological research but a putting into perspective of the vast materials of musical research and knowledge, which people actually must and do

---

† Numbered notes are collected at the end of each chapter.

11

acquire. Certainly we can never have recourse to the philosophical dimension of musicology simply as an escape from the hard work that goes with the study, e.g. of the history of musical notation — against a background and analysis of the pertinent historical treatises from medieval times through the renaissance and the baroque. For such a study, however, there is required a knowledge not just of the philosophical perspective these documents often give us, but also of the several languages in which they were written. That is perhaps the fascination of the study. Otherwise, it might become sheer scientific drudgery. All of this means a serious study of music and musicology. And this seriousness of purpose can never be labeled mere "severity," as J. Westrup has pointed out.[2]

I

More than ever before interdisciplinary give-and-take is required, since it may be the only way we are going to be able to effect the vast new synthesis of knowledge, which is perhaps *the* task and responsibility of academia today. In this new synthesis musicology will take its honored place among the arts and sciences in western culture and world culture as well. But how can this be accomplished without a *philosophical* dimension? H. Hüschen brought this out in his paper, "Past and present concepts of the nature and limits of music."[3]

Perhaps a look at the definition of musicology is in place. W. Apel regards the main task of musicology to be constant and thorough research into the history and literature of music.[4] All of us, who have struggled manfully through his history of musical notation together with the manuscripts and treatises that form its background, know full well what an important task that is. In his essay on musicology in American institutions of higher learning the late M. Bukofzer points to historical studies and stylistic criticism as the central occupation of musicology today. The study of musical esthetics is also regarded as a musicological approach.[5] Yet, though this can indeed deepen and broaden our appreciation of music as an art, it is especially here that the philosophical dimension is necessary.

Can we speak of new "philosophical" horizons in musicology? If so, we must first look to a definition of musicology as we know it now. Yet, what is a definition of anything? Are things really definable at all? Or to what extent? Will we ever be able to give a closed definition of musicology and its area of competence and, if we do so, is there ever any hope of incorporating it into a "philosophy of culture"? Rather, ought we not attempt to give horizon rather than "definition" to our speciality? The ordinary definition of anything, including music, usually defines and at the same time unduly confines the subject. It thus blocks the eventual *interdisciplinary fusion* that must take place, in order that the various specialties and their corresponding university departments do not become compartments, but rather that they eventually open out onto one another and onto the cultural foundations of western and world civilization. As things stand, however, departments have become estranged from one another, and sometimes one dare not be interdepartmental or risk the wrath of the whole system. This is, of course, difficult to comprehend, especially when the student has been enjoined to study two minor subjects along with his major. If the student actually becomes competent in one or both of his minors, why should this be cause for alarm? And if one of his minors emerges as another major, surely this should be a cause for rejoicing. But too often the situation is otherwise. This is a typical case of rigid categorizing, which can become an effective though unconvincing attempt to escape the interdepartmental and interspecialty problem. It also proves to be psychologically useful in overcoming the anxieties that an interdepartmental challenge inevitably causes.

However that may be, a philosophical definition of anything — at least from the perspective of phenomenology[6] — does not define and thus confine, close in, or shut off the subjects under discussion. Rather, a definition of something should open out onto horizons and into the situation of the other, however frightening this might seem to be. A definition means this also for the pre-Platonic Greeks, whose word, *horizō*, means not "to define," as we have translated it, but "to give boundary to something." This boundary was not conceived as shutting off but as a "horizon" that beckoned. Only in giving horizons to a thing and in discovering ever new horizons can we hope to merge our various perspectives of reality, academic and otherwise, into one meaningful culture.

And surely the history of music shows us this tendency to reach out for ever new horizons. Especially in music the word, new, is of particular importance. It is perhaps only in this field that the newness of an area is so emphasized, that we name a new era *ars nova, nuove musiche,* or *neue musik.* Of course, this can be and has been overdone. The late L. Schrade complained of the extension of the term *ars nova* beyond the small area of fourteenth century music it actually stands for.[7] U. Günther has brought this out again in a recent article in *Die Musikforschung.*[8] A. Schoenberg actually became caustic in *Style and Idea* about the journalistic use of the term *neue musik,*[9] just as P. Hindemith complained of the term, *Gebrauchsmusik.*[10] But it is only the journalistic minded that abuse terms. And even a good journalist knows when to stop. Musicologists and philosophers have learned to be more cautious, because they realize the importance of the concept of newness and the meaningful competence of terms. They may be tempted to agree with Jacques de Liège, that not absolutely everything new is automatically good.[11] We do not want to be guilty of what A. Liess in his biography of C. Orff calls in "historicism of the present."[12] And surely it is only a philosophico-musicological seriousness that can prevent us from becoming too rash in submitting uncritically to the dichotomy of new-old. C. Orff mentions that he makes use of old materials in his compositions not because they are old but because they are valid.[13] A philosophical validity factor should be our musical loadstone — not archaicism or mere novelty. But this is not the validity factor of traditional

value philosophies. Rather, we speak from a phenomenological perspective and outlook. This means an overcoming of
traditional values. Horizons are what lend perspective to our
present and past positions and musicological stance.

II

In so far as the study of musicology tends to be preoccupied
with the historical aspects of music, what are the possible
horizons that lie beyond this valuable historical tradition? We
might say that beyond history, or rather within it, lies the
musical *experience* and *phenomenon*. We might even make
bold to interpret this musical phenomenon in a phenomenological manner and even come to speak of musical subject
and "being."[14] Musical "being," of course, does not connote
some new form of mysticism or an esoteric ontology. It is
rather a serious and concrete going *within* the musical phenomenon, not beyond it to some ideology or abstract world
apart from this one. It is not unlike what G. Marcel calls
"inwardness" as the new transcendence. But this inwardness
is not introspection or introversion. It is a concrete entering
within the phenomenon of music, in this case, so that the
phenomenon be allowed to speak for itself, to reveal itself
to us, *as it is*, i.e. phenomenologically, rather than as we
categorize it.

What do we imply when we speak of a transcendence
over tradition and history, as such? Here we apply to music
the distinction between history and *Geschichte*. History, as
we know it, is a recounting of data from the past and present.
It relies heavily on scientific methodology and on the western
trichotomy of time. According to this, time is projected onto
metaphorical space and is divided into three segments: past,
present and future. It seems natural for us *not* to question
this established trichotomy, just as it seems natural to us (but
is in reality a part of our cultural conditioning) not to
question the body-soul dichotomy, or its secular version
of anatomy-reason. Yet philosophers through Augustine,

Husserl, Heidegger, Sartre, and Merleau-Ponty, have questioned it.

Geschichte is not "historicality," as the translators of Heidegger's *Sein und Zeit* tell us, or even worse, "historiology." Perhaps a better translation is simply a *happening*. Phenomenologically, this means that something *is* or happens in time but not necessarily only according to the western trichotomy of time. Past, present and future are subsumed into "existential-ekstatic" time, with special regard for the thrust of the future. Obviously, this is also of great import for a musical composition, which seems stretched out in space (on paper!) and progresses from past into the present. Without this spatial metaphor our present concept of musical form is inconceivable. It remains to be seen what kind of "form" emerges from a consideration of a nonspatial view of time. Being, understood phenomenologically, is not static but ek-static, i.e. it is a continual *becoming*, in which the modalities of present, past, and future are brought together not spatially only but as the emergence (ek-sistence) of the musical phenomenon. Obviously we can only hint at all this in an introductory chapter. It is a question of new horizons — even beyond phenomenology (which can only be regarded as "transitional"). In this new understanding of history we attempt to transcend the western dichotomy of old-new and search for what *is* valid. This can be done, of course, from any number of philosophical perspectives. And if the writer may be allowed a phenomenological heresy it might even be possible from the viewpoint of philosophical analysis. The present writer prefers to hope with Professor Khatchadourian and others that there is a common meeting ground for both phenomenology and analysis.[15] Perhaps phenomenologists need to pay more attention to the correctives of philosophical analysis. The opposite may also be true. But if one happens to be of phenomenologist leanings one can be excused for approaching problems philosophical and musical from this background.[16]

Phenomenology attempts to overcome the classic dichotomy of mind and body, showing that mind is bodily and that body is not just the physical. Overcoming traditions such as this does not mean destroying but rebuilding with the aid of new and perhaps radical insights into a more fundamental unfolding of musical subjectivity and being. For phenomenology is not merely a standpoint or a perspective but a radical attempt to let reality speak (or sound) for itself. When we speak of standpoints and perspectives we speak ordinarily of some individual's view. In phenomenology it is not just a question of someone's viewpoint. It is a question of letting "reality" speak in and to us. Reality of this kind is not just "opinion," especially since it takes in much more than the thinker's perspective. The ontological dimension, as phenomenological, rather than as metaphysical, is not an abstract absolute but the concrete, flesh-and-blood dimension of being fully and openly human. We let things — including other humans — speak for themselves instead of dictating to them from prefabricated cultural and metaphysical categories. Thus instead of trying to cast music in a spatial form, which is visually oriented, we let it speak in its own form. And above all, we stop dictating western forms into music, as such. We allow reality its own language and voice. We allow it to "sing" in its own modalities and forms. For when we study it, we do not force it into our own scientific categories.

That is why the truly phenomenological attitude is one of *listening*.[17] It is a musical attitude, if indeed listening is important in the musical world. A phenomenologist would not judge the music of, e.g., P. Boulez with categories based on traditional harmony and analysis; neither would he expect late compositions of Stravinsky, e.g. the *Canticum Sacrum* or *The Deluge* to sound like early Stravinsky, certainly not like *Le Sacre du Printemps*. In other words, one does not pre-categorize anyone's work but lets it be what it *is*. This letting-be is the core of the truly phenomenological attitude. The philosophical attitude is thus basically a musical one. Phenomenological philosophy is an attempt at openness and true listening. Openness in this case means not just open eyes and sight but open ears and hearing. For this reason a phenomenology of sound is important not only for musicology but also for philsophy as such. We allow musical being to unfold its "life-movement" in its own modalities rather than in accordance with outdated conventions. This is absurd, of course, to many people. But if the writer may be allowed to give A. Camus' concept of the "absurd" a phenomenological twist, we might say that the absurdity of listening instead of dictating is for our civilization of an "off-key" attitude. For the word, absurd, like many other words is a musical one and means "off-key." Hence if a composer like Boulez or Stockhausen plays in a musically off-the-usual-key idiom, we can be quite happy, philosophically speaking, to partake of their "absurdity" and protect them from reactionaries, whether we agree with them or not.

Unlike students of pure science we do not objectify reality and thus reduce it to a preset category; neither do we, as students of the science-of-music, i.e. musico-logy, distance ourselves from the *musical* phenomenon, even as we pursue "phenomenological" studies. Surely even though we are "musical scientists" (*Musik-wissenschaftler*), we cannot afford to adopt a cold, impersonal attitude toward living music. Music is, after all, more art than science. Life, but particularly musical life, is "warm" not cold, and our encounter with musical phenomena must be "subjective" and personal. How often do we not destroy the love of music by our scientific analyses of it! Music as a human phenomenon is the language more of heart than head. By heart, of course, we do not mean sentimentality but rather the full *human* dimension as opposed to the merely rational and scientific. This does not mean neoromanticism. Even if it did, what would be wrong with that? We see the neoromantic strain in such contemporaries as the late Bartok, Prokofiev, and even in the "classicist" Hindemith. Surely we do not want to remain forever in the category of antiromanticism. That period has passed. If Schoenberg is right, there is need for some "romanticism" in every man, if he is to remain human.

Ernst Kurth, as psychologist of music, said of the essence of music, "Music is the emergence of powerful primal forces, whose energies originate in the unheard. What one usually designates as music is actually but its echo."[18] This is strong phenomenological language, though its author was not a phenomenologist. A student of Heidegger might regard music as the direct or indirect "*call* of being," i.e. of the existential-ontological dimension, which has more to do with sound than many phenomenologists realize. "Being" is a powerful force that speaks to us literately but without letters, not from without some otherworld of abstractions or mysticism but from within the concrete depths of phenomena minus the intervention and consequent distortions of an exaggerated intellectuality. In this sense music as being (and being as "musical") is regarded as "irrational." However, this is a poor word, since it makes everything nonrational a deviation from "reason," as though the latter were an absolute norm. If it is true, as H. Hüschen seems to think, that we lack a philosophical focal point today,[19] perhaps phenomenology can be of service. For the heart of phenomenological philosophy is *sound* and *hearing*. And here it may take a musician to realize the philosophical implications.

Very often nonmusician philosophers, such as Santayana,[20] speak to us about music without firsthand knowledge. Perhaps it takes a musician to point out that the area of sound can have its own philosophy. Yet what have we done as musicians and musicologists? We have had recourse to sight-metaphors to explain musical phenomena. We rely, even in the most advanced modern music, on spatial and visual concepts. As musicologists we rely far too heavily on word, as scientific. We speak of "form" and of musical "materials." And here we almost borrow a page right out of classic philosophy. In musical esthetics we have borrowed terminology wholesale from the visual arts. In western civilization — like no other — music has tended to employ visual means and consequently to be distorted by it. This reliance on the visual (including all musical notation!) has given western music a kind of unnatural twist that it lacks elsewhere. Other peoples are content to listen to sound rather than to see it — whether on paper or mentally through musico-philosophical concepts and "form." We need a new musical conceptuality and vocabulary.

III

Heidegger, who in *Sein und Zeit* opens up a completely new horizon of thinking that prepares the ground for an over-coming of traditional thought and its metaphysical categories, is also the philosopher who perhaps better than any other helps in the overcoming of traditional esthetics — which M. Bukofzer had considered the next step in musicological research. Unfortunately, traditional esthetics is based on a historical development of classic critical metaphysics and/or rationalism. Esthetics is the logic, understood in its broader meaning. In similar manner ethics is the logic of ethos, as metaphysics is the onto-logic of physics. Here, of course, we do not speak directly of formal logic, which begins perhaps only in the twelfth century. Aristotle is wrongly called the Father of Logic. He is rather the Father of Syllogistic Reasoning, if he must be the father of something. By "logic" we mean that development by which the pre-Socratic logos came to be an *epistēmē logikē* and the eventual basis of medieval theo-logic and onto-logic.

As we shall see in detail in a later chapter, Heidegger gets away from the "philosophy of beauty" and makes us aware of art as the emergence of ontological *truth*.[21] Esthetics is not a question of "ontic," i.e. of traditional meta-physical concepts of beauty, but rather of existential-ontological *truth* — an entirely new dimension. As a result, esthetics cannot be the next step in a phenomenology of sound. A phenomenology of sound is already its own esthesis and ethos. It is already its own musical *logos* rather than an object of musicological investigation. It is already its own method. Method is not an abstract procedure one "applies" to a set of "objective facts" in order to set them going. Method is rather what the word itself says: a being *underway* or on-the-way in the unfolding of musical subject. It is a question of being underway in a "life-movement." And surely it is understandable for us to regard music as the life-movement of sound and the whole area of the human psyche (understood as "body-subject") that is inaccessible to classic philosophy or psychology.

We see then that in phenomenological thinking an attempt has been made to rebuild and reunite. It is an attempt to let the musical phenomenon speak for itself as musical tone rather than as material for some intellectual category, making use of visual metaphor. Word is musical word and the spoken word has a music of its own, even though it does not fall under the academic definition of music, as we know it today. It is not the literal word that conveys meaning, as much as the "tone" in which it is proffered. We tell from the musical sound and the intonation whether the spoken word is "true" or not. This is hardly a question for linguistic "analysis," but of phenomenological "facticity." Facticity does not denote factualness, but suggests that "facts" point to an ontological dimension. Ontic facts need to be "re-facted" as ontological, i.e. the rules of the tradition need to be overcome and transformed at a wholly new level. "Re-facting the facts," in this case the musical facts, means plumbing their depths and fullest meaning. And it must be admitted that our idea of the "essence" of music is very limited. To a large extent we have lost not only philosophical horizon but even the full musical dimension. As students of music history, we are familiar with the difficult problem of the ethos of Greek music. There is probably more to it than what C. Sachs called the tension between thetic and dynamic *mesē*.[22] Rather it is a question of a "tensor-factor," which is not unlike a phenomenological intentionality, though conceived from quite a different starting point.

IV

In the middle ages, musical number held all things together, as becomes evident at least from a study of Jacques de Liège's encyclopedic work, the *Speculum Musicae*, which is not just a musicological document, but a highly elaborate mathematico-philosophico-musical treatise. We know of the division of music from *musica divina* to *sonora*, which is music properly so-called. But this definition of music is dependent on a philosophy of number based on metaphysics, as the encyclopedist takes great pains to point out. Since that time music gradually came to be restricted more and more, so that in the last century with the help of German pedagogy the meaning of music was reduced to the *practice* of music, and the cleft between theory and practice became almost unbridgeable. Music still suffers from this artificial state of affairs. But more and more we are beginning to sense the meaninglessness of any gap between practice and theory and are attempting to broaden our meaning of music. Yet can this be done without the help of philosophical studies? For they show that the dichotomy of theory and practice is based on Christian metaphysics, which needs to be overcome. Perhaps this distinction can be dealt with in phenomenology, and instead of postulating a "practical theory" and "theoretical practice," as advocated by Jacques de Liège, we will achieve a musical *praxis*. In a living *praxis* "theory" is already contained. Theory in this case is a "closer look" within the concrete *praxis*, not beyond it into a world of abstractions.

There can never be a musical practice which develops independently of either meaningful "theory" or of historical sources, as A. Mendel has pointed out in his lucid article on the services of musicology for the practical musician.[23] Neither can there ever be musicology for musicology's sake. Even Jacques de Liège tried to bridge the gap between theory and practice, as we saw. Perhaps in our day we can find a plausible solution to the problem in phenomenological philosophy, which is not abstract like traditional philosophies of being but looks to the concrete situation, in this case the musical experience of the creative subject. This "looking into" is precisely the meaning of the word "theory." When we look into something, we do not look away from it or beyond it. There is no abstract musical world lying serenely beyond the musical phenomenon itself. Looking into and entering into the musical situation means "getting next to it." If this is so, a musicology based on such theory is always within the living musical experience itself and never departs from it. There must be no short-circuit between head and hands, because they both belong to man.

In pre-Socratic thinking (to the study of which Nietzsche, Heidegger and others invite us), man is not cut in two, i.e. into mind and body. Rather, as in biblical times, man is conceived as one living and undivided being, who feels no need to be put back together again by all the scholastic king's horses and all the psychoanalyst king's men. For Humpty Dumpty never did push him off the wall and break him in two. Humpty Dumpty in this case was metaphysics. There is no need for any "relation" between soul and body, because they are already one. The soul is the life of the body, but it cannot be conceived apart from it. It is very difficult to find such a dualistic distinction in the pre-Socratics, though it has been read back into them.[24] Not even Parmenides is a "pioneer for Plato" and his idea of "mind" is currently being drastically revised and de-Platonized. There was at that time no distinction between a theoretical mind and a practical hand, let us say. For Anaxagoras the mind is but a more refined kind of "sensing." He and Empedocles emphasize the fact that we think with every member of our bodily being. This is, obviously, a most musical thing. Surely the organist is not just a bundle of behaviouristic impulses impelled by a mind, when he finds himself in the midst of a Handel concerto or a Hindemith sonata. In fact, he had better not theorize too much or he will lose the music completely and grind to a halt. Instead of his theoretical mind guiding his practical fingers and feet, he thinks, i.e. muses or makes music with his whole body, but especially his hands and his feet.

This kind of thinking is parallel to modern phenomenological thought. It would be particularly fruitful to work out a musical phenomenology, based on the "body subject" of M. Merleau-Ponty. We are not embodied minds but "bodily beings." The "psyche" or soul is the life breath of the body, i.e. it is not just the physical inhalation or exhalation of air, but the total *movement* of the human being as he literally "lives and *breathes*." But this bodily movement, or "soul," can hardly be separated from the living person. (Theologians tried to do this by making "soul" the focal point of their theories of transcendence, and thus they often destroyed the very life they were purportedly saving.) And thus also in music. Music theory must not be something abstract but grounded in our life-movement. A serious study of this musical movement must not be merely scientific and abstract. It must aim at the unfolding of a basic subjectivity.

Certainly contemporary philosophy is rife with insights for a possible new horizon in musicological studies. Is it not time we began work in this largely uncharted area? We will have to forget for a while about side issues and concentrate on music in depth. This means studying its concrete philosophical dimension or the *musical phenomenon* itself. It is only from the musical situation as such that purely historical studies (in the traditional sense) can be placed in proper perspective. Perhaps this can turn out to be the foundation of a new musicology, as a truly musical rather than scientific study, a new "humanism" that will reunite man with his concrete world of music and the arts. For if this is a "broken world" as G. Marcel writes,[25] perhaps music can help restore it to its truer self. This is far more than mere "therapy." This — along with parallel insights from other idioms of thought — may well be the key to a rejuvenation of our musical culture and to the enlivenment of musical and musicological thinking.

Endnotes

1.   C. C. Pratt, "Musicology and related disciplines" in *Some Aspects of Musicology* (New York, 1957), p. 72.
2.   J. Westrup, "Editorial" in *Music and Letters*, April, 1962, p. 101.
3.   H. Hüschen, "Past and present concepts of the nature and limits of music" in *Report of the International Musicological Congress, New York*, 1961, p. 286. Cf. also W. Wiora "Musikwissenschaft

und Universalgeschichte" in *Acta Musicologica*, XXXIII, 1961, p. 84.

4. W. Apel, "Musicology" in *Harvard Dictionary of Music* (Cambridge, 1947), p. 473.

5. M. Bukofzer, *Musicology in American Institutions of Higher Learning* (New York, 1957).

6. There are many definitions of phenomenology. Its modern founder, Edmund Husserl, regarded it as a "first philosophy" attained by crossing the threshold out of the "natural" world into the realm of "eidetic essence." This realm is not a Platonic otherworld, however. Instead it means laying bare the "things themselves" by means of the "eidetic reduction" or *epoche* in which the incrustations and sediment of history, theory, and mere opinion fall away or are "bracketed." In Heidegger's writings phenomenology means freeing the essence of phenomena from pre-set categories and frameworks. The thing, as phenomenal, is allowed to present itself, as it *is*, rather than as we force it to be according to some preconceived system of thought. Letting-*be* announces the ontological dimension in the phenomenon, and this leads us into the "existential-phenomenological" depths of the thing examined. The thing is allowed to emerge (ek-sist) as it *is*. Our mentors in this philosophy are also Sartre and Merleau-Ponty, who, together with Husserl and Heidegger, at least in this study are not given merely in doxographical manner, but, it is hoped, in living dialogue. Other philosophers who are indispensable for this study are Kierkegaard, Nietzsche, Marcel, Camus, Dufrenne, Ricoeur and others.

7. L. Schrade, "The chronology of the ars nova" in *Les Colloques de Wegimont* II (Paris, 1959), p. 38.

8. U. Gunther, "Das Ende der ars nova" in *Die Musikforschung* XVI, 1963; cf. also *Bericht uber den internationalen musikwissenschaftlichen Kongress Kassel 1962*, pp. 108-9.

9. A. Schonberg, *Style and Idea* (New York, 1950).

10. P. Hindemith, *A Composer's World, Horizons and Limitations* (Cambridge, 1953).

11. F. J. Smith, "Jacques de Liège, an Anti-Modernist?" in *Revue belge de musicologie*, 1963; "Ars Nova — a Re-definition?" in *Musica Disciplina*, 1964, 1965; *Iacobi Leodiensis Spoeulum Musicae, A Commentary*, I (Institute of Medieval Music, New York, 1966); "Le contenu philosophique du Speculum Musicae" in *Le Moyen Age, Revue d'histoire et de philologie*, 1968; "The Division of the Speculum Musicae" in *Tijdschrift van de vereniging voor nederlandse musiekgeschiedenis*, 1968.

12. A. Liess, *Carl Orff, Idee und Werk* (Zurich, 1955).

13. A. Liess, ref. 12, p. 35.

14.   Here we distinguish between Husserl's phenomenology of the subject and phenomenological ontology, especially that of M. Heidegger. Cf. *Sein und Zeit* or in the translation of Maquarrie and Robinson, *Being and Time* (New York, 1962). Cf. J. Wild's review in *Review of Metaphysics*, Dec., 1963.

15.   J. D. Wild, "Is there a world of ordinary language?" in *The Philosophical Review*, 1958.

16.   J. Wild (Yale) and D. Folesdale (Harvard) attempted to find common ground between phenomenology and philosophical analysis. This is also true of the dialogue between the present writer and H. Khatchadourian (University of Wisconsin): Wild was a noble dilettante, uneven in scholarship and ambitious to promote phenomenology, turning out books of often hopeless philosophical journalism. "Sed de mortuis nil nisi bonum".

17.   This connotes an overcoming of the sight-metaphor in philosophy and the study of existential openness for reality as a sound-phenomenology, i.e. openness for the "voice of being."

18.   E. Kurth, *Musikpsychologie* (Bern, 1947).

19.   H. Hüschen, *Report of the International Musicological Congress, New York*, 1961.

20.   W. Austin, "Santayana as music critic" in *Musical Quarterly*, XI, 1954, p. 497.

21.   M. Heidegger, *Der Ursprung des Kunstwerkes* (Stuttgart, 1960).

22.   C. Sachs, *The Rise of Music in the Ancient World/East and West* (New York, 1943).

23.   A. Mendel, "The services of musicology for the practical musician" in *Some Aspects of Musicology* (New York, 1957).

24.   F. Nietzsche, *Vorspiel zu einer Philosophie der Zukunft*. M. Heidegger "Der Spruch des Anaximanders" in *Holzwege* (Frankfurt, 1950). Cf. also many other works, such as *Vorträge und Aufsätze* (Pfullingen, 1954); G. Kirk and J. Raven *The Pre-Socratic Philosophers* (Cambridge, 1960). This excellent study relies unfortunately on outdated translations of the fragments. Last century philosophical vocabularies are thus uncritically read back into the pre-Socratic thinkers. This is obviously a stumbling block to the understanding of what these thinkers wanted to say for themselves.

25.   G. Marcel, *Le mystère de l'être* (Paris, 1951).

Chapter 2

A CRITIQUE OF VISUAL METAPHOR IN PHILOSOPHY AND MUSIC

I

What is phenomenology? This is a question which has to be asked over and over again, not unlike the question, "What is philosophy?" Husserl kept asking to the very end what "eidetic reduction" was, and Heidegger keeps asking the question of being. In the avant-propos to *La Phénoméno-logie de la Perception*, Merleau-Ponty lists several definitions of phenomenology — which takes in the whole situation up to that time. Thus he mentions that phenomenology is the study of essences, a transcendental philosophy, a philosophy that is an exact science in the broader meaning of *wissen*, a thinking that has spawned the ontological-existential dimension, a phenomenology "for us"; and we would now add, a convincing phenomenology of the bodily dimension (*corps propre*). While it is true that phenomenology is divided "politically" into the pure phenomenology of Husserl, the eksistent ontology of Heidegger, the existentialism of Sartre, and the bodily phenomenology of Merleau-Ponty, it is difficult to belong only to one of these camps, if one is to believe in a "phenomenology for us." For the scholar is capable of seeing merit in all these approaches to phenomenology only because we ourselves in a sense *already know* and *already experience* what it is to be "phenomenological," even though we may never have articulated this premeta-physical fact.

Rather than become merely Husserlians, or Heideggerians, or Sartrians, we ought to be simply phenomenological thinkers, although it is obvious that in being this we certainly will not regard these philosophers as "equal." Some will be more convincing to us that others. In no sense do we want to create a homogenized phenomenology, which erases all the differences and settles for a kind of phenomenological scholasticism, in which everything has been reduced to a pedagogical system. The phenomenology of the German, French, and American thinkers is obviously differently colored. Keeping the differences, we can still learn from them all, for all of them can help us look into ourselves (not just look into myself) in our world and on this earth in interpreting the phenomenology, which is not only "for us" but which we ourselves *are*.

And yet it is necessary to do more than *look* into the situation. And perhaps it is precisely here that our great teachers "fail" us, in that they still make use of *visual* metaphor and the language of *sight*. In seeking the full phenomenological spectrum we may have to do more than just *look* into things. We may have to *listen* to things. Aristotle may not have been speaking for everyone when he wrote in the introductory paragraph of his *Metaphysics* that sight is man's keenest and most important sense. I am not sure that the musicians of that time, whose ear was attuned to far more subtle tonal nuances than ours, and who had no such reliance on written music as we do (though it existed), would have been able to agree with Aristotle. For most musicians feel that the sense of hearing is far more perceptive and inward than that of sight, since sound reaches the very center of our being. Even Hegel recognized this, when he wrote that music penetrates to the very core of man's soul and is one with his proper subjectivity.

But with few exceptions even traditional phenomenologists seem tied down to a fixation on sight and light metaphors, though, to be sure, the phenomenon of sound is hardly neglected.[1] The history of philosophy since Aristotle seems largely bound to sight and light. How a thing *looked* or *appeared* concretely to the sight, be that of the eye or of the mind, was the most important approach to what a thing *was*. The key to philosophical *being* from Aristotle through Heidegger is a study of "phenomena," i.e. what appears-in-light. From Plato to Husserl (and, of course, Husserl was not a Platonist), the *eidos* of a thing was the starting point to the discovery of essence. In Latin Aristotelianism intuition became important, i.e. how the mind's eye "intuited" or *looked* into the essence of things. From a medieval intentionality it was but a few steps, however important and unexpected, to an intentional intuition of essence in the phenomenological sense, and the Husserl's *Wesensschau*. And Heidegger writes of that *Sicht* which is fundamental even to a phenomenological intuition of essences. He also speaks of being as "lightened up" (*"Sein ist gelichtet"*). Even as late as his curious essay on *Zeit und Sein* (1962) he makes *Ereignis* a central theme. But elsewhere he has analyzed this as an *er-aügen*.[2] Thus "event" is really *insight*. The citations can easily be multiplied to show that, even though sound is not ignored, the light and sight metaphors carry the main burden of metaphysical and post-metaphysical conceptuality and vocabulary. From Plato and Aristotle through phenomenology in its traditional forms we are dealing almost exclusively with the phenomenon of actual and metaphorical sight, literally dominating what a thing *is* by how it *looks*.

In seeking to broaden the spectrum of phenomenology, we thus realize the need to expand its conceptuality and language beyond light and sight metaphor. This must then lead to a redefinition of phenomenology in terms of not only phenomena but also of *akumena*. It is true that Husserl makes use of musical tone in his lectures on time and that retention is regarded also from the viewpoint of musical retention. It is true that he writes of the essential link between expression and voice, that he attempts to cope with the disadvantages of metaphor, and that he does a future phenomenology of sound the favor of bracketing in advance sound as sonorous. But it is also true that the phoneme turns out to be the "idealité maîtrisée du phénomène," to quote Jacques Derrida's fascinating study of Husserl, *Signe linguistique et non-linguistique chez Husserl*.[3] In other words, even though sound was influential in Husserl's thinking and even though he appreciated the place of voice as phonetic expression and thus as meaningful linguistic sign, when he gets to the heart of the matter, to the essence of things, he uses visual terms to explain them.

This is true of Hegal also, as Derrida points out in an essay on Levinas' prophetic philosophy of visage, "Violence et métaphysique."[4] Perhaps it is Levinas who appreciates the necessity of a philosophy in which sound is brought to the fore. For visage is not just the countenance of the other as seen but *as speaking*. Speech is a thing of sound, not a phenomenon but an *akumenon* in our experience of the lived world,[5] as we discourse with one another. Were I to speak with you and to you now at this moment, nothing I would now say could *appear* to you *in light* except my countenance; but it is not this that brings you the full sense of what I aim to *be* at this time. My words, as alive, as "acoustical phenomena" – or more properly as *akumena* – are what bring meaning, in that they are spoken by me and heard by you. Perhaps you may read them somewhere in print later on. But that is only a secondary instance. The live discourse is now at this moment, and the conveyor of meaning is voice and sound. The *visage parlant* is, however, more in the tradition of biblical prophetism than of western philosophy. In prophetism the sense of hearing is foremost, for the prophet must listen to the god and then in turn must speak for the god to the people. It is the dialectic of listening and speaking that is at the basis of a phenomenology of prophetism. Perhaps this existential dialectic would also be at the heart of a phenomenology of sound, even though the religious prophetism would have to be bracketed.

There are a goodly number of philisophical leads in Husserl, Heidegger, and Merleau-Ponty, which could serve as primers in the working out of a phenomenology of sound. And here, of course, sound as merely acoustical would have to be reduced to sound as musical, though not by eidetic reduction as much by what might possibly be called "echotic" reduction, since we would not be interested in the *eidos* of musical sound but rather in its phenomenological *echos*, as sonorous essence. For, we would not begin by reducing a phenomenon but by reducing an *akumenon*. Perhaps we would no longer use the word, phenomenological, at all, though that is unlikely. I am not sure that a substitute term, such as, e.g., "akumenology," would be necessary or required, to say nothing of acceptable to phenomenologists. And yet in keeping the term "phenomenology" we would *not* want to make the phenomenology of musical sound simply a subdivision of phenomenology, as such. Rather it is that which broadens the horizons and the language of phenomenology. Phenomenology itself is redefined in broader terms and according to the full spectrum of the lived world, which must also include the haptic and the dance.

A traditional phenomenology tied to light-metaphor needs to be overcome, just as it has overcome traditional metaphysics. In fact, until it has accomplished this, it cannot truly be said to have overcome metaphysics at all, since it has not overcome the chief "category," that of light and sight, as the key to phenomena and essences. It is true that Merleau-Ponty speaks of "seeing sound" and "hearing sight," i.e. that he realizes the need to broaden out the dimensions of the entire *corps ontologique*; but he, too, stays pretty well within traditional light-language. Perhaps the opposite of light, i.e. darkness, as brought out in Heidegger's thinking can lead us toward the explanation of reality in terms other than those of light. For in darkness we cannot see, and thus we must begin to hear. In this case the akumena, as things heard, are obviously more important than phenomena, as things seen, since things seen depend on light for the eye or on clear distinct concepts for the mind. But in darkness which is more than just the opposite of light, which is in a manner of speaking the womb of being, our traditional conceptuality and metaphors fail us. It is then that the silent *cogito* begins; it is only then that we can speak of the voice of silence. And in this silent situation we are attuned to world ever yet, as we listen and harken to the call of "being." [6]

II

In his *Phénoménologie de la Perception*, Merleau-Ponty states that it is the task of phenomenology to get to the root and meaning of "reason" and "objectivity" by uncovering a more fundamental and primordial *logos*, which will make any *cogito* understandable. For the primordial world of *logos* is not light but darkness, and in this darkness it is not the eye but the ear that counts, not sight but the living voice that carries meaning. And it may be here that we seek the basis of a phenomenology of sound or of a phenomenology that in overcoming its over-dependence on sight symbols becomes *also* a tonal and haptic phenomenology. Thus we go back again to Aristotle and, while admitting the importance of seeing, accept at least the equal importance of hearing. And thus we no longer look for the essence of things only from the way a thing looks but also from the way a thing sounds. Thus coming to Husserl we would no longer speak only of eidetic reduction but also of a phenomenological in-hearing. A further development would be the *synthesis* of eidetic with echotic in order that our perception, as humans, be truly "bodily." We would no longer think of what essence is under the aspect of light and sight language, however carefully we try to bracket language and metaphor; instead we take things as they actually *give* themselves to us, as they show themselves to us; thus *as* eidetic, echotic, haptic, and whatever else makes up the total of human experience and world, *as* lived. It is only from this full bodily spectrum that a complete phenomenology is possible.

This cannot be done by making sight "stand for" all the senses, as it does in Plato's *tópos horatós*, in Augustine, in Husserl's *eidos*, in Heidegger. Hearing and touch cannot properly be adjudged from the standard of how a thing looks. The *eidos* itself needs to be bracketed. We know how long Husserl worked on the meaning and understanding of eidetic reduction. We know how strong an influence musical tone was in some of his writings. But we also know that to the end he never did succeed convincingly in what I call bracketing *eidos*, so that the world of *échos* may be known and appreciated for what it is in itself, and not just in reference to the visual phenomena.[7] I believe a bracketing of the eidetic and of phenonema might well lead us to the "echotic" and to akumena. But here again we would not want *échos* to mask out *eidos*. Rather, some sort of meaningful dialectic between sight, hearing, touch, etc., needs to be worked out, to help phenomenology not only arrive at a fuller meaning of itself but also to be more meaningful and acceptable in the world of art, music, and the dance: and to *life*, as the "dance of being."

Perhaps at this point Heidegger may be of more immediate service. For though he speaks of being in light metaphor and of "sight" as fundamental even to *eidos*, he does have some fascinating insights into hearing and sound that could aid in the establishment of the fuller phenomenology we seek. And here again we arrive at *logos* in its fundamental and primordial meaning. While I do not and cannot intend to go into this Heideggerian insight in a more adequate manner here, some indications of progress in this work can be reported. The larger work awaits further research and writing.[8] Suffice it for our present purpose to outline certain insights that are helpful in the discovery of a phenomenology of sound from Heidegger's position. Elsewhere I have tried to show how despite his nearness to the Greek meaning of things, Heidegger fails to acknowledge a very fundamental fact; that the *logos* is not just a primordial source of reason and thus crucial to the redefinition of man (not as "rational animal" but as the "living being who *is* logos-thinker") but that the Greek logos is indeed a *logos mousikos*. And thus man is not only the logos-thinker, but one who speaks and shapes his speech in musical sound. In writing about *Rede*, which has been translated more or less unsatisfactorily as "discourse," Heidegger calls this the basis of speech. It is interesting to note that music is called in German one of the *redende Künste*, i.e. one of the "talking arts."[9] Perhaps the primordiality of speech as a *musical* phenomenon can be worked out best in the light of the "talking arts" and the origin of the work of art, such as the music of poetry. Poetry and art have traditionally been called the "communicative" arts, and of course this must include also what we call formal music. The original logos is the "discourse" of Euterpe, the goddess of music, one of the Muses, who gives the first musical word, which makes it

possible for man to become the "talking animal," i.e. for man
to receive the *logos mousikos* and break forth in poetry and
song. This mythological imagery may well aid us in a discovery
of the primordial oneness of music and speech and abet our
efforts to discover the logos (and thus man, as logos) in its
full color and sound.

Thus in *Sein und Zeit* [SZ], *Rede* is the ontological
word which makes it possible for man to speak at all in ontic
words. It is the ontological word of silence, which is essentially,
we might now add, a musical silence, not as mere absence of
sound but as the womb of sound and speech and thought: of
all that makes man truly man. Thus it is possible for man to
discourse both with gods and with man and it is equally possible for Hermes to bear the word of the god to man, i.e. to
"lay out" (*Auslegung*) the word of the god before man. And
this may be the fuller meaning of an existential "herme-
neutics." *Rede* is the articulation of understanding and comes
before any interpretation or verbal statement, as expression.
Understanding, as existential-ontological, is already structured,
even before it is unfolded in explicit verbal form. This
pre-structuring, which *Rede* articulates, is the entirety of
relationship that the phenomenological world reveals. It is this
which gives meaning to words, as we know them, i.e. not to
mere words but to musical words. For primordial word cannot
be split into spoken or written word and sung word. Living
speech *is* musical. Word, as unmusical, is an abstraction at best
or an alienation from reality at worst. Perhaps Frenchmen
and Italians understand this better than we staid and sober
English speakers, who level everything out and regard any show
of musicality or emotion a thing of poor taste. *Rede* is the
discoursing of world, not only as what appears in light but
primarily as that which is unfolded in living sound. In discourse the world speaks forth as the whole world of structured
relationships that make meaning possible at all.

The reason why men can talk at all is that world already
discourses within him. As in-the-world, and I add from insights
taken from Heidegger's *Der Ursprung des Kunstwerkes*, as on-
the-earth,[10] man is already oriented toward and in being.

As it were, he already talks before he has spoken a word. It is in this *a priori of silent speech* that ontological thing is (i.e. "Ein 'ist' ergibt sich, wo das Wort zerbricht"): the ontological dimension of speech is there where the ontic word fails and falls apart.[11] And the shattering of ontic word is precisely that "step backward or aside" on the way toward the unfolding of a more primordial thought and language. Talking does not mean just verbal formulation or statement of abstract conceptual thoughts; and the traditional description of man as the "talking animal" falls short of the discovery of the basis of speech itself. Rather, man shows himself to be that living ontological being which already knows and speaks from world. This is his "world language," even when he harkens in silence. For in communing with rather than in merely communicating with the other it is required that man hear as well as speak. But at the primordial level hearing and speaking may be identical. Hearing belongs to discourse as constitutive, Heidegger writes. Hearing means being open for one's own ontological being and that of the other. Without this existential hearing there can be no "communication," no sharing of world, no communing with one another, i.e. becoming one with the other. *Rede* is thus not some sort of external communication nor does it depend on the spoken word, as such. Unless there *already* is a sharing of world there can be no communication nor communing, despite all the external communiques in the world. When we do not share a world, talk becomes idle talk and gossip; and, I might add, this is possible also at the academic level.

III

"Conscience," in *SZ*, is, of course, the "call of [ontological] being," essentially the voice. It is not a voice which berates us with moralistic prattle, but the call of ontological being as the mode of discourse, speaking and articulating the understanding of authentic being only in silence. Here it is even more evident that any "call" or cry of being is that of logos as "musical." The bickering voice of legalism or scrupulosity is not a true conscience but rather a disease. Real conscience speaks wordlessly in meaningful silence. The cry of "being" is the note of discord in our harmonious and concordant world of the "One," where one does what one does, says what one says, and thinks what one thinks, rather than follow the silent "discord" of being. Instead of listening to the call of being we may turn a deaf ear to it, temporize, negotiate, ignore, rather than take courageous action. The call of being reveals itself as the call of caring for our ownmost potential and that of the other. It is here where Merleau-Ponty comes to our assistance, when he speaks of the other as a "discord," i.e. as discordant with the concord and consonance of my unshared world.[12] The discordant voice of the other calls me to a sharing of world, to an ontological solidarity, to a true metaphysics, i.e. to a going outside and *beyond myself* by offering my hand, my heart, even my whole bodily being to the other in love. And thus the logos is not only musical in a formal sense; rather it is the very heart of human intersubjectivity. The logos is a song of love and friendship. And it is only in this world of life and love that meaningful word and thought take shape. Only in this living *praxis* is truer subjectivity and world to be sought. But for this we have to go farther than Heidegger. And it may well be Merleau-Ponty who indicates the way.

Logos as discourse, as the ontological basis of both reason and musical speech, is not only eksistent but temporal as well. And yet *Rede*, as the articulation of the understanding, does not show itself in any special ekstasis, and if so perhaps only in the present as a pre-senting, i.e. as making ontologically pre-sent rather than just being ontically present in time. [13] If we call *Rede* a world-discourse, as the discoursing of our being in-the-world (and I add "on-the-earth") we are also brought before the problem of the transcendence of world. *Dasein* (as "being-there") is the place where world transcends, *as* world discourses within us. Transcending and discoursing are what open up the world. Transcendence is thus not just a going outside ourselves to the other (and certainly not a going-beyond into a Platonic otherworld); it is a discoursing *within* which one speaks to the other. And thus *Dasein* is not just where my world "worlds"; rather it is where *we* discourse and share a world, thus transcending in presence to one another, as we listen to the *Logos*. And thus we come into world and being and life. This mutual coming-into is the existential-ontological temporality of being-there in a mutual listening and sharing of world and earth. And this is what Merleau-Ponty calls "the living bond of myself with myself and of me with the other." Thus any transcendence or "metaphysics" is not a system of concepts, but is just the opposite, for true metaphysical consciousness dies in contact with static absolutes. Rather transcendence is "musical": the discourse of the living dialectic between me and you, and this living dialectic is conveyed only by living word as meaningful sound.

In his essay on "logos" in *Vorträge und Aufsätze*, Heidegger emphasizes the necessity of *listening* to the Logos.[14] We cannot hear at all with our ears unless we already harken. An ontological harkening precedes any ontic hearing. Thus, we can hear not just because we have physical ears; rather we have ears because we are already hearers in that we already so listen to the logos, that we can be said to belong (*gehören*) to logos. Only then can we hear (*hören*) words and sounds. Otherwise we turn a deaf ear, even though the sounds penetrate to us physically. Forgetfulness of ontological being is often simply not harkening to being. Thus the essence of language is not taken just from physical sound. In order to say anything and in order to listen, the recollection or ingathering of logos is a prerequisite. Thus the *logos mousikos*, which makes any physical sound and hearing possible.

Similarly with reason, as a derivative of logos. Though in many places Heidegger uses light and sight metaphors in explaining *Vernunft* as a *vernehmen*, it is obvious that the ordinary usage of *vernehmen*, as hearing, is not lost on him. The restoration of this meaning to the German *Vernunft* is even more easily deducible in Kant, for whom practical reason was essentially, he writes at the end of his life, "a thinking that is a speaking, and this a hearing." For practical reason is the *Donnerwort*, the categorical imperative, speaking and telling man what he *ought* to *do*, and in his book on the philosophy of religion Kant shows that the idea of God is viable only as a symbol of the originality and unconditionedness of the law of reason itself. But man's task is to "listen to reason," i.e. in order to give horizon, unity, and purpose to his natural existence, man ought to live *as though* his religious symbols were operable. This *als ob* cannot be translated by the negative "as if"; for the "as if" is a phrase implying pretence and even despair. The *als ob* is positive: it means that traditional religious symbols are no longer taken in static, dogmatic, and even childish literalness, but that they become creative and workable symbols. And thus man, as reasonable and rational, ought to harken to the "voice of reason," or in our terms, ought to heed the logos.

This German meaning of *Vernunft* lends itself to an existential-ontological understanding of logos as musical, i.e. as the musical discoursing and sharing of world. For in the dialogue of sharing a world listening is everything. In a sense this is truer to the thought of Heraclitus, who tells us to listen to the logos. This does not mean just to take the logos *"in Acht,"* as Heidegger writes; it means, it is true, to at-tend to the logos. But this attending to the logos is also an *entendre*, a listening or hearing that goes deeper than even an ontological at-tending. Truer to the Greek meaning is not a concrete attending but an in-hearing, which is similarly concrete-ontological, i.e. it is not a question of physical sound but of musical sound. Sonorous sound, as purely phonetic, i.e. as the result of *phonē*, or as physical-sensual, is ontic. In a phenomenology of sound it is only musical sound that can be the ground of the akumena. Sonorous sound has to be bracketed, in order that a phenomenology of sound can be founded.[15]

This is, of course, reminiscent of Husserl's treatment of sound, as phonetic expression, i.e. as more than indication (*Anzeige*), rather as meaningful phonetic expression

(*Ausdruck*). But language as expressive form is seçondary for Husserl; it has to be led back to an original bedrock of pre-expressive meaning. And this brings us to the absolute silence of rapport with self, which implies the double reduction of the rapport to the other in me in indicative communication, and that of expression as ultimate stratum of meaning. It is in the context of this double reduction that voice is dicoverable, as Derrida points out. The ideality of the object cannot be expressed other than in the element whose phenomenality is not in the form of worldness; for, ideality means *being-for* the nonempirical consciousness. Now voice (*Stimme*) is what this ideal element is called. My words are alive, as words, because they never seem to leave me or escape my being, my "breath." Given the essential and necessary link between expression and voice or *phonē*, we see the phenomenological value of voice in concatenation with myself and my "breath." Thus: myself, my breath, and phonetic expression. This expression cannot be bracketed without endangering Husserl's whole endeavor. Thus, we see that meaningful expression is closely linked to sound as phenomenological. Perhaps from a closer study and presentation of such thinking within Husserl's otherwise visually oriented phenomenology insights for a phenomenology of sound can be deduced, that do not have to be led back to visually colored "ideality." Granted that there is already a nascent phenomenology of sound in both Husserl and Heidegger, it is evident that it has not been convincingly worked out, perhaps because both these great teachers did not have a certain musical awareness of reality.

IV

If a new understanding of sound can be of service in the broadening of the phenomenological spectrum and as a corrective to visual imbalance, phenomenology, even as visually oriented, can be of immense help to musicology, as the science-of-music. For musicology is still caught up in a "natural" and intellectualist philosophical tradition. And thus even as it purports to be the theory of the theory of music, i.e. basically the basis of any fundamental understanding of musical history and literature, it still makes use of traditional metaphysical conceptuality and terminology. Faithful to its metaphysical base, traditional musicology has explained sound in terms of speculation that has depended completely on visual metaphor. This becomes even more obvious in the study of musical esthetics, in which structures and terms are borrowed wholesale from the visual arts. And yet music is not a visual art; it is audial. Accordingly, any science that wishes to describe and analyse it really ought to make use of a musically oriented conceptuality.

The *ars musica* of medieval times, stemming from treatises by Aristides Quintillianus, Boethius, Cassiodorus and Isidore of Sevilla through the mediation of the *artes quadriviales*, relied on a philosophy of number as its rational basis. And this philosophy of number in turn relied on metaphysics. Number, whether *in se* or *ad quid*, falls under the metaphysical category of quantity, and thus music and philosophy are essentially bound together. Traditional metaphysics treats of *ens qua ens* and of *ens supremum* (later to become "theology"). Music treats of *ens numeratum*, not as separate from but as one with metaphysics. It is into this intellectualist grid that raw sound must be fed to emerge as *musica sonora*, i.e. as musical sound, based not just on raw sound but on numbered sound, as metaphysical and mathematical. It is not living sound itself that tells us what sound is; it is theoretical speculation that does.[16]

Especially here we see the deep split between the phenomenon of sound and its intellectualisations. But this intellectualisation, though counteracted in phenomenology, is not overcome insofar as phenomenology itself is still firmly embedded in the visual. It is obvious that all phenomenology has added is an overcoming of traditional metaphysical and scientific categorization. And that has been crucial. Yet more remains to be done. Phenomenology still has to move convincingly back to the living fact of sound, and it is here that its real contribution to traditional musicology will be made. Sound still must be allowed to reveal itself to us *as it is*. Even though we no longer bring musical sound under a metaphysical category as in the *ars antiqua*, we still look at it from the category of light and sight, as it were. But how does musical sound thus become comprehensible? A radical new unfolding of musical sound as a phenomenon is thus called for, especially when we begin to realize that musicology no longer preoccupies itself with European music, a music particularly influenced by western ideas of time and space.

It is perhaps in facing nonwestern music that the musicologist feels the inadequacy of his traditional categories. And it is not certain that a light-based phenomenology will help him out of such an impass. It is not sufficient just to say or decree that eidetic reduction covers all cases. If we maintain this, then we have failed to overcome the basic traditional category of metaphysics: dogmatic stance. Perhaps musicology can teach philosophy the hard facts in this case: that our western way of doing things, though it has always striven for universality (and often ended up simply postulating it), is but *one* way among many of approaching reality. And I am afraid this is true also of phenomenology, which despite all its major breakthroughs remains at heart quite western, even though it has reached the point where it allows of a number of windows leading toward something else. Thus a phenomenology of sound will have to expand itself beyond the traditional western conceptuality and vocabulary of German and French phenomenology, if it is to have a truer universal character.

Traditional musicology relies heavily on the visual. We see this best in the German concept of musicology as a *Wissenschaft*. The German word *wissen*, probably derives from the same root as our cognate word, vision, both words going back via various linguistic avenues to the same Indo-European root, meaning "to see." We would have no musicology, as the knowledge of music, were it not for the development of the visual metaphor in Greek and German philosophy, from which we finally conceive of *Wissenschaft* and thus of *Musik-wissenschaft* as the science-of-music (and Husserl's phenomenology as a "strenge Wissenschaft"?). The word *wissen*, is cognate with the Greek *eidénai*, meaning "to know." *Eidénai* is a verb formed from the word, *eidos*, familiar to phenomenologists. When Aristotle says that "all men are by *physis* aroused to know," he knew that this meant knowledge in the sense of catching sight of the essence of a thing, of gaining access to what it was by means of its *eidos*, i.e. how it *looked*. And thus sight is the keenest of all the senses and even is made to represent them all at the high court of metaphysics.

But surely we can begin to admit, that the light and sight metaphor has been worked to death; perhaps after Heidegger's magnificent use of light metaphor with regard to existential-ontological being nothing more remains to be done on this level in philosophy. Heidegger expanded the metaphor, making it apply to the existential-ontological dimension and reintroducing even the imagery of the Black Forest, when he speaks of *Lichtung* as a "clearing" in the forest, thus an area of light, a mixture of brilliant sunlight and the twilight that eternally inhabits the daytime forest. And this open area is where darkness and light meet in primordial conflict. Many paths lead from the darkened forest into the clearing. And anyone who knows the Black Forest realizes what an impact a brilliant clearing can have as you suddenly emerge from the misty depths into the light. *Lichtung* (or, as in his first Kant book, *Rodung*) is thus not just an abstract lighting up of being; rather it is intimately bound to the mystery and adventure of a journey through the Black Forest, not excluding the whisperings of earth, the threatening storm, the danger from marauding animals, the sudden silences, the weird shapes that lights and shadows can conjure up in a tangle of bush and trees, the discernible cries of birds and the strange and unidentifiable rumblings in the distance, the play of the wind through the pines.

All this is what Heidegger meant by the imagery of the clearing. What a fruitful period would lie ahead in both phenomenology and musicology, were we to allow sound to speak ear-language, a language that could even imitate sound, or at least make use of metaphors of sound. Then our terms for music and logos as musical would not be eye-terms, and our music would not be a kind of philosophical *Augenmusik*; rather it would be meant for listening. Thus music and words about music would be identical. And the original unity of music and philosophy, known to the Greeks, would be recovered.

A musical phenomenology, perhaps of use to both philosophy and musicology alike, might recognize that the greatest areas of human existence and the human phenomenon lie not in light and therefore in the domain of clear and distinct concepts, whether metaphysical or scientific, but in darkness and twilight as well. While it is true that Husserl, Heidegger, and Merleau-Ponty philosophize about the vague, the dark, the unclear and the obscure, they do so mostly in reference to the philosophy of light that is their *pharus*. In the area of darkness and the vague, which is not just the opposite of light and clarity but is the very womb of phenomenology, in this area where eyes and vision fail us (and thus every theory of knowledge or philosophy built thereon) we must, like the "blind," learn to *feel* our way through the darkening night, to *listen* our way through enveloping shadows. It is precisely in this area that sound and sound metaphor are important and that phenomenology is eminently a philosophy of sound as well as of light, or perhaps more accurately a phenomenology of aboriginal and primordial sound.

Thus phenomenology means not only letting things *appear* as they are in light, but also letting them *sound* as they are. This may seem strange: to expect things to sound rather than to appear phenomenally, so that we can perform an eidetic reduction on them. Nietzsche, as great music lover (and mediocre composer!),[17] knew that this "insight" had nothing whatever to do with sight. He was not an iconoclast who went about smashing things for the pure fun of it. The Nietzschean hammer-blow is thus not nihilistic. Nietzsche struck at things with his prophetic-philosophical hammer not to smash them but to "see," i.e. *hear*, whether or not they *rang true*. We thus approach philosophy as we approach a bell or fine china, to test its tone. We do this with crystal wine glasses. The approach is wholly different than just looking at these things and gaining access to what they *are* by how they *look* or appear. We gain truer access by listening to how they *are*, as they *sound*. (And more often than not this is the case in dealing with people as well.)

Here we see the place of the phenomenology of living word and spoken dialogue, of song and poetry, of drama and fable. Surely this field of darkness and musical sound within the human psyche and within world is also of moment for the musicologist, too. Is this not precisely where traditional psychology falls down, since, whether as scientific or even as existential, it is more or less blandly tied to light and sight metaphors and to an ontology of science or being that is almost wholly dependent upon but a fraction of the total human spectrum and facticity? The psychologist leaves out the whole area of sound and never-the-less expects to "sound the depths" of the human psyche, when even psyche itself means not "mind" or "soul" but the *breath* or bodily movement of the *corps ontologique*, thus something much closer to phenomenological voice than to rational mind. Using music as an external therapy is no substitute for neglecting the dimension of sound itself.

V

Is this not what G. Marcel is trying to tell us, when in *Le mystère de l'être* he writes, that he is thinking and writing not in logical but in "musical" manner? In *Homo Viator* and the *Journal Métaphysique* he also takes his cue from musical composition, as temporal. Heidegger uses the musical tone as pivotal in the understanding and effecting of the ontological leap in *Der Satz vom Grand*.[18] In *Der Ursprung des Kunstwerkes* he gets away from both esthetics (the logic of esthesis) and philosophy of beauty, making us aware of art as the emergence of ontological *truth* in the primordial struggle between world and earth. As seen in the musical work of art this struggle or conflict gives rise to the creation of a musical composition, but it is likewise the ground of language, as such. We might be justified in saying that nowhere is a musical logos more at work than in the pro-ducing (the bringing-forth) of the work of art. But here again Heidegger is more aware of Van Gogh and Greek temples than he is, let us say, of Hinemith or the so-called ethos of Greek music. Yet what made a temple come alive if not the music and dance of its devotees? What gives the full essence of the peasant maiden's shoes in the painting of Van Gogh, if not her actually using them to plod along, feeling the good earth underneath. The "musical" silence of these shoes is what makes them what they are to the maiden. Were they only to be seen, or were they to sound when worn, they would not be what they are. But their silence is significant, and it is only from the logos as essentially musical that we can grasp this.

In the Greek times, of which Heidegger is so fond, music and thinking were not so sharply distinguished as now. The word, music, had a much broader meaning. We still retain vestiges of this fullness of meaning in such words as musing, museum, musicals, etc. Musing is thinking. In *Was heisst Denken?* Heidegger tells us that Mnemosyne, the Mother of the Muses and of music, is not to be translated as "memory." Perhaps the mythological rather than the facultative definition of "memory" brings us closer to the problem we now have of relating thought to memory. Perhaps the Mother of the Muses simply teaches us to muse, i.e. to "make music," as living thought rather than as theoretical abstraction. (And again "theory" means *looking* at and into a thing.)

In the middle ages music had a broader meaning than today: it meant that the philosopher or thinker, as *musicus*, took delight in the philosophico-mathematical play of proportions that made music possible at all. Thus the medieval *musicus* cannot be translated as "musician." He was indeed the "muser." Since that time music gradually became more and more restricted in meaning, so that in the last century with the help of German pedagogy the meaning of music was restricted to the practical musician and practical music. The cleft between musical theory and practice became problematical. Music still suffers from this schizoid condition, as does philosophy itself and many an academic field. But more and more attempts are being made, and perhaps this rather than historical and esthetical research is the truer task of musicology, to bridge the dualism between theory and practice in convincing manner.

I feel that phenomenology can be of service at this crucial point by showing the need not only to build a bridge but to overcome the dualism, as such. Instead of the provissional solution as of a Jacques de Liège, who speaks of a theoretical practice and a practical theory in his *Speculum Musicae*,[19] we may be called on to apply to music and the arts what is discoverable in phenomonological context as a living *praxis*. In a living praxis one not only sees the world but *"does* the world"; and perhaps this doing of world — and here I obviously rely on Merleau-Ponty — is a more pertinent phenomenological stance than either seeing or hearing the world, or a complex of both. Perhaps the basis of this phenomenology, which includes the akumenal context as well as the phenomenal, is for both musician and philosopher alike the *corps ontologique* in quality of *logos mousikos*. For we want to avoid what the composer Hindemith called the short-circuiting between head and hands — and on a larger scale, between man, himself, and his world.

Certainly contemporary thinking, especially along phenomenological lines, is rife with insights for new horizons in musicology. But perhaps musicology itself, as it comes to deal more convincingly with the live fact of sound, can remind phenomenology of the danger of remaining too caught up in its visual orientation. Perhaps our regarding man, his musing, and his music, from out a living *praxis* rather than mere theory or mere practice, can lead us to the point where man is reunited with the live world of thought, speech, music, and the arts. Perhaps this is the key to a rejuvenation of our philosophical and musicological endeavors: to discover that thinking and musing are at root the same thing, and thus that philosophy and the musical arts are really one. For if philosophy leads us out of the *monde-en-idée* into the *monde-lui-même*, will this live world not be one in which man learns to sing again? And is not song part of the "dance of being"?

VI

In his *Metaphysics* Aristotle criticizes his teacher Plato for his apparent hypostatization of the world of ideas. And thus the return to *prágma*, to the "thing" as something to be done, rather than any continuance in the world of *idea*, i.e. of abstract "forms." Aristotle's coming back to this world from an ideational one is a step in the right direction, if indeed Plato did take his other-world as seriously as did christian neoplatonists. That he did do this is, of course, a moot question. Plato was too much a Greek to actually believe that his other-world was anything more than a symbol. It was left to christian theology to take it literally, and we might add, materialistically, some scholars feel. Hence, Aristotle's supposed criticism of Plato is one that is based not on the Greek but on dated translations of Aristotle, translations couched in languages that had received a rather heavy metaphysical overlay. Whatever the case may be, it is not so much this purported criticism of Plato that preoccupies the modern student of Greek thought, as much as something more important for the whole sweep of western philosophy: Aristotle's confirmation of the primacy of sight and insight in the life of man and in his thought and culture.

For already in the first paragraph of the *Metaphysics* Aristotle claims that sight is the keenest of man's senses, and it is interesting to note that the Greek word, *eidénai*, to know, is derived from a visual word, *eidos*, which means the way a thing looks; and thus its "essence." And so when

Aristotle states that "every man is aroused by his very nature to know," it means that he finds it urgent to gain sight of things and thus to know them by means of intellectual insight. We begin with the *prágma*, it is true. This brings us out of theorizations for their own sake back to things as they give themselves to us in perception. But the language in which this process is couched is heavily influenced by and depends on what we would now call visual metaphor. "Meta-phor" means literally that which is "carried-over" from one stratum to another; and thus things caught *sight* of become the object of *insight*. What is seen by the eye becomes material for the "mind's eye," as it seeks to "see" into things and question them. The primary question for Aristotle, of course, was "What is a being" and "What is beingness (*ousía*)?"

It appears that Aristotle set the pace for subsequent classic philosophies. It is true that Plato had spoken of clarity (*lamprótes*) as the goal of thought, and had used a further visual metaphor when describing the two *tópoi*, thus the *tópos horatós*, i.e. the "place" or region of the senses, sight in this case standing for all the senses. But it was Aristotle, who in confirming this visual orientation of his master and mentor, influenced the entire history of classic thought and its linguistic expression. And so Augustine also, though apparently influenced more directly by Christian Platonism, made sight stand for all the senses, as Heidegger has pointed out in *Sein und Zeit*.[20] From here it is but a step to the confluence of Platonism and Aristotelianism in the "intuitional" theories of the middle ages. An *in-tuitio* means, of course, insight, literally a *looking-into* a thing. From here through Kant, Hegel, and Husserl to Heidegger and the continental phenomenology of today is a long stretch of history but a short step in the expansion of the visual metaphor in the expression of philosophical thought. For if we examine key concepts in these classic philosophers, we find such words as *Anschauung, Wesensschau, Sicht, Ereignis*, etc., all having to do with some sort of intuition, insight or the sighting of what a thing is. We need not go into the radical difference in the use of such a word as "intuition" between such philosophers as Descartes, Kant, and Husserl. For that is common knowledge. But the general visual orientation of such language is evident enough. Perhaps it takes a musician to raise an objection to this overemphasis on sight and insight. For a musician appreciates the place of hearing in the understanding of the live word, as opposed to the merely written or mentalistic one, as he also appreciates metaphors which have their origin not in the things of sight or insight but in the raw sounds of nature.

Music, musicology, and words

For the Greeks there was no such sharp distinction between music and thought. J. Lohmann, writing in the *Archiv für Musikwissenschaft* on the "origin" of music, deserves credit for pointing out this historical fact, along with a few other philologists both here and abroad.[21] Greek poetry is a good example of the unity of music and word. It is only in its metaphysical alienation from living sound that word takes on a spurious existence of its own. It is only in the departure of Aristotle's *epistéme* from concrete *logos* that "special language" is made possible: language that becomes a thing apart from living man, an abstraction that begins to take on an existence of its own. Yet we cannot accuse Aristotle. Again, he too, was too much of a Greek to allow a beginning logic to spin itself out of the real world into a shadow existence in some mentalistic arena. The real split between living word as musical sound and word as a mere entity to be manipulated by rhetorician and dialectician came about in the gradual rise of Christian Platonism and Latinized Aristotelianism. The "alienation" is most easily seen in the clever distinction of Abelard between voice (*vox*) as the spoken word which signifies things but is not a thing in itself and the word (*sermo*) which is the word of man that originates any universal meaning not to be found in things or in a given *vox*. Thus "voice" is of nature, whereas "word" (*sermo*) is of man's making. Logic has to do only with the word, as instituted by man, and it is only here that any universal term can be found.[22] In our own day attempts have been made by various philosophers from different schools to reunite logic with logos, i.e. the abstract with the concrete. Hegel made the classic breakthrough out of mentalism and returned to logic as dialectical.[23] Husserl speaks of formal logic as "objective" rather than as mentalistic.[24] If logic has indeed become a form of alienation from live reality, perhaps its usefulness as a word, heavily laden with classic metaphysical meaning, is at an end. In certain strains of contemporary phenomenology one would not be interested in mentalistic logics as much as in the "logic" of things, whether real or ideal. Such "logic" would interest itself not in the traffic regulations of the flow of thought or the grammatical pre-occupations of some philosophical school marm, as much as in the *structure* of things, real or ideal. Thus the structuring of speech, as it is being spoken, as "musical" sound, would again become important. And the unity of abstract and concrete world would be achieved.

In similar manner the word, *mousiké*, which for the Greeks was concrete and much broader in meaning than our word (which we naively use to translate the original), also fell prey to a metaphysical alienation. To begin with, the Greek word was an adjective. Music, as a word, did not become a noun until the early renaissance. One sees this quite easily in the Latin musical treatises of the middle ages, where the Greek *téchne mousiké* is rendered *ars musica*, as one of the liberal arts in the medieval quadrivium. It was the French who introduced the word *la musique* as a noun having to do exclusively with what musicians do when they perform. German and English followed suit. Music becomes a cultural and later a pedagogical specialty. Its meaning gets narrowed down to what we now call formal music. In our times philosophy and music are far apart indeed. But it is only an un-overcome metaphysicism that blocks their being reunited as they were in their very origins in Greek times.

The live word that we speak to one another every day is a sound word, a word that sounds in "musical" cadences,

easily identified by the student of language. It seems strange
that this truism should have to be emphasized. It is strange,
that, granted this apparent fact, one would complain of too
much visual metaphor in ordinary speech and in literature or
philosophy. Even the visual word, "intuition," must be
spoken in order to be heard and understood. And yet it refers
not to hearing but to sight. Our philosophy was thus built
not on the live word but on what it signified. And what it
signified was expressed in a mode carried over from what we
see; thus "sight" and "insight." Sight stands for all the
senses, even for hearing, although the actual words we use to
explain this orally are rendered in live sound. Is there not a
radical imbalance at work here? Not that we would want to,
or could ever, abolish visual metaphor. What is hinted at here
is the possibility of counteracting an overemphasis on it, an
emphasis which has apparently suppressed many other
possibilities built on the word as musical or living sound.

And what is the situation of musicology in all this? Apel
has defined it as study and research in music history and
theory. Bukofzer would go a step further into esthetics.
Some people would include the work of Kurth and Wellek
in the psychology of music. Musicology, born in an atmosphere of scientific objectivity, needed to have resource to
the "subjectivity" of esthetics, in order to restore a balance,
in order not to sacrifice art to science. And yet esthetics,
too, can be regarded as a form of metaphysics. And thus at
least Heidegger returns to a more concrete *aesthesis*, using
the Greeks again as a mode.[25] But *aesthesis* is no longer mere
sense perception nor is it a theory of beauty or of pleasure.
We have no word to translate "*aesthesis*." The imposition of
metaphysics upon language with its concomitant suppression
of concrete native words has seen to that. The closest one can
come is "feeling," but that word has an unfortunate history.
Has metaphysics ruined our chances of expressing our experience of art and music in meaningful language? Or ought one
not lapse into silence before the work of art! Certainly one
should keep silence during a musical concert. And subsequent
analysis, musical or philosophical, risks running a solid

appreciation of the art, as musicology with all its severe
historical scholarship has often brought about an alienation
of the scholar from his art, despite the extensive contribu-
tions he has made to the practical musician.

The return from all these alienated mental words to live
sound and living word is crucial if there is to be a reuniting of
the various branches of learning. Or is the fragmentation to
continue indefinitely, until what little communication there
is between the disciplines vanishes so totally, that we think
and talk past one another as though we actually did live in
special worlds separated from each other by a chasm! Musicology has been called "words about music," which is the most
damning thing a practicing musician can say about the work
of the scholar. The tendency of philosophy has always been
to be caught up in a web of words. For even though Aristotle
did return to the *prágma*, this was not philosophical for him
until it was caught up in speech. Philosophy started out as
words-about-things. This still seems to be what it is. And yet
while this may be quite satisfactory for the philosopher, it is
not so for the musician, who knows that verbalizations,
important as they may be, are not everything. The artist
tends not to verbalize his art, unless he is a poet. At least the
painter and the musician are too preoccupied with the work
of art itself to verbalize about it. The work of art, whether
it be Rodin's *Lovers* or Stravinsky's *Agon*, speaks for itself.
Verbalizations may come afterward, but they are not overly
important or impressive to the artist himself. And surely it is
presumptuous for the overeager non-artist to put words in
the artist's mouth for him. Musicologists and estheticians are
not too popular with artists. Of course, there are some cases
where the musician, thinker, and musicologist are combined
in one person. Perhaps Egon Wellesz is the best example of
that. The trend today is to unite musician and musicologist.
But the bringing together of musician and philosopher of
music is still a distant ideal. The latter is too often a well-
meaning dilettante; the former may appear anti-intellectual,
and not without good reason.

Phenomenology as an overcoming of metaphysics

But how does a phenomenology of sound figure in all this? What indeed is "phenomenology"? In Husserl it is an attempt to break out of what he calls the "natural attitude" in which classic metaphysical and scientific thought had trapped itself. In his later works, which are models of style and clarity compared with the early writings, in which he was struggling with the inadequacies and limitations of traditional metaphysical language, Husserl speaks of phenomenology as a "conversion," not to be taken in any religious sense, of course. A conversion means simply a change of attitude, in this case a freeing of oneself from a tight categorical mentality so that one can encounter reality afresh, so that one can indeed get back to the "things themselves." Husserl also speaks of the phenomenological attitude as an awakening to life[26] out of the torpor and rigidity induced by classic metaphysical categories. The phenomenologist is to develop an awakened awareness of himself and others, in short of life and world.

In Heidegger one secs an attempt to break out of what he calls the "ontic" order of thinking and things. This means a break with the Aristotelian question of being; for Aristotle narrowed philosophy down to the ontological theme, to the preoccupation with beings (*tà ónta*) and categorial forms. The word that is meant to signify Heidegger's breakthrough is *das Sein*, which is no longer trapped in the order of beings as such, and thus one is freed to pursue other horizons and can even become "ontic" in a more meaningful sense. From Heidegger's early work, when he, too, struggled with the language problem, to his later works one sees a struggle to overcome metaphysics. For some, Heidegger's later works, models of style and expression, are regarded as "poetic." But Heidegger himself would regard this as an ontic evaluation, i.e. one made by a thinker still caught in the thought forms of classical logic and ontology. Be that as it may, what we seek to do here is not to give an appraisal, one way or the other, of either Husserl or Heidegger. Our point is that, while

they sought to overcome metaphysics, they may have succeeded only to a degree. For, the chief metaphysical "category," that of insight as a visual symbol, remains essentially
un-overcome. Both Husserl and Heidegger, despite the fact
that they occasionally deal with sound, still bear witness to
the classical tradition that expresses philosophical thought in
words which rely heavily on visual metaphor. Thus Husserl
writes of the "intuition of essence" (*Wesensschau*); and
Heidegger speaks of that sighting of things (*Sicht*) which is
basic even to any phenomenological intuition of reality.
Much of current phenomenology, of course, no longer makes
great use of the breakthrough language of either Husserl or
Heidegger. And thus both intuitional essences, which Husserl
conceived as un-metaphysical, and Heidegger's so-called
"eksistent" ontology are regarded as but part of the early
history of the movement, though indeed in America these
works are just beginning to be studied as they were in Europe
in the twenties and thirties. And yet even such a contemporary phenomenologist as M. Merleau-Ponty also relied on
visual metaphor in the expression of philosophical thought.
It is true that he advanced the study of sound and even of
music itself, yet in the final analysis, he, too, stands in the
classical tradition.

What phenomenology needs is an expansion beyond its
preoccupation with the *phenomena*, i.e. those things which
appear-in-light and thus are the object of *sight* and insight.
Phenomenology must yet develop a more convincing attitude
towards things *heard*, i.e., if we must describe them in the
terms of continental philosophy, towards *akoumena*. And a
word is primarily not something to be seen in print or to be
thought about in accord with what is now being called the
"Gutenberg Complex": a word is first and foremost a thing
to be spoken and to be listened to. Yet, even the title of this
paper starts with the word, "insight." And as the author tries
to break out of too much visual metaphor, he searches in
vain for a word to replace insight. We will never know what
akoumenal words were suppressed during the evolution of
our language, so that we might find ourselves in our present

impasse. And the speaker hesitates to introduce a neologism such as "in-hearing." Such things are frowned upon in English, though they are acceptable enough in cognate Germanic tongues. Only poets are allowed such licence. Philosophers are limited to the *status quo*, until someone like Cicero gives us a neologism as the word, "quality"; or some translator like Boethius puts the words, "nature," "form," "essence," or "substance" into the stream of Western language; or until some illiterate American president calls for a return to "normalcy."

As both Hegel and Heidegger have pointed out, classical metaphysics was caught in propositional language which was the result of one-directional thinking, i.e. which was trapped in spatial-linear metaphor. For whether we look to time, as stretched out in linear space because of its being defined in terms of spatial metaphor, or to the general language of positivistic metaphysics, one sees the same phenomenon. It is especially the category of time, so important for music and for recent continental philosophy, that needed to be delivered from its spatial prison. And in similar manner the word of the thinker needed to come out of the special world created by intellectualism and rejoin the world of the poet who appreciated not just the dry meaning of it but also its actual sound as it was born in dynamic time as well as in intellectualized space.

Some cogent themes in detail: sound and "insight"

What, then, is sound as such, if we grant that words may be spoken and even sung, if we grant that meaning is imparted not just through abstract cogitations but in concrete relationship with the total nuances of words *as* they are being proffered in speech or song? Sound has been variously defined and categorized. Writers speak of physical sound and scientists have written books on "acoustics." Thus the "electric oscillograph," a term readily grasped by the speaker of ordinary language, becomes important, and thus sounds are graphed *visually*, so that they can indeed become an *object* of scientific study. It is obvious that though the phenomenologist and the musicologist (who has had to study acoustics!) are aware of the value of such researches, they also do not look to acoustics for a viable definition of music or for insight into the possible significance of the musical experience of e.g. the performer or the composer. To regard sound only as physical means to view it from an intellectualistic position. For one sees the not-so-hidden dualism between the mental and the physical, i.e. between the meanings imparted by the mind and the significance that arises from a consideration of a raw phenomenon of nature. It is precisely this dualism of mind and matter that troubles the phenomenologist. From the historical viewpoint he may justly regard it as a kind of un-overcome medievalism. The classic example of this medieval dichotomy is evidenced in the *Speculum Musicae*, the high point of medieval music theory. But in this encyclopaedic musicological manuscript one sees clearly depicted the rationalistic metaphysics of the *ars antiqua*, the last grand manifesto of classic dualism: mind over body and nature. For music gets its meaning not from the spoken or sung word itself but rather from the rational speculation concerning the nature of musical consonance, defined in terms of exact and exacting mathematical proportionality. The *musicus* is therefore not to be translated as "musician" but as mathematician-philosopher, who literally delights in the interplay of classic proportionality in the analysis of consonance and its subconcepts. The *musicus* need never really *listen* to any music; he already knows all about it mentally. And thus physical sound has no meaning in itself; it has meaning only as material to be fed into an intellectual grid. The practicing musician is reduced to being called one of Guido d'Arezzo's *bestiae* or to sitting at the feet of the Christian metaphysician, there to learn his mathematics and metaphysics. It is apparent that neither master nor disciple will have much time left over either to sing or to play the lute. The true intellectual has little to do with such a thing as live sound, whether it be "voice" in the sense of the logic of Abelard or in the sense of a medieval *chanson.* Certainly he would never attach any meaning, especially of universal intention, to it.

In the history of musical theory one can trace the same alienation of meaning from actual music as one can trace the separation of live word from metaphysics in the history of · classical philosophies. Meaning is imparted from on high, from outside the musical experience, from beyond the musical word. And thus the gradual alienation of physical sound from what is defined formally as "music." The pheno-menologist sets himself the task of becoming aware of this case of double vision and of correcting it by a return to the basic unity of experience and expression thereof, whatever the time sequence be.

In the ordinary spoken language we make use of a number of metaphors and idioms that may prove worth looking into — or perhaps even worth hearing. In contrast to always referring to the "mind's eye" and to insight we sometimes speak of "sounding a thing out." Boatmen take a sounding to ascertain the depth of the channel and to judge what course to plot. Sometimes we say that a thing "sounds right" or "sounds somehow wrong." We gain adequate access to the meaning of what a given individual says to us not only from the abstract consideration of a dry proposition but from the tonal nuances of the statement itself. Often the statement may remain the same, word for word. But its meaning can be drastically altered by the particular tone and the circumstances under which it is pronounced. And thus while a given statement, such as "You are quite a talent" may be grammatically and logically correct as a given proposition, the tone of sarcasm or irony prevents one from a naive acceptance of the statement at its face value. The sound of a statement cannot be ignored if one is looking for the full meaning of what someone says to us or perhaps mutters to himself. And thus, though the statement is quite correct, it just does not "sound right" to us. And we part company with our friend, sure of our intellectual categories but quite confused as to what was really said. And thus because the statement has not *sounded* right to us, we mutter, "I wonder what he really meant by that!"

Some initial conclusions

Perhaps the overcoming of metaphysics can be abetted by an attempt to put into perspective our over-reliance on the visual metaphor in philosophical and musicological language. It is the correction of this imbalance, and only this, towards which the present effort is bent. What can take the place of some of the tradition's visually oriented words is not yet as evident as we would like. Perhaps this indicates not our inability to devise some meaningful "substitute" but the possibility that the visual metaphor represents a kind of dead-end for which no substitute is desirable. But one thing is certain: the proper use of visual metaphor and the restoration of other kinds is part of an overcoming of metaphysical alienation. If we start at the beginning with Aristotle we might want to disagree, at least those of us who are also musicians, that sight is the keenest of the senses and that it can stand for all the other senses without further ado. A number of reasons, including geography and climate, pre-conditioned the Greeks to put such emphasis on and advance such claims for sight. But we are justified in asking if even such students of Aristotle as the musical theorist, Aristo-xenos, really believed with the master that sight was all that keen. It is a known fact that the Greek musical ear was attuned to far more subtle nuances than is our own and that musical theory was far more complex not because of meta-physical considerations but because of just such subtlety of perception. It is certain that medieval metaphysics took one away from the brute fact of musical sounds as such. In our time efforts are being made to come out of intellectualisms of all sorts toward a more fundamental appreciation of musical sound in its own right rather than as mere material for some intellectual grid, of whatever kind.

As to phenomenology, while there have been a good

number of allusions to sound, and while musical tone has
even been crucial to Husserl's own early treatise on time as
well as to Heidegger's "existential leap," it remains true that
the fundamental metaphor of sight and insight is unovercome; and all else hinges on that. In early Heidegger *Sicht*
is presented as fundamental to his entire philosophy, as basic
even to that *Wesensschau* which is the controvertible cornerstone of Husserlian thought. Yet in the later Heidegger the
situation remains basically unaltered, despite occasional
eloquent passages here and there about hearing and listening
(in this case to the *logos*); for, the later Heidegger emphasizes
a new cornerstone, that *Er-eignis* or *in-sight* which is essential
to all thought. The purpose of the present paper is not to
give a complete critique of the use of all possible visual metaphors in classic philosophies but only to begin to point out
a number of key terms that are essential to such thinking.
And in so doing one notes the predominance of sight and
insight in the language employed. The working out of this
critique will obviously take a good deal of time and further
research. But in the meantime the possible range of phenomenology, as expandable beyond its apparent imbeddedness
in the visual, is envisioned.

Above all the restoration of words as living sound,
rather than as mere items for metaphysical and other propositions, is called for. Words, as live sound, are crucial not just
to the poet but also to the musician, who works both with
musical sounds and with words as such. One need hardly
recall the important influence of words on music and vice
versa, the easiest example being the series of sketches made
by Beethoven of the opening theme of the last movement of
the *Choral Symphony*, where he labored over the word,
"*Freude*," until he found the correct balance between the
word and the theme. It is only the inveterate metaphysician
who cannot see this, and he is the kind of thinker, of whom
Sartre wrote, "Wherever he treads, the grass stops growing."
The phenomenologist does not examine only the inert
propositional deposit of language but the structure of the
living word and statement *as* it is being spoken. In order to

do this properly his attitude cannot be that of the traditional philosopher, whose key terms are expressed as visual metaphors. In a certain sense propositions and the language of visual metaphor exist only in the head of the philosopher, for we search in vain for the real existence of a word or statement as merely printed or as merely mental.[27] The only "real" thing is man speaking and thus stating in temporal sequence what he wants to say or sing. And even this sequence cannot be conceived as merely linear or serial, i.e. as extended in a metaphorical line, so that the "mind" can bring it together as a "statement." The live voice is the place to begin, not the written or printed sequence which at once becomes an object for sight and thus for "insight" as well. The influence of writing on the history of Western music is well known, but it is not realized how thoroughly many of our supposed thought modes also depend on the printed or written line. Yet the written line and its after-image, which often qualifies as propositional thought in the sense of Hegel, is only a record of a past statement by a speaker. Merleau-Ponty calls attention to this when in his *Phénoménologie de la Perception* he writes, that the *cogito* has no existence whatever, except when I speak it and think it. In similar manner the written scores of a given symphony are not music until they are restored as live sound by musicians. Obviously, the written note and the written word are but aids or symbols. But they are neither thought nor music. The living man is required for there to be either philosophy or music. And living voice is the means by which he communicates with the other.

   If we have been troubled by the overdependence of classic intellectualism on the visual metaphor and visual symbols in the expression of its content, what is a symbol, what is a metaphor? Allow me to give but a partial and exploratory reply. A symbol is not just what merely "stands for" something, or in a German sense merely sensibilizes a concept (*versinnbildlichen*). Symbol may be a kind of "presence." Thus the written word is the second presence of the spoken word. Spoken word is the first presence of *man as speaker*. First presence is effected in the sound of the spoken word. Second presence is only seen in the written or printed word. And it is there that we object to reducing all sound symbols and metaphors to the visual. The phenomenologist, more aware of the akoumenal than the phenomenal aspects of reality, regards language symbols primarily as "musical," i.e. the appearance in sound of the living word. Language is thus not mere symbol as the medium of expression, as though it existed somewhere apart from the living man in some special metaphysical world. Language, as spoken, means the human being as speaker or even as singer. It is living man, not some higher logic that regulates and affects language when spoken. And all else, including classical logic and grammar, is secondary, however important an achievement it represented. They are "secondary," i.e. consequent upon the primary presence of the spoken word. And thus man is the "symbolic animal," to use Cassirer's words, not merely because he uses a given set of pre-existing symbols as though they lay about somewhere waiting to be picked up and used as "tools," but because man himself sym-bolizes or puts-together the phonemes of words in accord with patterns he has learned from his forebears, patterns he re-shapes in accord with his own environment, his needs, his limitations, his ambitions, his errors.

To conclude, though traditional phenomenologists have dealt with sound and traditional musicologists have studied music in all its ramifications, historical and esthetical, all are apparently still caught up in systems whose *key terms* are borrowed from the visual, are carried-over (meta-phor) from the vocabulary of sight and thus are imposed on the vocabularies of the other senses, which do exist, but which may have been prevented from flowering because of this imbalance. Our aim here is not to criticize negatively but only to sound out the possibilities of working more closely with sound, whether that be the voice speaking a philosophical sentence or singing a melodic phrase. In a sense this is both philosophy and musicology used against themselves, with varying degrees of success and failure.

Endnotes

1. Cf. Don Ihde, "Some auditory phenomena" in *Philosophy Today* (winter 1966); also "Discussion: Sound and Music." comments on a paper given at the IV Lexington Conference on Phenomenology by F. J. Smith (1967). Ihde works within the framework of phenomenological psychology. A recent essay by A. Pike, "A Phenomenology of Music" in *Philosophy and Phenomenological Research*, Dec. 1966, is a presentation of materials from L. Meyer concerning music and Gestalt psychology. It is not phenomenological, nor can Meyer be called a phenomenologist. This seems to be the opinion of Meyer himself, in a communication with the present writer. It is true that A. Gurwitsch has regarded Gestalt psychology as phenomenological in a "pre-phenomenological" sense. But even he admits the need of phenomenological *reduction*, missing in traditional Gestalt theory. Cf. Aron Gurwitsch, "The Phenomenological and the Psychological Approach to Consciousness" in *Essays in Phenomenology*, edited by M. Natanson (The Hague, 1966), pp. 40-57.

   Convincing essays on the subject are those of Eimert, "Zur Phänomenologie der Musik" in *Melos, Zeitschrift für Musik*, 1926, pp. 244-45, and H. Mersmann, "Zur Phänomenologie der Musik" in *Zeitschrift für Aesthetik*, 1925. Perhaps the most convincing work of all is "Das Musikwerk" in R. Ingarden's *Untersuchungen zur Ontologie der Kunst* (Tubingen, 1952). Cf. also A. Schutz, ed. F. Kersten, "Fragments on the phenomenology of music" in *Music and Man, vol. II, nos 1/2, 1976*, pp. 5-71.

2. M. Heidegger, "Der Weg zur Sprache" in *Unterwegs zur Sprache* (Pfullingen, 1959), p. 260.

3. J. Derrida, *La voix et le phénomène: Signe linguistique et non-linguistique dans la phénoménologie de Husserl.*

4. J. Derrida, in *L'écriture et al différence* (Paris, 1967), p. 117f.

5. In using the term, "lived world," I wish to dissociate it from an existentialist interpretation of Husserl's *Lebenswelt*. The latter means first and foremost a primordial *doxic belief* or trust in world; existentiality of whatever kind is secondary to *Urdoxa*, as such. This is brought out clearly in Husserl's *Krisis der europäischen Wissenschaften*.

6. The present writer hesitates to capitalize the English word, being, in an effort to render Heidegger's distinction between ontic being (*das Seiende*) and existential-ontological being (*das Sein*). Capitalization tends to make "being" look like some sort of metaphysical absolute, perhaps like the one Levinas fears, writing in *Totalité et infini*, an absolute which goes on "independently of beings."

7.   *Echos* is taken to mean "primordial sound," everything from the
      sudden crash of thunder or the roar of a waterfall to the gentle
      lapping of alluvial waters against the shore. Such sound is not yet
      "musical." Musical sound is *tonos* for the Greeks, tonus for
      medieval music, and tonality/atonality for us.
8.   A section of the larger work was presented at the IV Lexington
      Conference, April 7, 1967, repeated at Washington University,
      June 24, 1967: "Toward a Phenomenology of musical Aesthetics."
9.   This is not in agreement with Kant's division of the arts in *Kritik
      der Urteilskraft* (ed. K. Vorländer), 1951, p. 175f. Cf. footnote,
      p. 176, where he specifically leaves the question open and does
      not pretend to fixate the arts in some sort of dogmatic division.
10.   Cf. the present writer's contribution, "In the world and on the
      earth: a Heideggerian interpretation," in *Heidegger and the Quest
      for Truth* (Quadrangle Books, 1968).
11.   M. Heidegger, "Das Wesen der Sprache" in *Unterwegs zur Sprache*
      (Pfullingen, 1959), p. 216.
12.   M. Merleau-Ponty, "La métaphysique dans l'homme" in *Sens et
      non-sens* (Paris, 1948) p. 171.
13.   Ontological pre-sence or "presential being" is a rendering of
      Heidegger's *Anwesenheit*, which in turn is his interpretation of
      the Greek, *ousia*.
14.   M. Heidegger, "Logos (Heraklit, Fragment 50)," pp. 214-15.
15.   By "sonorous sound" is meant mere physical or acoustical sound.
      But *musica sonora* also means metaphysical sound, if we look at
      Speculum Musicae of Jacques de Liège. Both physical and meta-
      physical sound must be bracketed, in order that sound may
      merge in its primordial sensuousness and richness.
16.   Cf. the present writer's *Iacobi Leodiensis Speculum Musicae, a
      Commentary, vol. I* (Institute of Mediaeval Music, 1966), pass.
17.   H. G. Hoke, "Nietzsche, F. W." in *Die Musik in Geschichte und
      Gegenwart* (Kassel, 1961), vol. 9, pp. 1521-26. The author is
      shocked at Nietzsche's "immoralism," without really under-
      standing that it is a profound Christian-prophetic critique of
      Christianity's dubious position.
18.   M. Heidegger, *Der Satz vom Grund* (Pfullingen, 1957) pp. 95, 117f.
19.   Cf. the writer's "Ars Nova, a Re-definition?" in *Musica Disciplina*
      (American Institute of Musicology) 1964; 1965.
20.   Cf. S7 no. 36, p. 171, from *Confessiones*, X, cap. 35, "vide quid
      sonet ."
21.   J. Lohmann, "Der Ursprung der Musik" in *Archiv dur Musik-
      wissenschaft*, 1952, Heft 12, p. 161.
22.   P. Vignaux, *La philosophie aux moyen âge*, (Paris, 1958) ch. II pass.
23.   G. F. Hegel, *Wissenschaft der Logik*, I, Die objektive Logik, pass.
24.   E. Husserl, "Formale und transzendentale Logik. Versuch einer
      Kritik der logischen Vernunft" in *Jahrbuch dur Philosophie und*

phänomenologische Forschung, X, 1920; separately, 1929.
25. M. Heidegger, *Der Ursprung des Kunstwerkes*, (Stuttgart, 1960). Intro. by Gadamer.
26. E. Husserl, *Die Krisis der europäischen Wissenschaften und die transzendentale Phänomenologie*, (The Hague, 1954), ed. W. Biemel.
27. R. Ingarden, *Untersuchungen zur Ontologie der Kunst*, 1962, Das Musikwerk, no. 3, Das Musikwerk und die Partitur, pp. 23-26.

Chapter 3

WORKING PROPOSITIONS IN SOUND: A BAROQUE SUITE

ADAGIO

1) As a word, ana-lysis means the breaking down (or literally, the "loosening-up") of anything into its component parts. This is the original Greek meaning, one that seems to have perdured more or less intact to our own day. Thus today we "analyze" a sentence from some book or essay or a musical statement from a sonata by Beethoven or a section of some compact composition by Anton Webern. Analysis is an ancient word, one originally not proper to ordinary English, but a word that filtered down into common parlance from the discussions of academicians. Even to ordinary people today "analysis," as a word, conjures up the earnest chemist, the musical theorist, the therapist, and in general somewhat extraordinary people, one of whose chief tasks seems to be to "analyze" things or people. Philosophers set about to analyze language and, going beyond to "extra-linguistic" areas, they claim to analyze also "objects," thus drawing closer to their scientist colleagues, for whom they seem to have considerable admiration.

2) Analysis is an ancient and yet contemporary word. Without the Greeks, from whom we once borrowed the word, we could not speak of analysis at all today. Philosophical analysists love the Greek word *analysis* as much as Husserl loved the word *eidos*, and Heidegger the *logos*. The only difference was that the two latter words never filtered down into ordinary language in their original forms. But they did come down to us as *idea* (a variant form of *eidos*) and as

"logic." The Latin translation of *eidos*, i.e. *essentia*, also found its way into English as the word, *essence*. Philosophers would be in a bad way without Greek and Latin loan words and derivatives. Yet what does "analysis" really mean to us? Granting what poor shape we would be in without the translations made by Boethius (which gave us the words, essence, form, matter, etc.), what does "analysis" mean to the working philosopher of today? Does a given statement (or a given musical composition) "break down" naturally and of itself into component parts or must it be broken down by the "mind" in its analytic activity? It is at this point that we seem to differ from the Greeks. For we tend to cut things apart according to mental categories, whereas for the Greeks *things* fell quite naturally into their component parts. And, of course, the word *thing* had a much broader meaning than our present English usage, which seems confused with the word *object*. There were several kinds of "things" in Greek: a thing to do (*pragma*), a thing to be "handled" (*chrema*), a thing to be acted out (*drama*), etc. All these "things" were forced together in the Latin translation *res*, from which we get our word "reality", which we like to call (tautologically?) "objective reality," as opposed to the "subjective" creations of mind as over against object-things. Thus, there has been an impoverishment of meaning and a kind of flattening out process, which has given us the rather unimaginative word "reality." We no longer stand at the center of this Latin loan word. We understand what it means only from the circumstances in which we have heard it *used*. And so we also feel justified in using it to translate the various Greek words for "thing."

ANDANTE

3) The Greek attitude is "phenomenological" despite its incipient intellectualism. It is not mentalistic. Mental categories are more the product of post-medieval thinking than they are of Greek "logic." And this is why phenomenology

insists on bracketing out (but not thereby destroying) logical categories: not merely to attain a better understanding of Greek philosophy, from which we have gotten so many crucial words and notions, but to get "back to the things themselves," whether these be the "things of the mind" or object-things, i.e. whether they be "ideal" or "real" things. Thus phenomenological "analysis" is not first and foremost a logical technique for breaking down sentences or objects of experience. These very structures of the "mind" need to be held in abeyance in order that a simple observation and description of the thing itself be made possible *as it resolves iself* into its component parts. Hence such analysis is not a "mental activity" but the disengagement of typically western categories in order that the thing, whatever it may be, may *present* itself adequately to the thinker. Mental activity needs to be bracketed out if the "natural structure," e.g. of a musical composition, is to be *heard* as what it "really" is, rather than to be "seen" by the "mind's eye" with the aid of traditional visual symbols ("notes").

4) What are some concrete examples of things "falling naturally" into their component parts? We observe fuel burning and being emitted from our cars as water, carbon monoxide, hydrocarbons, lead particulate, etc. (thus becoming a severe ecological problem), snow melting, a carcass decomposing, a symphonic movement that falls into sonata form (AABA), or a "theme" that resolves itself quite naturally into various figures, e.g. a theme from a work of Vivaldi or of J. S. Bach. The opposite of this "natural resolution" can be seen in the build-up of a theme out of component motives as, e.g., in Beethoven's *Fifth Symphony* or in Stravinsky's *Symphony in C*, modeled after it. We also notice that sentences fall into a certain kind of "articulation," i.e. into certain component parts. We ought not to force statements into a given mold; we ought simply to observe and describe what is happening, not so much when language, as written, becomes visual and linear as when it is actually being spoken, i.e. language as an *audial phenomenon*. When language is

examined from the linear viewpoint it seems to fall into an S P relationship. Regarded as linear, language is "syn-tactical," that is, it is "put together," in that something is predicated of a subject. Regarded as an audial phenomenon, that is, as actually spoken, statements need not be described in linear manner. Rather they are *heard* as audial phenomena. Words do not come out in ready-made statements; rather they come out one-*after*-the-other in an "additive" manner, thus not syntactically but "paratactically." This applies particularly to musical rhythm; but it is obvious also in the observation of speech rhythms. The clean, faultless proposition is not a result of ordinary language, as it is being spoken (often disjointedly); rather, it is the result of a definite process post factum. We think "contrapuntally," as is our common experience; but grammarians force us into expressing ourselves in monolinear fashion. Often a jumble of thoughts gets expressed in a jumble of words, especially in extreme situations. But in the "normal" situation we maintain that thought and its expression is a steady flow of regularized propositions in S P form.

5) Language, whether ordinary (which is often merely prosaic) or extraordinary (which is often "poetic"), is meant to be spoken, not merely to be read or seen in propositional form on a printed page. Perhaps the "Gutenberg Complex" is at work in our preoccupation with the propositional form of language. However, if the propositional form of language (a form which owes its development to a very definite historical process, begun in medieval metaphysics) is viewed as what it probably is, i.e. simply an important level of language, then the results of its analysis can indeed prove fruitful.

6) The propositional analysis of language began with Abelard, reached a high point in Ockham, and received its first significant critique in the *Logic* of Hegel. From its earliest beginnings right into Hegel propositions were important as a part of a definite theological system. Post-Hegelian philosophy had recourse to science for its badly missed

"objectivity." But it kept the preoccupation with the propositional form of language, as such. Whether the coveted objectivity (and "truth") has been attained by wooing science is, of course, a moot question, granted the crisis science itself has been in for the last decades, a crisis that is evidenced in a rather large literature.

7) At the pre-propositional level language seems to be paratactical. But one may ask whether it is entirely syntactical *in itself* even at the propositional level, whether a good bit of this logical and grammatical order is in the actual hearing of the philosopher or only "in his head." If this is so, there arises the problem of psychological and historical preconditioning in the study of language. At the syntactical level statements are analyzed as falling into the subject-predicate relationship. This, too, is the result of an easily traceable historical development in Greek and Latin grammar, which was imposed on the Germanic tongues (the most savage imposition having been on High German). One is thus justified in asking how much analysis of this sort is due to an unawareness of a definite historical conditioning and how much to what we actually *hear and understand as we listen to the spoken word* being preferred at this moment, whether such speech comes out in a jumble of words (as with children) or in logical propositions (as with an Oxford professor).

8) As *seen* by the physical eye or by the "mind's eye" in a linear statement, sentences seem to fall into subject-predicate relationships. They then can be subjected to the categories of the mind. But as *heard*, the words of any whole or half statement come out one *after* the other, *next* to each other in temporal sequence (which is more often than not an irregular sequence, rhythmically speaking), disconnectedly: paratactically. They seem connected only in the mind of the logician and the traditional grammarian; but they may not be connected in fact. Words are separate entities, disjoined, even on a printed page. They must be put together consciously

and with a certain mental viewpoint in mind. But a Frenchman and a German put the following statement together in
a considerably different manner: "O singe fort." For the
German it means: "Oh sing forth"; but for the Frenchman
it means: "Oh strong monkey." It is only the *sound* of this
phrase, the French and the German pronunciation of these
words, that spells the difference. But the printed proposition
is quite ambiguous. In this case "meaning" is quite a precarious thing indeed!

9) It is particularly in musical analysis that analysis *as
such* becomes questionable. An absurd example, of course,
is the quandry a harmonic analyst of the tradition is in when
attempting to analyze the *corde printanière* of Stravinsky's
Le Sacre du Printemps. This juxtaposition of two hands on
the keyboard was never conceived intellectually and defies
classic analysis in terms of functional harmony. Less easy to
criticize is the intellectual analysis presented by, e.g., Jan La
Rue in his *Guidelines for Style Analysis* and elsewhere in the
journals. Analysis has been the musician's and the musicologist's manner of coming to grips intellectually with the
experience and shape of musical sound. He does so traditionally with visual symbols and intellectual categories. Yet in
bringing such symbolism and categories to the musical
experience, the analyst sees how unsatisfying a surface
analysis of the musical statement can be. Schenker tried to
reduce the surface and get at the underlying layers of
harmonic sound, but he failed to bracket the basic categories
that had become problematic in the first place. La Rue is well
aware that analysis is "only a part of the task of understanding music," but he neglects to follow through in the
discovery of experiential layers in his approach to style
analysis. To understand the musical statement, which, as
Wittgenstein[1] himself avers, is not at all unlike the verbal
sentence, it is necessary to bring to the experience of sound a
good bit more than logical categories.

And in order to grasp music *as such* it is necessary to
bracket out analytic categories, if one wishes to get past the

intial layers of symbolism and structure, *as* statemental. Today we have come to a point even in music history where speech and music are considered as essentially different. This is a phenomenon of modern history only; for, from the Greeks through the middle ages, music and language were not considered apart. And in the middle renaissance, reaching a climax in the baroque era, music and speech were held to be the same, so that music was meant quite literally to "talk." This is common musicological knowledge. Language was in fact the model employed to understand music, and figures of speech were adopted and modified to become figures of music, as late renaissance treatises such as the *Musica Poetica* of J. Burmeister (1606) and the baroque treatises of Mattheson clearly demonstrate. The rhetorical model displaced the mathematical model of the middle ages and the constructivist principles of the renaissance as a port of access to an understanding of the musical phenomenon itself. Only in the last century (with Hanslick) did music criticism adopt the formalist approach; and the work of musical analysts like E. Kreft (*Die späten Quartette Beethovens*) and J. La Rue represent the culmination of an era of intense intellectual pursuit of detail and form. The problem musicians face, however, is to what extent this type of intellectuality and symbolism adds to or detracts from the experiencing of musical sound, and thus with regard to an understanding of the musical experience as such.

10) It is the "mind" that puts words or musical notes together in syntax (cf. Burmeister) through its "synthetic activity" and that pulls them apart in its "analytical activity." Just as the mind is the measure of motion in time, it is also that which puts words and/or notes together into a given statement. It therefore appears that syntactical order depends essentially on the dualism of mind over against reality, in this case the reality of given words which become words only as the *body* speaks them. (And here we do not restrict ourselves only to oral movements but include general gestural movements as part of the expression of "meaning"

and not as a mere obligato expressiveness.) The mind-body dualism (and truth defined as relational) seems to be a presupposition of analytical technique with regard to syntactical sentences. Yet in its origins this was an ancient theological dualism, one that survives in the mind-matter dichotomy. Whether such a dichotomy is the result of historical conditioning or whether it is discoverable in the manner in which we actually experience ourselves, or in this case in the experience of sounding words, is another moot question.

SCHERZANDO

11) "The dog runs." Running is predicated of a dog, as subject. Yet there exists no such thing as disembodied "running" except in the "mind." "Running" cannot be separated from the dog. The predicate cannot really be separated from the subject in this case. The subject-predicate dualism is the product of a long metaphysical history: a "substance" has some quality or "accident" predicated of it. But "predication" is a jargon word. In ordinary language we predicate nothing, we simply say something, like: "The dog is *said* to be running." "Predication" as a term is the product of a definite academic development, but it has little to do with ordinary speech.

12) If science has been in deep crisis for some decades now, which seems to be the case judging from the literature, then "Scientific propositions are true" is just as ambiguous a statement as "God exists." In fact such a statement may be even more of an abstraction, since the deity — as a religious symbol (however "deity" be interpreted) — is at least felt to be an experience (like "love"). But objective "scientific propositions" seem to be logical constructs. Yet already in Kant such "objectivity" was seen to be reducible to subjectivity. The problem of classic theism was to postulate a "really existent" divine object corresponding to the subjective

religious experience, and thus all the hassle about whether
"God exists in reality." A similar difficulty is seen in the false
problem of whether "being is a real predicate" (Kant, Hegel).
The problem of philosophy still seems to be "theological":
it wants "proof" that something "really exists." And the
scientific proposition (admittedly better grounded) rather
than theological dogma is now the gateway to this realism.
Such philosophy evades a basic experience of reality *in the
subject*, and it looks outside for proof. But how can the
objects-of-science reassure me about my own basic subjectivity, or to use a more comprehensible word, my own basic
humanity? All science does is to show me that I am surrounded by a world of objects. Could this not become somewhat dehumanizing? How do I prove scientifically that I
am? Is not my presence to myself and others sufficient
"proof"?

ALLEGRO MA NON TANTO

13) "Don't think, just look," writes Wittgenstein. In
this statement he brackets out metaphysical thought and
tells us to rely on what we actually *see* and experience *as*
seen. In other words, we are told to disengage our mentalistic categories and open ourselves up to what is actually
seen and experienced *as* seen. We are told to disengage our
speculative categories and open ourselves up to what is
actually going on, i.e., to *see* people and things for what
they really *are*, rather than for what we have merely been
conditioned by our mental sets to regard them. This could
be an example of what Husserl called the "epoche," i.e.,
the withholding of judgment in the sense of pre-judgment or
"prejudice." Yet, like Husserl, Wittgenstein was also caught
in the language of visual metaphor, a language born of classic
metaphysics (since the first lines of Aristotle's *Metaphysics*).
Instead of looking we ought to *listen* to words *as* they are
being spoken and experienced as heard. For in so doing we
may hear language as quite paratactical. We might even

bracket out all "meaning" and become enamoured of the musical quality of the words as such. It is obvious that this was the case with the composers of melismatic plainsong in the middle ages. Stravinsky used Latin this way in his *Oedipus Rex*. The "sexy voice" of the beloved is more important to many men than the proposition "I love you." It is often the voice that makes such a statement ring "true" or "false." In looking at things or at statements, too often we conceive language as unilinear. We become captive of the visual, especially the printed word and statement, particularly when such statements also represent established political power and power struggles (thus the statement of a corporate manager, a general, a president, a "kept intellectual"). If we give too much credence to statements, we fall prey to the forces that put such statements together — perhaps only in their interest, and not in the interests of serious thought. Language thus becomes "syntactical." But there are more things in a syntactical statement than mere logic or grammar! Marcuse makes a decided point with regard to the need for "linguistic therapy." This means more than cleansing language of metaphysicisms.[2]

14) Propositional language is unilinear and one-dimensional. But "experiential" thinking is often multilinear or "contrapuntal." Only classic metaphysics, whose positivistic impasse Hegel criticized, tried to force the natural ebullience and "irrationality" of thought and its expression into one easily analyzable line. Our actual experience is that we think not only in logical categories (and unilinearly) but in para-categories and in no categories at all. We have "scattered" thoughts; and thought-themes do an amazing counterpoint in our heads. Thus in ordinary speech we often "blurt things out," and under stress this is often done "incoherently." This seems quite natural. "Logical" thought, which must be striven after, often seems somewhat contrived and artificial. And thus also its linguistic expression. Arranging thoughts and statements into systematic propositions seems — from the prepropositional level — to run the risk of becoming a

construct. This does not mean that such a procedure is use-less. But it can become misleading. Some "truth" may be obvious to someone who thinks only within a given system. But it is a truth whose logic may be more contrived than real. Thus with the "clear and distinct concept" and with the exactly parsed sentences, the bane of many original thinkers.

15) The proposition becomes "public," especially when set in type or promulgated by a king, a president, a pope, or a professor. But "experience" is only "private." Hence we must build only on the public facts. For "private experi-ence" cannot be verified. But is private experience merely subjective and personal and thus incommunicable? There must be a ban on all privacy! Persons who indulge in private experience must be brought before the high court of public philosophy and ideology. Only public experience may be allowed to serve as a basis for "thought," especially as "philosophical." But if all our thinking must be forced out into the public forum through verbalizations in propositional form, could this not be regarded as quite "obscene"? Some public court, comprised of the best public factualists, must pass on all private experience and its communicability factors. Is not the dichotomy of private vs. public world (and thus the problem of "private language") not an un-overcome metaphysicism? Advocates of "public verification" are uncritical dualists: mind against body, subject against object, person against "fact," man against a threatening outside world. But out of "facts" come only more facts. Yet facts are there only *for man*. Man himself is the nearer "fact." Objects are there only for the subject who made them such in the first place. "Scientific objectivity" seems to be a "subjective" attitude toward things.

ASSAI SOSTENUTO

16) The history of philosophy begins with Plato's *dis-trust* of the shifting forms of *sense*-reality. Mind was thus

constructed as an idealistic escape. Critical philosophy begins in Kant's *distrust* of *mind*-realities, i.e. of the mentalistic speculations of classic theological and metaphysical traditions. It is precisely this radical distrust that makes western philosophy a basic skepticism, as philosophers still look everywhere, but particularly in statements, for "mistakes." Is this not an anxiety-ridden world to live in, one in which thought is reduced to hunting for errors of mind and senses, and the elusive search for "truth"? It would be better to begin with a basic trust ("primordial *belief*") which overcomes the metaphysical dualism of mind and senses and thus its historic dilemmas, false problems, and general skepsis. The basis of such thought, whatever its ambiguities, is not a distrust of first the data of senses and then the speculations of mind. It is a thinking not based on such a historic dualism at all. It is belief based not on philosophical theory or theological faith but on the experience of life as *lived* in the world and on the earth. A basic logos (as "structuring principle") rather than a theoretical "logic" is uncovered. It is a radical Yes to the experience of living and thus of thinking in a life context. And only from such experience can any meaningful thought forms arise.

17) But what do we mean by "experience"? In everyday speech (rather than "ordinary language") we make use of the word "experience" in any number of ways. The various uses tend to exemplify, i.e. are concrete examples of, what such a word "means." The word "experience," as such, seems to subsume all the various facets of meaning that usage makes manifest. For Husserl this would be the "essence" of the word, as an ideal type for various usages. Usages manifest what the word, *as such*, signifies. Scientists deal with experience as empirical. Experience itself can become the object of scientific inquiry as empirical, i.e. as that which is a part of a scientific experiment or itself becomes thematic, empirically. Such "objective" experience is what both Husserl and Heidegger characterize as "outer experience," i.e. external testimony concerning the experiencing subject.

Phenomenological consciousness is understood only when empirical states of mind are reduced to fluid "states" of the thinking and experiencing subject. To experience means to undergo something. This ancient meaning has perdured into modern times.

Language is indeed like a European city with its Old Town and modern city built around it, as Wittgenstein relates. But the road of experience, as expressed in language, seems to connect these two cities, and this vital link might indeed prevent both the deterioration of the center city as well as the alienation of the suburbs of thought and language. Phenomenologically, the living subject undergoes an experience *as his own*, not merely as the object of an analysis that comes after the fact or accompanies it in mental detachment. But since man is also a social being, he shares basic experiences with others, thus "verifying" them. However, even publicly unverifiable experiences are experiences as such. The human sub-ject is that which under-lies experiencing anything whatsoever; and since the subject underlies, it can undergo. Subjectivity eludes the objectivist not because it does not "exist" but because it resists being objectified. The technology of traditional psychology is not yet subtle enough to discover subjectivity.

18) As philosophers we sometimes seem to pursue the one true doctrine; and thus we are very scrupulous, self-examining, self-conscious, critical of every ideal, symbol, and model, occasionally argumentative to the point of becoming ludicrous, given to some sort of "realism," e.g. as "scientific." It is difficult to see why we cannot take our thought models, some of which are rather interesting, as provisional models and nothing more. Alas, the shades of some sort of "true doctrine" and a basic insecurity bedevil us. Yet "truth" seems to withhold itself from the doctrinaire, and certitude seems to haunt the insecure. Betimes there is a total lack of sense of humor, as among bickering theologians; and in the dead-earnest hunt for the right approach to "objective truth," the philosopher reveals himself as a literalist

at heart. He seems to be going the same way as his blood-brother, the theologian, from whom he learned that man could indeed attain a knowledge of objective truth. But "truth," like Mona Lisa, only smiles, as she hides herself from his awkward efforts. Dogmatic objectivists are probably as awkward at love-making as they are at wooing truth. They seem to be disappointed theologians, searching for the "truth," i.e. the Holy Grail. Perhaps after all Nietzsche was right about philosophers.

ALLEGRO MODERATO

19) How do we "analyze" a "statement," when the latter never exists *as such*, except as the written or mental afterimage of words that have been uttered. There "exist" no statements at all. There are only momentary words, one after the other, as it were, "paratactically." A complete "statement" like a musical theme exists only in memory or in anticipation. But at each single moment only a phoneme, the basic building block of words, exists in reality. Then it dies off into nothingness, to make room for the next phoneme or word. "Statements" exist only in the mind of the grammarian but not in reality or in fact, anymore than a musical composition exists all at once *in toto*. Yet, despite this, we continue ignoring the temporal sequence of phonemes and words and pretend that a sentence exists *in toto* all at once, to be analyzed. Is this not simply a mental fiction? There exists no such thing as a given statement *in toto*. It comes into existence word by word and passes out of existence in the very fact of its being *spoken* in temporal sequence. A statement is and is not; i.e. it comes into being and passes out of being, but never exists *as such*, except in dead print or in our activated memory. There exists only *man as live speaker, stating* in temporal sequence what he wants to say. And even this "sequence" cannot be conceived except as linear and serial, i.e. as extended in metaphorical space and line, so that the "mind" can *bring-it-together* (*syntatein*:

syntax) as a "statement."

The *live voice* is the place to begin analyzing, rather than the written sentence, which is only a record (minus the sound) of a past statement by a speaker. But the live voice does not exist disembodied from the living man as speaker. Hence we begin with *man as speaking* in time and in "tonality." And thus his silence, his utterances, his "half-statements," etc., are also part of the picture. Logical analysis of statements is mostly a matter of a *post factum* event.

20) A spoken sentence is syntactical and thus material for analysis as a "proposition" only in the mind of the grammarian. Words, as alive, come out *in time*. They are primarily in paratactical order, though this need not mean simply "additive" in the sense of certain primitive musical rhythms. Words are indeed linked together as they issue from the speaker. But it is the speaker, who as a *bodily* being unifies his utterances; it is not just a case of disembodied mind, or of mind somehow put together with body. Thus, words are put together not because of the "mind" of a grammarian, but go together of themselves, in that the same bodily person utters them.

21) Is reason chiefly analytical? Or is this but an emphasis, i.e. philosophy's last hope, as it views the debris of classical systems? Perhaps it secretly hoped that the theological and/or metaphysical entities really existed after all. Mistaking creative fantasy for the production of "real entities," reason ended in disappointment that none of the creative castles were, after all, very "real." So it looked elsewhere for "reality," that chimera of the metaphysical mind. So now it must de-construct statements, to see whether there is any reality and truth to them. Can reason never construct anything again? Must the philosopher be forever incapsulated in the prose of "ordinary language"?

22) Perhaps it is true that classical reason has run its course and after the collapse of all its metaphysical systems

can no longer construct anything meaningful. The tragedy of classic metaphysics was to posit truth outside things in a Beyond of some sort, whether theological or mental. Even Hegel, the grand summator of all western metaphysics, remained a metaphysician even as he consciously imposed his fascinating and brilliant system on things, rather than reading the structure out of things. Perhaps only he who gets at the roots of reason, i.e. to "thought" as the hitherto unthought and unthinkable, can show us the possibility of a more convincing construction and reconstruction of our ruined intellectual worlds. But as things stand, only the artist and the poet seem to be constructing anything worthwhile. The philosopher may want the poetry to "really exist." He has come no farther than his father Anselm, the great onto-logist and theologian, who demanded that deity be existent.

23) Consciousness is a structure, i.e. a continuous self-structuring. Hence "conscious reason" *as* self-structuring (even at the analytical level) is a constructing reason: it continually shapes and con-structs itself. Analysts also construct as they de-construct, as they dismantle the "ontological slums." Heidegger also spoke of a "destruction" of meta-physics (*Sein und Zeit* 1927); but now (*Zeit und Sein* 1968) he tells us to let the metaphysicians to themselves and have done with "overcoming" metaphysics. Heidegger leaves the "ontic slums" and creates something new. But the Being he creates is not a "real entity." Heidegger is no theologian or logician. He does two things: (a) he lays bare beneath the old metaphysical ("ontic") constructions the structure of Being that would not be suppressed through mentalisms, and (b) he makes it possible for a new philosophy to grow from the debris of the old. But this "new philosophy" is not proferred dogmatically. It is called what it is: *one* way of being "on the way" to the discovery not of "reality" but of non-meta-physical Being. It is meant only as provisional and as prepara-tory to something else in the future. Its attitudes are thus probing and creative, not metaphysical.

24) Analysis seems to examine the inert (objective?) propositional deposit of language but not the structure of living words as they are spoken. It thus leaves unexamined the structure of consciousness of the speaker (the "subject") and ignores the source of propositions. Phenomenology looks to the pre-propositional act as well as to the proposition. And the latter needs to be "bracketed" to avoid metaphysical residues.

25) Philosophy was the constructive creation of the Greeks. They developed a "special language" and coined new words, since ordinary language failed them in their philosophical games. Neologisms like the words "energy" and "entelechy," the former so important to science, crept in and were accepted. Today the special language of the Greeks looks abstract and artificial in English. Hence the recourse to ordinary language, with the exception, of course, of scientific jargon. We are back where the Greeks started, but minus their historical achievements, excepting, of course, the surreptitiously retained words like "logic" and "science." Once again we may find common language unable to serve as expressive vehicle for philosophical thought and creativity. So we renounce creativity and only analyze. Is it the preoccupation of an observer of the philosophical "game"? The player of this "noble game" (Huizinga) must do more than analyze. He must play the language game, but not "too much" (Greek: *lían*). Secure in their world and culture, the Greeks did not have to be so deadly serious about philosophy as Christians and post-Christians were to become. They could afford a certain sense of humor and generosity, evident in Plato's dialogues. We seem to be in full humorless pursuit of "truth." When generosity is restored, humor and "true" philosophy will accompany it. But truth will not be what is pursued or only becomes verbalized in propositional form. It will be the truth of a shared generosity of living in the world together. And philosophy will again be the creative "play" (Huizinga) of young spirits rather than the arena for embattled metaphysicians and their opponents. In playing the

language "game" the philosopher, relieved of his anxieties, will help create new words and concepts. These are the beginnings of a new philosophy built not on distrust but on a shared "belief." Or was philosophy but the one-time creation of the Greeks and our activity nothing but shadow-boxing and jousting with windmills?

26) A statement is syntactical, and thus subject to the rules and laws of logic and grammar only post factum in the mind of the logician and of the grammarian. Concretely (in "bodily" manner), however, a statement is quite paratactical, as an audial phenomenon, not unlike the musical composition whose hearing must precede analysis. This need not mean that words are merely additive, i.e. in additive *taxis* or order. They are indeed linked to one another but not merely in accord with the linear conception of a sentence, as a given "line" of words to be analyzed. The link is non-linear; the *bodily articulation* of the actual speaker, or even of the reader of a printed proposition. This problem was grasped by the Schoolmen, who distinguished between "voice" and "word" (*vox* and *sermo*). It is the body that joins words together, not abstract mind. Thus paratactical, not merely syntactical statements. Yet regarded as a part of the statemental process, the post factum residue of the paratactical process, syntactical propositions leave room for useful analyses of various kinds, scientific and non-scientific.

ALLEGRO APPASSIONATO

27) Certain philosophers, who have a naive faith in the "cold light of reason," insist on the difference between the cognitive and the emotive levels. They are quite emotional about the cognitive dimension and are not overly cognizant of the emotions. They do not criticize the artificial distinction between knowing and feeling, a distinction visited on us by the classic metaphysical tradition. Knowledge must be utterly unfeeling; and in feeling there can be no knowledge

whatsoever. Yet for the Greeks reason was not a cold light. It was white hot. Only the celibate monks and the classic metaphysicians took the fire out of knowing truth and kept this fire from them in utter fear, calling it by that intellectualistic and paternalistic term the "emotional level." In other words, soul against animal nature. The "true me" is only in my soul or mind (Descartes); the body is the area of the "dark and obscure." Cognitive, non-emotional, truth might well be only the emasculated knowledge of the monk, the solitary, the man alienated from life and art. It is the last futile stand of the mere intellectual against the overwhelming fact of exuberant, colorful, musical, emotive life. *Logos* not logic!

STRETTO

28) One worried about being "carried away by passion" or emotion. One did not seem to fret over the gross illusions and delusions of mind in its frenetic and pathetic pursuit of "truth."

29) Especially, one did not worry about becoming bereft of emotion, humanity, and thus of any solid understanding of what it could mean to be a man in the world and on the earth.

30) Cognitive truth is of and for the mind. Emotion originates in bodily feeling and passion. Truth vs. feeling: mind vs. body. The same old metaphysical dualism of tradition!

ANDANTE

31) The distinction: cognitive vs. emotive, like the Cartesian dualism, is the wreckage of an unsuccessful phenomenological reduction (epoche). What some philosophers do

not see is that the cognitive must also be "bracketed out." If we bracket out both cognitive and emotive levels we overcome the classic metaphysical dualism which spawned them. Cognition, as bracketed, makes *understanding* possible, as opposed to sterile intellection. Emotion bracketed makes the identical understanding possible. For understanding is neither objective nor subjective, thus neither merely "cognitive" nor merely "emotional." Rather, understanding is rooted in the *subject thinking* as a whole man, as one living bodily unit. The cognitive level is actually a phenomenological bracketing out of the emotional level. Hence, analysts do understand what "reduction" is after all! But they do not go far enough. And thus they are left with a faulty dualism and with the dilemma of two "levels." Yet cognition, bracketed or reduced, would lead to a non-metaphysical understanding of reality, just as emotion, as bracketed, would lead to a rediscovery of a fundamental *movement* of bodily man, a "movement" that is not essentially different from understanding. This is the Greek *pathos* as opposed to Christian "passion."

32) Philosophers, who lay too much emphasis on "truth," may be overlooking the "game" of language, the sometimes purposeful labyrinth, the initiation rites, the need to dissemble rather than "tell all," the essential puzzle and enigma which was the very origin of philosophy (Huizinga). For philosophy began not in the Christian search for ultimate "truth" but in the Greek appreciation of riddles. In normal language there is a withholding as well as a giving of information, for even if we try we cannot really "tell all." Most people conceal as well as reveal when they speak. There are conscious and subconscious censors at work. Only the metaphysician demands unequivocal verity, i.e. the "straight truth" without any of the game, the fun, the fancy of human speech. Life is subtle and many-faceted. Language hides as much as it reveals, even in propositional form. Any language, that is not the product of speculations but is the result of living in the world must mirror the complexity of living itself.

Clarity is a myth. Not utter clarity of mind but the *chiaro-scuro* of living on the earth! Living means being caught up in the drama and interplay of light and darkness; and a living language reflects this play. Is language only a tool to be made use of? Do words really just lie about in a mental dictionary waiting for us to use them to match our thoughts? Is standard usage the only acceptable manner of using words to "fit" our thoughts? If standard usage is our guide for philosophy, the presupposition is that everyone already understands everything. We may not think or say anything that everyone does not at once comprehend. Otherwise it is misleading. Thus a line of Rilke is "meaningless," because it is neither ordinary nor scientific. This applies also to a theme of Beethoven, a sentence out of Mallarme, of Heidegger (who also employs "everyday speech"), in short to anyone who does not share the presupposition, that what *one* says and what *one* means is what *one* ought to think and say. The use of language cannot be an absolute norm for philosophy, because language has often been flattened out and deprived of its richer meanings. Moreover, political and religious forces have forced certain words to mean this or that in "practical" usage. "Usage" means the way *one* speaks a language. The "One" is impersonal and empty. It relies too much on the state of things and allows too little room for creativeness. The world needs its Rilkes.

33) Usage is not the only key to the total understanding of language or of music. The theorist Guido d'Arezzo distinguished between a *musicus* who "knows" what he is doing and a *bestia* who only "does" but does not know. The latter only makes *use* of the creation of others; the former is an "artist" because he does things "not through use but through art." The only trouble with such "art" was that it became metaphysical. Yet is looking for "logic" in syntactical language any less metaphysical than the intellectualistic art of the middle ages? Not "logic" but the *structure* (*logos*) of words, speech, and music. Thus "to the things themselves." Only out of such a situation can we really know how to

"use" language creatively, whether or not we coin new words.

Leave language just as it is. Thus Wittgenstein. If this connotes not tampering with language in the sense of political exploitation of it or in the sense of using language to build a false system or to invent spurious problems in philosophy, I can understand it. But if it means restricting language to its present status in our *use* of it, I do not comprehend. For languages change *in their being used*, as linguistic science confirms (cf. E. Bourciez, *Elements de linguistique romane*). It was from this *change in usage* that e.g., classic Latin gradually broke down into all the dialects we have today from Spanish to Romanian. Moreover, classic Latin itself developed from a more practical and rudimentary Italic dialect into a major literary language through the good services of literateurs, lawyers, and poets from Livius Andronicus and Plautus through Cicero. These writers were greatly influenced by classic Greek literature and introduced many neologisms into Latin.

In the middle ages Italian became a classic language at the hands of Dante and Petrarca; German developed at the hands of Luther in the renaissance. As to English, after the Norman invasion in the eleventh century, it gradually became a new language, so that now we have to study Anglo-Saxon as a foreign idiom. But in becoming a cosmopolitan language English also became metaphysical, in the sense that abstract overlays were imposed on ordinary language in the high middle ages particularly. And in becoming a high language German also became quite metaphysical, though for other reasons. Perhaps this historic fact is what Wittgenstein was unwittingly fighting. A knowledge of some history could have abetted his efforts. It is tragic that English became a metaphysical language, particularly in its heavy reliance on Latinisms of all kinds. By contrast, in becoming a high language, classic Latin never became metaphysical, since it was never subjected to Christian speculative influences in its crucial formation period, as was English. Latin remained a natural language as it passed from being a practical rustic

dialect to becoming literary and poetic. Medieval Latin is
another matter entirely: it became a metaphysical language
in intent. And this is the source of most Latin loan words in
English, as well as of "category mistakes."

Language never remains "as it is." It is always changing
as it is used by different peoples. Language develops *as it is
spoken* (cf. E. Bourciez). The evolution of spoken sounds is
what makes the difference. Man's bodily embouchure,
affected by various internal and external conditions, is what
brings about the ever continuing historical changes. This is
common knowledge in linguistics. In order to be properly
grounded in reality, it would seem to me that philosophy of
language must begin here and not just in criticism of the
speculative blight visited on certain languages, like English,
by metaphysics in all its overt and covert forms.

34) What can logic continue to mean, if it is no longer
tenable as a predominantly mental technique, whatever
"relation" it has to things? If there is a logic of things rather
than of symbols, perhaps the word *structure* is more apropos.
This is both a return to *logos* as the historical etymological
source of logic and a more convincing contemporary interpretation. The word *structure* seems more acceptable to
those working in the realm of the arts, which includes the art
of language. The trend toward things and away from mentalisms is to be seen both in the logic of Hegel and that of
Husserl. But this does not mean merely turning from subjective mentalisms and solipsistic speculative systems toward
"things" as "objective." The subjective-objective dichotomy
itself must be overcome. A "thing" is not merely a rock
object. It is not merely "material" as opposed to "mind."
"Logic," which began in Abelard's theologico-intellectual
world, is a word whose history has been far too mentalistic to
be salvaged for our present needs. Perhaps we should look at
the *structuring* of things, whether "real" or "ideal," rather
than have recourse to "logic." Perhaps we seek a convincing
contemporary *logos* as the substructure of our statements.
For the Greeks this was a "structuring principle" within

things themselves. It was non-metaphysical.

35) "Logic" may not be the absolute answer in the search for the principle of structure in thinking and in things. It may be a left-over metaphysicism to look for the logical substructure in thought and language, one that is supposedly articulatable according to formal rules. Human consciousness is far too subtle in its ebb and flow for that. In human consciousness there is no solid ground that endures long as "ego," no perduring rules that regulate the organization of experience, of sense data, or of thought. That has been a metaphysical ideal but not necessarily a fact. Language, too, had logic imposed on it, as well as Latin grammar. But language itself is hardly very logical for all the surface-level success of S and P. Language is fluid and alive; grammarian-logicians would freeze the flow of rhythm and encapsulate the natural linguistic phrase within the S P categories devised by classic speculation. It becomes a way of controlling man's thinking and speech. And that is one reason why propositions have been so important to classic theologians.

36) Logic arrests the flow of consciousness at a given moment, makes an artificial cross-section of it, freezes words in propositions to be analyzed, and claims to see a given logical set of rules at work. So to arrest the movement of thought and speech is to make but an artificial analysis rather than a "natural" one. It would be like arresting a waterfall, a ballerina, a tight-rope artist, a concert pianist in mid-air or in mid-performance to analyze what is happening. But what is thus analyzed apart from the global experience of the given phenomenon is no longer alive and real. It is a distortion at best, a contrivance of mind at worst.

37) Husserl's writing (especially in *Ideen*) is organized in sections and chapters. But it is not clear and distinct nor apt to please traditional logicians or grammarians, though he aims specifically at clarity as such. It is, not unlike *Ulysses*, stream-of-consciousness writing, a writing in sometimes

complex counterpoint. For Husserl not only wrote *about* consciousness in delivering it from psychologism, he was in his writings of the period faithful to the natural multilinear flow of consciousness in his style and expression. But this is all maddening to the inveterate logician.

CODA

38) These notes on the meaning of analysis have not necessaily been irenic either in intent or in fact; but neither have they been meant as merely eristic. Perhaps analysis is actually a part of phenomenology (or vice versa?), but if so, its propositions need to be "reduced." It is to be hoped that philosophers will one day find out more about the implications of philosophical thinking, so that a "dialogue" may become possible within the ranks. Hopefully, philosophers of a given school will not fall into the classic impasse, that "error has no rights." If we are dealing with philosophical thinking and not just with a primitive struggle within a given profession (which could thus be *any* profession), then there is hope that out of the difficult present situation a decent future will emerge for philosophers. Otherwise they may be condemning themselves to irrelevance as they go the way of petty theologians, for whom a system became more important than the deity they had originally built it around. The system went on a good long time after the death of the deity. Perhaps this is really what we are witnessing in contemporary philosophy. And so philosophy ceases to be of much relevance for people in either the sciences or the arts and becomes simply the graveyard in which the dutiful historian of human culture and thought can dig for an endless variety of fascinating cadavers.

One would hope that the chasm could be bridged, so that philosophy does not come to such an end. But if a bridge is built, the "middle ground" may be the source of a new creation in philosophy. A certain maturity and detachment is thus called for on all sides. We may have to give up a good deal of the baggage we bring to this project. And this applies especially to phenomenologists.

Endnotes

1. *Philosophical Investigations* [*PI*], No. 527, where Wittgenstein expressly states that understanding a sentence and understanding a musical theme are more related (*verwandter*) than one suspects. The word, related, implies a family resemblance (*PI*, No. 65) between musical understanding and the understanding of propositional language. *Verwandtschaft* is a family relationship in the sense of *relatives*. It is thus not a merely abstract relationship.

2. From different viewpoints both linguistic scientists (as, e.g. E. Bourciez) and philosopher-literateurs (as, e.g., B. Parain) point out (a) how political history affects language and usage directly, and (b) how political systems make *use* of language to maintain control of the established situation. The political dominance of Imperial Rome made possible the emergence of the Latin dialect as a world language. (The same may be said, mutatis mutandis, of imperialist English.) The decline of Roman power and the invasion of "barbarians" in the fifth century insured the development of Romance languages as separate but cognate tongues. And, as is known, sixty percent of English vocabulary is based in some way on Latin, thus making English a Germanic dialect with a Latin overlay. As to controlling the language, we might make use of an American model: Pentagon-English. This special language makes particularly heavy use of Latin derivatives and avoids pithy Anglo-Saxon stems in covering up its policies. Thus in place of bombing, P.E. speaks of "protective reaction," a Latinism that is meant to keep ordinary speakers from understanding what is really happening. Another example is "new direction" for rout or retreat, etc. Political and religious establishments seek to fixate meanings by means of key words and phrases. Madison Avenue advertising does the same in a more blatant manner. Propositions are thus a cornerstone in the maintaining of given systems. To be unaware of historical and political influences on language and syntax is to be either naive or given to some abstract method or approach, i.e., to a metaphysical mentality, which deals neither with things nor with living language "in situation."

Chapter 4

MUSICAL SOUND, A MODEL FOR HUSSERLIAN TIME-CONSCIOUSNESS

INTRODUCTION

Akoumenology, or the phenomenology of sound, is a relatively young branch of general phenomenology. It is also a science emergent from the principles of phenomenology coupled with the experience of musical sound. It is a study long overdue. In the past there were more or less sporadic attempts to thematize sound and to develop a phenomenology of sound; yet, to mention but one philosopher, Ortega y Gasset considered it a scandal that this fruitful area of thought had not already been worked on by philosophers of his era, and this in thorough, systematic manner. R. Ingarden's ontology of the music work of art is the closest we have come to a systematic presentation, but to the musicologist his musical contribution is that of a learned amateur, to be revered mostly for his philosophical insightfulness.[1] Within the last years several of my colleagues and I have shared writings and insights,[2] but it is still true that there exists no comprehensive and satisfactory work on the phenomenology of sound, whether applied to music or to language as a system of auditory symbols. The study of language has been a preoccupation of our era, but it is usually done by linguistic scientists interested in morphology, or by language analysts interested in laying bare the conceptual structure embedded in everyday speech.[3] Neither has given sufficient attention to the paratactical flow of the sound of the human voice, as it builds sentences in syntactical structures. Moreover, it seems that a comprehensive work can no longer be the result of individual effort; it may have to be a common project under

91

editorial direction. There are those of us, whether acousti-
cians, musicologists, linguists, or philosophers, who could
coordinate our efforts in order to produce the desired synthesis. Such a work would take in all sound phenomena and
thematize them phenomenologically, stressing music and
language.

Our theme is necessarily restricted. But I feel it is a
theme which is significant for any phenomenology of sound,
a sort of modest prolegomenon. Its significance is partly
attributable to the fact that it takes shape in dialogue with
the fundamental work of Edmund Husserl, the founder of
contemporary phenomenology. There are scattered references
throughout Husserl's writings bearing on the subject of
musical sound, but it is not our present concern to catalogue
such references. Rather, we shall refer to several of his works
that seem to be crucial to the background of any phenomenology of sound, his lectures on time-consciousness, his
writings on passive synthesis, and to some extent his treatment of judgment and experience.[4] For, it is clear, that in
his treatment of both time and of synthesis the musical
model is central to his thought, for he deals with the single
tone, the musical phrase, melody, and even with the extended symphonic form. In all of this, we do not base our
study on Husserl, in such a way that we end up only giving an
exposé of his thought. Rather, even an "original contribution" takes full cognizance of basic texts, for they formulate
insights that must be known and employed by anyone working
seriously in the field of akoumenology. This paper is thus not
an exposé of texts, but it does relate to them. For, whatever
we might excogitate on our own out of pure exuberance can
hardly be indifferent to the writings of the founder of
phenomenology. Phenomenology is not journalism. Moore
has a point when he separates philosophy and literature,
though I personally feel philosophy suffers when so divorced.
There is nothing wrong with philosophical journalism,
provided it does not become a substitute for serious effort or
an excuse for not familiarizing oneself with basic materials.
Husserl is basic to *all* phenomenological research.

1. THE POSITION OF THE MUSICOLOGIST

In this age of specialists there is a felt need for interdisciplinary studies and research, of a wedding of insights from science and philosophy. The marriage of phenomenology and musicology seems to me to be a particularly natural one, and the offspring of such a union will probably be more practical than the former and more theoretical than the latter. Both the practical musician and the musicologist have shown signs of considerable intellectual distress within the last decades. Today the situation seems urgent. There is widespread dissatisfaction in the ranks with classic musicological methods and a need to break out of especially historic and scientific moulds, so that the experience of musical sound can be properly thematized. Husserl himself would recognize this as an attempt to deliver musical experience from the scientific and positivistic frameworks of classic science, for musicology is *Musik-wissenschaft*, the science-of-music. Classic musicology seems entirely imbedded in the "natural attitude." Since the middle ages music theory has been based on a mathematical model rather than on an experiential one, and even in the baroque era the musical *Affektenlehre* had a rationalist base. What Husserl styled "die Mathematisierung der Natur"[5] took place in music theory long before it took hold of physical science, as the *Speculum Musicae* aptly demonstrates.[6] Ever since the theory of musical proportionality was formulated by such mathematicians as Johannis de Muris and by Jacques de Liège, both of the *ars nova* (early fourteenth century), and made more practical by Gafforius (fifteenth century), musicians have played in accord with a detailed musical mathematics. Indeed, the interplay of proportions is still used by Kant in *Kritik III* to explain musical form, even though it had subsided into the background in music theory as such.[7]

Functioning in their role of objective historians and guardians of musical esthetics, musicologists have made the modern world aware of medieval and renaissance music, and this in formidable studies that are important to the modern scholar. Their message is apparently of import also to certain contemporary composers, like M. Babbitt, who loves to play with mathematical formulae, it appears. There is, in fact, a curious continuity of interest between the mathematicizing of (musical) nature, as conceived by historical figures, and as presently being effected by theorists of a certain slant. Even in the baroque era, the time of Bach, there was a strong and persistent mathematical stratum operative beneath the overt affectivity which made music "the language of the emotions." The question asked by the thoughtful musicologist is, to what extent does this idealized world of numbers (called "sounding numbers" in the renaissance!) actually relate to, aid, or obstruct the musical experience? Does mathematicized consciousness block perception? Or does it merely structure it too rigidly? At this point the musicologist is already a potential phenomenologist, as clearly needs to be stated. To what extent does any cognitive framework aid or block the experience of any sound? In the middle ages sound qualified as musical sound only after being subsumed into the mathematical system. In our age John Cage has effectively demonstrated that any sound can be utilized for musical purposes. To what extent do mental sets help sharpen our intellects for analysis, and in how far do they dull our perceptivity, especially with regard to musical sound?

It is obvious that the services of the phenomenologist are required at this juncture. For although the musicologist can muster a formidable array of knowledge with regard to sonata, symphony, and quartet, he needs more than the facts of music history, more than what the psychology of music can offer him in its interpretations of musical consciousness. Facts need to be "refacted," made over, delivered from remaining only "facts from which come more facts." The latter phrase is obviously Husserlian and any beginning student can identify its source. If one is plagued by such problems, one has two options: (1) to think entirely for oneself, independently of sources that are available, or (2) dialogue with fundamental sources, as one continues with one's own inspirations. I believe the practical musicologist will opt for the second solution, even though the first alternative tempts one's natural impulses to "go it alone" and relieves one of the need for background studies. Such studies need not dominate or obstruct original insight; it may well fructify and amplify one's own theorizations. Indeed this was the path followed by our phenomenological mentors themselves; and in their apprenticeship with great teachers like Brentano they launched their own speculative endeavors. For Husserl one such great teacher was also Carl Stumpf.

2.   THE EXAMPLE OF CARL STUMPF

Professor Stumpf is known both to phenomenologists and to musicologists, though this fact itself seems to be unknown to either of these groups. Every introductory student of musicology hears of Stumpf's theory of consonance, the amalgamation of musical sounds (*Tonverschmelzung*), and graduate students in phenomenology know that Husserl dedicated his *Logical Investigations* to Carl Stumpf. Moreover, the word, *Verschmelzung*, i.e. the fusion or amalgamation of objects in perception, figures constantly and importantly in Husserl's treatment of passive synthesis, making it a kind of theory of philosophical as well as of musical consonance. But until H. Spiegelberg's history of phenomenology few philosophy students knew that Stumpf's tonal psychology figured significantly in the early days of phenomenology itself,[8] in that Stumpf departed from the acoustical preoccupations of Helmholtz and began to clear a phenomenological path toward the understanding of the *experienced* amalgamation, as opposed to the merely physical fusion, of concordant tonalities. Unfortunately very few musicologists get to know the importance of the philosophical dimension of Stumpf's work; and our greatest and most voluminous musicological encyclopedia omits all mention of Husserl in its article on Stumpf, though it does give deserved prominence to musical students of Stumpf, such as Hornbostel, Sachs, Lachmann, et al.[9] These are well known musicological names; but they are largely unknown in philosophy. (We live in adjacent but hermetically sealed compartments in our departments of philosophy and of musicology!) Musicologists are likewise aware of Stumpf's musical background, and of the fact that he can be considered one of the chief founders of ethnomusicology. But they fail to learn of the important link between Stumpf and his student, Husserl, the founder of phenomenology.

     Neither do students register the importance of the dedication of *Logical Investigations* to Carl Stumpf. It is not an idle dedication. Rather, it is a dedication that embodies the devotion of the student for his great mentor, a devotion to Stumpf's own method and a proposal for the way out of psychology as such, including Stumpf's tonal psychology. In his book Husserl could have brought Stumpf out of psychologism toward reductive phenomenology, which is *in specie* different from Stumpf's own phenomenology. That Stumpf had negative feelings toward Husserl's type of phenomenology, as it gradually unfolded, is sufficiently well known, thanks to Spiegelberg. This is not unlike Husserl's own negative feelings for the work of his student, Heidegger. Stumpf was primarily a scientist, and he held philosophical speculation, divorced from scientific studies, in suspicion. To Stumpf with his background in music, both as an art and as a science, the work of Husserl must have looked like pure speculation, just as Heidegger's work must have appeared to Husserl as a "metaphysical adventure." Yet from our vantage point Stumpf appears as a prephenomenological figure. We can learn from him, and not just as a historical figure. For, his method of working is still a model viable for those who would bring phenomenology to the arts and sciences, without thus turning it into a "service philosophy." Stumpf's psychology of musical sound was the more convincing to his era because its creator worked actively in both music and psychology. To Stumpf phenomenology was not an independent research, carried on apart from the facts of art and science; rather, the phenomenological method he espoused was a fundamental stratum of his musico-psychological studies. In this sense it was a pre-science, which kept science as such from being denuded of philosophical insight, as it became preoccupied with empirical data. Hence, there seems to be more than what Spiegelberg calls the "common ground" obtaining between these two types of phenomenology. Rather, regarding phenomenology as a basic stratum in our study of reality, including that experienced in the arts, may be an effective way of keeping us "practical" as philosophers, by helping us keep our theorizations "down to earth" and relevant, as we work in the areas of a phenomenology of science or of sound.

This essay adopts Stumpf's insight into the manner of working in a given science. The musicologist thus remains a musical scientist (as the psychologist remains a psychologist), and follows Stumpf's manner of working, while relying on Husserl's method. The essay is thus Husserlian in character, but hopefully it will maintain the practicality and relevance characteristic of Stumpf's work. This seems the only meaningful approach for a working musicologist, who identifies both with science and with philosophy in evolving a phenomenology of musical sound.

3. AKOUMENOLOGY OR THE PHENOMENOLOGY OF SOUND

In order to understand the significance of Husserl's use of musical sound as a model both for intuition and for time-consciousness, we must speak briefly of akoumenology as such. It is a musico-philosophical science of sound that has predecessors in historic music theory, in acoustics, and after Stumpf — in phenomenological psychology. But it is also an expansion of classic musicology and is understood best from this source. The intellectualist position of music theory, as best represented in the *Speculum Musicae* (1330-40), is philosophical in the extreme, i.e. it is a meta-physical adventure. But this medieval metaphysics of music, fascinating to the musicologist and student of culture for its amalgamation of philosophy, theology, music, and mathematics, in effect stressed the cognitive level to the detriment of perception. Physical sound was subsumed into an intellectual grid and became mathematicized. Thus not the sheer esthetic perception of sound but "numbered sound" (*sonus numeratus*) became essential. The musician was not one who played an instrument as much as one who delighted in the interplay of musical proportions that constituted musical consonances. The educated listener thus departed from a concert intellectually rather than esthetically satisfied. One suspects that ordinary listeners simply enjoyed the music. Medieval music theory was a kind of rationalization of musical practice. In the baroque era the theory of proportions was still in the background, but now everything was subservient to the theory of musical affectivity, called *Affektenlehre*.[10] According to this theory music was the "language of the affects," meant to move man's soul. In *Kritik* III Kant still bore witness to both musical proportionality and to the theory of affects, though by now it was musically obsolete; for the musical world had already been enjoying Mozart at his best.[11] With Kant the mathematicizing of music was replaced by esthetics. And yet philosophical esthetics regarded musical esthetics as a poor relation, to the point that a musicological pioneer like F. Chrysander advised musicians to create their own theory of musical esthetics, to correspond with their experience rather than with some crystal palace of philosophical speculation. At the same time — with the rise of the sciences — acoustics became important, and Helmholtz became famous. It was here that Carl Stumpf made his entry into the history of music theory, making an incipient phenomenology of sound possible.

In a twentieth century definition of musical sound one has to take into consideration such diverse people as Schoenberg, Stravinsky, Ussachevsky, John Cage, Xenakis, et al. They are all totally different from one another. It is impossible to speak of a unity of styles, as it may have been in, e.g., the classical era, with Haydn and Mozart. A phenomenology of sound would have to be redefined in terms of the experiences of twentieth century music with all its contradictory phenomena. A unitary mathematicizing of musical experience seems impossible in a century such as ours. Frustrated at not being able to find a category to cover all cases, theorists feel at sea. And yet, though we need a general theory of twentieth century music, there is no need for us to go begging at the portals of mathematics or esthetics for some regulative or unifying idea that will save us from utter fragmentation. Instead of searching for yet another intellectual grid, we might look at *sound as such*, and make it primary. Its rich diversities discourage intellectualization but invite phenomenological analysis, in that it gets "back to the things themselves," in this case to sound, relieved of the theoretical sedimentation imposed by history. Instead of feeding sound into some intellectual grid, there to be converted into "musical" sound (as opposed to the ordinary sounds of life and of work), we might follow John Cage's indications, that *all* sounds are material for musical composition. In the presence of sheer musical experience intellectual grids seem to be automatically reduced, i.e., they do not hold up in the face of actual experience. Experiencing Cage's *Indeterminacy* or Xenakis' *Akrata* is sufficient to illustrate the point.

Akoumenology thus examines *sound as such*, whether it emerges as language or as music, and this in ordinary life and work. An analysis of what John Cage has done in his various musical "works" will lead one to suspect, that for the traditionalist he is a kind of anarchist, or a court jester. For, in *Indeterminacy*, which is "scored" for any and all sounds, including the narrator's voice, mere intellectual meaning seems irrelevant. And even as one understands the words of the narratives, one realizes that the mere sound of the narrator's voice is what is significant, not anything he has to "say," however amusing the anecdotes. Thus the "sense" of the narration is often "senselessly" interrupted by random sounds, produced by a piano, a radio, the tape of a dog barking, noises concocted on an electronic synthesizer, etc., making it clearly difficult and occasionally impossible to "follow the meaning" of the words. In this composition, as in others like it, the sounds are all that count, whether they be noises, instruments, voice, or a catch-all of random sounds. In other words, *only sound* emerges as a proper *phenomenon* for phenomenological analysis. All else, including "meaning," is bracketed. Only sound is thematized. Hence there exists no meaning in the traditional sense, and one begins to realize what Husserl's conception of noema implies for such a study as this. Any merely semantic meaning is secondary to the sound in its noematic significance. Husserl himself was a musical traditionalist, and he employed the example of classic tonality as his model for time-consciousness and for passive synthesis, as temporal. But we could hardly have expected Husserl to envision the achievements of Cage, Babbit, Davidovsky, or Penderecki. His model is thus dated, as far as the contemporary musician is concerned, but phenomenologically it is still full of import for our studies on musical time and synthesis.

4. HUSSERL'S MODEL: MUSICAL TONALITY AND MELODY

Husserl modeled his conception of time on the "protensive" character of a musical melody, extending in sequence from past through present into the future, and leaving a "retensive" trail in memory. Musical time was originally taken from a metaphysical conception, as is again evident in the *Speculum Musicae*; and, according to this, now-points succeed one another in a series starting in the infinite past and proceeding into an open or "empty" future horizon. Because of Stumpf's influence Husserl did not begin either at the physical (acoustical) nor at the metaphysical level, i.e. in objective time. Rather, he began with time as actually experienced in the temporal sequence of a musical composition, as it builds toward musical form in its successive moments, thus in time as "subjective." Husserl, the general

phenomenologist, was more radical than Stumpf, the phenomenological psychologist, it goes without saying. Yet Stumpf
spoke more convincingly from musical experience than did
his student. For all his expert handling of the subject of
musical consciousness Husserl speaks more from speculation
than from actual musical experience. Nevertheless, his pene-
tration into the core of the conscious experience of time is
crucial to a re-evaluation of musical time as such. His
"speculative" analyses are phenomenological, not ontic.

Concretely, what was Husserl's model? In different contexts, specifically in his treatment of time-consciousness and
of passive synthesis, Husserl continually makes use of musical
tonality. Because he writes of musical "tone" one should not
conclude that he is working, like an acoustician, with a single
tone, though this can be one meaning. Instead, musical tone
must be taken in terms of general musical tonality and the
phrase-building that begets melody. The latter word is frequently used, and it implies a sequence of tones, rather than
a solitary one. In fact the temporal sequence of single and
multiple tones is the heart of this musical model. A given
musical melody, as e.g. Schumann's "Du Ring an meinem
Finger" from *Frauenliebe und -leben*, is extended in the time-
consciousness of the experiencing and perceiving subject, in
this case a husband in love with his wife (a fact we will not
bracket!). The extension is not that of a *res extensa* but of
the subject expanding in consciousness, the latter interpreted
also affectively. As he knew from experience and as he
learned more in detail from Stumpf (for Stumpf knew his
music theory), musical time as represented in the printed
score is not merely linear. The score is only meant to abet the
restoration of an experience, in this case one in which affectivity is primary. And it is to this re-creating that performers
give all their time. The experience of musical time embodies
a whole network of temporal phenomena in a pattern of
thrust and trail. Whereas the objective score is linearly
conceived — and in traditional music it is quantilinear — in
the consciousness of the perceiver it becomes a "subjective"
experience. The music is like a comet plumeting through

subjective space, leaving a trail of after-echoes, a musical tail
(*Zeitschwanz*) that is retained in memory.[12] But memory is
not merely an electronic storehouse for sense-data; memory
is a part of consciousness, in that it is a form of elemental
awareness. Even the original word tells us this (*memor esse*
= to be aware of). This memory awareness is a sublevel of
consciousness, into which the patterns of perception temporarily vanish, until they are consciously recalled or are
suddenly awakened, often passively without any activity of
the mind. But musical memory is not to be taken as a thing
apart from the consciousness of the perceiving subject, as it
seizes on the passing musical moment, creating, as it were,
a *moment musical*. The forward thrust of musical time builds
a horizon of expectations and possibilities for the composer
and for the listener; and, as the musical tone unfolds in its
forward movement of "protension," it leaves in its wake a
whole series of tonal shadows (*Abschattungen*), that spread
out in ever diminishing diagonal lines behind it. The nature of
musical time serves as an apt model for the philosopher, in
this case Husserl. Combining what he had learned from his
teacher, Carl Stumpf, with his own experience of sound,
and analyzing it with his phenomenological method,
Husserl produced the treatise known as the lectures on time-
consciousness.

If we examine Husserl's model even more closely, we
discover interesting details, important both musically and
philosophically. In the lectures on time-consciousness Husserl
expressly pays a debt of recognition to both Brentano's
philosophy and to Stumpf's tonal psychology.[13] But he parts
ways with natural psychology as well as with Kantian subjectivity, as he unfolds his conception of immanent time as
"phenomenal" (*erscheinend*). The first example he gives of
phenomenal time, i.e. time as it appears-in-experience, is that
which occurs in the process of tonal duration. A musical
phrase or melody appears in consciousness as a "serial
phenomenon" (*Nacheinander*), i.e. in a temporal sequence
specifically different from objective time. For our awareness
of musical sound is not limited to linear objectivity; we hear

globally, synthetically, not as the mind actively turns toward phenomena conceived in linear terms, but passively as the melody takes shape in audial perception.

At this point we might digress briefly concerning the little there is to offer on musical sound as a model for intuition as such. Textually, it is little; factually it is most significant. In his famous *Logos* essay on philosophy as a strict science, Husserl delivered his epoch-making pronouncement on the "naturalizing of consciousness," in which he criticized psychology as the science of experience, proposing a phenomenology of consciousness as a means of overcoming empiricism, a "pure" consciousness to counteract scientism, an intentional line of temporal experience as opposed to the chronometric line.[14] In pursuing this theme he states that phenomenology seeks to present the "essence" of things in the same immediate manner "as one hears a (musical) sound."[15] In this direct and unencumbered manner we seek to intuit (*schauen*) any essence whatsoever. The immediate intuition of musical sound as an object of experience is thus the ideal model for the intuition of the essence of any phenomenal thing, whether a visual object, or the essence of an ideal entity such as judgment or will. The primacy of audial perception and intuition seems to be clear to Husserl at this point, though he never developed the insight in radical and systematic manner. The reason for this is that his classic vocabulary, heavy with visual metaphor, masked out the audial models and images; and thus *Wesenschau* took precedence over hearing, even though at least in this one significant instance he had modeled the former on the latter. What Husserl bore witness to at this juncture was the supposed effortless experiencing of sound as opposed to the more difficult intuition of real or ideal objects. For the visual world is mostly a world of clear and distinct things, and its correlative mental world is one of clear and distinct concepts. Even in phenomenology we speak of the "ray of light" which the subject casts on the given object to reduce it to noematic meaning. And this ray of light rather than a global wave of sound is the symbol of phenomenological intentionality.

Moreover, the ray is cast by the subject in its intuiting of reality; in the experience of musical sound there is passivity at work, a deeper layer of experience, a hidden stratum of the same intuitional intentionality.

Yet even had Husserl stayed with his audial model and developed a more convincing akoumenology (less fascinated with the activity of the subject and more with the "passivity" of hearing), his musical model would have remained more convincing to the phenomenologist than to the musicologist. For the latter knows that, at least historically, intellectual filters of various sorts already described were capable of interfering with perception. We must conclude that perception is a subtle and delicate affair that can be obstructed or masked when intellectual categories grow too powerful. Mental categories seem to function as a perceptual depressant and are probably suppressant of the natural erotic content of musical sound. Few musicians in western history were capable of the pure perception of sound precisely because of such mental blocks. Hence it is difficult to agree with Husserl that pure perception is as automatic as he postulates as regards musical sound. In fact it is now necessary to conduct seminars, in order to help musicians reduce their intellectual categories, so as to let the pure experience of sound as such break in on them, aiding them in disengaging their theoretical prejudices as a prelude to the reception of sound for its own sensuous sake. Husserl himself admitted that the "naturalization of ideas" makes intuition (and we might add, inhearing) difficult; yet he claimed that intuition was no "mystic secret" if we understood perception.

And, of course, this may apply also to language. In a little quoted passage in the *Logos* article Husserl makes startling statements that one would expect from John Cage himself. For in defending himself against charges of scholasticism, he writes that the phenomenological analyst does not deal with judgments based on words, but rather that he looks *directly at the phenomena* which speech conjures up.[16] In other words the phenomenologist is not intent on building a conceptual empire, as was scholasticism. Rather, he looks at things themselves, as they begin to appear in the web of words we weave about them. Words, as it were, have no other function than to serve as indices for a whole context of *phenomena*, for a whole world of noematic meaning. In themselves words are and remain only *sounds* that indicate things in a world context, but not in the manner of Augustine or Abelard. This position appears to have some affinity with that of Wittgenstein, one is tempted to state. Husserl's point is that a final fixation of scientific language and meaning presupposes a completed analysis of phenomena; and such a final analysis has simply not taken place; nor will it ever. This might well hold also for ordinary language in an allied sense, insofar as it represents a static world of words and objects. Husserl calls for an analysis of things rather than of words only, and this might qualify as "extra-linguistic analysis."[17]

Musical tonality is thus important for the cardinal concept of *Wesenschau*; but the musical model is traced out much more in detail in the lectures on time-consciousness and on passive synthesis. For here consciousness is regarded as a temporal apriori, which the author seeks to clarify through analysis of musical tones. In presenting and criticizing Brentano's theory of time, Husserl thematizes musical fantasy and imagination.[18] He is aware of the possibilities of tonal modulation as a crucial part of musical fantasy, though here he classifies himself as a traditionalist. Yet his conception of musical fantasy is open-ended, and he postulates the possibility of transcending ordinary modulation "toward musical sounds never before heard." Indeed, had Husserl been more aware of contemporary music, he could have fleshed this out in considerably more detail. And were he alive today to hear the unusual sounds of an electronic synthesizer or of a traditional orchestra playing Penderecki or Xenakis, he might have had additional problems about musical sound itself.

In discussing tonal apprehension (*Auffassung*) Husserl follows W. Stern, emphasizing the fact that apprehension is not instantaneous, a thing of the moment, but that it builds

up gradually.[19] A melodic line, though indeed a series of
tones, is in reality a gradual build-up even for the faculty of
apprehension. In other words, progressive apprehension is a
facet of the temporality of consciousness; it is not merely an
automatic fact of momentary response to stimuli. A series of
musical tones builds a successive unity, which is apprehended
as such.[20] This, I feel, is significant for the proper understanding of such a thing as sonata-allegro form, particularly as
illustrated in the symphony. This need not be a classical
symphony; perhaps such a symphony as Sibelius' IV illus-
trates it even better. For this composition, though analyzable in strict sonata form — except that the recapitulation
commences with the second rather than with the first theme
— is hardly recognizable to the classic ear as sonata form.
Instead the symphonic form builds gradually from motives
enunciated by the cello in the opening bars. Sibelius expressly intended form to take shape gradually, to build, to
synthesize, to constitute itself, as does nature itself. This
building process is more immediately true of the themes
introduced in the classic and romantic symphony. For a
theme is not just a series of notes physically independent of
one another. Rather, a good classic theme builds toward an
arch, as easily exemplified in Mozart, Beethoven, and later in
Bruckner. The unity of such a theme is a matter of perceptive
consciousness rather than of physical unity or of intellectual
form. The form of the sonata is not a mould to be filled with
content but rather a progressive building of temporal unity
in the consciousness of the composer and perceiver, a unity
held together as primary impression, memory, and expectation. Any building of form counts heavily on expectation,
and the sonata form as such depends on memory for the
reprise of the principal themes. Tones are in themselves, as it
were, dead entities, regarded acoustically, easily identifiable
as the same continuous tones; but in phenomenal flux,
as they appear in immanent time, tones are alive and fluid;
and so is the form they thus generate.

The importance of temporal unity in musical tonality
becomes thematic in Husserl's treatment of passive synthesis,

and detail emerges more convincingly.[21] Again, it is useful to recall that this essay is not merely expository in character, an exposé of accessible works of Husserl. What is treated here is only what is found to be useful to clarify the musical model he had in mind. What is "passive synthesis"? And in what sense does this bear on the musical model being employed, i.e. the musical tone as extended in subjective space from past through to future, building a progressive unity, that in musical composition becomes form? Both in his work on passive synthesis and on experience and judgment Husserl grappled with the difficulties of the word, passive, in his attempt to portray what was happening phenomenologically. Passivity is not merely passive behavior (*passives Verhalten*), and this is apparent in the musical experience, specifically in listening to music. In *Erfahrung und Urteil* Husserl called for a more radical concept of passivity, one not confused with cognitive conceptuality, one explainable more as affectivity, as passive "belief," as passive *doxa*.[22] This seems eminently adaptable to the musical situation; or rather, the musical situation can serve as an excellent model for such theorization. For here cognitive aspects seem secondary to the musical unity which is passively effected, before a given composition, as, e.g., a classical sonata, is analyzed by the activity of the mind. What is presupposed in active analysis is a transition from a primordial *aisthesis*, i.e., from pure sensual awareness, to the cognitive categories of evaluation.[23] The engagement of cognitively oriented analysis presupposes the activation of this fundamental *aisthesis*, of passive *urdoxa*, which Husserl calls "the primary stratum which is the basis of all experiencing in the concrete sense."[24]

The pure awareness of sound brought about by the musical experience is not mere passivity, any more than perception itself is mere sense-perception, i.e., mere receptivity for sense data. According to Husserl perception has its own type of intentionality, independent of mental activity, and it is in fact a precondition for any such activity.[25] Sounds come together, as it were, of themselves, without the intervention of an active agent. The synthetic character of perception must be thematized, for it is a stream of impressions, not an isolated phase. And in musical sound original impression, retention, and protention acquire a synthetic unity of their own in a temporal process of continual self completion independently of what we traditionally call conscious activity.

And here the language used by Husserl is illuminating. If heretofore he has made use of (or rather coined) the tribal language of phenomenology, he now departs from it and employs ordinary language to describe the unifying process of passive synthesis. Accordingly, he writes that a thing "builds itself" (*sich bauen*) in consciousness, a thing "produces itself" (*sich herstellen*), "fulfills itself" (*sich erfüllen*), "achieves itself" (*sich leisten*), and "constitutes itself primordially" (*sich ursprünglich konstituieren*).[26] One notices immediately that these are all reflexive forms of the verb. Passivity is self-action, and the "passivity" of the musical experience is a shaping up of the music *itself*, as it presents itself to consciousness. This synthetic "activity" is a prelude to the more complicated discussions on the fusion of sounds (*Verschmelzung*), so important to Stumpf and now also to Husserl in his explanations of what happens in musical temporality, as exemplified in a melody or symphony.

Let us take a closer look at both words in the phrase, passive synthesis. Husserl showed great uneasiness with the classic distinction between active and passive voices. Here we see the difficulty of expressing insights in ordinary language. The rigidities of classic grammar wished on us the speculative distinction between activity and passivity, between analysis and synthesis. In modern languages it is hard to grasp not just the subtlety but the utter necessity of a middle voice between the poles of activity and passivity, a voice that mediates between the polarities imposed on language and thought patterns by the classic tradition. Taking the advice of an analyst friend who admires the subtleties of classic Greek, I shall allow myself a short diversion into something lost to philosophy in the English translations of Greek thought: the middle ground between active and passive as embodied in the Greek middle voice. In classic Greek there was no "relation" between subject and object, the establishing of which led to the discovery of truth. Rather, there was a mediation between the passivity (*pathémata*) of the soul and things-to-be-done (*prágmata*). The passive mind and active things came together in a process in which the mind was "assimilated" to things, so that passivity became in fact a "likening" to things (*homoiómata*). Thus Aristotle's definition of truth has little to do with the relating of the subject to the object; rather he speaks of the "passive assimilation" of the soul into the world of things.[27] This passivity of the mind was best expressed by the middle voice, in which strictly speaking there is neither mental activity nor mere receptivity. The middle voice emphasizes the *subject* acting either for itself or for others, we might say, intersubjectively.[28] This self-action is expressed in modern languages by means of the reflexive form. The Greek word, *phaino*, means simply to demonstrate or show; but the middle form, *phainomai*, means to show oneself, thus to appear. To the Greek philosopher *phenomena*, or things that appear, were conceived as appearing on this middle ground, as being there in appearance, as showing and constituting themselves prior to any mental activity or receptivity. And this seems to be the case as regards listening to musical sound. This experience of things as they appear on middle ground, as they become phenomenal, so to speak, by appearing in phenomenal time (*erscheinende Zeit*), is already phenomenological, at least noematically. (And as I have pointed out elsewhere, the word, phenomenon, also means things that *ring clear* as sound as well as appearing-in-light.)[29] The mediation between subjective listener and objective sound is a kind of passive intentionality, a passive "belief," in which the subject is drawn into the world of sound and becomes part of it, "assimilated" to it, as it were. This passive intentionality is perceptually affective and prepares the ground for many fruitful epistemic achievements.

As to the word, synthesis, it is a word the Greeks made considerable use of, and mainly in the middle voice. Something "happens to me," is constituted for me as a unified and structured happening. Musical sounds fall together or *pull themselves together* (*sich zusammenschliessen*) for me in synthetic patterns in the experience of listening to a sonata or to the sonata-allegro movement of a given symphony. I am thus "passive," in that this symphonic happening comes over me, though I am not overcome. Rather, I am "affected" by the experience, though not merely passively. It goes without saying that this excursion is meant only to employ the classic Greek middle voice as a model; it is not an attempt to restore ancient Greek. For, it is obvious that this linguistic modality is irretrievably lost to us; and we can only look with admiration and some nostalgia at the subtleties of ordinary Greek as used by Plato and Aristotle. And it fills us with mixed feelings with regard to the present and future of less subtle languages. The genius and subtlety of English lies in other directions.

It is the middle ground between the arbitrary poles of active and passive that such a thing as the musical experience takes place; and it is on this middle ground that Husserl's notion of "passive synthesis" was conceived. We note that throughout his treatment of it he continually refers to musical sound as a temporal phenomenon. He seems to model his conception on the facts of musical experience, where notes *put themselves together* for us in perception and offer themselves as such to consciousness. This putting-together is literally synthesis. Tones and colors are depicted as hyletic data in the consciousness of immanent time; and these data *constitute themselves* (Greek middle: *syn-tithontai*) in a process of continuous becoming. Tonalities are not mere *data* in the sense of empirical data: rather they are *Gegebenheiten*, i.e., they are *given* to us in transcendent manner. In this case "transcendent" means an overcoming of the empirical level of ontic science, so that the data do not remain merely objective but can be subsumed into the immanence of the subject. Now the natural correlate of any giving is a receiving; and it is said to be better to give than to receive. But in order that giving can be accomplished a basic receptivity, an ability to perceive and receive, is required. Even medieval philosophy recognized this. Such receptivity is thus a correlative necessity, if data are to be taken into the subject's consciousness as *Gegebenheiten*, as givens. To receive a proffered gift, we extend the hand with the intention of taking the gift. The image of the extended hand, significative of intentionality, connotes the activity required to constitute proper receptivity. Receiving is therefore not inert passivity. The hand must close on the gift, else it will fall to the ground. Similarly, in order to listen to either spoken language or to musical sound, we have to "lend our ears." Listening is not merely passive reaction; it is its own kind of activity. It has its own kind of intentionality, seen embodied in the sudden erecting of the ears when the dog hears its master's voice. In sound the voice or the music shapes itself and presents itself bodily to us as hearers. It is there *as given*; it is not merely a question of sense data affecting our audial apparatus.

On the middle ground of the listening process we hear words or music "take shape," i.e., they constitute themselves in our awareness; and the receptivity of the listening subject is a necessary correlate to the activity of the speaker or of the musician. Aaron Copeland spoke of the "creative listener," who is necessary for the sensitive performer. Heidegger has put it rather forcefully, stating that we do not hear because we have ears; rather we have ears because we can hear.[31] We are dealing here with what Husserl calls pure passivity, the most fundamental stratum of pure subjectivity.[32] It goes without saying that this is not a flight to the extremes of mere subjectivity; rather, it is "pure" in the sense of having been purified of mundane content, which includes being delivered of the rigid dichotomy of active vs. passive.

For the sake of detailing our thesis, let us examine an example used by Husserl. In his treatment of associative synthesis, after both praising and criticizing Kant for his masterful treatment of transcendental synthesis ("Transcendental Deduction" in *Kritik* I), Husserl states that we need to go beyond this point to the laying bare of the constitution of the inner world of the subject, of its stream of experience.[33] We have to plumb the depths of the subject as such, i.e. the subject *for itself*. For, in the process of living from moment to moment the subject achieves an ever higher degree of synthesis.[34] Here we see, that without being consciously aware of it, Husserl does indeed put himself on the middle ground we spoke of, viz., that of the subject-for-itself. And it is on this ground that the subject constitutes itself in passive synthesis and builds the synthesis in a process that is neither active nor passive in the ordinary sense.

The musical example Husserl employs to describe this is illuminating. Musical sound perdures from moment to moment, he writes, and it is synthetically one throughout all these individual moments. The temporal synthesis comprises the retentional tail, the momentary Now, and the protensional edge, fusing them into one continuously conscious structure. Hence tonal duration is not a mere series of sounds, and reality is not just a series of facts. Rather, the musical tone is identical with itself throughout all the individual moments that could fragment its identity. Moreover, we are not dealing with only a single tone, studying it, as does the scientist, with the aid of electronic instruments. For in musical composition, obviously, more than one sound may enter, whether we look at such entries vertically as a harmonic chord or horizontally as with the entries of a fugue. In the example Husserl describes there is an interplay between any one tone and all the others that are also present in the temporal process and in synthetic unity. Thus the problem of the simultaneity of time (*Gleichzeitigkeit*) is discussed.[35] For, each musical entry does not have its own isolated time apart from all the others. Instead, all the various entries together form one continuous temporality, achieving identity as one musical composition, however disparate the parts. To initial audial impressions are added additional ones, and they build a continuous temporal unity. Thus there are not as many times as there are entries, but rather there is one time, in which all the temporal processes take place. Time-consciousness is thus the primordial place (*Urstätte*) for the constitution of musical identity and unity, as well as the source of the connective forms of coexistence and succession of objects in consciousness.[36]

Time-consciousness is, in fact, the origin of what we know as "form," for in it entities shape themselves in passive synthesis for consciousness.

For the musical analyst such a conclusion is significant. And even for that classic form known as sonata-allegro the example and the explanation are important. The analyst will be tempted to say that the symphonic form is simply there objectively in the musical score. Actually, it is constituted in passive synthesis at the pre-analytical stage in the perceptive consciousness of the performer and of the listener.[37] Of course, with the larger form of the symphonic sonata-allegro we have the problem of "appresentation," i.e. only segments of the symphony are present at one time to the hearer, and it required some effort to pull it all together into a larger form.[38] Still it is consciousness that makes even this possible, and first-movement form was conceived with a double exposition of themes precisely to give the listeners a chance to register the thematic entries twice, so that they could be retained and become part of the developmental and recapitulatory process that was to be built on the exposition.

When Husserl speaks of the synthetic unity of the sound process, stating that notes share their time though individually fragmented, he speaks from within the concept of the unity of consciousness. This hardly militates against the known facts of music history, according to which the medievalist can easily discover exceptions to the rule. He could object, for instance, that voices in medieval compositions are conceived, composed, and performed independently of one another. And yet even the musicologist knows that these individually conceived voice parts are meant to sound together in accord with the principles of mathematically conceived consonances. Here we see that in the *ars antiqua* especially the mathematicizing of musical consciousness did not go against the actual ensemble sound of the musical composition, as, e.g., in the *Codex Bamberg*. But the perceptual process was formalized and subsumed under the aegis of a medieval theory of consciousness which was pre-psychological, i.e., it was mathematical and metaphysical.

Thus, though the individual voice parts were conceived as independent voices, as it were, none-the-less by force of the mathematically conceived theory of musical proportionality they were meant to come together in consonances, and that at given places above the foundation voice or *tenor*. This lower voice, probably instrumental, was not a *basse fondamentale* in the sense of the baroque music theorist and composer, J. Ph. Rameau; nor did it beget functional (or pretonal) harmonies in the sense of the pedagogy of the nineteenth century. But it was indeed the base of a consonantal column or "pillar" (*Säule*), which the other voices — for all their independence — were expected to help build.[39] What we have here is an architectural model based on exact mathematical proportionality. And this was considered to be the structure of musical consciousness. This rigid structure is a long way from the stream of consciousness advocated in Joycean manner by Husserl. Though mathematically conceived, such consonances were meant for the ear's perception and enjoyment. Despite the greater independence of individual voices in the middle ages (I think specifically of the *ars antiqua* and of the *ars nova*, thus of the later thirteenth and the first half of the fourteenth centuries) forming consonances pleasant to the ear was a principal preoccupation of the composer, as he devised ways to amalgamate the individual voices into one harmonic structure. The intellect may well have delighted in the interplay of mathematical proportions, as Jacques de Liège relates in his encyclopedic *Speculum Musicae*, but the ear's perception was at very least the port of entry to such mathematical consciousness.

Finally, a word on the importance of Stumpf's and Husserl's notion of fusion or amalgamation (*Verschmelzung*). The word, *Verschmelzung*, occurs a good many times in Husserl's treatment of passive synthesis.[40] By it Stumpf had meant the fusion of two simultaneous tones to make a consonant interval in the perception of the listener. Thus the musical interval of a fifth did not consist merely in two concurrent tones, e.g. one at C and the other at G. Rather, they sounded together and in so doing fused together as a new entity, which the harmonic analyst calls a fifth. But Stumpf's conception of consonance was fundamentally different from the mathematical conception of the *ars antiqua*, for it was psychologically conceived and was incipiently phenomenological. For Stumpf the concept of sensation (*Empfindung*) is central; it is not merely a matter of psychological consciousness. Fusion is something *given primordially* in perception; thus it is not a conscious activity in the sense that we consciously put tones together to make a consonance. Rather, tones enter consciousness *as already fused* or amalgamated in perception.[41] Improving on this phenomenologically Husserl distinguishes two types of fusion, (1) formal or necessary, and (2) affective.[42] Formal or necessary amalgamation has to do with primordial continuity and is a hyletic fusing evident in the successive and continuous unity of perception within a given field of sensation. Such fusion is a progressive building of unity (*Einheitsbildung*), particularly in temporal sequence. Affective fusion has to do with the sense data that directly affect consciousness, even though they may never actually attain the conscious state. In such a context contrast is stressed by Husserl. Thus consciousness is affected by a sudden change, and one cannot but help think of the terrace dynamics of a baroque concerto grosso or of the dramatic diminished seventh chord at the close of a Bach fugue. The latter has the immediate effect of making the entire fugue present in consciousness, and Husserl might go along completely with such an explanation. The diminished seventh chord so employed was crucial to the baroque *Affektenlehre*, consciously used by Bach. *Affektion* is, of course, not "affect" as such. Rather it denotes being "struck" or affected (*affiziert*) by the sensation. It is constituted for consciousness in passive synthesis, which is a primordial stratum in the progressive build-up of consciousness. Fusion (*Verschmelzung*) is a constitutive and unitive process, a plural consciousness (*Mehrheitsbewußsein*) based on a sensuous context (*Zusammenhang*).[43] And, while Husserl is intent on using musical tone as an example for passive synthesis, he provides us with a phenomenological version of Carl Stumpf's theory of musical consonance as such.

CONCLUSION

Phenomenology and material ontologies stand in close alliance with one another, Husserl writes at the close of his treatise on passive synthesis.[44] One sees how important a musical model was for the founder of phenomenology, and how important phenomenological insights can be for musicology. Phenomenology seems to be a necessary stratum of one's studies, if one intends to break out of classic frameworks, thus out of historicism and psychologism. And yet phenomenology needs the concreteness of such a material ontology as the science-of-music, for ontic sciences have a way of pinning us down to realities, despite their theoretical naivetes. In musicology one gets pinned down to opus numbers, dates, and scores, as well as to manuscripts from the middle ages and the renaissance. However "narrow" science's purview may appear to the philosopher, the fact remains that we need this scientific and scholarly reality, lest we get caught in foggy postulates and end in irrelevance. Yet the scientific factualist also needs the insights and fluidity of phenomenology, lest he become imbedded in empiricism for its own sake. Without science philosophy risks floundering and becoming mere speculation; without philosophy science overlooks primary questions that may be crucial even to scientific investigation for its own sake. What is needed on all sides today is the interdisciplinary approach; and the philosopher must identify with his colleagues in the sciences, and bring them to a recognition of the horizons philosophy envisions.[45] This was the ideal of Carl Stumpf, and the musical models he employed became significant in the unfolding of his student's methodology.

Endnotes

1. R. Ingarden, *Untersuchungen zur Ontologie der Kunst* (Tübingen, 1962), Das Musikwerk, pp. 3-138. Cf. Zofia Lisa, "Einige kritische Bermerkungen zur Ingardenschen Theorie des musikalischen Werkes" in *Studia Estetyczne*, 3, 1966, pass.
2. Don Ihde, "Studies in the Phenomenology of Sound: I. Listening" (with T. F. Slaughter), "II. On Perceving Persons, III. God and Sound" in *International Philosophical Quarterly*, X, 2, June 1970, pp. 232-251. I have also had some correspondence and discussions with H. Spiegelberg on Husserl's musical background. Cf. also, Thomas Clifton, "Music as Constituted Object" in *Music and Man*, Vol. II, Nos. 1/2, 1976.
3. This does not imply that analysts are uninterested in the paratactical structures of speech as spoken.
4. E. Husserl, *Zur Phänomenologie des inneren Zeitbewußseins*, Husserliana X (The Hague, 1966—); *Analysen zur passiven Synthesis*, Huss. XI (The Hague, 1966). These volumes go together, as it were. The first represents Husserl's work from 1893-1917, the second from 1918-1926. Cf. also, *Erfahrung und Urteil, zur Genealogie der Logik*, ed. L. Landgrebe, 1939.
5. *Erfahrung und Urteil*, p. 72.
6. Cf. F. J. Smith, *Jacobi Leodiensis Speculum Musicae, A Commentary*, II (New York, 1970), pass.
7. I. Kant, *Kritik der Urteilskraft* (ed. K. Vorlander), p. 184.
8. H. Spiegelberg, *The Phenomenological Movement*, I (The Hague, 1965), p. 53f.
9. *Die Musik in Geschichte und Gegenwart* (ed. F. Blume), XII, col. 1640f.
10. H. H. Unger, *Die Beziehingen zwischen Musik und Rhetorik im 17. und 18. Jahrhunderten* (Berlin, 1941), pass.
11. F. J. Smith, "Mozart revisited: K550. The problem of the survival of Baroque figures" in *The Music Review*, XXXI, 3 Aug. 1970, p. 201f.
12. E. Husserl, *Zur Phänomenologie des inneren Zeitbewußseins*, Beilage, VI, p. 114.
13. E. Husserl, ref. 12, p. 4.
14. F. Husserl, "Thilosophie als strenge wissenschaft" in *Logos*, I, 1910/11, ed. W. Szilasi, in *Quellen der Philosophie* (ed. R. Berlinger) (Frankfurt a.M., 1965), pass.
15. E. Husserl, ref. 14, p. 42f.
16. E. Husserl, ref. 12, p. 26.
17. Cf. H. Khatchadourian, *A Critical Study in Method* (The Hague, 1967), p. 210f; cf. also, the present writer's review in *The Journal of Value Inquiry*, Summer 1974.
18. E. Husserl, *Zur Phänomenologie des inneren Zeithewußswins*,

        p. 13f.
19.   E. Husserl, ref. 18, p. 19f.
20.   E. Husserl, ref. 18, p. 21.
21.   E. Husserl, *Analysen zur passiven Synthesis*, e.g. p. 78.
22.   E. Husserl, ref. 21, p. 51f.: *Erfahrung und Urteil*, p. 61.
23.   E. Husserl, ref. 22 (EU), p. 67.
24.   E. Husserl, ref. 24 (EU), p. 67.
25.   *Analysen zur passiven Synthesis*, p. 54.
26.   E. Husserl, ref. 25, pp. 66, 72, 76, 104, 125, 126, 157, 218, 252, 319, etc.
27.   E. Husserl, ref. 25, p. 102; but cf. Heidegger, *Sein und Zeit*, p. 214, where Heidegger translates *pathémata* as *Erlebnisse* and *homoiómata* as *Angleichungen*.
28.   Cf. E. Husserl, *Analysen zur passiven Synthesis*, p. 126, where he speaks of the subject as "für es selbst seiend"; later this comes to mean the being of conscious constitution. In stressing the self Husserl is in effect on "middle ground," where according to both Kaegi and Smythe the Greek middle voice is conceived.
29.   F. J. Smith, "Toward a phenomenology of musical aesthetics" in *Aisthesis and Aesthetics*, eds. Straus/Griffith (Pittsburgh, 1970).
30.   E. Husserl, *Analysen zur passiven Synthesis*, p. 105.
31.   M. Heidegger, *Der Satz vom Grund* (Pfullingen, 1957), p. 87; cf. p. 95, where the ontological leap is illustrated by musical modulation from one key to another.
32.   E. Husserl, *Analysen zur passiven Synthesis*, p. 118.
33.   E. Husserl, ref. 32, p. 125f.
34.   E. Husserl, ref. 32, p. 126.
35.   E. Husserl, ref. 32, p. 127.
36.   E. Husserl, ref. 32, p. 128.
37.   Sonata-allegro form was recognized as such only in the nineteenth century, when with A. B. Marx pedagogues began analyzing classical symphonies.
38.   E. Husserl, ref. 32, p. 202.
39.   German musicologists coined the word, *Klangsäule*, in this context.
40.   E. Husserl, ref. 32, pp. 141, 142, 155, 159f, etc.
41.   H. de la Motte, "Uber die Gegenstände und Methoden der Musikpsychologie, ein geschichtlicher Überblick" in *The International Review of Music Aesthetics and Sociology*, I, 1, 1970, pp. 83-90.
42.   E. Husserl, *Analysen zur passiven Synthesis*, p. 159f.
43.   E. Husserl, ref. 42, p. 399 (Beilage XVII).
44.   E. Husserl, ref. 42, p. 222.
45.   Particularly useful for such purposes is publication of A. Schutz' "Fragments on the phenomenology of music," ed. F. Kersten, in *Music and Man. An Interdisciplinary Journal of Studies on Music*, vol. II, 1/2, 1976.

Chapter 5

CARTESIAN THEORY AND MUSICAL SCIENCE

A phenomenological analysis of "thinking" must include also a musicological examination of the traditional *cogito*, particularly since music theory was heavily influenced by Rameau's Cartesian orientation. It is a truism that Husserl emphasizes the *cogito*, while Heidegger underscores the *sum*. And yet this does not mean that Heidegger's interpretation of the *cogito* ignores the phenomenological moment in favour of the ontological. Indeed, despite the risks entailed in any ontology within phenomenology (and thus any application to the "phenomenon" of music), it can be said that Heidegger's existential-ontological interpretation of thought is not "un-phenomenological," even though it seems to depart from what loyal Husserlians would call a "pure" phenomenology. Granted that being is *a* theme within phenomenology, and that ontology may well be made possible only within phenomenology (Heidegger's thesis), it is evident that Heidegger's existential-ontological interpretations of the *cogito* are something new and original, unlike the "ontology" present in Husserl's work or the study of being which is the main purpose of traditional post-Aristotelian metaphysics. A true and complete phenomenology of thinking (and thus also of musical thought) would imply an unfolding or manifestation of the whole range of thought, rather than just the purely phenomenological in its eidetic meaning. As a result, the philosophical and musical *cogito* cannot be considered outside its philosophical and musical context, even though this is done at the risk of a kind of "objectification" of the *subject*, as thinking.

1. A CRITIQUE OF THE TRADITIONAL INTERPRETATION OF THE COGITO

Jean Phillipe Rameau was part of the rationalist scene in Descartes' time. He made a fundamental revision of music theory — resurrected in the pedagogy of the nineteenth century — based on Cartesian thought forms and the basic structure of the *cogito*, as rational base for musical composition. The *cogito* has very little to do with a theory of knowledge, with skepticism or a merely subjective thinking. Rather, the *cogito* emerges in a discussion on first philosophy in Descartes' *Meditationes de prima philosophia*. It is thus a metaphysical rather than an epistemological situation, based on a *mathesis universalis* rather than on any universal "doubt" in a skeptical sense. Thus "mathematical" clarity not universal skepticism was the goal. Descartes' "doubting" was in effect a re-examining of the metaphysical foundations of thinking. It is therefore not a question of establishing one's existence because one cannot deny thought itself.

Since the entire thrust of Descartes' "doubting" was to establish a universal clarity, his *mathesis universalis* becomes the basis for a wholly new approach to metaphysics. (We leave in abeyance the Husserlian critique of the failure of the initial epoche in Descartes' philosophy and the resultant wreckage which emerges in the history of philosophy as the Cartesian "dualism," so treated even by Heidegger in *Sein und Zeit*.) This "mathematics" was to have been the standard and grounding of *all* thought, and thus Descartes set up rules for thinking in his *Regulae ad directionem ingenii*. It is for this reason that method became all important. Method is no longer simply an abstract process but rather a procedure in which the subject "makes" objects. Method is not mere procedure but the very ground from out of which and upon which we begin to know what can become an object for us, and how it becomes an object. The entire method "consists in order and disposition" and the reduction of the obscure to the simple by means of clear intuition. *Scientia universalis* is not attained in any other way than by deducing from this basis whatever can be clearly intuited, including (for Rameau) musical ideas.

This is therefore not a psychological situation but rather the attempt to re-ground metaphysics and music in "mathematics," i.e. on a new philosophy of number. Such attempts are to be found, of course, before Descartes. In the hitherto unanalyzed *Speculum Musicae* (1330-40), for example, Jacques de Liège wrote that the object of traditional metaphysics was not just *ens qua ens*, as it is usually presented in our manuals of history, but the *ens numeratus*. Number is thus recognized as the basis of the question of being, a number which in turn is based on *mundus*, understood in pre-Copernican context as a world centered upon men and universally intelligible by man's reason. Now Descartes tried again to found metaphysics, i.e. to rediscover its ground in *mathesis*, in order to give knowledge a more solid foundation. This is not being "subjective," but is the "objective" grounding of the *subject thinking*, even as the "objective" world depends on the subject as ground. The mistake Descartes made was to put this grounded subject in what Merleau-Ponty calls the *monde-en-idée*. The Cartesian *cogito* is thus truly metaphysical in a traditional pre-Kantian sense, for it is but a *cogito pensé*, a thought-*cogito*, rather than one grounded in-the-world and on-the-earth.

Since for Descartes the grounding of things is the task of the *res cogitans* or "thinking-thing," axioms and assertions are important. Things are regarded not in their bodily situation for themselves but only in the light of clear and distinct concepts and assertions about them. The assertion rests on mathesis. The assertive statement is grounded in the subject, *as* thinking, and the subject grounds itself upon an "objective" philosophy of number. The subject-thinking is the fundamental or the ground-statement itself. But this does not mean that the subject is "subjective." When I make a statement, "I think," it is not meant as a premise leading to the conclusion that "*therefore*, I am." Rather, the *cogito* has little to do with existence or nonexistence. Instead it seems to mean that I posit or "set" myself intellectually. And this "primary and most certain of all statements" is a self-stating statement, a self-positing, a 'proposition" that results from such a metaphysical positing. I state myself: I set or posit myself before myself and thus I come to "be." Hence being is not the conclusion to a logical argument; it is the intellectual ground and not the result of thought. Being, conceived intellectually rather than phenomenologically by Descartes, is therefore the sub-ject or ground of thinking. In accordance with this, the translation of *cogito ergo sum* is not "I think, and *therefore* I am," but rather, "I *am*, as thinking," i.e. I am when I state or posit myself as the ground or subject of my own being. This fundamental positing is also the source of Rameau's "fundamental tone" as the principle of musical composition, the subject for a later detailed study.

The ground-statement, "I posit myself," is a rational ingathering of self and thus a *res cogitans*, or thinking-thing, is a reason-thing, thinking. *Cogito* means: I think rationally and thus ground my own being, securing myself inwardly. In order to ground my being on clear and distinct thought-concepts I must not find myself in contradiction. The predicate must not say anything against the subject, since the subject is ground; and an assertation based on the grounding subject cannot go against itself. Thus the axiomatic principle of contradiction, which is not logical but metaphysical or onto-logical. While the attempt to reground metaphysics was necessary, our modern objection to Descartes is not that he was a skeptic or a subjectivist but rather that he founded subjectivity on reason and thus not in a logos-based matrix, insofar as traditional reason, even though made possible by logos, is a departure from the primordiality of logos. And thus though the Cartesian *cogito* is "ontological," rather than either logical or psychological, it is not yet founded on bodily logos. For the Cartesian *res cogitans* is quite separate from the *res corporea*, even though it is expressly stated that the soul is not a pilot in a ship but is somehow confusedly one with body. Neither the intellectual *cogito* or the *res corporea* is bodily in a phenomenological sense, and thus presents great difficulties for musical analysis.

The Cartesian *cogito* is at best an embodied thought, and in this sense the *res*-philosophy of Descartes is not wholly unlike traditional metaphysical realism. Any being in-the-world is indirect in such thinking. For though Descartes speaks of *res*, as thing, it is the mind or soul which is the "true me," as thinking thing. Body, as corporeal thing, is what situates me in a world of objects, for it is body as extended and as capable of locomotion that places me in the *res extensa*, as external *world*. Thus the "true me" is only indirectly in-the-*world* and is in a real sense quite world*less*. The ego is self-incapsulated. It is *solus ipse*, surrounded by a world of objects with which it has real contact only through despised body. It is for this very reason that it must reach out intellectually in order to make the metaphysical escape from solipsism, which is at the heart of this "first philosophy." Instead of emerging out of world our natural self posits itself from out a worldless *monde-en-idée*. And from here it reaches out to the extended outside world via corporality. But such being *in* the world of idea means being *out* of phenomenological world, as such, since idea is a metaphysical abstraction, something speculative reason abstracts from the concreteness of physis. And thus it is necessary for me to reach out into world, to per-ceive it intellectually, to force the dark and the obscure into the metaphysical forms of distinctness and clarity.

In addition the whole structure rests on a theological basis, though it is possible to dispute this. It is possible that in grounding his thought in a metaphysical mathesis Descartes "brackets" the theological presuppositions. Yet whatever subtleties lie between the lines, it seems clear that overtly at least Descartes postulates the deity to hold to-gether soul and body, thus guaranteeing my being also in the outside extended world by means of the *res corporea*. The foundation of such *res*-philosophizing is substance — which God is only analogously. Now substance is a thing "which so exists that it needs no other thing to exist." Yet substance as such as inaccessible. Substantial being cannot really affect us; it is unknown and not a real predicate of the subject. Here we see how Cartesian philosophy is wholly ontic. Ontological being lies hidden and covered over beneath the system of Descartes, even as it purports to be a "first philosophy." And once more we can see, with Heidegger, that a theologician cannot ask the fundamental question concerning ontological being.

Descartes' *cogito* means "I perceive or have an idea." To perceive thus means to *set* something *before* me, i.e. to re-present something to myself. I make it secure and thus found my own certitude; I must do this, if I start from such a metaphysical solipsism as that of Descartes. I have consciousness of the object in the act of perceiving or grasping it. Thus grasping is really my securing of the object. The thinking thing secures its place in the external world, as extended thing. This conceiving, as a per-ception or grasping, includes will, affects, actions, and passions, in short as Descartes himself writes, "all those things which happen consciously within us and to us . . ." A thing is perceived, i.e. it *is*, as secured and ordered (in Leibniz as perfected). A thing "exists" only when I have secured or grounded it in my rational subjectivity, even as the latter relies on the "objectivity" of a metaphysical mathesis. Man is therefore no longer the measure of things in the sense that he measures up to things in dialogue with them; rather man *is* the measure or standard of all things, as he founds himself in "mathematical" subjectivity. Things now become the object of this self-grounding subject. The *res extensa* is made the object of the *res cogitans* — and thus any "dualism."

"I am" means "I ground and secure myself" and thus I also secure things: I subject things to myself as grounding subject, because *I* am rational subject, i.e. *I* am that which under-lies any perception. I am the *hypo-keímenon* or ground of perception. "I perceive" means that I order, arrange, dispose, organize. Such a "hominized" rather than "subjective" metaphysics is possible, of course, only with Christianity in the background. Certitude and the need for it is characteristic of traditional Christian philosophies, as is a very definite solipsism. For everything must indeed be "secured" in a world in which the Christian man is or would be the un-disputed center. Per-ception means taking possession of a thing, for, Descartes tell us, we are to be "possessors of nature." To take possession means to ob-ject the world, i.e. to re-present or make a thing present to myself as an object: to ground and secure it in my own solipsistic subjectivity. Thus I give things their rationale for existing. In Leibniz I find a *sufficient* reason and erect this into the *grande princi-pium*. I make a thing objectively present to myself as subject: I put it into my rational presence, and I do this, of course, in accord with *my* categories, since I alone am rational sub-strate, i.e. the ground of judgment and certitude concerning all things that can be objectified. What we call "subjective thinking" is born: not out of the subjectivity of the thinking thing so much as out of the objectivity of the thing thought. Re-presenting a thing means making it present or visible; this visible re-presentation is an "idea," especially as "made by me." And this also includes any musical idea, such as Rameau's *ton fondamentale*, as an idea heard by me.

Thus *cogito* means to *bring* things to mind, i.e. to the rational ego, thinking and grounding itself. This bringing entails an examining of the thing, a calculating according to the correct rules of thought, or of composition. And it is this that leads us to the precise meaning of "doubting." To doubt does not mean to destroy by means of a skeptical denial of things. It means to re-examine: to re-ground. (The *cogito* and the *dubito* are interchangeable, Sartre writes in *Situations*, II, in his essay on Cartesian freedom.) All thought is a "doubting": a re-examining and securing of things. There is therefore no universal doubting in Descartes, as though he were a philosophically doubting Thomas; instead there is a universal re-grounding of things — just the opposite of what easy introductions to philosophy tell us. Instead of a uni-versal doubt we must speak of a universal assurance given by the re-grounding of the thinking subject in a *mathesis universalis*. This universal *scientia*, of course, implies the *con-scienta sui*, i.e. a self-assuring or self-securing. To stretch a point, it is a kind of *presence-à-soi*, i.e. making self distant from self, so that it can be presented-to-self. This is a kind of re-assuring or re-securing of presence. We see then that the *cogito* is not primarily psychological but rather metaphysical in the first philosophy of Descartes. I think on what *is*, even when this is my own subjectivity, philosophically or musically.

According to Heidegger it was Nietzsche who interpreted Descartes' statement as "psychological," since he himself takes up the "physiological" position, as the antipole of traditional metaphysics. But even here "psychological" means metaphysical. It can be thus understood best in the wake of Kant, who called Descartes' idealism empirical and gave a critique of the empirical ego as such in terms of a transcendental metaphysics rather than of theory of knowledge or of "psychology." The "physiological" in Nietzsche's writing was still enmeshed in the ontic order, Heidegger states. But in reality it may well have been the first step out of the metaphysical or ontic order of things, even though it never attains the level of phenomenological ontology, as eksistential, nor the dimension of the *corps propre*. Nietzsche objected to Descartes' presuppositions on existence, thought, and certitude. But his more cogent objection is felt in the identification of *cogito* with *volo*, as the will-to-truth: knowing or thinking means a conscious attempt to control reality. Knowledge as a *con-scientia* is a self-willing, a self-justification. This is more evident in the thought of Leibniz, where perception is appetitive: an active force that goes out of itself to possess the world. It must be admitted that this has obvious roots in a Christian voluntarism that no serious student would call into question. Nietzsche claimed that Descartes' *cogito* was a hypothesis that gave the feeling of power. Will was of prime importance for Nietzsche, influenced as he was by Schopenhauer. And thus also the will to power, even though "power" is meant as the will to *fullness-of-life* rather than to control. In Nietzsche feeling is in and of the "body"; but Descartes' *cogito* is only in the *res animata* as soul-thing. It is the life of the soul not the fullness of bodily life that makes us truly human and thinkers.

Nietzsche's critique thus leads to a better understanding of the beginnings of the "bodily" dimension, though his insights remain at the pre-phenomenological level. The *cogito* is not "psychological" but "physiologically" based. Mind is the "little reason," whereas body is "great reason." Humanness is not grounded in a rationalistic solipsism, as religious and metaphysical, but rather in the body, which is of the earth. The human is that which emerges from ontological earth, from that *physis* which gives birth to the "physiological," from that *humus* which is the source of both humanity and humility. Ontological earth, whether conceived in the pre-phenomenological terms of Nietzsche or in terms of Heidegger's "conflict" between world and earth, is neither fatalistic nor naturalistic. It is that to which we return from out the ideational world for its own sake, from out that half-a-world which begot half-gods and half-men. However, we must be careful to add, that in the *Discours de la méthode*, Descartes asks whether instead of the speculative approach he pursues there be not some sort of *pratique*, by which we can know the reality of the body. This is surely an important Cartesian insight and an opening in his otherwise metaphysically conceived thinking. Does it prepare the ground for what we might nowadays style a "bodily praxis"? It is sad that Descartes could not pursue his insight and that it became lost in the actual rational course he did follow.

2. THE PRE-REFLEXIVE AND THE BODILY LOGOS

Consciousness of self is not that of a subject for an object, phenomenologically speaking. We do not objectify self when we become conscious of self, even as we seek the ontological basis of self. Rather, there is an immediate rapport of self to self and of the pre-reflexive *cogito*, which is the condition for any Cartesian *cogito*. Thus I do not know myself because I reflect, instead I can reflect because I am conscious. Hence consciousness (of) self is not a new consciousness but rather, Sartre writes, "the only mode of existence possible for consciousness of anything." Consciousness is not produced as a singular example of an abstract possibility but arises from within being itself, as the fullness of existence. It is necessary therefore to renounce the primacy of "knowledge" and find the *being* of knowledge: the "absolute" of existence. The possibility of a parallel between the pre-reflexive *cogito* and Heidegger's "self-anticipation" (*sich-vorweg*), which is the eksistential meaning of "care," suggests itself. Both are in a sense attempts to re-ground metaphysics and to overcome the rationality of the Cartesian *cogito*. Care (*Sorge*) is that which *is*-there before any "reflection." We might add, that the existential-ontological dimension is there prior to reflection upon it, be this the reflective process or the reflecting of self on self. Especially when this self-anticipation is bodily, it is clear that a merely psychological reflection has to do with abstract intellection or knowledge primarily. In this case reflection is an abstraction of that concrete bodily being which makes any reflecting of self on self possible at all. Reflection, as rational, roots in the bodily logos as pre-reflective. Heidegger's "self-anticipation" connotes "standing in one's own way." I am thus "before myself" ontologically rather than only "for myself," in that I not only confront myself dialectically at the level of knowledge but "anticipate myself at the level of phenomenological ontology."

Consciousness is therefore not substantive, and Descartes' error may well have been to make it a substance. Yet Cartesian substance, Heidegger points out, is inaccessible. And thus even when Descartes defines thought as thing and as substance, it is not "substantive" in the traditional sense, contrary to Sartre (who also makes Husserl pose as a "phenomenalist"). Sartre felt that Husserl remained incapsulated in the phenomenological *cogito* and that the transcendental ego was not an overcoming of ordinary solipsism. Yet it is difficult to state that Husserl remains enclosed in the *cogito*, when he performs a series of difficult eidetic reductions, thus overcoming not only Descartes' *cogito* but also his own egological position. Hence not only the "substantive" ego of Descartes but also the objectionable solipsism is reduced, making the intersubjective dimension possible.

Sartre takes over and adapts the Hegelian distinction between *an sich* and *für sich* in a dialectical explication of phenomenological consciousness. Thus the *en soi* is that which is in itself, as self-contained, a kind of massive density, full positivity and indissolubility. That which is in itself is full of itself; and there is no fissure or opening through which what it is *not* could appear. The *en soi* is not conscious. And here we must remind ourselves of the difference between self-consciousness, as *wissen* in Hegel, but as phenomenological consciousness, ontologically based, in Sartre. The transition from self-knowledge to phenomenologically ontological self-consciousness is enormous. But the dialectical process re-introduced by Sartre, and perhaps possible only in a phenomenological ontology of consciousness (rather than in a Husserlian subjectivity of consciousness), recoups the movement of Hegel from self-positing through creative nihilation. Only now the positing is not metaphysical but phenomenologically ontological. In order to become conscious and attain presence to self it is necessary to gain distance from this compact oneness and in-itselfness. An opening must be found, one covered over by "knowledge" in its systematic self-explication. The opening in being makes it possible to be *for* itself and not just *in* itself. Thus what is in itself must nihilate (not annihilate) itself, rather than only reaffirm its oneness with self. It must open out to what it is *not*, in order to recoup the lost negative moment, which it then must take into itself. It must therefore lose itself, absorb itself, sacrifice itself, decompress itself, in order to become phenomenologically conscious of self and other and so enter into world. Though Sartre would have us believe so, *Dasein* is not *en soi*, for the ground of its being-there is not self-affirmation but rather no-thingness — even though this negativity is not fully developed in *Sein und Zeit*. Hence *Dasein* is hardly "full positivity." Moreover, it is not monolithic unity but a continual "dialogue" between the ontic and the ontological.

Heidegger calls this area the "difference" or the "split" in being. Ontological being is the "open middle" in the ontic beings. To *be*-there means to be caught up in this openness. The influence of Hegel is evident in *Sein und Zeit*, though hardly so overt as in *L'Être et le Néant*. Under such circumstances it would be difficult to maintain with early Sartre that *Dasein* is only *an sich*, and thus also *en soi*.

The *pour-soi* is what guarantees our being in the world; and of its very nature, this means becoming body. The escape from the *en-soi* world of empty abstractions and closed system effects itself in the form of an involvement with body in the world. Such a world is not a desert, a world of mere concepts without living man, but is the concrete world of phenomenologically bodily reality. Even soul and reason are basically bodily and can be abstracted from body only by a metaphysical withdrawal. The self, which *is* body and of the earth, Nietzsche writes, laughs at the handsprings of ego, because self is in reality the very source of "soul" and ego. Here Husserl comes to our aid, when he writes in *Ideen* II, that "body, as the here and now, is the place from which pure ego contemplates the sense world." Soul and body in this case are anti-polar rather than dichotomous.

Heidegger gains knowledge of "body" not so much from such insights as from a dialogue with the pre-Socratics; thus he writes of *physis* and *logos*. Man is not a "rational animal" or an ensouled body (*sóma émpsychon*). He *is* the living logos. And logos is not conceived rationalistically by the pre-Socratics. It is the task of phenomenology to get back to the primordial logos, more fundamental than objective thought, the logos that makes the *cogito* itself possible. And Heidegger does this when he restores the Greek sense of the classic definition of man as the *zôon lógon échon*, as well as in his attempts to get at the meaning of Parmenidean and Heraclitan fragments. The classical definition underwent a major shift in meaning when it was translated as "animal rationem habens," and thus as the "rational animal." Heidegger cuts through this rationalistic and metaphysical definition of man, which splits man into soul (mind) and body, and lays bare a

more primordial logos, which man has/is. Logos is a fundamental ingathering or as-sembling, which only in post-
medieval fashion can be interpreted metaphysically as
"reason." Granted that "reason" is one interpretation of the
primordial logos, it is not the only one, and is at best a
derived and deficient mode of logos. Thus rationality must
always return to its fundamental logos, in order that it not
become a form of metaphysical alienation from primordial
ground. Thus a Cartesian *cogito* is interpretable as a *co-
agitatio*, i.e. as an as-sembling or ingathering by the subject.
But in this case it is *ratio* as the *res cogitans* which does the
ingathering. A more fundamental as-sembling is the definition
of *logos* itself, as that which as-sembles (*vor-sammelt*) or in-
gathers. Thus the *cogito*, as that which brings together or
as-sembles, is in a sense coextensive with logos itself, as that
which in-gathers (*légein*). *Cogito* is thus the "ingathering
thought" of the logos itself. Any return out of mere
knowledge to consciousness must eventually end up at the
primordial level of the logos, as that which makes both
consciousness and knowledge possible at all. Thus man is not
the "rational animal" divided into body and soul. Rather,
man is *bodily* as the "living being which has/is the *logos*."

Fundamental meaning grounds itself not in reason alone
but in the living man as a whole, as ontological body, as
logos. The bodily dimension is a phenomenological overcoming of the "dualism" of rational and corporeal, thus of
the *res cogitans* and the *res corporea*. In Cartesian philosophy
the "true me" is the ego, as mind or soul. But this is in reality
but a me-in-idea, which resides in a world-in-idea rather than
in world as such. The ego of Descartes cannot *be* truly in
the world except indirectly through speculative reason, newly
grounded on a universal mathesis, or in a *pratique* which
remains undeveloped and covered over. Yet phenomenologically speaking ego is but an abstraction of body, or as
Nietzsche puts it, "something of the body." Phenomenological intentionality is in the bodily logos, as primordial,
rather than in abstract soul or reason. "It is I who reconsti-
tute the historical *cogito*," Merleau-Ponty writes. This means

that I take up the bodily movement of a *cogito*, rather than seeking to embody it in the manner of traditional metaphysical realism. My taking up of the bodily movement of the *cogito* is the return to primordial logos, as such. This bodily movement *is* man moving *as* logos. It is evidently not mere abstract thought but logos thinking itself. Thus thought is not mere rational process but a bodily matter. We might ask how one takes up the bodily *cogito*. Bodily thinking means not just thinking things over abstractly and then judging them in accord with the arbitrary standards of some ideal or ideological system of thought. Bodily thinking or logos-thinking is a weighing of matters (pensare). This entails not just "weighing" facts abstractly and "objectively"; it means actually holding them in my hands, getting the "feel" of them, experiencing in my whole body the weight of a situation in which I am involved. Abstract thought is a way of escaping involvement in world and earth. But being bodily in the world, as logos-thinker, rather than just speculating about being in the world, means that when I "think" I gather myself together in confrontation and anticipation of self within the primordial logos that I have/am.

Merleau-Ponty's critique of Descartes is somewhat similar to that of Nietzsche. Descartes reduced thinking to metaphysical hypothesis, to system of thought, to "psychology." The *cogito*, if not grounded in ontological body, is a closing in on one's own solipsistic world and a retreat from world as such. Thought is not something abstract, absolute, or "eternal" in the traditional sense of "eternal truths." The *cogito* takes place in time. Eternity is a hypocritical concept, in that it is a derivative of time, which refuses to acknowledge its concrete philosophical and historical source. Phenomenological eternity is but the atmosphere of time, and I partake of this atmosphere.

Cogito as vision cannot be but a speculative or theoretically intuited thinking *about* sight. Yet intellectual insight is not just the abstract intellection of abstract ideas and forms, even of a metaphysically conceived mathesis. Vision is an acting out, prepared by my primordial or bodily ekstatis and openness to the field of transcendence. I must "see" the eksistent world appear *before me*, as I "anticipate" myself. This bodily ekstasis or standing-out into world-itself (and away from world-in-idea) is a "vision" that does not merely contemplate things but rather *goes out* to them. Thus *cogito*, as the ingathering of the primordial logos, can come to mean the movement of transcendence which is my own bodily being in contact with, i.e. *one with*, concrete world. I "throw" myself into things. Such "doing" the world rather than merely thinking it begets a "certitude" impossible for the traditional epistemologist to conceive of, for it is a certitude not based on the securing of a world of objects. Instead it is an ontological certitude based on the primordiality of an original logos.

In this case certitude does not mean a hard core of convictions, based on anxiety, but the capacity to accept what we are *not* as well as what we *are*. It means not resting content on an imaginary fund of eternal truths but becoming involved in the nihilation of being bodily in the world as on the earth. It means the capacity to "doubt," i.e. to affirm not a world of abstractions but the bodily world in which exist. The best way to stop doubting is to "doubt" effectively: to become honestly involved in the phenomenological experience of doubt. "Doing" the world implies grounding oneself bodily in world. This existential grounding begets not an abstract or "moral" certitude; rather it opens out of a mere self-securing into a sharing of world. Doubting demands that I re-examine the foundations of my metaphysical solipsism and stand *before myself* in good faith. But to stand before myself I must return to the primordial logos which makes both the pre-reflective *cogito* and the *sich vorweg* possible. Only then can I "think myself" and thus "know myself."

3.   MUSICOLOGY, AS "MUSICAL THINKING"

A musical composition, especially a symphony, does not
exist in the dry notes of the musical score, as presented or
even restored by the working musicologist, that writer *about*
music. We know that a good musicologist does not merely
restore the correct scores of past centuries but also, as musician, attempts to recall the concrete milieu and the artistic
mind of the composer himself, so that the composition may
be safeguarded against often misleading "practical" interpretations. It is especially the musician-musicologist who
must "take up the movement" of the musical *cogito*, in order
that the musical logos as "composition" may emerge in its
concreteness. In restoring old music we do not aim at
"objectivity" in a purist sense, as we combat the errant
subjectivity of many an unjustifiable private interpretation
(as e.g. the romanticising of Bach). Rather we try to lay bare
and return to the musical *subject*, as such, as it is born in the
creative activity of the composer, and as it emerges in his
concrete "historical" situation. Thus, in order to render the
notes of Beethoven, Bach, Hindemith, or Schoenberg, we
have to try to enter into their "bodily" movement, as it were.
This is especially true when the composer was also an outstanding interpreter and performer, say a Rachmaninoff.
Thus we recoup a bodily logos.

Musical notes, like the written *cogito*, are never regarded
as having value in themselves. They have neither real nor
ideal existence *as* music, Ingarden writes. But it often seems
that written words, unlike written notes, have some sort of
priority over bodily movement, whence they originated.
Words, and then thoughts about words, have been split off
from the living, bodily reality of man, as speaker or as singer.
The written word has become an abstraction, justifying its
priority on the postulation of an ideal world of essence and
meaning. This has been a problem in historical musicology
from the start. But it is a problem for all the sciences, of
which historical musicology would be an honored one. In
order to circumvent the tendency of alienation of written

word from living logos, as musical or as anything else, perhaps we ought to be aware of the gradual process of alienation that has taken place in the theoretical sciences. A given statement, once the "bodily movement" of the speaker or singer *as* speaking and/or singing, came to be written down. The purpose was laudable: to preserve the proverb or the song for posterity or simply for repetition, when the given word was a part of ritual or ceremony. But this letter, which is a kind of "first abstraction," gradually seemed to become more important than the living word itself, so that finally the living word ended up as just an "instance" of the new "ideal" word, as such. Once written words, as subsumed into an ideal existence, were erected into definitions (such as the rational definition of man) and systems of definitions, and were then regarded as "thought," an important "second abstraction" took place. With the first abstraction our attention was diverted from the living word, as logos, to the *littera*, as written, and thus as "material" or "real" word, a word that could be "preserved," and thus could be regarded as lasting and eventually as "eternal." In the second abstraction, or withdrawal from logos, we depart even farther from living reality and begin to construct systems upon systems of "pure thought," gradually convincing ourselves that this is reality in its purest form. This is the common danger of any idealism. Then to convince ourselves completely, we proceed to "embody" the abstract word. This is most evident in legal word. Yet merely re-embodying abstract word is insufficient. It is an ineffectual return to logos, for it keeps up the illusion of the superiority of abstract thought and of the split between the concrete and the abstract. Hegel was eminently aware of this problem.

But rather than essaying "absolute knowledge" in a Hegelian sense, as spirit objectifying itself in nature and subsuming nature into itself in dialectical manner, we try to lay bare the primordial logos, as that which makes "knowledge" possible at all. This is the recovery of living word itself, phenomenologically speaking. For abstract thought, like musical notes or musicological theory, is but a derivative and deficient form of primordial word, as such. Not disembodied verities but rather the truth of bodily logos itself is the norm of thinking, and thus "being and thinking are the same." For any meaningful *cogito* must be based on the primordial logos, of which it is the "conscious expression," understood phenomenologically. Thus abstract philosophical and scientific theories, including musicological research — to say nothing of theological excurrences into a "higher life" or an after-life — need to be checked constantly against the bodily logos we *are*, as in the world and on the earth.

It is therefore insufficient just to think or talk the *cogito*. I must throw myself bodily into living world, especially the living world of musical sound. I must *do* this world, *as* logos. Such a bodily logos does not mean merely "certain modulations of my body." Rather it means that "I *am* my body," as Marcel writes both in the *Journal Métaphysique* and *Refus à l'invocation*. A musician finds this easy to comprehend. Though he may have composed and/or analyzed a given composition, he will not attempt to dictate intellectual forms to his fingers. For he thinks with his fingers, and not just with his head, even as his finger movements are coordinated in his head. They are still finger movements, and his head is, after all, of the body. Fingers in contact and dialogue with the concrete possibilities and limitations of a keyboard (or any instrument) is what gives birth to living music rather than to cerebral effusions or pedantic exercises.

Coming out of abstract world means overcoming an abstract *cogito* with its excessive demands and intellectual chatter. It means breaking down the artificial solipsism that causes the ego to overdemand and chatter at its world of objects, which it seeks to control by means of "thought." The continual chatter of the solipsistic *cogito*, as expressed psychologically or even musicologically (witness the plethora of scientific research on music!), must all fall silent, as when we fall speechless in the limit-situation. This speechlessness and "thoughtlessness" is the "silent *cogito*": the silent call of primordial being. At this moment the utter limitation of abstract thought or merely verbal word — in short, the whole world of ontic facts and words — becomes suddenly apparent. At this moment of anxiety we are jarred into wordlessness and into world: into *listening* to the call of ontological being as primordial logos. The "silent *cogito*" is thus the musical logos. When this logos speaks (or sings?) the ontic concepts, categories, and alienated words, no longer mean anything. We are rendered speechless and thoughtless: we fall wordless, as we cease to chatter at our world of controlled objects, as we "lose control," begin to *listen* to the logos, and thus begin to share in the world of *Mitsein*. We thus face the nihilation of all we had relied on heretofor, as we reappraise in silence our entire situation. When ontic words become useless, we must set them aside and face, naked, the living, bodily, logos of being and being-with. This is the musically ontological moment, when we either eksist bodily or face annihilation. There may be no time for "reflexion." Perhaps we begin to see the possibilities of the ontologically pre-reflexive dimension as *cogito*.

When I think, Merleau-Ponty writes, "I am (one) with myself, as I am in the world." The world is not object but pro-ject; but this is not a subjective projection, born of solipsism. We do not realize selfhood except by becoming effectively body and thus by being bodily in the world. Marcel formulates it somewhat differently: I cannot be truly "spiritual" except under condition of becoming flesh. But this is not mere embodiment. And "flesh" is carnality only to the misguided ascetic. We deal not with corporality but with the bodily dimension as ontological, i.e. with primordial logos. This is not a body conceived in a world-in-idea. Such a "body" is disembodiment: it can be re-embodied with or without success and rather surrier for the process. Abstract thought or word is but a rationalization of that primordial faith which is involvement with world and earth. Thus "faith" is not merely a rational assent to a disembodied set of religious or scientific doctrines; faith is rather doxic belief as trust in primordial world and earth, from which bodily logos emerges. Thus a proposition or assertion is valid only

insofar as it is an expression of the logos, and to the extent
that it is rooted in life-world as the source of all "objectivity"
in the sciences. Statements, whether musical or verbal, which
are rooted in concrete world are not rational assertions but
phenomenological descriptions of bodily experience of life
and primordial doxic belief. This is particularly evident in
music, which seems closer to phenomenological subjectivity
than the sciences or the visual arts. For the latter seem to
make objects; whereas music has no objects at all. It is pure
subjectivity.

A musical situation also begets intersubjectivity, for
making music means sharing musical logos with the other. It
is not a question of my forcing my experience on the other
but of unfolding it. Hence mere dialectics are useless, as we
conduct an "existential dialogue." In this intersubjective
dialogue, which means that one logos unfolds its essence
through and in the other logos (thus *dia-logos*), it may
happen either the one or the other is more open to the play
of being itself. And thus the need for mutual forebearance.
If, as two musicians, we play music together, we must share a
world and overcome any solipsism. In the creative situation
there is no room for either ego or abstractions. The solipsistic
ego would destroy the work of art, whereas the sharing of
logos is what makes it possible for musicians to "make
music" together and thus play a sym-phony. The essence of
a symphony is not first and foremost abstract AABA form
in the first movement or the general overriding structures of
the symphony, as such. The phenomenological essence of a
symphony consists in the intersubjective logos that allows
a making music *together*: thus the symphony as a "sounding
together." It is the task of the musico-logist to lay bare this
symphonic logos, for only then can he gain perspective with
regard to "form."

4.   RELATIONAL AND PHENOMENOLOGICAL TRUTH: MIND AND THING

Truth has been described as the "relation between mind and thing." *Cogito* thus means "I relate mind to thing," or "I relate thing to mind." In the framework of truth, as relational, the *relating* of mind and thing is crucial. This re-lating is a carrying-back upon one another of mind and thing. Mind and thing seek to be rejoined to one another. The *I*, as subject, is the basis of this relation; for the subject, *as* thinking, is that which carries thing back to mind and carries mind forward to thing. The relational definition of truth has obtained since the middle ages through Descartes and up into Kant himself. It is first challenged perhaps only by Heidegger, who questions the "dualism" and is dissatisfied with the subject relating. For the relational definition of truth presupposes that mind is a thing somehow apart from world and thing, and indeed in Cartesian thinking mind is indeed a "thing" thinking, *as* apart from the world of objective thing. Because of this apartness (which need not be interpreted exclusively in terms of the classic "dualism") there arises the need to establish some kind of realistic relationship with things. This relationship is in Descartes the "realism" of a *res*-philosophy. But it is precisely here where Descartes may be accused of having erected a hypothesis. For mind is *already* a bodily thing, and the clarity of mind rests ultimately in the "obscurity" of body. This phenomenological apriori, i.e. the "already-ness" of mind *as* bodily, is what founds the possibility of "mind," as rational. Mind is grounded in and is one with body, as the primordial logos. Mind and body are not discontinuous; they are polar. And re-embodied realism of the "relationship between mind and body" is but a pale shadow of the original ontological unity of the fundamental logos. The burden of "proof" lies not with him who experiences himself as a basic unity, but with him who asserts that man is dichotomous. A phenomenological statement, based on the experience of the essential bodily oneness of man, is not an "assertion," but rather an unfolding of what is already *there*. Thus when I *say* "I am bodily, as logos," it is not merely a grammatical or logical statement; instead it is a manifestation of myself in concrete situation, as experiencing the basic unity I *am*. Thus *"Sage ist Zeige"*: "Saying is a showing." I show myself to be that which I *am* in myself. An ontological "statement," as the manifestation of self-positing is not an assertion, but rather the eksistential ex-positing of man, *as* logos.

It is not a question of "opinion" but of phenomenological "fact." It is not a subjective assertion but is grounded in my bodily subjectivity, as phenomenological, i.e. as the appearing-of-the-logos that I *am*, as sub-ject. If we live in this body and world rather than in a body-in-idea or world-in-idea, what we "say" is not mere assertion but is an eksistential manifestation of our bodily movement. If we speak from out an abstract world, whether ideological or scientific, what we say is but an assertion. Only the rationalist is capable of assertion, since he alone is alienated from a more primordial logos and thus needs the assertive statement. And thus the problem of musicology as the "science" of music, or as "words *about* music." While it is unnecessary to denigrate the task of the musicologist, it is evident that musicology must always lead us toward the uncovering of the full musical experience rather than lead us away from it into the abstractions of historicism and esthetics. The purpose of musicology ought to be to lay bare the primordial logos, as musical. The study of form, time, history, and esthesis, ought all to lead to this subject.

"Mind" is but a further refining of the bodily dimension. It is a "sensing" which is not metaphysically separable from the "senses" but is one with them, even though at a different "level." Mind is grounded in and *is* body, as primordial logos. This is suggested also by a Heideggerian interpretation of Anaxagoras, for whom the *nous* is the "most refined of the senses." ("Senses" is a translation of *chrémata*, as "things-in-hand," thus as the handling of things, as the taking of things *in hand*, thus of feeling and sensing them.) Mind *is* bodily; it does not need to be re-embodied. Its separation from body is at worst a theological artifact or at best an abstraction. When we say that mind *is* body, the "is" is not a logical copulative particle merely linking or relating mind to body. The "is" in this case is phenomenologically onto-logical, as the unfolding of a bodily "fact" of experience. This "fact" is not an "objective thing" but the experienced subjectivity of the speaker, who is bodily alive and speaking from out the flesh-and-blood world of a truer earthly trans-cendence rather than from a false or material transcendence. In this case "truth" means not an abstract coherence of subjective mind with objective thing but rather a remaining bodily *true to* our being in the world and on the earth. It is in effect a primordial doxic trust in world and earth, rather than a "relation" between mind and things in a world of objects. Thus thinking and thing are the bodily situation itself: at one in primordial faith with world.

All ideologies and ideational abstractions of one sort and another are attempts to create a world apart from the living one. But it is an endeavor doomed at the outset. This holds also for the "practical" attitude which so often turns out to be but vulgar theory. What passes for common sense and practical knowledge is often enough nothing but a lack of critique and insight. Hence the need for both theory and practice to be firmly grounded in a fundamental logos, to which any *cogito* must return to find true transcendence and the "festival of life." And this festival is musical, as rooted in the *lógos mousikós*, in the creativity of musico-logical subjectivity.

Endnotes

This essay was written using the following background materials:

1. René Descartes, *Discours de la méthode, Regulae ad directionem ingenii, Meditationes de prima philosophia, Compendium musicae*, and *Les passions de l'âme*.
2. Martin Heidegger, *Sein und Zeit, Holzwege, Die Frage nach dem Ding, Vorträge und Aufsätze, Nietzsche*.
3. Edmund Husserl, *Ideen* I and II, *Cartesianische Meditationes, Erste Philosophie, Krisis der europäischen Wissenschaften*.
4. Jean Ph. Rameau, *Traité de l'harmonie*.
5. Jean P. Sartre, *L'être et le néant, Situations* II.
6. Maurice Merleau-Ponty, *La phénoménologie de la perception, Sens et non-sens*.

In addition some of my own materials were marshalled, particularly my critique of Rameau *redux* in "Traditional Harmony — a radical Question" in *The Music Review*, 1974. The dialectical critique of phenomenology begun in two of my essays (viz. "The phenomenology of sound: Akoumenology" in A. Motycka, *Musico-Aesthetic Education: a Phenomenological Proposition*, GAMT Music Press, Jamestown, 1975, and "Music educating as phenomenologist: an overview" in A. Motycka, *Music Education for Tomorrow's Society*, Jamestown, 1976) awaits further needed development that takes criticism of phenomenology into consideration, such as in M. Iovchuk, *Philosophical Traditions Today*, Progress Publishers, 1973 et al.

Chapter 6

MUSICOLOGY IN NEED OF NEW HORIZONS

If one scans the contents of one year's musicological journals one is both amazed and appalled at the sheer amount of effort being expended on music and musicians great and small. One is amazed to realize what a scholarly group one belongs to, a group that has treated not only of the obvious greats in history but has also unearthed composers, instruments, theories, and practices, never heard of before in the annals of music history. One is appalled by the realization that (1) one could never catch up on all this work, even if one spent every day of the year trying to do so, and (2) that even if one could, it is not so sure it would be a completely worthwhile effort. It is safe to say, that musicologists know what the historical method is and what a plethora of theses and essays it can produce! All this encyclopedic effort dwarfs the genius of a Bach and would even make Mattheson look like a simpleton. For that is indeed what it is: encyclopedic historicism. Not that we do not want such authoritative work as, let us say, *Musik in Geschichte und Gegenwart*, which stands out in a number of ways for sheer excellence. Not that we do not want or need good historical essays, to be published in the proper journals. Yet it may be possible to conclude, that historicism in musicology has pretty well run its course. The piling up of musicological minutiae no longer makes a convincing study of music. Something more is called for.

1.   A PROPOSED PASSAGE OUT OF HISTORICISM

It may be necessary to overcome preoccupation with the "objective" historical method, if musicology is to be more than a field for painstaking and pain-causing specialists. Curt Sachs voiced this same warning almost thirty years ago, when he pleaded with musicologists to emerge from over-specialization and help musicology make its proper contribution to humane studies.[1] It is doubtful whether musicology can make this contribution to general culture if it remains within the framework of traditional scientific historicism and the philosophical categories that presupposes. To be sure, there have been some notable efforts along such lines, but a more concerted effort may well be needed. Musicology may have to catch up with other disciplines in its definition of "history," for it still seems imbedded in concepts of history current in the last century, when "science" and "objectivity" became the criteria of scholarship. Since music, as such, seems to be largely the activity of the creative *subject*, it can readily be seen why musicology took flight to history and its "historical" personages. And yet the "history" of music need not be only the passing in review of centuries of composers and their works, though it is obvious that this must be done. There are different definitions of history, but musicology seems imbedded in the objective historicism that Von Ranke made popular. This essay wishes to propose not doing away with such obviously necessary work but the broadening of the musicological spectrum to include the musical *subject*: the working musician, not as a biographical item (and thus as an "object"), but as an historical subject defined in terms of his creative subjectivity. It is in such terms that we can then approach his "work," which in turn is not a lexicographical opus or object, but is that "musical truth" which emerges in the creativity of the musician (whether composer or performer) as *working subject*.

The problem is compounded, however, because musicology has regarded itself as a "science" of music. And science deals with objects, whereas music can be regarded (from the

viewpoint of contemporary phenomenology) as pure subjectivity. Such "subjectivity" evidently does not mean the
"subjective" in the popular sense of the word. Subjectivity
refers to human consciousness and creativity: in this case
to the "process" in which music, as we know it, comes
about. It therefore has to do with what is *happening* in
music, and in this sense it is "historical" (*Geschichte* rather
than *Historie*).[2] But musicology, as the science-of-music,
arose at a time when the historical sciences were the pace-
setters, and thus musicology was born in objectivity, not in
any philosophical theory of the creative subject as such.
This was quite understandable, however, since at this
particular time philosophy and its metaphysical theorizations
were justly held in disrepute. Hence musicology looked
askance at philosophy and any theory of the subject it might
offer toward the more inviting objectivity of both science
and history. Our task today may be the recovery of the
human subject in the objective history of music, which would
make both our biographical efforts and our musical analyses
of given works more convincing. Some of this has been
attempted in the "psychology" of music, but this seems
largely imbedded in an unovercome intellectualism or in
traditional esthetics.

It is doubtless true that most contemporary musicologists are well aware of the dead-end that mere historical
studies can become. Today, therefore, there is a trend away
from psychologies of music and away from overintellectual-
izations toward music itself. And thus the combination of
musicologist and musical performer is being emphasized. The
pendulum has swung away from theorizations toward
practice. This is certainly a healthy move, for one not only
unearths e.g. medieval *nakariu*, one can also beat upon
them without worrying about any sesquialtera proportions.
And yet, though the restorations of medieval musical
instruments is without a doubt an important and necessary
endeavor of musical scholarship and performance, the
problem of traditional musicology is not solved by shifting
from historicism to the practical level.

Our chief problem seems to be the classic dichotomy: theory and practice. It seems we can abandon neither, but in keeping both we seem to be a house divided upon itself. The dilemma has been with us since the Greeks from whom we get both terms. Yet in Greek music there was no real split between theory and practice, so that one could have, as we do, people specializing in "musical theory" and people who make "applied" or practical music their major effort. For the Greeks "theory" meant literally *looking into* what was being done, whether it was a question of philosophy or music (though there was no split here either). "Theory" was thus a *sighting* and therefore "insight" into what was being done; but what was being *done* was captured in the word, *praxis*. Thus any "theory" was always a looking into or insight gained into what was being done. But this was not yet speculation at a distance. It was rather insight gained from *within* the "practical" situation. Hence any *praxis* always gave birth to its *theoria*, or: theory emerges only from within the "practical" situation. It is not a product of abstract speculation or theorization from without. In music, one could not theorize, as did Aristoxenos, unless one were actually a performing musician. But it is evident that such performance was not blind practice: it was not divorced from theory but gave birth to theory. Perhaps in the recouping of what we call the "creative subject" in this essay we will be able to draw on this insight of the Greeks.

In the middle ages, however, with the advent of Christian metaphysics a split was introduced between mind and body. It is this specific philosophical distinction that is behind the modern dichotomy of theory and practice, for one "thinks" with the "mind," but one makes music with one's "body." In this metaphysical conception of reality a radical split was introduced in the definition of man as "rational animal," and thus in man's culture, musical and otherwise. The tendency today — from various viewpoints — is to regard man not as a unification of mind and body (with its obvious implications for music) but as an essential *unity* as *living subject*. Body and soul are in this concrete way of thinking but two possibly divergent poles of one basic life movement, of one fundamental *logos*. For it seems that the unity of musical theory and practice must look to a philosophy of logos for the principles of an expanded study. And thus the musico-logist is not caught in the study of objects but becomes a student of a musical logos fundamental to musical experience, theory and practice. He becomes, as it were, the musico-logos as creative subject, rather than the musico-logist as objective scientist.

Medieval theorists, such as Jacques de Liège, were familiar with the difficulties the dichotomy theory and practice produced, and it was for this reason that he wrote of a "practical theory" and a "theoretical practice" in hopes of bringing the two convincingly together. But such efforts were more or less doomed at the start on account of his metaphysical commitments. For, it is eminently true that for Jacques de Liège, the *musicus* is first and foremost the musical metaphysician who delights in the mathematical gymnastics of that *ens numeratum* which makes musical consonance possible. The musical performer is given short shrift. At worst he is one of the "bestiae" mentioned by Guido d'Arezzo; at best he must sit at the feet of the Christian metaphysician to learn the intricacies of metaphysical mathematics. In all this there is little time left for what we would call musical performance.

2.   MUSICAL ESTHETICS AS AN ATTEMPT TO DELVE INTO MUSICAL SUBJECT

In his critique of musicological training M. Bukofzer wrote that it is the task of the musical esthetician to get at the "inner meaning" of music.[3] But his own brilliant efforts were mostly in the areas of history and stylistic criticism. Yet he saw that the factualist and the analytical approaches to music were not enough, and thus his brief comments on esthetics and its place in the curriculum of music schools. But certain recent trends, enunciated at the IV Lexington Conference on Phenomenology, chaired by the late psychologist, Professor Erwin Straus,[4] showed up some of the insufficiencies of traditional esthetics in an approach to the "inner meaning" of things, music included. The present writer sees such inner meaning not so much in classic and traditional psychology or esthetics but in a phenomenological "esthesis." Put simply, this is a return to the *musical experience itself*, which implies an overcoming of the merely theoretical and abstract approach to things. For esthetics has really been the "metaphysics" of esthesis, i.e. it has led us away from the primordial experience of music as such into the realm of intellectualisms, and this under the guise of restoring to musicology some of its lost subjectivity. For the subjective studies of esthetics furnished the proper counter-balance to an exaggerated objectivity. And yet (at least in the eyes of a phenomenologist) traditional esthetics leads us only to the portals of a fuller subjectivity, i.e. to the beginnings of a more complete study of the *human subject*, as musically creative (whether as composer or performer), and to the musical *work* as the result of the creativity of the subject. The musical work is thus not an *object* of art. This connotes a recouping of primordial musical world in which any theory or practice is not the result of speculation *about* an art experience but in this case emerges from a description of the akumenal experience itself. Traditional esthetics has described music as a *phenomenon* and has brought to the task the whole visually oriented vocabulary bequeathed on it since Kant. Yet music is not something to be studied with the mind's eye; it is an akumenal and not a phenomenal experience. And thus even phenomenology needs to be expanded beyond its present imbeddedness in the conceptuality of western thinking, as phenomenal, i.e. as the study of what appears when *seen*. For music is meant to be heard. Even phenomenology (which we do not present in dogmatic manner but only as *one* way of doing things) needs the corrective of the musical experience. And it is particularly here that only the musician can make such a contribution.

What is this transition from esthetics to esthesis when it

comes to music, and how is this a broadening of the musicological method? Briefly it means a return to the *thing itself*
as it presents itself in bodily perception. By "bodily" perception we mean that we are aware of things not just
intellectually but as they *give themselves* to us "in person"
in the *living* context of primordial experience. The primordial musical experience is that which arises out of our
"first" encounter with musical sound *before* any "esthetic
judgment." But this presupposes a definition of man which
emphasizes his basic oneness with himself and world; it
therefore implies a critique of the traditional classification
of man as the "rational" (and therefore as the "esthetical")
animal. Man is therefore not an "esthete" but the *aisthétes*,
i.e. the "sensing" being who encounters in this case musical
world and being. His "sensing" is not artificially separated
from his understanding or mind: rather these are but two
facets of one vital activity. And thus the study of esthesis is
neither the pursuit of esthetical theories of beauty nor of
pleasure as based on "sense perception." For the essence of
the esthesis-experience is not first and foremost the quest for
either beauty or pleasure, but rather the emergence of
musical *truth*. The Hegelian and Heideggerian overtones
of this definition are evident enough to the student of
philosophy. Evident also is the fact that we are not talking
of propositional truth, such as can become an object of study
for analytical philosophy. In an essay such as this, meant for
musicologists, the difficulties of any entente between
phenomenology and analytical philosophy must be held in
abeyance. Suffice it to say that phenomenology studies the
pre-propositional level of things, in order to lay bare the
roots from which grows the philosophical tree. It may also
be true, that musicology, which was born of continental
thought, might well find continental phenomenology more
congenial to the expanding of musicological method than
the analytical philosophy of either Britain or America, though
these latter can also be of undoubted service in an often
necessary critique of some of the unwarranted postulates and
excessively complex language of phenomenology as such.

3.   THE "INNER MEANING" OF THE MUSICAL EXPERIENCE

Can the "inner meaning" of music, if there is one, be attained by a study of esthetics, as suggested by Bukofzer, or by a psychology of music, as presented by Ernst Kurth and others? Or are linguistic analysts correct in dismissing the question as "meaningless" since there can be no "inner" meaning of anything that is not evidenced in the examination of propositions and ordinary language? It is apparent that such a question awaits an additional study. For our present purposes it suffices to present the phenomenological view-point as a corrective to the esthetical. But it is helpful to mention in passing that even such luminaries as John Austin felt that analytical philosophy had to get beyond mere linguistic analysis and gain access to phenomena, as such.[5] However this be interpreted, it is a fact that as musicians we understand what Bukofzer was saying when he spoke of the "inner meaning" of music, even though this needs analysis, and even though our understanding of the phrase is not too closely defined but lies in the area of what phenomenology might call the "*an*exact" or the "vague."

Esthetics apparently fails to get at the full inner meaning of the musical experience not because of its lack of good will or intellectual acumen but because it lacks the *method* necessary for delving into the meaning of the creative *subject* as such. This is best seen in the third *Kritik* of Kant; for in writing of the esthetical judgment, Kant did not mean either juridical or intellectualist evaluation of the work of art. He refers rather to the subjectivity of the person judging. Yet though he breaks ground for philosophical subjectivity, he himself was unable to break completely out of a residue of Christian metaphysics and rationalism, which subverted his efforts to get at the meaning of "transcendental" subjectivity. Perhaps Edmund Husserl was the first to attempt this in dialogue with Kant, though he did not apply it to what we call esthetics. (In addition it was Husserl who went beyond the subjectivity of the subject to the development of that intersubjective experience which makes human encounter possible.) And the method he evolved is known as the "eidetic reduction" of phenomena, or in this case of akumena. This "reduction" means simply cutting through the sedimentation of history and theory and returning to the primordial experience itself. In the case of music, it would mean laying bare the fundamental musical experience that has been covered over by too much history and theorization. With regard to esthetics it would connote "bracketing" the intellectualism of so much esthetic theory so that we can get through to the "inner meaning" of music as an akumenal phenomenon. Far from destroying traditional esthetic theory, the "phenomenological" method (which means laying bare the essence of things in themselves) can abet such studies, and in addition can serve as a corrective to the tendency to overintellectualize.

The "inner" meaning of music is thus *music itself*, stripped of the accoutrements of mere history of scientism, music appearing as the Muse of the creative subject, as the very source of history and theory. This Muse, which emerges in the "reduction" of all history, science, and esthetical theory, is not unlike an Istar being relieved of her seven veils. When the last has been taken away, she is revealed in all her native beauty. The phenomenological method thus manifests the essence of things in their "bodily selfness," as Husserl put it. But this essence is unlike the essence of classic metaphysics, which in destroying concreteness arrived at a mere abstraction. It is not a question of pealing the rings off an onion, so to say, and expecting to find the "essence" after the last ring has been removed and *nothing* remains. The inner meaning of music is thus revealed as a primordial bodily experience. Music is thus experienced by the subject, but not merely intellectually; similarly it is not a question of a merely empirical experience. The dichotomy of intellectualism vs. empiricism is thus bridged, as the source of both is laid bare. In addition, this is no longer a merely subjective experience. It is rather intersubjective, for music more than any other art or experience demands the overcoming of egotism and a reaching out toward the other. In music, as inter-subjective, the creative subject encounters the *other*. Thus the composer does not compose just for himself or for an abstract career. He needs and wants listeners. Thus also the performer, who plays better with an appreciative audience. In the interplay between composer and listener, between performer and audience, the primordial experience we seek to describe comes about. It seems to me that musicology is valid only in the description of such an experience, one that takes place not just abstractly in the mind or objectively in the pages of history but in a living *praxis*, where subject dialogue with musical subject and the meaning of music is known *before* we speak or write of it. For, though music may well be a "language," it is one that is spoken at the pre-predicative stage, i.e. it is there before any ordinary language. Ordinary language can only describe it after the fact. But the fact itself comes before the word or the proposition. Traditional musicology has too often been "words about music." Perhaps the phenomenological method can abet its efforts to overcome its traditional verbosity and its preoccupation with the written word, as historical, as musicology comes closer to the primordial musical experience itself. And thus the Muse within us supplants the historian. This will not destroy history. But it will bring history closer to its own origin in the *happening* of the musical experience.

4.   THE QUESTION OF MUSICAL "FORM"

If we employ the reductive method, as described, it may well transform a number of our musical concepts. The most obvious of such concepts is that of musical "form." Musicology gets this word from the history of philosophy, originally from the Greeks, who also gave us the word, music.

It was especially Aristoxenos, the student of Aristotle, who gave the word, *eîdos*, currency as musical "form," i.e. as "generative idea."[6] But in medieval music theory form came to mean something akin to empty mould into which to pour "content," following the lead of philosophy in which idea or form was an abstract generality under which a concrete item could be subsumed. It is not our purpose to trace this complex history in such an essay as this, but the fact remains that music historians continue to write about form and content, as though there were no contemporary critique, especially phenomenological, of such terms. Perhaps we can sketch a possible transformation in the meaning of musical form, which will serve both to update its use in music history and also aid us in recouping the more concrete and primordial significance of the term.

In so doing it might serve our immediate interests better, if we dealt with a more familiar music form, such as "sonata form." The classic AABA form can be graphed visually. And it is at this very point that our phenomenological critique must begin, for musical form should be meant primarily not for the eye but for the ear. This was certainly the composers' intention. The fact that western music is grasped or written down in musical notation sets it off as an art peculiarly influenced by *visual symbol and metaphor*. For the audial experience is literally transferred over to an intellectual grid that originated in things *seen*, whether by the physical eye or by the mind's eye. And thus in a larger sense western music history has been the story of a veritable *Augen-musik*, which makes the ordinary use of the term seem quite harmless. But the reason for this can again be traced in the rise of music theory, as it took its terms from philosophy. And classic philosophies are all visually oriented, ever since Aristotle claimed that sight was the keenest of man's senses.

The predominance of the visual in western thinking has greatly altered our musical experience, for the traditional classic categories did not emerge from an akumenal source but from a phenomenal one. It will be the reduction especially of visually oriented theory and vocabulary in music that may become our greatest task in our attempts at stripping away secondary features in order to arrive at what we have been calling the "primordial musical experience." For the primordial musical experience, while it does not exclude what may be called a syn-esthesis with the other senses, is itself primarily audial and not visual. It is paradoxical that this simple insight, easily acknowledged by the musician and composer, could have been covered in music theory, whether historical or esthetical, by an overlay of visually oriented concepts and categories. But that is part of the history of what happened in western thought. It is only more evident in the field of music. And thus the need for a critique of traditional musicological method, as embedded not only in the historical or the esthetical but primarily in a visually oriented conceptuality. And so with the word, form.

Form is grasped in visual space, allowing us to *see* what it is. But do we understand form by seeing it? Or has musical space, which is not visible, been neglected? Perhaps we ought to explain such form in terms of the audial, if we want to get at the "essence" of the experience of musical form. If we begin with our own history, starting with the Greeks, we may be able to recoup the idea of audial space and thus of audial form. For if it is a question of musical form, it is also a question of *tónos*, configurations of which give birth to "form." The word, *tónos*, which has perdured through medieval *tonus* up to and including both tonality and "atonality," has to do exclusively with an audial experience. It is directly related to the tuning of the Greek *kithara*, as later on medieval music theory with its definitions of *tonus* turned to the monochord, as a pedagogical device to determine intervals. But this *tuning* had nothing to do with a visually conceived form until medieval music theory was wedded with metaphysics, particularly in the *Speculum Musicae* as the prime example.[7] For the Greeks, even though they made use of a rudimentary tablature, played music "by ear" and not by following a written notation visually. This means that for them not the visual but the audial was the more important. For tuning had to do with various degrees of the tenseness of the strings, as every string player knows in his fingers. Thus the tablature, though mediated through the eye, was really a contact between the fingers and what I would like to call a musical *tensor*. And thus the performing subject was in direct touch with the very heart of music: with musical "tensility," and thus with musical "space." The Greek *tónos*, the building block of western music, was thus a tensor first and foremost. And a tensor, *as a vibrating unit in the primordial experience of music*, is meant for the ear. It is in the realm of tensility and not of the visual metaphor that the essence of music is captured and the Muse revealed within the creative subject. This must affect both our theory and our practice, as we attempt to overcome traditional intellectualism. And thus the visual symbols of traditional music history, while hardly excluded, are made to play a subservient role. They can no longer dictate musical or esthetical conceptuality, as they have in the past.

If the AABA of sonata-allegro form is to be heard and not graphed, we must describe it in terms of a more truly musical apperception. The architectonic structure of AABA form, if experienced in its inner musical tensility or dynamism (especially in the interplay of tensions between themes and keys) can be regarded as a unique perception of the audial, freed of the encumbrances of visually oriented theory. For the musical "themes" can be regarded as tensile coils that unleash their dynamic energies against the overarching roof of AABA form. Each part of sonata form, but particularly the tonal pattern within each symbolic letter, thrusts and comes to bear upon various focal points, whether this be within the theme or in the flow and modulation of modalities. The focal points of this tensile activity are presently graphed by us in visual symbol, signified by letters such as AABA. And within the letters the tonalities are also graphed with TDT depending on the part of the sonata or symphony we are analysing. But these visually graphed highpoints (which with the aid of the score can be fleshed out in a far more complex graph) are in reality focal points of the musical tenor, specifically of the musical "tone," in the sense explained. Perhaps a different graph, showing this tensor factor, would be of aid in understanding this simple fact of musical experience. But that would defeat the whole purpose of this critique of the visual metaphor.

Suffice it to say that, awaiting a much fuller study, form must be understood as an audial and not as a visual phenomenon. Thus musical compositions which employ such form ought to be analysed accordingly. Instead of a visual graph, perhaps a verbal description should suffice, which must include the tensility *felt* by the listening subject (and thus an audial esthesis) as well as by the composer or performer. It is this very "infeeling" (which is the result not of analytic in*sight* but of a more fundamental "*inhearing*") that we mean when we speak of esthesis as the phenomenologically "esthetic" experience of primordial musical sound. But such an experience is neither an intellectual analysis of the given form nor a psychological or esthetic experience in the traditional sense. In a sense this is a recouping of the Greek idea of form as "generative idea." For in the generating of the tensions between strings, that thus define what *tónos* as a tensor is, the "form" emerges in its various configurations and patterns. Form is therefore the result of musical tonality. It cannot be imposed from without. Form is thus not "empty," waiting to be filled with musical "material." Nor should it be visually graphed, since the visual graph applies to *any* sonata. But no given sonata is *any* sonata. That is classic metaphysical procedure: the "universal form," which exists in an otherworld apart from concrete reality. Musical form is not "universal" in the old classic sense. Yet the traditional graphing of musical form presupposes it is.

5.   MUSICAL TIME: A CRITIQUE OF LINEAR TEMPORALITY IN MUSIC

As with musical space and form, time has also been conceived in accord with visual, in this case with spatial metaphor. For time, as philosophical and thus also as musical, has been conceived in western thought as "extended in space." We literally draw time out in linear manner, and thus we can measure what Hegel called the successive "now-points" of a given line of time. It is obvious what western music theory has succumbed to: the linear interpretation of time. It has done so more completely than any science, for its musical notation has been literally linear from the start. The entire history of musical notation is one of an uncritical acceptance of temporality as linear, for we literally follow the notes like now-points across a spatially extended printed page. As with regard to form, musicology seems totally imbedded in a period definition of time, as though there had been no critique thereof, as though other sciences were not already working with different and more viable concepts of temporality. The "more viable" concepts of time which will be suggested in this essay are phenomenological, i.e. concepts that emerge not from classic definitions of space and time but from more recent efforts of such men as Husserl, Heidegger, and Merleau-Ponty.[8] These concepts are felt to be more workable in music because they respect the inner subjectivity of the musical experience.

Traditional linear concepts are based on the mathematical and visual conceptions of reality. Linear time is to all purposes "objective" time. It is the mind's measuring of objective events in an objective world, as they progress in proper succession along a given horizontal line. And yet music is hardly a horizontal experience. It has its "vertical" depths, as Husserl showed, in writing of protentions and retentions. It has its "circular" or what I call *vortical* movement in the manner of Heidegger. The vortex in this case is the "whirlwind" of reality. Music can indeed be forced into the linear dimension; but it is legitimate to ask whether the raw musical experience is not rather "vortical," emerging from a veritable whirlwind of the creative activity of the artist subject. Such activity becomes linear only under certain controlled conditions. There is nothing wrong with linearly conceived music; but it must never forget its origins. Music is also "bodily" in the sense of Merleau-Ponty, who was keenly aware of the musical possibilities of his thinking, though he did not spell things out. Linear conceptions of time are the result of mentalistic elucubrations; circular, vortical, and "bodily" time is that which emerges in the lived musical situation of the subject, as a human unity.

Here specifically, what do we mean by the "vertical" rather than the linear-horizontal approach to musical time? Husserl, onetime student of Carl Stumpf of *Tonverschmel-zung* fame, gained his insights into the nature of time not only by a thorough meditation on Augustine's treatise but particularly by an analysis of musical tone. He introduced terms that are now classic, which need not be taken over into musicology, but might well be worth studying: pro-tensions and retentions. Thus time is not simply linear: it is a whole network or tissue of experience that thrusts ahead or pro-tends itself and leaves a trail of after-shadows. Thus the experience retains itself and each given new-point stands not in isolation but in the pattern of thrust and trail, almost in the manner of a comet. But the musical tone is the best example, and Husserl describes retention as a musical "tail," or as a series of after-echoes exemplified in the flight of a bird. As the forward thrust of time builds a horizon, it leaves in its wake a whole series of tonal "shadows" (*Abschattungen*), that spread out in ever diminishing diagonal "lines" behind it. And thus musical time spawns the idea of phenomenological time for Husserl. One sees how important musical insights are for philosophers. But are they just as important for musico-logists? Such a philosophical break-through with regard to the definition and explanation of the concept of time is hardly revolutionary for musicians. It simply describes what we know already, especially what can be the more easily demonstrated with a piano, yet it describes the musical experience of time in truer terms than the usual linear considerations employed by musicology. This conception of time may be called "vertical" though it is obvious that the flow is diagonal: and though it is graphed in one dimension, it obviously is a circular flow out and behind the thrusting edge of musical tone as it makes its "time."

But "circular" time is described convincingly also in the thought of M. Heidegger. In fact it is mostly from him that contemporary philosophy has derived the idea of

circularity in this matter. But what does "circularity" mean
when it comes to the concept of time? It obviously does not
connote a mere circle, especially a "vicious circle," as a
counterbalance to classic linear conceptions of time. The
"circle" of time is in this case more like a whirlwind or
vortex — and here I embroider the thought of the Freiburg
philosopher. Time can thus be called "vortical," in that it
takes shape within the whirlwind of Being, as it unfolds itself
in "ekstatic temporality." The *ek-stasis* of time is simply the
standing-out of temporality in its various modalities of
future, present, and past. For the thrust in this case is from
the future, as that which is to come, as that which is to come
about or happen, as that which in this case a musical tonal
pattern can be-come. There is no need to go into an extended
exegetical interpretation of texts at this point. Suffice it to
say that the concept of time is considerably expanded by
such thought. The musical applications are not difficult. It is
easy to interpret the musical *tónos*, as a tensor, in terms of
ekstatic temporality, though it need not be explained
exclusively in such terms.

The before mentioned tensor factor is directly related
to time, both as "vertical" and as "vortical." For it *is* the
dynamic nucleus that thrusts ahead creating the musical
horizon and leaving in its wake the after-echoes of its musical
tensility. It is what begets and abets artistic creativity in the
subject. Thus musical time is no longer conceived exclusively
in terms of a linear metaphor or of visual space. It is no
longer "durational" in this classic sense: there is no longer
merely a succession of given now-points extended in
imaginary space. Rather music becomes "timeless" because
of an expanded notion of time. This has direct application to
musical notation, which has been a series of notes written in
succession across a lined page. In fact, this conception has
even given birth to what we call a "theme," which is not a
nucleus or pattern of sounds but has been regarded as a
succession of individual notes which go to make up an
interesting and viable musical composition. Counterpoint is
based entirely on this linear premise, but so is traditional

harmony. (As to recent exotic efforts in the area of notation I am not prepared to say anything, pending a further study.) It is evident what a tremendous influence the visual, in this case as the linear, has had on our musical experience in the history of the west. And in this criticism of linear theme in music we may be able to break through to an understanding of why rhythm is the more important element, for the rhythmic nucleus is what begets any "flow" of sound, later measurable with the calibrated linear conceptuality of western temporality. Classic theme has been a static *positing* of a linear succession of musical tones. Phenomenologically, musical "theme" would have to do first and foremost with the dynamic heart of rhythm, as the pulse of a more fully liberated musical "time." It is apparent how much work remains to be done on such a topic as this!

Finally, musical temporality can be conceived as "bodily." Thus it is not a question of mere abstract or "objective" time. It is not a time that is conceived in some metaphysician's head but rather the musical time that pulses in the very body of the performing and creating musician. "Body" in this case is not just what remains after "mind" has been abstracted. Rather, it means the whole man as one living and in this case creative subject, regarded not as a unification of mind and matter but as a concrete human unity attuned to the living world of musical sound. Bodily temporality serves as a corrective to merely intellectualist interpretations of time. And thus also the tensile nucleus of musical time is not just an abstraction one writes or talks about: it is rather the living cell that generates music and that gets the entire man going, not as he contemplates music from afar (from his musicological study) but as he participates in the live experience of music-making, whether as composer, performer, or creative listener. The musical experience is something the musician knows in his fingers and arms, in the movement of his whole body. Any description, which is not based on this total involvement of the musician in tonal world, leaves out a crucial part of the musical experience or describes it insufficiently. The musicologist will say he has been describing

just such a world. But with the tools of traditional intellectualism can he truly succeed in doing so? In the "bodily
involvement" of musician in the world of primordial sound
the tensor factor is essential. For *musical* sound does not
exist except in and through the musician. If the musical tone
is the result of a given tension factor, it is a tension originat-
ing in and produced by the musician's own "bodily being."
Not only his whole musculature is involved in the bringing
forth of musical tone, rather his entire personality as subjectivity (leading immediately to intersubjectivity) is
engaged. Musical tone does not exist at all unless I give it
its bodily musical existence as composer or performer. Unlike
the classic *cogito*, musical tone is not the product of mentalistic efforts. Music can be examined speculatively, as in the
classic case of Jacques de Liège, but it has no true existence
apart from the musician *as* he "makes music." Music, either
as metaphysical in the sense of the *Speculum Musicae* or as
an "esthetical" experience, is music only "in idea." *Music
itself* emerges in its bodily essence only when we, as bodily
beings, give it existence: in a living praxis.

6. THE REUNITING OF MUSIC AND PHILOSOPHY: THE EXAMPLE OF THE GREEKS

Music has always had its "theory." But music theory, beginning in the medieval music treatises, became progressively
alienated from musical practice. In our times attempts of
various kinds have been made to reunite theory with practice. But perhaps a living *praxis* out of which emerge both
"theory" and "practice" would be more convincing. Music
and philosophy, both creations of the Greeks, were originally conceived as basically one phenomenon. Their separation from one another can be traced in the history of thought.
But even as late as the middle ages music was conceived as
having a definite metaphysical base in the *ens numeratum*,
which comprised philosophy of both being and of number.
It has been only relatively recently that, thanks in part to

German musical pedagogy, music was separated from cultural and philosophical studies. And thus our present need, so poignantly expressed by the late Curt Sachs, of bringing music and thought back together again. It was understandable that musical pedagogues would shy away from metaphysical theories, not only because of the lack of theoretical bent on their part but largely because too many such philosophies of music were in the last analysis irrelevant to the musical experience. But neither the philosophy of the Greeks nor contemporary phenomenology is an abstract mentalistic thinking. Thus neither at the beginning nor at this end of history have music and its philosophical underpinnings been considered as separable or as separated. Our present felt need to put music and thought about music back together again in a healthy reaction against the Christian metaphysics of the middle ages and the rationalism that took hold in the wake of Descartes. And even Kant with his critical philosophy and his break-through into esthetic subjectivity did not succeed in breaking out of a rationalistic view of world and culture.

Phenomenology looks for a logos more concrete and convincing than rationality, a logos which in fact is the root of rationality, as such. Its purpose is not to destroy but to lead back to sources and origins, in order that the "reason" given for anything may be more truly convincing to the extent that it is more firmly rooted in world and life. The implications for musicology are evident.[9] The historical rationale and the esthetic rationalizations of the musical experience need to be grounded in a more fundamental principle that is dictated not from some abstract source outside the actual musical experience but that arises from within it. And the logos-thought of phenomenology may well provide access to such a primordial principle, for the logos is not an abstraction. The logos *is* the creative subject. For man has been defined by tradition as the *rational* animal: he has been divided within himself between mind and body. Yet this is but a period definition and actually a distortion of the classic description of man as the *zôon lógon échon*, i.e. as that *living being* which has and is the *logos*. And this logos is is the "bodily" principle of unity which arises from out the creativity of the live subject and ingathers the dynamic and tensile forces, in this case of sound, in the bringing forth of the musical work of art. Hence man is not the "rational animal." Instead of "animal" he is a *living being* (*zôon*) that operates not because of "reason" as much as by the unifying and creative principle of the logos. The further story of how philosophy turned the logos into logic (and thus eventually also musico*logy* as the "logic" or science of music) is a chapter in the decline and distortion of this original insight. Current phenomenology attempts to recoup this lost moment and restore the arts and sciences to the primordial experience of world and life.

The phenomenologists are aware of the musical implications of philosophy, though far more extended studies are needed. Such studies are handicapped from the start, because few philosophers have the needed knowledge of music history and musical esthetics, to say nothing of feeling the music in their fingers in a live performance. It may take the musician and musicologist to include such studies in his researches, in that in using philosophical method, especially as described here, he will not be distracted from his musicological studies but will be aided in the understanding of what he is doing and in the necessary critique of musicology as the "science" of music. In addition it will help him recover the musical logos, as the unifying nucleus of the musical experience, a logos that seems covered over and neglected in the present rationalistic and scientistic attitudes of musical scholarship. In all this it must be repeated that phenomenology is not suggested in any other manner than as a methodological aid to musical studies. It is not set forth as a new dogmatic approach, nor does it in any way leave out philosophical critique provided by other trends in current thinking. But it may well prove to give access to musical experience in a more fundamental way, as we musicologists describe and write about the musical world.

Endnotes

1. Curt Sachs, Editorial, in *The Journal of the American Musicological Society*, 1949, pp. 3-5.
2. Martin Heidegger, *Sein und Zeit* (Tübingen, 1960), ninth edn., cf. chapter V, "Zeitlichkeit und Geschichtlichkeit," p. 372f.
3. Manfred Bukofzer, *The Place of Musicology in American Institutions of Higher Learning* (New York, 1956).
4. *Aisthesis and Aesthetics*, ed. Straus/Griffith (Pittsburgh, 1970). The present writer gave a paper entitled "Toward a phenomenology of musical aesthetics," April 6-8, 1967. Lexington, Ky.
5. John L. Austin, "A plea for excuses," in *Proceedings of the Aristotelian Society* (1956-57), reproduced in R. R. Ammerman, *Classics of Analytic Philosophy* (New York, 1965), p. 379f. H. Spiegelberg calls attention to this essay and its possibilities for phenomenology in Alexander Pfänder, *Phenomenology of Willing and Motivation* (Evanston, 1967), appendix B, p. (86)f.
6. J. Lohmann, "Der Ursprung der Musik," in *Archiv für Musikwissenschaft* (Tressingen, 1959), 1/2, p. 161.
7. F. J. Smith, "Le contenu philosophique du Speculum Musicae" in *Le Moyen âge, revue d'histoire et de philologie* 1968; cf. also *Iacobi Locdiensis Speculum Musicae, a Commentary*, vol. I (New York, 1966) pass.
8. Edmund Husserl, *Vorlesungen zur Phänomenologie des Zeitbewusstseins*, ed. M. Heidegger (Halle, 1928) pass. (Cf. recent edn. Nijhoff, The Hague, 1966.)
9. F. J. Smith, "Vers une phénoménologie du son" in *Revue de métaphysique et morale*, (Paris, Aug., 1967).

Chapter 7

A PHENOMENOLOGY OF MUSICAL
ESTHETICS: THE CONTINUING
REDEFINITION

It seems necessary to continue asking what we mean by
"phenomenology," especially in America, where due to the
earnest efforts of a number of professors it has begun to
find its "place in the sun." The word itself has a rather
interesting history in modern philosophy all the way from
the *Neues Organon* (1764) of J. H. Lambert, where it means
the philosophy of appearance, through Hegel's phenomenology of spirit, up to Husserl and his students. It seems useful
to ask once again what phenomenology may come to mean
in America, where (despite the warnings in Husserl's
Phänomenologische Psychologie)[1] it is applied sometimes
meaningfully and sometimes dubiously to a wide range of
studies from an examination of the transcendental ego and
consciousness in W. James to an attempt to turn Gestalt
psychology into a phenomenology of music.[2] Kant, from
whom both Husserl and Heidegger learned much,[3] kept
asking to the very end what "transcendental philosophy"
connoted. And, as is well known, on the very vigil of his
death Husserl was ready to begin all over again in quest of
a truer phenomenology. And though we do not want to
remain only with an exposition of primary sources, it may
well be useful from time to time to remind ourselves of
the fundamental literature and the main issues of phenomenology.

The style and complexity of Husserl's and Heidegger's
language make their works more often than not inaccessible
or at least formidable to many intelligent Americans, who
may not have had the chance to learn German either at home

or abroad. And translations, while useful, can never function as an adequate substitute for the original, as Heidegger has communicated to the present writer.

1) Phenomenology was meant originally to meet the crisis of both philosophy and science.[4] As such phenomenology was a critique of what we may call traditional metaphysics but also of empirical and positivistic science, which was really a kind of "outrunner" of metaphysics. Husserl attempted to rediscover a convincing "first philosophy" and his approach was through the suspension of judgment which he called "eidetic reduction." While it is true that this may be regarded as commonplace, it is nevertheless a fact that Husserl himself kept asking to the very end what eidetic reduction connoted. In this sense it is always possible to rediscover new meaning in terms that are apparently well understood. The full implications of eidetic reduction are just now beginning to be realized, as with the steady publication of primary sources we witness a renewed interest in Husserl, even after the experience of Heidegger, Sartre, Merleau-Ponty, and now (finally) also Max Scheler.

Given that there is a whole series of eidetic reductions to be made in phenomenology — some of the more complex ones to be witnessed in the question of transcendental ego and in intersubjectivity as the basis of any objectivity in the sciences — what can "bracketing" mean when it comes to the musical phenomenon, especially as "esthetical?" It is here that we can no longer simply expound the text of Husserl. Instead we are challenged to "apply" phenomenology; and in this very application to musical phenomena there may be an implied critique of eidetic reduction *as* eidetic. For, what can *eidos* mean when predicated of music, which is in essence not a phenomenon but an *akumenon*? For Husserl, who does us the service in advance of bracketing any metaphor including the visual, the eidos is meant simply as the "essence" (*Wesen*) of anything whatsoever. Insofar as it is a question of essence, eidos may refer indifferently to any sort of phenomenon, whether visual, haptic, or audial. And thus the "ideality" of anything whatsoever takes in the entire range of phenomena, as such, whether they "appear" as visual or audial.

It is true that after Plato the word, eidos, is used in the description of the Greater Perfect System of Greek music, as J. Lohmann has pointed out.[5] It was especially Aristoxenos, the musician pupil of Aristotle, who gave us eidos as a musical term, as an "analytical" concept which is the result of the theoretical approach introduced by the Greeks. The eidos or "form" is a subdivision of the genos, which is not a "genus" but rather that special complex of fundamental tones, semitones, major and minor thirds and microtones which went to make up the diatonic, chromatic, and en-harmonic tetrachords, that were the building blocks of the Greek scale. Hence we see some historical justification for the use of a visual term to explain the inner workings of musical system. Yet, it must be noted, that Aristoxenos was the student of Aristotle, and it was especially Aristotle who put forth the theory that sight was man's keenest sense and that it stood for all the rest. By way of contrast Lajos Szekely, who has contributed a theory of the bipolarity of sensation, holds that the sense of hearing is closer to the subject, whereas the sense of sight is closer to the object.[6] Whatever the merits of this theory, it may be true that western philosophy developed into a visually oriented thinking at the expense of subjectivity and to the short-sighted advantage of objectivity. Thus it seems to me that phenomenology will not discover a truer subjectivity until it becomes more convincingly akumenal. But historically speaking, sight stands for all the senses through the entire history of philosophy. It is seen at its clearest in Augustine, in medieval philosophy, and perhaps in Husserl and Heidegger.

2) Whatever the case may be, and despite the fact that Husserl brackets the visual as metaphor, musicologists are increasingly restless with the visual, bracketed or unbracketed, in describing the live musical experience. For both as musicologists and practising musicians they know that music is first

and foremost not a phenomenal but an akumenal experience, despite the obvious influence of the visual in western music and both musical and philosophical theory. I would therefore like to suggest that bracketing the visual or visual metaphor is not enough. The musician feels the need for a transition to a new key, the possibility for which is surely given in the eidos. Husserl gives what might be called an eidetic critique of western philosophy and by postulation of any and all philosophy. Yet he remains pretty well within the tradition itself, though he radically reconstitutes its horizon, conceptuality, and vocabulary. Husserl makes first philosophy viable, as it were, but at least to this student of music and philosophy it remains quite "western," if by that term we may designate Greco-European thinking. It is for this reason that making use of audial vocabulary to describe musical experience may be regarded as a radical break-through as also a break from western philosophy both in its Greek origins and in its phenomenological form as first philosophy. And yet to a musician this "break" is merely a return to the primordial thing itself, i.e. to music as akumenal. And thus we would not talk so much of eidos as of musical *tónos* or of a fundamental *échos*, that describes things not only as seen but as felt and heard. For echos, as sound, takes in everything from the tumultuous roar of the ocean and the grandeur of a summer cloudburst to the specifically musical *tónos* of Greek music, the *tonus* of medieval music, and the tonal/atonal systems of modern history. In short, echos takes in what we call primordial world, as it sounds and swells all about us and within us, as we are borne aloft on the crest of life. A phenomenological eidos seems far too "intellectualized" a process to render convincingly the primordial world of raw or of musical sound. It is far too cerebral, like certain kinds of contemporary music. In a sense it is even philistine, in that it can be the antithesis of the work of art. For, philosophy and *belles lettres* have not often courted one another. And *belles lettres* are not just beautiful letters and literature: they are also meant to be read aloud, where their musical essence can reveal itself.

Musical sound is more than just raw sound. The roar of the ocean is not yet music, though it is primordial sound. Raw sound becomes musical sound only after it has been processed, as it were, through the grid of definite categories. We may be allowed to take a specific example from music history, a history which at this point seems inseparable from the history of philosophy. Jacques de Liège, the protagonist of the *ars antiqua*, i.e. of the metaphysical theories of the middle ages, wrote his encyclopedic *Speculum Musicae* (1330-40) during the *ars nova*, at a time when the middle ages were waning and the renaissance beginning to dawn.[7] What began as a reactionary treatise decrying the *ars nova* in music ended up as a vast metaphysical and mathematical treatise, the summation of all music theory from Boethius through the middle ages. In this work Jacques de Liège gives one of the clearest statements in history on the difference between raw sound and musical sound. It is the difference between physical sound and what he calls "sonorous" music (*musica sonora*), i.e. music properly so called, as musical consonance. For only in differentiating musical consonance from physical sound does one discover the building blocks of musical composition, from the *tonus* through the *diapason*, or as we would put it today, from one end of an octave to the other. It is interesting to note two things: a) that musical sound is called "sonorous," and b) that this means not "sensuous" but rather mathematico-metaphysical. For medieval music has to do not just with "being" but with "numbered being." It is only in being "processed" through a metaphysics of number and proportion that raw sounds can emerge as the building blocks of music. Thus not raw sound but metaphysico-mathematical categories are responsible for what medieval theorists called music, as an art. And this harmonic modulation, this interplay of musical proportionality, carried through the history of music and philosophy all the way up to and including Kant, who in the *Kritik der Urteilskraft* writes that the essence of music, as the free play of sensations in conjunction with esthetical ideas, really lies in the pertinent mathematical proportions of the faculty of understanding.[8]

And so we arrive at the portals of phenomenology. Husserl brackets sound, as sonorous, Jacques Derrida states.[9] As far as I am informed, this means that Husserl reduces or brackets sound as physical and acoustical, and thus as "sensuous" in an ontic or physical sense. But what really needs bracketing is not just physical sound but particularly the categorical grid, i.e., the pertinent musical metaphysics, as typified in the classic example of Jacques de Liège or any such rationalist. Both physical and metaphysical sound, thus both acoustics and the categories of the intellect, need to be reduced, in order that music may emerge in its "bodily selfness." Obviously, it can easily be argued that Husserl does this. Both the real and the ideal need bracketing, in order to lay bare the truer ideality of the musical experience. And yet the "ideality" of the musical experience is not rediscovered at the expense of what I would like to call the "phenomenological sensuousness" of the akumenal experience. To retreat from the sensuous in music would be the old error of a metaphysics of music. Phenomenological sensuousness differs in kind from mere physical sensuousness, from the merely empirical, or even the sensual-erotic in Kierkegaard's interpretation of Mozart. For, sensuality like traditional ideality is an abstraction, introduced by Christian metaphysics. Kierkegaard writes how sensuality was brought into the world by Christianity.[10] For the sensualist is the child of the idealist; and Don Giovanni is indeed the natural but unacknowledged child of the ascetical monk, as pornography is the natural result of too much hagiography. And somewhere between these abstractions the human being is lost. Indeed, it was an ascetical monk, Tirso de Molina (Fray Gabriel Tellez), who reintroduced the Don Juan theme into drama and literature. And from *El Burlador de Sevilla* Don Juan begins his trek through modern literature and music, from Molière through Byron, Kierkegaard, Unamuno and Richard Strauss. A phenomenology which treats of the akumenal experience of music does not allow the innate sensuousness and richness of music, like Stravinsky's *Rite of Spring*, to fall between the traditional abstractions of sensuality and ideality. Rather, as in colorful poetry, the musical word is laid bare in the full surge of its eros, in the full range of its sacral springtime primordiality.

3) In postulating a primordial echos, as possibly more convincing to musicians and musicologists, we need not thereby imply that it is a substitute for the eidos. Merleau-Ponty is of service at this point, for it was he who wrote of a *syn-esthesis*, which would take in both the visual and the audial.[11] And thus it is possible to "see sound" and to "hear sight," strange as this may sound at first flush. It is not a question of "color music," as it is known in music history, or of the rather odd experiment of Scriabin in his less than lucid moments. The synesthetic enhancing of sound by sight and of sight by sound might well be best exemplified in the opera, for as musical drama it is meant to be both seen and heard simultaneously, and the unity of the two (by no means always achieved!) is what makes it a work of art, however apparently hybrid. In his important work on the ontology of the arts and of music, Roman Ingarden avoids the opera, as a work of musical art.[12] For, he seeks the more obvious musical work in elucidating and exemplifying his original phenomenology of music. And thus he settles for Beethoven and Chopin, for orchestra and piano. Yet the same problem would arise in Beethoven's *Pastoral Symphony*, insofar as it is "representational." The problem returns in *Fidelio*, his only opera. As far as I am informed only Kant among the classic philosophers has dealt with the opera as a work of art, when in his third *Kritik* he writes of the conjunction of fine arts in one and the same artistic production. He also includes the oratorio.[13]

Perhaps it is only Merleau-Ponty who has seen the possibility of synesthetic perception, not as psychological but as phenomenological. This may be the key to the perplexing problem of opera or of any conjunction of the visual with the musical, be it a pastoral symphony, the fountains in Rome or anywhere else, a locomotive, or a steel foundry. Composers through Beethoven, Respighi, Honegger, and Mossolov have worked on such representational themes, to the alarm of purists who hold to the autonomy of music as opposed to heteronomy. And yet even classical sonata form is not pure. For both the concept of theme, as such, and its being built into the architectonic of first-movement or sonata-allegro form, depends more than is realized on the visual and spatial. Perhaps in a closer analysis of the meaning of synesthetic perception we will begin to realize that we are not looking for an eidos as much as a transcendental logos, which is the fundament of philosophy, science, and the arts. Perhaps a primordial logos is the unifying basis of any eidos or echos, and thus of the visual and the audial, whether in general or specifically in the arts. But one looks in vain in Husserl's works for this kind of "esthetics." One finds it, however, in Heidegger, when he deals with the origin of the work of art.[14] Yet Husserl's whole conception of time is dependent to a great extent on what he learned of musical tone. We must recall that Carl Stumpf, whose theory of *Tonverschmelzung* is known to every student on introductory musicology, was Husserl's teacher. His influence seems to show up in such treatises as Husserl's lectures on the consciousness of time. Apparently, the protensions and retensions of time are not only illustrated by allusion to musical melody, they seem to be spawned by an analysis of musical tone. (This becomes particularly clear in *Beilage VI.*) Husserl's search for the structure of consciousness could easily have been abetted by an attempt to analyze musical consciousness and time, for he would not have fallen into the psychologisms of E. Kurth or G. Anschutz any more than he would have lapsed into some of the philosophisms of N. Hartmann.[15] Yet, at least judging from available materials, Husserl never quite reached a critique of "esthetical consciousness," particularly as musical. And yet the raw materials seem to be present in his works; they could be developed, even as "esthetics" is bracketed.

2. MUSIC AND MUSICOLOGY: THE NEED FOR NEW FOUNDATIONS

1) If we are to ask about a "phenomenology of music," we must inquire not only into the meaning of phenomenology but also of music and musicology, as they stand today. It is not the easiest possible task to give a clear and distinct definition of either phenomenology or musicology, and one goes limp when asked to give a short account of either, but none-the-less I shall attempt the impossible, braving the scorn of the gods. In *The Harvard Dictionary of Music* the eminent scholar, W. Apel, takes the term through its various possible meanings and connotations.[16] He settles for the idea of research in the field of music history "in which there are still so many facts to discover and clarify." In this factualist approach to musical history he seems to agree with M. Bukofzer's critique of the place of musicology in the university system.[17] The list of musicological objectives which Bukofzer drew up seems to focus more or less on research in the field of music history — the traditional "scientific historical" approach — and thus the many excellent scholarly studies done on music from the Greeks to the present. A former tendency to be preoccupied with "old music" is now being overcome, though "old music" is not being neglected. Musicology is also beginning to discover its present and future as well as the rich heritage of the musical past. But it seems to need a new methodology, and it is here where phenomenology may be of great service, in that it does not merely analyze music but allows music to manifest itself in its inner subjectivity and being.

For Apel both acoustics and esthetics are regarded as adjunct fields of musicological endeavor. They are probably the same for Bukofzer, though he does state that the task of the musical esthetician is to give the inner meaning of music. I see this inner meaning, however, not in a musical esthetics but in a "phenomenological esthesis," as will be explained. Bukofzer tended toward stylistic criticism both in theory and practice. He mentioned this task also in his book on baroque music, a masterpiece of musical scholarship and a perfect demonstration of what he held.[18] All of this recalls the editorial on the need for an esthetic criticism, written in *The Musical Quarterly* by its editor, Professor P. H. Lang.[19] In another editorial in *The Journal of the American Musicological Society* the late C. Sachs pleaded with musicologists to come out of an incapsulation in their individual specialities and to work on an esthetics of music which would show it to be an essential part of a larger culture.[20] My own question is simply this: Is all this possible if one remains within the framework of traditional philosophical and esthetical conceptuality and vocabulary? It is my personal conviction that the inner meaning of music and its place in humane culture can be seen (heard!) and expressed more convincingly, if we equip ourselves with phenomenological method. This cannot be done by "ignoring historical phenomenology." For it is only thus that music can emerge in its "bodily selfness," in its primordial nudity as the *lógos mousikós*. And it is here that music is seen to be at one with primordial world and thus as an integral part of our "culture."

2) The methodological difficulty of traditional musicology is that it has approached the musical experience as an *object* of study. In thus concentrating on objectivity it has impaired the essential subjectivity of music, whether we look at the human subject or music as a subject for study. Especially after Kant esthetics points us from the object to the subject of an art. The beautiful and the sublime are not to be found in the objective world but rather in the esthetic judgment of the subject, which regards the form of things and has to do chiefly with the free interplay of the faculties of understanding and of transcendental imagination in the acting subject itself.[20] And even though Kant defines music as the free play of sensations, its essence is recognized as lying in the proportional play of harmony and thus within the subject judging. (This "judging" is neither logical nor juridical, and thus "evaluative," but rather esthetical in the sense of subjectivity.) The emphasis on the

subject, as transcendental, is pre-phenomenological, i.e. it is no longer a question of what Kant himself calls the empirical idealism of Descartes or the visionary idealism of Berkeley, yet it is not a truly phenomenological subjectivity in our sense. Husserl felt that the necessary reductions failed. Perhaps it is only in an analysis of a phenomenologically transcendental subjectivity, as in Husserl, that the truer subjectivity of the musical experience can be laid bare, not as esthetical in a psychological or even in a post-Kantian sense, but as "transcendental" in a post-Husserlian sense. And thus the work of Roman Ingarden, whose ontology of the work of art is not opposed to Husserl's phenomenology but necessarily complements it.[21]

The problem of finding a new method for musical scholarship is intensified when we realize how musicology has not only tended to make an object out of music but that it has regarded itself as a "science." Musicology as the science-of-music (rather than the study of the logos of music) arose at a time when the positivistic and historical sciences were very influential and philosophy was perhaps justifiably held in disrepute.[22] Thus musicology looked away from the subjective views of philosophy toward the objectivity of both history and science. It was a situation quite the reverse of that of the *Speculum Musicae*, the classic example of a metaphysics of music or a musical metaphysics, and even of the rationalistic tendencies that perdured into the high baroque. Musicology turned to objectivity on the one hand and then became acutely aware of the contribution of post-Kantian esthetics on the other, with its fund of subjectivity. In the objectivity of science it found its methodology; in esthetics it found its soul, as it were, but from esthetics it also took an additional fund of visually conceived vocabulary. But in neither science nor esthetics has musicology been able to lay bare the inner meaning of music. Perhaps in a return to phenomenological subject, particularly to the creative consciousness of the artist (whether this be a composer or what Aaron Copland has called the "creative listener"), we can hope to recover a more fundamental meaning in musical scholarship. But then it will have ceased being the "science" of music, since we will be dealing with art and artist and thus with the artistic fundament, which seems to be at the basis of what we call being a human being. For the Muse is in everyone to the extent he or she is human, though it slumbers in many. The recovery of phenomenological subject means reawakening the Muse within us, whatever we may be.

But in the rediscovery of this Muse within the subject, it is necessary to bracket traditional musical categories and methods, which have been given us in music theory, esthetics, and in a philosophy of number. Only through a phenomenological reduction can the Muse be awakened and thus emerge in artistic consciousness. For while we may keep the distinction between raw sound and musical sound, we will realize that the categories that have made sound musical for us may also have kept us from a more fundamental musical experience. The most obvious example of this is the *Speculum Musicae*, which is a minute examination of the proportional relations of musical metaphysics. For the *musicus* is not one who plays an instrument or sings; rather he is the "muser," the philosopher-mathematician who delights in speculation concerning the harmonic modulations and the proportional interplay of consonances.[22] It is true, these consonances are the building blocks of any musical practice; but a preoccupation with them might well keep one from any listening or musical composing. Indeed, com-position meant not what we call musical composition today, i.e. of a vocal, instrumental, or orchestral piece. Rather, it meant the putting-together or com-positing of numerical proportions that went to make up a consonance. Specifically *com-posito* meant the componibility of one number with another; and thus the *musicus* is in reality the philosopher of number, the metaphysician, who sees and admires first and foremost the interplay of mathematical proportions in music.[23] He sees all this; but he does not hear the musical art work, at least not first and foremost. And thus he is kept from a more fundamental musical experience. Hence the need to bracket the musical categories. In this we see the difference between a great classic philosophy of music and the beginnings of a phenomenology of musical sound. For the latter considers the musical experience first and foremost (but as consciousness, not psychologically), as it attempts within the live musical experience to lay bare the intentional structures of musical consciousness and creative activity.

3) In order to discuss the act of musical composition, as understood in a modern sense, we need to take a brief look at the question of theory vs. practice. This is both a philosophical and a musical problem. Since the time of the Greeks the distinction between theory and practice has been with us, receiving its first truly significant critique in the writings of Immanuel Kant, [24] though in the *ars nova* Jacques de Liège had written of a "practical theory" and a "theoretical practice."[25] The distinction between theory and practice begins as a philosophical and seems to end as a linguistic affair. For Aristoxenos the eidos of music was not merely theoretical or abstract, although it was a kind of "analytic" concept that came about through the observation of the musical system of the Greeks. Instead it was a "regulative idea," analyzed as part of the essential substance of the musical opus itself.[26] This idea was still preserved in Athenaios, a second century B.C. theorist, in whose *Deipnisophistai* the phrase *"kat' eîdos,"* means not "according to ideational theory" but "according to (musical) pattern." It is possible that our modern distinction between theory and practice, which has wrought so much havoc in music education as well as in philosophy, is reducible to our inability to analyze a given pattern as unity in basic complexity.

Gestalt theory is a new beginning in the recovery of complexity in unity, yet it remains pretty well imbedded in psychology. It is not yet phenomenological, as Merleau-Ponty has shown convincingly.[27] The *whole* experience, whether musical or philosophical, is neither merely theoretical nor merely practical. It is a baffling combination of both, an intentional pattern or structuring which eludes the theoretical and the practical as two separate approaches. There can be no artificial distinction between thinking and doing. And thus we work out a musical praxis which is more than just the reunification of theory and practice in "theoretical practice" or "practical theory." Rather it transcends both theory and practice, as the primordial logos is laid bare. Within this logos theory is not just intellectual speculation but rather the concrete meaning which emerges in living practice. Thus there can be no musicology for its own sake, or philosophy in an ivory tower, divorced from creative activity. Similarly there can be no blind practice which only does but never thinks or knows. The interplay of both theory and practice in a living praxis is best seen in the art of keyboard improvisation, where mind leads fingers and fingers lead mind in an exhilarating musical experience. It is here that a musicologist and practising musician realizes that one thinks with one's body, in this case with the fingers, which Stravinsky called his "inspirers."

The classical example of all this is Stravinsky's *augures printaniers* chord, which defies mere harmonic analysis.[28] It is quite useless with only the techniques of traditional theoretical analysis to analyze this juxtaposition of a dominant seventh chord in E flat in the right hand and a chord of F flat major in the left hand. It is very simple: there is no harmonic analysis called for; it is simply a question of how the composer placed his hands on the keyboard. It was this bodily positioning of the hands which gave birth to the complex of sound, and not some theoretical idea that made it possible. Out of this nucleus of harmonically clashing chords grew the inspiration and motifs of *The Rite of Spring*. Here we see how a merely intellectual analysis arrives at an impasse and even appears ridiculous. Phenomenologically speaking it is a question of "body thought," not just of psychological Gestalt: in this case the composer's hands moving on the keyboard. And his movement is his orientation to musical world and primordial sound. The intentional links are not theoretical but bodily. It is not a question of "reason" or of mere body but of bodily logos. And thereafter all that remains to be done is to spell out and develop the motifs that have been posited and suggested in this bodily positioning of hands on keyboard, in this bodily evolving of world.

Composition, like temporality and eros, which are of its essence, is a whole intentional structuring of the subject and of world, in which the subject does not merely relate to world but evolves world. And here it may be useful to recall that music is an intersubjective experience, not a solipsistic one. The evoking of world in the work of art, in this case musical, is the result of the reduction of both subject and object. Therefore the composer needs his audience, his creative listeners, in order to be truly a composer. It is not just a question of playing down to or merely playing for an audience, as it were, to feed the audience into one's boundless ego. Rather the true composer plays for and with his listeners in an intersubjective dialogue which reduces mere ego and all its external concomitants, such as fortune and fame. The same ought to be able to be said of the creative philosopher.

4) An attempt to explain the creative process in music cannot succeed if we remain only at the predicative level. At least in ontological phenomenology we study the prepredicative and prestatemental levels of speech and music, i.e. that which preceeds or comes before the predicated or the statemental, in that it makes them possible at all. It may be particularly in this area that philosophy and music come together rather than in a metaphysical philosophy of number, as in the classic theories of music, such as the *Speculum Musicae*. It may be that in phenomenology we draw nearer to that which makes both music and philosophy possible, however different they emerge at the statemental level. I use the word, statemental, advisedly, since there is such a thing as a musical statement, though it is not recognized as such by many a philosopher, even by R. Ingarden. The most obvious case of musical statement is what is called a theme, i.e. the positing of a musical subject, the use of melodic types in the building of musical configurations. It

was always recognized that music was derived from number. But the concept of theme was slow to develop and is essentially a modern idea, beginning perhaps in the renaissance, when the composer posited the musical *soggetto* as distinct from the natural *numero harmonico*. The only problem is that, instead of furthering the truer subjectivity of music in a phenomenological sense, this led toward the positing of theme as objective, i.e. as a musical object for both composer and hearer to focus on. But music has no objects, as sight does. And thus a phenomenology of music would move away from such thematic objectivity toward the restoration of a truer subjectivity, and thus to musical logos rather than to musical statement, as a kind of logic or expression of natural musical number. And here we see the importance of the restoration of musical rhythm as the heart of the musical experience. *The Rite of Spring* or Messiaen's rhythmic innovations exemplify this.

If we take the era of the Viennese Classics, we have a good enough model of the statemental in a traditional sense, for it is here that we see the high point of sonata or first-movement form. The overarching AABA structure of the sonatas and symphonies of Haydn, Mozart, and Beethoven is a commonplace to students of music, as are also the places first and second themes take in this structure over against the harmonic changes from the tonic to the dominant and return. The score of Beethoven's *Eroica* reveals a number of internal and external innovations, instrumental and harmonic (as well as the wedding of sonata with fugal form), but the general structure remains pretty well the same. The phenomenologist would be interested in the intentionalities that make this overarching structure possible. In this case we have music without words.

In philosophy we believe we have words without music, but this is true only at the statemental level. And yet, as musicological research reveals, there is a primordial unity of word and music, one known, e.g. by the Greeks not only at the pre-predicative but even at the predicative level. For at least classical Greek is a musical language, and it is by far not

the only such language known to man. At least in Greek
poetry there is no such thing as the alienation of language
from musical sound. The accents in classical Greek are not
just stress accents; they are quite musical. A Greek "statement," particularly as poetic, is both verbal and musical at
once. This influence carries over into formal music, as may
be seen in the "Skolion of Seikilos," an early second or first
century (B.C.) drinking song, transcribed from an epitaph
engraved on a column at Aidin in Asia Minor, which Ramsay
discovered in 1883.[29] Though this is a relatively late
example, it may not be unwarranted to note that on almost
every acute accent there is a raise in musical pitch, on every
circumflex a lengthening and a cadential figure. A transcription of the first phrase may be used as a sufficient example:

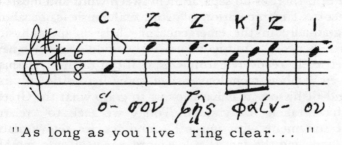

"As long as you live   ring clear... "

This is obviously only a transcription. It cannot really be
given on the well tempered keyboard, since the pitch intervals are quite different. It can only be sung by a trained
expert. The Greek letters above the music are the vocal
notation that accompany the words. It is interesting for our
research into synesthetic perception to note, that in this
drinking song we are admonished to "ring clear" while we yet
live. The actual word is *phaínou*, which means "to appear" or
"to shine forth." Here we have the musical and the visual
united in one phrase. Actually, the verb, *phaínomai*, means
"to appear," either as sight or as sound, though it usually
means the former. We can grasp this the better if we realize
that our word, clarity, is not only a visually oriented word,
though we use it much more for sight than for sound. Yet the

poets tell us of the clarion call that rings out loud and clear. We speak of a clear voice. And there are not only clear and distinct ideas; but they must also be spoken clearly and distinctly. Since we are dealing with a drinking song, it is obvious that the otherwise apparently visual word, *phaínou*, is meant to the rendered not as "appear" but as "to ring clear." After all, during a drinking bout there is a good bit of toasting, accompanied by much loud and clear merriment.

Examples of earlier Greek music, such as the *stásimon* sung by the chorus in Euripides' *Orestes* (fifth century B.C.), though less interesting than our drinking song, might illustrate more faithfully how Greek accents are musical. Whatever the case may be, it is obvious that at least in the Greek language, where both philosophy and music as we know them were born, there is no separation between word and music of some sort. The separation of word and music came about only gradually in the emergence of Christian metaphysics, which spawned the music theory of the middle ages. We have not yet really recovered from this artificial dualism, perhaps not even in phenomenology, as we know it traditionally. At this end of history it is hard for us to grasp what the Greeks may have taken for granted. Today we seek to "relate" logical statement with musical sound, or we set words to music, ignoring the fact that live word sets itself into musical expression. The Greeks knew that logic was not just "mental," and that it was inseparable from primordial musical word. Yet we need not go back to the Greeks, except in the sense that we are searching for a convincing model. We can take the spoken word as it is in use today. As I read these words aloud, for example, I cannot escape their natural musical sound, and it is only this which enables me to speak and you to hear. The musical phrases and cadences of speech are essential to live word, and only live word is the basis for intersubjective communication. The word, as read, is always secondary or after the fact.

5) In effect, music is the "bodily selfness" of word, as alive, i.e. as in-the-world. No reduction is desirable here. The

eidetic reductions to be performed would have to do only with the abstractions of acoustics or of my ontic ego and yours.[30] And "logic" as phenomenological is inseparable from the concreteness of the transcendental logos itself, as musical. Perhaps Hegel can be of help at this point, insofar as he calls form the "becoming of concrete content," or when he writes that *Dasein*, as self-concretizing, is immediately "logical." This is, of course, very Greek, as it was meant to be. However it floats in a concept of consciousness that lacks sufficient reductions and fundament. In living dialogue (*dia-logos*), i.e. in the sharing of the logos which makes any intersubjectivity of dialogue possible, live word as meaningful musical sound is what unites us. For only in it do we give ourselves "bodily." Reading words in print is at best a substitute or a post-factum. "Logic" as merely propositional or statemental is a kind of rootless and groundless word. And thus we recoup the prelogical grounding of any logic, musical or philosophical, by recovering the transcendental logos which makes any logic whatsoever possible at all. In building any new logical system we cannot ignore this prelogical level, otherwise we literally build on sand.

The phenomenology of the prelogical (or protological) must provide the ground for any philosophical or musical logic (or onto-logic). While the phenomenologist does not deny the many branches of the philosophical tree, he is most interested in what makes such a tree stand: the roots and the ground into which the tree has sunk its roots. The prelogical is thus not some sort of mystic postulate but rather the logos itself. Heidegger has traced the gradual alienation of the *epistéme logiké* from the logos which gave it birth. When any logic becomes an ontologic (or theologic), as metaphysical, it runs the risk of spinning itself out of primordial ground, and, loosened from its roots, it may take on an alienated existence of its own in a fantasy world with or without much relation to the original ground. Only a logic, expression, or predicate, that does not cut itself away from its primordial source can expect to retain and evolve meaning.

3. MUSICAL "ESTHESIS" AND THE "ESTHETICAL EXPERIENCE" OF MUSIC

1) We are stressing the difference between "esthesis" and "esthetics" in our discussion of phenomenology vis-a-vis the esthetical experience. It is only proper that we now reveal ourselves for what we are when we speak of a "phenomenology of musical esthetics." In reality we no longer mean traditional esthetics at all, not even in a Kantian sense, though we admit a great debt to Kant. At this point we cannot be blamed for waxing Heideggerian, since it was apparently Heidegger who made the break-through out of esthetics into an ontological esthesis in *Der Ursprung des Kunstwerkes*. Briefly, he criticizes esthetics as the "logic of *aisthesis*," i.e. as the metaphysics or onto-logic derived from a more fundamental esthesis. But, as derived, esthetics is also deficient. And thus the call for a return from philosophies of the beautiful and from traditional ontic esthetics to the work of art itself, as the emergence of truth (*a-létheia*) in the primordial conflict of earth and world. As musical esthesis this would mean a return out of musical esthetics, as we presently know it; it would be a recouping of the primordial world of the *akumena*, i.e of the akumenal logos.

It is here that sounds emerge as "phenomenologically sensuous" in the richness of a primordial eros, as best exemplified in Stravinsky's savage and primeval *Rite of Spring*. We want no monkish *epochés* here! Though there are other examples, let this more obvious one suffice for our present purposes, for in this epoch-making composition of the younger Stravinsky (before he became an ascetical dodecaphonist!) all the eros of springtime, all the intense rhythms and the white heat of the sacral puberty rites of pagan Russia are portrayed in music so lush and overwhelming, that it caused a veritable riot on its first public performance in Paris. No place here for the ascetical analyst or the mere theorist! And the key to this masterpiece is not just the exotic orchestration or the cataclysmic harmony but rather the revolutionary break-through in rhythm. And the orgiastic pulsations of this composition portray a musical eros which is perhaps the best expression of what we might call a true transcendental logos as opposed to a merely intellectualized one. It is a commonplace and yet a musical fact worth further study that Stravinsky broke through not only the theoretical categories of harmony but especially the tight metrical categories of traditional musical rhythm. In fact, rhythm takes precedence once again over musical theme and melody — perhaps for the first time in music history since the isorhythmic compositions of Guillaume de Machaut in the *ars nova* (14th century). Musical rhythm is thus the key to this creation. It is a piece impossible to "keep time to" or to conduct in the usual manner, since the concept of time is radically altered. The most one can do is cue in the instruments, for there is page after page of highly irregular and inconsequential rhythmic pulsation, which gets its meaning not from any metrical measurements of linear time but only from what I may be allowed to call the "tensor factor" of musical time, as phenomenological.

2) This tensor factor is directly related to the dynamic intentional nucleus that begets artistic creativity in the subject. In this sense musical time is no longer conceived as extended in metaphorical or linear space and thus as durational. In *The Rite of Spring* the sense of "duration" is lost. One does not "count" such music, as one does not watch a clock while reading Rilke. It is, indeed, time-less. And only in this sense can "atemporality" be understood. This is not a psychological phenomenon but rather the emergence of the "timeless" logos of phenomenon. Neither is it a metaphysical "eternity," that hypocritical concept which the concept of time makes possible, only to be denied by it. The timelessness of music is concrete and not abstract: it roots in an overcoming of objective or ontic time and the unfolding of the subject in its fullest essence, as ekstatic. Thus musical time has little to do with the spatial or linear, despite the tradition of western philosophy and music which extends time along a line leading to infinity. And of course the west evolved

a linearly conceived musical notation! It best exemplifies in concrete practice the linear conception of time, but it is at best a derived symbolization of phenomenological time, whether we understand this in the sense of Husserl, Heidegger, or Merleau-Ponty. We make a great mistake when we take these symbols literally and predicate of the phenomenon of music a linear duration which it does not have in essence, for music is fundamentally not durational but "tensile." The ontological tensility of music cannot be graphed either linearly or even in the manner of protensions and retentions. "Tensility" can best be grasped if we understand phenomenological intentionality minus the spatial visualizations. For that is what they are: visual "realizations" of an akumenal phenomenon which cannot be so realized.

This notion of ontological tensility is also a closer approach to what the Greeks called musical tonos. For the "musical tone" is directly related to the Greek kithara and to the tuning of strings. But such tuning has to do with the various degrees of tenseness, as every string player knows in his fingers. And for this simple reason the tonos, which is the fundamental building block of western music since the Greeks, is actually a "tensor" first and foremost. Only then does it concern what we would now call pitch, especially as graphed visually on a scale. Greek instrumental notation, unlike our own, was a tablature, i.e. it indicated the positions of fingers and had nothing to do primarily with the visual representation of pitch levels, as conceived in our own linear notation. And thus music was liberated from the imposition of a spatially conceived temporality. It could be what it was: an interplay of strings of differing intensities, thus producing musical sound. This is phenomenological in the sense that music is allowed to present itself as it *is* in its truer subjectivity: not as something to be seen but as something to be fingered and thus as "no-ontic-thing" to be heard. Here the haptic and the musically audial go hand in hand. The visual symbols, which are but aids to the fingers, cannot become anything more than they are. They cannot begin to dictate musical conceptuality.

It is perhaps this tonos that best exemplifies a transcendental logos, whether we speak of the Greeks or of ourselves.
Were we to search for a suitable word to exemplify a phenomenology of music, as Husserl and Heidegger sought and
found the eidos and the logos, we would have to choose the
word, tonos, and this for reasons not dissimilar. J. Lohmann
must receive the credit for pointing out this historic fact:
that not only philosophy but also what we now call music
began as something absolutely new in the world of the
Greeks. And of philosophy, mathematics, and music, the
latter was the oldest.[32] The word that characterizes this is
tonos, as intimately bound up with the logos. Neither logos
nor tonos can be understood properly unless we make
passage from esthetics to esthesis.

3) What is this transition? In the *Nachwort* to his large
essay on the art work Heidegger puts it quite clearly: traditional esthetics has regarded the work of art as an object,
literally, we might add, as an *objet d'art*.[33] Art is thus an
object of esthesis, understood as sense perception in a broad
sense. This has then been interpreted as "art experience"
which is looked on as the source of both the production and
appreciation of art. "Everything is experience," Heidegger
writes. And perhaps this is the very thing which brings about
the death of true art, a death that drags itself out over centuries despite all the talk about undying works of art. Art is
not an object of experience but rather the emergence of the
truth of being in primordial conflict of world and earth. The
transition is thus from the ontic to the ontological, from the
objective to the phenomenological subject. But the return to
the eksistential subject is a departure from esthetics as
subjective, whether in a Kantian or psychological sense. And
thus a phenomenological esthesis is not just sense perception
or any kind of either psychological or esthetical experiencing
of the work of art. Rather, it is a phenomenological perceiving, i.e. original (in the sense of Merleau-Ponty) and intentional rather than intellectual or empirical. It is a question of
the intentionality of the subject which brings forth a work

of art and thus creates a world.

When the Greeks used the word, *aisthánomai*, it did not mean just "sense perception" in a modern sense, as though there were really a post-Cartesian division between mind and senses which spawned the split between intellectualism and empiricism criticized by Merleau-Ponty. There was no need even for a Kantian scheme to bind together the apriori forms of sense-intuition with the categories of understanding. Rather, man himself is the sensing being (*aisthētes*), i.e. the living being who is aware of being, as it unfolds itself to him in his encounter with the world he opens up. This man is no "esthete" who looks for esthetical pleasure or enjoyment. Art is not pastry. The essence of this phenomenological sensing of world is the emergence of ontological truth in the primordial struggle of world and earth. World opens out and earth closes in, but this is no metaphysical closure. It is a kind of dialectic between world and earth, and in this conflict of the Titans the truth of the work of art is brought forth. Pleasure may or may not be a concomitant. There is little "art experience" or "esthetical appreciation" here. Thus, in a certain sense Heidegger's insights begin to spell the "end" of traditional esthetics, as the completion of a historic period in philosophy.

However, there will be a good many esthetes who will not take too kindly to such an explanation of the art work or to Heidegger's statement in *Die Frage nach der Technik* that "on account of sheer esthetics we can no longer preserve the essence of art."[34] In this case the downfall of esthetics goes along with the particular trend that technology has taken in modern times. In our technological age everything, art included, becomes an object to be dealt with, an object that can have a value, esthetical or monetary, set on it. Technology is indeed one manifestation of *téchnē* (which we have translated both as "art" and as "technique"). But Heidegger returns to a primordial techno-logy (as the logos of *techne*), i.e. to a more fundamental bringing forth of being (*Sein*), a bringing forth which is more evident in the work of art as a manifestation of truth (the "un-concealment" of being) than it ever could be in technological science. Heidegger's approach is somewhat Hegelian, in that he brings esthetic problems back to a consideration of truth, as phenomenological, and away from theories of the beautiful. Truth and beauty are not just "convertible with being"; beauty is not just an "esthetical idea." Rather truth, as the disclosure of being (*Sein*), *is* beauty. The Husserlian objection at this point would be, Why being? If it is disclosure at all, it is that of subject not of being. But the problem of being and subjectivity we must reserve for another occasion. When we speak of the work of art in this essay, we are obviously speaking of ontological phenomenology, one that might be in need of considerable correction and supplement from an inter-subjective phenomenology.

4) How does "truth" manifest itself as art? How does it show itself not as "actuality" or "reality" (those bastard translations of *en-érgeia*) but as a work (*érgon*)? How is artistic truth not "real" but a "work" (not *wirklich* but *werkhaft*)? Truth reveals itself in the art work because the work is what initiates the conflict between world and earth.[35] Out of this creative opposition truth reveals itself, as being emerges. For the work of art holds open the region of world; it makes world possible and best exemplifies world. Yet another "principle" besides the opening up of world is required: the bringing forth of earth. A Greek temple is used as an example. Perhaps we may refer to the temple at Agrigento (ancient Acragas) as a refreshing change from the Acropolis. The "materials" of the temple, taken from the earth, are not just used in the erection of the sacred edifice, as today we use up so many tons of concrete, which is regarded as nothing more than so much material. Matter is not consumed in its being used. Rather the "materials" are brought out *as such* perhaps for the first time. And here we must recall that matter is to be interpreted mythologically as belonging to ontological earth, the mother loam.

And thus crude rock that has become a Doric column at the hands not of a technician but of an artist comes to thrust forward and rest against the capital and roof. The "artist" (*technítēs*) literally *brings* the fluted column *forth* from the mother rock, i.e. from "matter." Thus for the first time it becomes rock in the truest sense, for its strength and beauty have been brought forth into the light from out the darkness of concealing earth. And this is the task of the artist: to bring forth. One gets this idea particularly with the unfinished torsos of Michelangelo: they struggle to emerge from the rough rock, and only the hand of the artist can bring them out in all their strength and beauty as the truth which they are. Thus the rock, as a Doric column, comes to thrust against the temple roof in dynamic "rest" and becomes rock for the first time. In the same way rough ore becomes metal and receives a lustre and sheen it would never otherwise have; and now it can become a flashing blade in the hand of a warrior, or, if a precious metal, can become "brushed gold" at the hands of a Florentine artist. In like manner colors are brought out in the creation of the artist; and raw sound becomes music, not by its being filtered through an intellectual grid, but rather because in working with raw sound the artist brings out its innate musicality, so that we have music for the first time, as we know it in a Delphic Hymn, in a medieval chanson, or in a modern symphony. All of this is brought about because the work of art, as it opens world, sets itself back into earth: into the massiveness of stone, into the firmness of wood, into the lustre of bronze or gold, into the resounding of tone, into the magic power words have to name. The art work holds the earth into the openness of world and being, as it helps earth to become truly earth. World and earth are different from one another and yet never separated; they are distinguished but not apart. This is a oneness of creative opposition: the opposing factors mutually complement each other and essentially necessary to one another.

Insofar as an art work opens up world and brings forth earth, it initiates the conflict between them. It is a conflict in which the opposites become ever more opposing, so that conflict remains conflict and is not leveled out in a false peace. Yet this is not a sterile antagonism but a creative opposing; for out of the no-thingness of being truth is "created," i.e. is brought forth as a work of art. Thus Heidegger can write that "the being of an art work consists in its initiating a conflict between world and earth." The initiating of the conflict is precisely a gathering-into-movement which is characteristic of any art. And this is what we mean by "rest," e.g. the pillar "rests" against the capital and the roof. For in its thrust the Doric column gathers itself wholly into the movement of "resting" against the capital. Such rest is obviously not static repose. In like manner a musical rest is not just a pause between musical phrases; rather the musical themes come to rest all their weight against the overarching roof of AABA form. Here we see that "form" is no longer visual but dynamic in the sense of an architechtonic and musical tensor factor. For, while the AABA form can be graphed visually, audially these are but focal tensor points, at which the forces of the art work are gathered together, ready to unleash themselves again as the composition further develops itself. It is this dynamic tensility which we "feel" in a musical score rather than see in an analysis or on the printed page. Musical form is meant for the ear not the eye. And this "infeeling" as "inhearing" is what we mean by esthesis. Thus it is neither an intellectual analysis of music nor is it a psychologically esthetical experience, as such.

Truth emerges in interplay with ontological un-truth. Untruth is not logical or moral falsity but rather the "opposite"-of-truth in the sense of the closure and disclosure of being (*Sein*). When being discloses or reveals itself to us we call it truth; when it withholds itself, even as ontological presence, we call it untruth or closure. Being opens-out and closes-in in the emergence of the un-hiddenness (*a-lêtheia*) of truth. Being reveals of itself, it tells of itself; but it does not tell all, for it conceals *as* it reveals. And thus while world opens out, earth comes forth or is brought forth, concealing. To the "open middle"[36] of the primordial conflict between truth and untruth belong world and earth. Yet world is not simply the Open as earth is Closure. Rather, world is grounded

only on earth and earth thrusts only through world. The conflict of world and earth in the work of art is not identical
with the conflict of truth and untruth, but it depends on it
and issues from it, insofar as truth "sets itself into the work
(of art)." And thus truth is what works the work of art.
Truth stands in-the-work and thus we can speak of *enérgeia*,
which has little to do with "energy," and less to do with
"actuality" or "objectivity" in the sense of an object-of-art.

5) Heidegger identifies the conflict of truth/untruth as a
"Riss."[37] This means a fissure, a tear, a breach. In the conflict of world and earth, in their opposing tendencies to open
and close, the opposites belong essentially together and not
apart. This ontological fissure is not a splitting apart; for in
this tearing there is no rending asunder. It is a *"Grund-riss,"*
i.e. a fundamental breaching, a primordial distinction that
does not, as it were, extinguish the opposites but brings them
together in a fundamental unity of being, thus giving them
contour or "shape" (*Umriss*). The conflict is brought into
this breach, as world is "set back" into the earth and thus is
"set fast" into its shape. It is now evident that this shaping
cannot be understood in the sense of a psychological *Gestalt*.
Heidegger employs the word, *Ge-stell*, a rather violent neologism, which emphasizes the "setting-up of world," and
"setting forth" of earth, and the *setting* of the fissure itself.
Being is what *sets* things into "shape." And thus any *"Gestalt."* It is the hand of the artist, be he sculptor or musician,
that sets truth into its shape. This setting-fast is not a con-
gealing or a becoming rigid and motionless. It means being set
into movement, just as a composer sets to work with raw
sound, thus "setting an idea to music"; but this musical
"idea" is not just an abstract form. It is, as it were, "La
danse des adolescentes" in Stravinsky's *Rite of Spring* (which
is the antithesis of all the saccharine "Springs" one is used to
hearing), or as in the sadistic voice of R. Strauss' *Salomé*, as
she taunts the dripping head of St. John (one of the most
gruesome scenes in music). This phenomenological sensuousness cannot be the object of musical analysis or the subject

of esthetical experience. It can only be "felt" in esthesis. The total effect can be felt only in a syn-esthesis.

4.   SOME PROVISIONAL CONCLUSIONS FOR BOTH PHENOMENOLOGY AND MUSICOLOGY

1) Perhaps any conclusions we might reach in this essay would be the result of research into the meaning of syn-esthesis rather than of esthetic experience as the immediate experience of art, which takes place in the presence of the object of art itself, even be this a judgmental evaluation of art in a post-Kantian sense. And thus the transition from esthetics to esthesis is a passage from the "logic" of esthesis to the logos, which makes any logic possible at all. In music we found this logos intimately connected with tonos, as tensor factor. What then is the task of the musicologist, if he is to get beyond historical and esthetical research? It seems to me his task will be to give a phenomenological description (rather than just an analysis or stylistic criticism) of the musical logos as it unfolds itself in a musical work of art. But for this he may need to study the meaning of intentionality in Husserl and Merleau-Ponty and of logos in Heidegger. But as he studies phenomenology he may set a new task for it, in that he gives a critique of its predominantly visual conceptuality and vocabulary. Hence the task of the phenomenologist and the musicologist may well coincide in the logos. As a musician he will be aware of the essential sensuousness of his art; as a phenomenologist he will know that this sensuous quality is no longer physical or physico-erotic. Rather, in the emergence of the musical logos the abstractions of both traditional sensuality and ideality vanish, as the musical work of art reveals truth and essence in their original selfness, i.e. in the full primeval force of a springtime, or even in the savage pulsations of the rites of eros.

2) In a phenomenology of musical esthesis the original unity of music and philosophy (both creations of the Greeks)

is recovered. The critique a musician will make of the visual orientation of philosophy will be balanced by a return to a fundamental syn-esthesis, in which both sight and hearing are grounded. It is only in a "synesthetic perception" that we can appreciate not only the art of sound but all the arts together as one integral art work. For in synesthesis one not only hears sound but hears world, for hearing is a basic openness for world. And thus since one hears world one also sees it, and thus one "hears sight" and "sees sound." It is only thus that one can appreciate opera, for example. It is only thus that following the score of, e.g., Benjamin Britten's *Serenade for Tenor, Horn, and Strings* we can appreciate how he "set" words to music, in this case the words of Tennyson, Keats, and Blake. Here we both see and hear the words, as poetry and music: as *one*.

Ernst Kurth has written that "Music is the emergence of powerful primal forces, whose energies originate in the unheard. What one usually designates as music is actually but its echo."[38] We might say at this point that musical tonos is the echo of a primal *échos*, which is accessible in phenomenology, as the study of logos, but only if it becomes an akumenal phenomenology, i.e. one of primordial sound.

Endnotes

1. E. Husserl, *Phänomenologische Psychologie* (Den Haag, 1962), ed. W. Biemel, Abhandlung II, pp. 247-255. Here Husserl writes that phenomenology did not come about in the interest of psychology but of philosophy, to make it a strict science. Transcendental phenomenology and psychology, he claims, are quite different from each other in their fundamental significance and must be sharply distinguished and kept apart from one another. This is so even when on both sides the apparently same phenomena are studied. Even what we call a pure psychology in a phenomenological sense, i.e. thematically bounded in psychological-phenomenological reduction, is still a positive science, he continues. A clearer statement could hardly be given on the issue. Cf. also *Ideen* III pass.

2. In a recent article in *Philosophy and Phenomenological Research* (vol. XXVII, no. 2, Dec. 1966) A. Pike attempts to present the

work of L. Meyer, *Emotion and Meaning in Music* (Chicago, 1956) as an important work in the phenomenology of music. Perhaps this can be done if one dismisses the work of the founder of phenomenology, as Pike does in his first footnote, where he puts "historical" phenomenology from him. But it is a less than convincing attempt, especially since L. Meyer rejects phenomenology. His presentation is a case of Gestalt psychology and nothing more. In the musicological world Meyer's book was not exactly welcomed as a "highly important book," judging from such reviews as those in *The Musical Quarterly* (Oct. 1957, A. Lippmann) or allusions in such journals as *The Juilliard Review*. Some of these reviews were over-severe, but they did point up some essential flaws in Meyer's attempt to apply Gestalt to music. A considerably more felicitous presentation of this is given by Meyer in his essay, "On Rehearing Music," in *The Journal of the American Musicological Society* (vol. XIV, no. 2, Sept. 1961), pp. 257-267. But in no intelligible sense is this a "phenomenology of music," unless the word, phenomenology, is meaningless. Besides the brief essay "Zur Phänomenologie der Musik" by Eimert in *Melos, Zeitschrift für Musik* (1926, pp. 244-5) there is little written on this subject to the present writer's best knowledge. The only really significant work done on the phenomenology of music is that of Roman Ingarden, who in *Untersuchungen zur Ontologie der Kunst* deals convincingly both with music and with phenomenology. Cf. same (Tübingen, 1962), pp. 3-115, "Das Musikwerk." Cf. H. Mersmann, "Zur Phän. d. Musik" in *Zeitschirft fur Aesthetik*, XIX, 1925, p. 372.

3.   Iso Kern, *Husserl und Kant* (Den Haag, 1964) pass. Heidegger, M. *Kant und das Problem der Metaphysik* (Frankfurt, 1951); *Die Frage nach dem Ding* (Tübingen, 1952); *Der Satz vom Grund* (Pfullingen, 1952); "Kants These über das Sein" (1962) in a Festschrift for Erik Wolf, *Existenz und Ordnung*. Husserl, E. *Erste Philosophie*, I (1923/4) (Den Haag, 1956), cf. "Ergänzende Texte." This is but one of many references in Husserl's works. Cf. *Ideen* III, Beilage I & VI.

4.   E. Husserl, *Die Krisis der europäischen Wissenschaften und die transzendentale Phänomenologie* (Den Haag, 1954) pass.

5.   J. Lohmann, "Der Ursprung der Musik" in *Archiv fur Musikwissenschaft* (Trossingen, 1959) 1/2, p. 161.

6.   A. Wellek, "Musikpsychologie" in *Die Musik in Geschichte und Gegenwart*, Band 9 (Kassel, 1961), p. 114-1169 for general background; for L. Szekely, cf. H. H. Dräger, "Musikaesthetik," pp. 1000f., esp. p. 1001.

7.   F. J. Smith, "Jacques de Liège, an Anti-modernist?" in *Revue belge de musicologie* (1963); "Ars Nova, a Redefinition; some observations in the light of Jacques de Liège's Speculum Musicae"

in *Musica Disciplina* (American Institute of Musicology, Rome) (1964/65); *Iacobi Leodiensis Speculum Musicae, a Commentary,* vol. 1 (Institute of Mediaeval Music, N.Y.) (1966-).

8.   I. Kant, *Kritik der Urteilskraft*, ed. Vorländer, Phil. Pibl. B. 39, pp. 181, 186.

9.   J. Derrida, "La voix et le phénomène: signe linguistique et non-linguistique dans la phénomenologie de Husserl" (unpubl.).

10.   S. Kierkegaard, "Die unmittelbaren Stadien oder das Musikal-isch-Erotische" in *Entweder/Oder* (Düsseldorf, 1956), tr. E. Hirsch, p. 49f.

11.   M. Merleau-Ponty, *La phénomenologie de la perception* (Paris, 1945), pp. 264-5.

12.   R. Ingarden, *Untersuchungen zur Ontologie der Kunst*, p. 28.

13.   I. Kant, *Kritik der Urteilsckraft*, pp. 182, 52 "Von der Ver-bindung der schonen Künste in einem und demselben Produkte."

14.   M. Heidegger, *Der Ursprung des Kunstwerkes* (Stuttgart, 1960) Intro. by Gadamer, with a *Nachwort* and *Zusatz* by Heidegger. The *Zusatz* is a new addition, not to be found in *Holzwege*, where the essay originally appeared.

15.   N. Hartmann, *Aesthetik* (Berlin 1953), pp. 197-210, "Schichten des Musikwerkes."

16.   W. Apel, *The Harvard Dictionary of Music* (Harvard, 1953), "Musicology", p. 473f.

17.   M. Bukofzer, *The Place of Musicology in American Institutions of Higher Learning* (New York, 1956); cf. also his essay, "Historical Musicology" in *The Music Journal*, IV, 1946.

18.   M. Bukofzer, *The Baroque Era* (New York, 1949).

19.   P. H. Lang, *The Musical Quarterly*, Editorial, Oct. 1949.

20.   C. Sachs, *The Journal of the American Musicological Society*, Editorial, 1949.

21.   A.-T. Tymieniecka, "Editorial: the Second Phenomenology," in *For Roman Ingarden, Nine Essays in Phenomenology* ('s-Graven-hage, 1959).

22.   W. Wiora, "Musikwissenschaft" in *Die Musik in Geschichte und Gegenwart*, vol. 9, p. 1195 "Grundlegung als positive Wissen-schaft."

23.   *Jacobi Leodiensis Speculum Musicae*, I, ed. R. Bragard (American Institute of Musicology), cap. 8, p. 28, "Cui parti philosophiae musica supponatur." Cf. also II, p. 7, "Habet enim musicus dicere de quibuscumque sonis distinctis simul collatis consonant-iam facientibus quam inter se facian harmonicam modulationem vel consonantiam . . ."

24.   Kant, I., *Über den Gemeinspruch: das mag in der Theorie richtig*

      sein, taugt aber nicht für die Praxis (1793), ed. Gadamer
      (Frankfurt) 1946).
25.   Smith, F. J., *Iacobi Leodiensis Speculum Musicae, a Commentary*,
      vol. I, p. 45f.
26.   Lohmann, J., "Der Ursprung der Musik" in *Archiv für Musik-
      wissenschaft*, 1959, 1/2, p. 151.
27.   Merleau-Ponty, M., *op. cit.*
28.   Vlad, R., *Stravinsky*, tr. F. and A. Fuller (Oxford 1960), p. 30.
29.   Martin, E., *Trois documents de musique grecque* (Paris, 1953),
      p. 48 f; cf. Apel, W. *The Rise of Music in the Ancient World East
      and West* (New York, 1943) section five "Greece and Rome"
      p. 195 f.
30.   Husserl, E., *Cartesianische Meditationen und Pariser Vorträge*, ed.
      Strasser (Haag, 1950) pass. We deal here with the reductions of
      ego and *alter ego*.
31.   Smith, F. J., "The 'End' of Aesthetics" (unpubl.).
32.   Lohmann, J., in *op. cit.* p. 149.
33.   Heidegger, M., *Der Ursprung des Kunstwerkes*, p. 91, "Die
      Ästhetik nimmt das Kunstwerk als einen Gegenstand und zwar
      als den Gegenstand der aísthesis, des sinnlichen Vernehmens im
      weiten Sinn. Heute nennt man dieses Vernehmen das Erleben . . .
      Alles ist Erlebnis. Doch vielleicht is das Erlebnis das Element, in
      dem die Kunst stirbt. Das Sterben geht so langsam vor sich, daß es
      einege Jahrhunderte braucht."
34.   Heidegger, M., *Vorträge und Aufsätze* (Pfullingen, 1954) p. 44.
35.   Heidegger, M., *Der Urpsrung des Kunstwerkes*, p. 51.
36.   Heidegger, M., *Holzwege* (Frankfurt, 1957), "Wozu Dichter?",
      p. 260; *Der Ursprung des Kunstwerkes*, p. 59.
37.   Heidegger, M., *Der Ursprung des Kunstwerkes*, p. 71.
38.   Kurth, E., *Musikpsychologie* (Bern, 1947); cf. also "Musik-
      psychologie" in *Die Musik in Geschichte und Gegenwart*, vol. 9,
      p. 1148 f.

Chapter 8

ESTHETIC RE-EDUCATION: THE EXPERIENCING OF MUSICAL SOUND

For a long time now it has been common knowledge how many students have been "turned off" by traditional introductions to music. This seems to be the case both with regard to the general student who, whether as an honor student or a regular plodder, takes an introductory music course, and also with regard to the music student for whom music is a major. This is apparently true also of general introductions to philosophy. One begins to suspect that what happens in music and in philosophy departments may be true of more university departments than one cares to become aware of. In other words, and in plain language, at the very port of entry to music or to philosophy (and to other subjects?) the normal student, whether bright or dull, seems to be stopped cold. Or he may find himself in a comatose state through most of the course in question, waking up only for a cramming session at the end of the quarter. One hesitates to conduct a systematic survey of such courses across campus, for fear of being entirely disabused of the notion, that students can really be introduced to anything, without having their initial interest (and even enthusiasm?) diminished, if not utterly destroyed.

Part of this general debacle is doubtless the fault of students themselves, as they fail the courage to go into things in more than dilettante fashion, or they lack the ability to suffer through with a given professor. A good deal of blame must be chalked up to the "system." But the system is not an abstraction. It is comprised of people: the professor, the curriculum committees, the general administration, all of whom were originally intended to abet the educational effort rather than obstruct it. Both students and faculty often get the idea that they are caught in a mindless system that suppresses interest and participation in favor of sterile information and pseudo-intellectual categorizations. The esthetic impulses of the good student — to say nothing of his natural sensitivities — are indeed often subverted by over-intellectualization or, especially in music, under-intellectualized pedagogy. Since the middle ages western man has come to stress the cognitive levels of understanding at the expense of genuine esthetic education. Recent philosophers like Scheler and Hartmann have stressed the emotional basis which directs a man's cognitive needs. Still, generations had learned to be ashamed of feeling and artistic sensitivity, because they seem to defy direct intellectual thematization. On the other hand, in despair of ever becoming a part of the house of intellect, musicians have concentrated on doing to the exclusion of thinking, barring sporadic efforts. Thus the practical level is stressed as over against the cognitive. But in either case the esthetic experiencing of musical sound is blunted; for man, as an esthetical animal, is neither one who merely thinks nor one who merely does. Rather, he should be one who, as he acts, reflects on what he is doing, and in reflecting is impelled to a more concretely creative activity, especially in the arts.

When the philosophical impasse of theory vs. practice becomes institutionalized, the effects can be devastating for both teachers and the taught. Thus we have esthetic theory divorced, departmentally, from the performing arts. The theoreticians spin their theories generally without concrete reference to artistic practice, and the practitioners develop a narrow guild or trade mentality in their approach to their art, an approach that can go as far as to disparage even pertinent reflection about art and music. Both theorist and practitioner thus run the risk of becoming obscurantists, the one because he watches too many pink clouds float by, the other because, mole-like, he burrows into his art and, as it were, brutalizes himself with endless performances (cf.

Hindemith's *A Composer's World*), hoping by sheer quantity
to make up for his lack of thoughtful reflection on artistic
problems, to say nothing of pressing life-related issues (like
how our country is going to pieces). A massive esthetic
re-education seems called for in music at least, and the
present author will restrict himself to a critique of the
manner in which musicians (and musicologists!) are educated
at the expense of a more humane understanding of their art.

What indeed is "esthetic education," if one is to write of
the need for re-education? As university courses go, esthetic
education has come to stand for a number of things, not all
entirely commendable. At one end there is the truly knowledgeable professor, capable of imparting knowledge and
emphasizing the need to experience music as well as to know
about it. On the other end is the esthetics class, which may
degenerate into a catch-all for ambiguous nothings, taught by
a professor not noticeably cognizant of what is actually going
on in a given art, music particularly. In between we
encounter the well-meaning group of people who sincerely
desire to increase their esthetic potential. But all of this
describes only the courses in formal esthetics. The esthetic
education which counts even more should be imparted in the
degree courses in the given art, here music. In his study of
music theory and history the student should be enhancing his
esthetic potential; and courses in formal esthetics could then
wed knowledge with experience in a convincing amalgam.
As things stand, however, it is not unfair to say that music
students get absolutely no esthetic values from their formal
degree courses in music theory or history, at least where the
latter emphasizes the "objective" side of music. For the
typical music student must pass through a puberty rite, an
initiation ritual first and foremost, rather than be introduced
to the experience of musical sound or reflect on its basic
problems. What he is initiated into is not knowledge or
esthetic understanding but rather a guild, whose intellectual
and esthetic content is relatively low, however much activity
is evidenced at the practical level. The guild professors, of
course, are firmly entrenched in the institution, and they are

a formidable barrier to anything beyond the relatively narrow preoccupation that goes under the label of music theory. Yet in this essay I seek neither to deny the obvious need for good theory teaching ("some of my best friends are theory teachers . . .") nor even for rigorous training in the objective history of music. Nor do I opt for a return to inept and mindless courses in music "appreciation." Granting some essential place to both music theory and history in the music curriculum, I merely ask what is happening to musical feeling and sensitivity in the process of one's being educated as a musician. To begin to answer our initial questions, we might well first ask what education is supposed to connote, and what esthetics has to do with it, particularly in music.

1. WHAT IS "EDUCATION"?

The question, formulated in such a concise manner, is both mindboggling and pretentious. The present author does not intend to pretend he knows the answer to such a question. Yet one can reflect on certain facts of this troublesome query, for it is not only a formal philosophical question, it is also a matter close to the heart of troubled students and their critical mentors, not the least of whom sit in state legislatures. What is the present scene in music education? The present scene is a depressing one, like the general scene in this country. To focus on the educational scene in music schools, even good ones, would be to uncover some of the concrete reasons for the depressing feeling one gets in examining the American educational arena. One notes a systematic narrowing process at work, as musicians specialize in either theory or performance. This process is begun in their first year of being exposed to traditional theory and history. Perhaps the word "traditional" is crucial in this criticism. For the "traditional" pedagogy of nineteenth century pedants is still very much with us, though often in "modern" garb, with contemporary window dressing. The outdated mental categories of the last century, when form, analysis, and functional harmony became so all important (and all-engulfing when it came to music teaching), have not yet began to receive the necessary critique that is called for, if they are to be retained as modified parts of esthetic education. The fact is they seem to tend to obstruct both an understanding of music and any esthetic education on the part of the sincere musician.

"Traditional" music theory is not traditional in a genuine sense. What passes for traditional form, analysis, and harmony is to an uncomfortable extent a distortion visited on us by nineteenth century pedagogues. The distorting element was their preoccupation with and uncritical acceptance of most of the baroque theorist Rameau's naturalistic assumptions concerning the basic nature of harmony, i.e. that it did indeed originate in the bass and was understandable only as evolved from this foundation voice. Certainly this is a way of looking at things understandable for Rameau's times (though by no means entirely typical of baroque theory, which was occupied principally with the affective approach to music), but it hardly applies to the twentieth century, and there is some doubt it applies to the nineteenth. In fact, it is to an extent atypical of the baroque era in which it originated. It is, however, a fascinating reflection on Rameau's own music, and it is good to remember that he began first as a theorist (the "Newton of Music") before evolving into a significant French composer. That the nineteenth century pedagogue (living in a post-Newtonian era!) latched onto such a period definition of harmony may be understandable from several viewpoints. On the one hand musical pedagogy was unfairly regarded as a very low form of learning; and music had been pretty well read out of the crystal palaces of nineteenth century intellectualism, though when it was mentioned it was with some embarrassment (ranging from eulogies to patronizing remarks). In addition, toward the end of the nineteenth century music esthetics was caught in the crossfire of such figures as Wagner and Hanslick and was unable to develop in a normal manner, as an academic discipline. On the other hand teachers of music were justifiably confused by the all-engulfing fact of musical romanticism, and it was understandable that "lesser minds" of the last century concentrated on trying to make some pedagogical sense out of the welter of harmonies that characterized the era. And thus the theories of Rameau, rediscovered and revived (by Sechter and Riemann) must have seemed like a boon to the beleaguered pedant. It may have been survival technique that prompted good teachers to adopt such a method so uncritically. Whatever the case, such musical pedagogy (forged during the Enlightenment) with its false emphases and historic distortions came to be visited upon the body musical. Like some ancient reformation or counter-reformation catechism, it provided "some basis," some point of departure, for the neophyte. It was supposed to be "better than nothing," like its equivalent Fuxian theory in counterpoint. But such a basis, whatever its merits or demerits in the last century and at the beginning of this one, is hardly relevant musically or philosophically to the facts of life in the twentieth century. It is a shell musicians carry around on their backs, in imitation of the chambered nautilus. It has become, in fact, obstructive. Music theory needs not only updating; it needs drastic and radical critique in terms even of nineteenth century music, to say nothing of our era. It is obstructive both of a meaningful understanding of what really goes on in a given musical passage as well as of esthetic appreciation of it. It is a mis-educational ritual entrance to a pedagogical guild, rather than an introduction to music itself. It is the imposition of an outdated and never very well founded musical mentality on the living body of music of our era and that of others (for it is read back into medieval and renaissance music as well!).

If this is the discouraging scene, what could be done to introduce students to the musical experience as well as to understanding specifics of musical composition and techniques? Here, of course, we note that our attitudes must change. We can no longer impose an uncritical and anachronistic mental framework on musical experience; rather any categories that emerge must come from our fresh experiencing of music as such. Our understanding of musical facts will be based not on a detached musical metaphysics, which is both bad history and bad theory, but on musical sound as such, as it is shaped by the contemporary (or the historical) composer. Thus the student would no longer be indoctrinated in a given theory; the musical Muse would be led-out (e-ducated) and brought out of him through contact with the composer and the reflecting performer or musicologist. Specifically, for historical studies, I would have him study Zarlino and Burmeister and not the baroque theorist, J. J. Fux, concerning renaissance polyphony. In like manner I would have him understand Bach through theorists who expounded the meaning of baroque figures, rather than through some nineteenth century restorer of Rameau. I would have him study the scores of Mozart and notice the unselfconsciousness of such classic "form," rather than have him become involved with descendants of theorists like A. B. Marx and P. Goetschius, who were preoccupied with a static form that never existed anywhere in music history, particularly not in the classic era. Preoccupation with form and analysis is a mark of nineteenth century pedantry, continued on in far too many cases in the twentieth century. This, too, blocks both an understanding of music and esthetic education. One ends up with fistfuls of visual symbols and materialistic categories, that not only do not represent the music itself but preoccupy the student to the detriment of his even listening to music.

At this point the author might also give a progress report on his own handling of both honor and graduate students in his seminar, called the "Experiencing of Musical Sound."[1] Here the following steps are followed, steps that seem to suggest themselves as natural, if our goal is the music itself rather than mentalistic or trade categories. Briefly, the students listen to given selections of music from all eras (often performed by them), since the actual experience of listening is what everything else is built on. Then, instead of pouncing on the musical experience with pre-given categories (learned rather than formed in experience), the students are asked to give free vent to their impressions of the music at whatever level. Out of these verbalizations of the experience of musical sound arise a good many "finds" in terms of history, problems, questions, and categories. The analysis of the verbalizations, using contemporary analytical techniques, is what makes such "finds" possible. In this way one hopes to be introduced to music "for the first time" (honors students) or anew (graduate students) in such a way that the gains are those of esthetic appreciation and experience-based understanding, rather than in terms of some historic doctrine about musical form, harmony, etc. The results of such sessions have been startling, and in a sense it is difficult to render in print the "happenings" that have occurred. In summary, the stages traversed are: (1) the experiencing of a musical composition, (2) verbalizations of one's impressions on whatever level, (3) analysis of the verbalizations, which brings out the various levels (cognitive, emotive, etc.) and relates or criticizes them, (4) the emergence of problems and questions which demand the presence of composers and historians, and (5) the hoped for understanding of music itself, at least incipiently. The whole purpose of this approach is phenomenological, i.e. to allow music itself to emerge from under the overlay of theory and the incrustations of history.

2.   WHAT IS "ESTHETICS"?

Like the first question this one, too, can be only partially answered. And in fact, it may not be properly formulated; for, in asking *what* esthetics is, we may imply that it is a self-contained body of thought, and this bodes ill for its being accepted by artists, as relevant to what they are doing. We ought to ask *how* we react "esthetically" to a given work of art, rather than *what* esthetics might be as a philosophical discipline. Again, what is the present scene? Like the first scene described it, too, is far from encouraging. A good bit of what passes for esthetics in the appropriate journals is felt by artists to be simply irrelevant to their art, in this case music. Though this rejection of esthetic theory is often due to the natural obscurantism of the trade mentality, often it is simply the human response of one working in a given area to the mystifications practiced by one not at work in that area. The often unrelated and irrelevant articles published in the journals look indeed like so many "pink clouds" passing over in an otherwise clear sky; they are beautiful but say little to the working artist or musician. They often literally becloud the issues. On the other hand traditional "musical esthetics" is often related to what the artist is doing, but it seems provincial and second rate by comparison with the esthetic efforts of significant thinkers, even though the latter may not be musically knowledgeable. What we have here is not just a discouraging lack of communication but a depressing disorientation and lack of understanding on all sides.

What could be done to begin to remedy this seemingly impossible situation? First of all, it seems reasonable to state that this century will not see such a figure as Hegel, the summator of all knowledge and the builder of an absolute system. Moreover, we would not want another Hegel. The present writer feels that no one individual is capable any more of solving the problem on hand; but that with concerted effort and by pooling resources we can, as cooperating groups, begin to remedy the "bad scene" inherited from the last century. One approach to the esthetic question is to bracket esthetics out, insofar as it is a metaphysical remnant of the past. Instead of "esthetics" we would inquire about *aisthesis*; i.e. instead of placing our hopes in an intellectualized (or in contrast, sensualized) esthetics, we would ask about *how* man perceives, feels, and responds to the work of art, how he is aware, and why he may be unaware.[2] One easy reason for his unawareness and lack of *feeling* for music is obviously the fact that he has been educated away from it, and that systematically. He has been indoctrinated in an anachronistic theory of music to the detriment of the Muse that is within him. The Muse never gets out; its way is blocked by education in the trade harmony and history of the pedagogue. *Aisthesis*, rather than esthetics, is thus the *feeling response* of a person to the experience of a work of art, in this case a musical composition. And yet this response is not merely to a physical stimulus; rather it is that "bodily" sensitivity and awareness that lets the experience happen, that lets the sound in (past the border guards of theory and history), that lets the Muse out, lets it respond or call back vocally or instrumentally to the composer, as he works with his "sounding numbers" or with his natural or electronic sounding devices. This natural response allows for the cultural incorporation of man in the era in which he lives. He can "get with it" and be part of it, rather than be bogged down with a clutter of basically irrelevant categories from another age. *Aisthesis* is bodily response to the sound of music, a response that can mean one begins to dance or sing or remains in responsive silence. But this "bodily" response must not be understood only in the sense of a physical or physiological response. Man is not a composite of mind and body (or for the theologian: soul and body) but one living experiencing unit, who indeed experiences at different "levels" but is basically not dichotomized as a human being. We had to learn that we were dual. We do not experience ourselves in this manner. This becomes particularly evident in conducting a seminar on musical sound, as described above. If man is not dualistic but one live unit, then esthetics is neither intellectualistic nor sensualistic, though our split culture has indoctrinated us so to believe. The reality is that "third" dimension which philosophers like Berkeley, to use an absurd example, rejected even as a possibility. The third possibility is simply that man is *one*, uncomposed of "soul" and body, or as Nietzsche put it, of that superstitious leftover, "psyche." Delivered of the impositions of theology and its philosophical remains, man can breathe anew in the oneness of his bodily response to music, since he is a *bodily unit* by nature (though a duality of mind and body by indoctrination).

In using the word, *aisthesis*, instead of the metaphysical word, esthetics, we use the Greek word as a fascinating model, and as an interim term, until we can rehabilitate the word, feeling. In no sense do we attempt to restore the Greek world, which existed once and for all, but which in the brilliance of that once-ness became a model for all time, for all eras: the early Christian Platonic world of Byzantium, the middle ages, the renaissance, and perhaps once again for us. It is only in the sense of an interim word-model, that we conjure up the concreteness of the Greek word, *aisthesis*. Perhaps were we more aware of our Anglo-Saxon forebears we would have had recourse to the earthy words they gave us, some of which have survived, like the word, awareness. For in "sense perception" we are aware of musical sound, independently of any intellectualoid impositions or preconditioning. This awareness is not an item in a psychological theory but a bodily fact of life. It is precisely this general and musical awareness that is suppressed in conventional theoretical introductions to musical experience. In place of bodily awareness and sensitivity to esthetical values a pseudo-intellectual pedagogy is implanted, to keep the musician apart from that which he is doing, to become an intellectual and emotional block to the very quantitative occupation (music-making) he is engaged in. Such theory even builds up a reservoir of false guilt complexes in would-be composers, who in a naive moment may feel bad that they compose freely, rather than in accord with the pre-set categories they learned in class. In all of this, of course, the genteel theory professor will realize that the author is playing the devil's advocate. The better teachers in fact welcome such frank critique. Elsewhere the author has turned such criticism on himself and on musicology, which certainly demonstrates that "we are are all in this together."[2]

3. MUSIC EDUCATION AND MUSICOLOGY

We have described two "bad scenes," one in education as such and the other in esthetics. If we speak of both in terms of "esthetic education" one might expect that two bad scenes add up to some sort of catastrophe in music education (using that term to apply to all music educating, not just to what is known in the trade as "mus. ed."). But it need not be so, particularly if esthetics implies an awakened awareness, and education means not indoctrination but bringing out the Muse in us. The actual scene, of course, is one of fragmentation, a Kafkaesque situation in which purposely darkened ships pass each other in broad daylight in a "dark night of the soul." However, there are beginning attempts at enlightenment and cooperation between segments of music schools (musicologists actually speaking to anyone else) and within college or university departments (philosophers descending from their celestial chariots to speak with the music-making peasants). What could be is, again, fascinating.

Together, rather than apart, music educators, both in the general and in the specific senses, could work out a concrete philosophy and esthetics of music, that would be convincing both to philosophers and musicians, presupposed that both can "bend" a bit. Apparently philosophers and music educators in the specialized sense "think" more than ordinary plodding theorists and historians.[3] If such thought is not grounded in the basic musical facts of life, then it becomes a thing apart from the musical experience, with no relation to it, and thus is irrelevant. But if through joint effort a consensus could be worked out, initiated by marathon talkfests and even culminating in sensitivity and encounter sessions, perhaps there would be some hope that esthetics and music theory might one day not only meet but form the basis from which a more convincing theory could grow, a theory that addresses itself to the realities of the musical experience as such. Such a theory could be spelled out in its general principles as well as in detail, where music educator, musicologist, and musician suddenly experience that awakened awareness of reality which is the necessary predisposition of anyone working fruitfully in music theory or history.

This practical theory, emerging from the serious encounter of musical human beings (rather than from the alienated theories and counter-theories of pedagogues), could spell the difference between success and failure in our dealings with students, whether regular, honor, or graduate. Seminars would include a cross section of students and faculty in a colloquium that would bind people together and form the base of their mutual search. While it is not to be denied that some of this is already afoot, much more is needed; and enlightened individuals need to hear more about and from one another.

The conclusion to all this entails a closer focusing on the common musician, the special genius not excluded. Again, what is the "scene" with regard to the ordinary as well as even the extraordinary musician? Hindemith described the sad plight of the performer, giving endless recitals, endlessly pursuing the ever retreating phantom of fame, like his myriad counterparts, each conceiving himself as the center of the performing world. Meanwhile life issues are neglected or are seen but dimly on the periphery of this frantic and futile activity. Musicians are on a treadmill of epic proportions. And music schools are the ones that implant the false ideal of virtuosity and fame in the heads of every student, so that life becomes an endless series of unremitting stage appearances, even though the stages may not always be Carnegie Hall or Lincoln Center. Yet the musician rarely takes time to ask questions beyond the narrowest trade and technical problems, as important as they often may be. All this could be modified or changed, if during his graduate tenure he were able at least once in his life to plumb some depths and think some musical (and other) thoughts in addition to his obvious and often enviable performing technique. Even such an artist as Glen Gould has given up on the concert merry-go-round, restricting himself to solid study and select quality recordings. But treadmill activity is too often the musical "scene"; and the present description is not necessarily an absurd exaggeration of the actual state of affairs as it obtains on the American scene.

What could be — with a little communal effort — is a vastly different and more humane situation. Musicians could again become humanists who reflect on what they are doing and thus also become articulate both as teachers and even as writers. Even more, they could become conscious of the world around them to the extent of becoming involved in social and political changes, to which their very art could contribute greatly. As things stand now, it is the exceptional musician who is aware of anything more than the narrow range of activity which takes all his time. On the other hand, it is he, after all, who is bearing the brunt of performing, and even though he is on a kind of treadmill, he deserves more care and attention than what has been meted out to him thus far by the general and the academic society. He certainly deserves better by estheticians, many of whom seem to him unproductive, if not counterproductive.

What then is the ideal musician? Perhaps we must first ask ourselves what music is — another historic question. Though, again, we will be unable to answer the question to the satisfaction of either a Hegel or a Horowitz, the process of trying to answer will of itself yield some useful results. To a musicologist familiar with the history of music it becomes immediately apparent that our modern definition of music (and thus of the musician) is a narrow one indeed. Again we may be allowed to use the Greeks as a historic example, and perhaps as a useful model as well, for here the range of meaning granted to the word, music, is most enlightening. Without the Greeks we would not have the word, music, at all, as we would also lack the word, philosophy. The Greeks bequeathed their word on the cultural world of the Arabs, of the medieval ages, and on the modern world as well. The word, $\mu o \nu \sigma \iota \chi \eta$, is derived from the Muses themselves, who called man to the musico-cultural task of building up the arts and civilization. They called man to the challenge of discovering and cultivating both the arts and sciences. And music is usually an adjective modifying these nouns, thus: musical art, musical science ($\tau \epsilon \chi \nu \eta$ $\mu o \nu \sigma \iota \chi \eta$, $\epsilon \pi \iota \sigma \tau \eta \mu \eta$ $\mu o \nu$-$\sigma \iota \chi \eta$).

Thus music, as a word, has a broad cultural sense and refers alike to arts and sciences and to those dedicated to them. There was, of course, also a narrower meaning of music, as both vocal and instrumental (though the former predominated). Yet music was never considered a thing apart from life and general culture, something to be cultivated apart for the individual's own goals. Rather, the musician was one who felt himself as a part of his society; and the development of music went along with that of drama, dance, poetry, and cultic ritual. Musical potential (δύναμις) did not connote the possibility of virtuosity and fame but rather of character building in the sense of contributing to the ethos of a people, thus to be understood in a social rather than in an individual-istic or moralistic manner. Indeed, this is the way Plato himself understood it when in *The Republic*, IV, he inveighed against those musicians who would change the musical ethos, thus endangering the social order. We also note that for the Greeks music is not "esthetical." But it was part of their education, especially for the young, as the phrase, παιδεια μουσιχη, indicates sufficiently well. Music is thus not a sub-stantive either grammatically or culturally; it is an adjective that colors and qualifies general education, human potential, art, and science. Moreover it is a divine calling, as it were, to help the gods give character and shape to a people and to its cultural history. The Greeks were made of stronger stuff than our esthetes, and music pervaded the entire life of the state and of the individual.

Through the mediation of such figures as Augustine, Martianus, Capella, Boethius and others, Greek musical thought (though only fragments of actual music) became the basis of medieval and renaissance music theory, also con-ceived along broad cultural lines. It is from this source that we get much of our present musical vocabulary and concep-tuality, however modified by contemporary usage. For a medieval theorist like Jacques de Liège the *musicus* was not the vocalist or instrumentalist of today but rather the philo-sopher-mathematican who "delighted in the interplay of mathematical proportions" in musical consonances.[4] More-over, in the *Speculum Musicae* the entire universe from deity to diapente (the interval of the fifth) was mirrored. In the late renaissance and through to the high baroque era the musical model was no longer principally mathematical but rather rhetorical, i.e. music and speech (under the influence of the rediscovered Greek rhetorician, Aristides Quintillianus) were considered two facets of the same audial phenomenon. Music was meant to give the word more bodily meaning and finally to influence the whole man emotionally or "affectively." Here, too, music had a much broader meaning than in modern times. The narrowing down process actually began in the last century, when, overwhelmed with the output of the Romantic composers, pedagues took refuge to studies on form, analysis, and harmony. They, not humanists or composers, got control of music schools; and thus to the present day the music student is not educated in the humane arts, as described, but rather in the narrow pedagogy of the nineteenth century schoolmaster.

Hence, the way out of what *is* to what *could be* will certainly be fraught with political difficulties and tempests in teapots. But it is worth initiating such an effort, if musicians are to be part of their culture and world, as well as being expert guildsmen. Even the guilds of the middle ages demanded thorough knowledge of one's culture, though such practitioners of the various arts were unfortunately never accepted at higher social and academic levels. The story of the social emancipation of the lowly musician is one of pathos and struggle, as we trace the gradual progress made from the wretched jugglers of the Provence to the court musicians of the renaissance the baroque; and beyond this to Haydn, dressed in the livery of a common servant of the court of Eszterhazy, to Mozart, sitting with menials at the foot of the Archbishop of Salzburg's table (after his return from Paris). Apparently, it was Beethoven who first successfully asserted the social independence of the musician, and from him it is one gigantic step into the modern era.

Our title indicates that what we are proposing is an entire esthetic re-education for musicians, and by implication also for musicologists, philosophers, and estheticians. Beginning where the author is actually at, this means an awakened awareness to the experience of musical sound as such, and as an essential part of our whole culture. This re-education will have to be done by music educators who have re-educated themselves by pooling their resources with colleagues and students; for re-education can only be convincing as a communal affair. We teach one another. One learns a great deal from students in a seminar, and hopefully they learn something from you and from one another, particularly if the teacher does not dominate the communal sessions but guides them in the direction of listening and learning (rather than indoctrinates them in some method espoused by himself). In practice, it means that musicians are going to have to be a bit more "theoretical" than they are used to being, and philosophers and estheticians are going to have to be a bit more "practical."[5] In the encounter between theory and practice, perhaps we can attain a living *praxis*, which is the ground on which we build a truer musical and humane culture, one in which both thinker and doer unite (sometimes in one person), perhaps using the Greeks as a classical model. If this can be initiated, the present impasse can be countered, and perhaps we can find our way not only to a more convincing modern synthesis but also find our way back to one another as human beings living in the world and dwelling together on the earth.

Endnotes

1.   Cf. "A seminar on sound," forthcoming in *The Journal of Aesthetic Education*.
1a.   Cf. *Aisthesis and Aesthetics*, eds. E. Straus and R. Griffith (Pittsburgh, 1970); contribution by the present writer, "Toward a Phenomenology of musical esthetics."
2.   F. J. Smith, *Commentary on the Speculum Musicae*, II (Basel/NY, 1971), p. 139, "Does musicology need a new method?"
3.   A. Motycka, "Musicians in education or educators in music" in *Triad, Official Publication of the Ohio Musical Education Association*, May 1970, p. 7ff.
4.   F. J. Smith, "A medieval philosophy of number: Jacques de Liège and the *Speculum Musicae*" in *Arts Libreaux et Philosophie aux*

Moyen Age (Montreal/Paris, 1969), pp. 1023-1039.

5.   H. Khatchadourian, "Family resemblances and the classification
      of works of art" in *The Journal of Aesthetics and Art Criticism*,
      28/1, 1, Fall 1969, pp. 79-90. This essay is a good example of
      relevant writing with regard to the arts. What the author has to
      say on music (p. 80ff.) has been taken up by the present writer in
      "Mozart re-visited: K550, the survival of baroque figures in the
      classical era" in *The Music Review*, August 1970. One of the finest
      foundation philosophies is to be found in R. Ingarden's *Unter-
      suchungen zur Ontologie der Kunst* (Tubingen, 1962), Das
      Musikwerk, pp. 3-138; cf. also H. de la Motte, "Uber de Gegens-
      tande and Methoden der Musikpsychologie" in the *International
      Review of Music Aesthetics and Sociology* (Zagreb, 1970), 1.
      1, pp. 83-89.

Chapter 9

IMPLICATIONS OF PHENOMENOLOGY FOR MUSIC EDUCATION

To a greater extent than is realized outside the specialty music education is the philosophy of "music in action." By contrast music theorists or musicologists often rely too much on a received deposit of faith, as it were, and much effort is given to the technology and content of these specialties without too much energy being spent on a philosophy of music that would underlie what lies ahead. Obviously, there are exceptions, but generally music theorists relegate philosophy of music to the sidelines in favor of "doing" even theory. Music educators — despite inadequacies and failures — have at least sought to reflect on both the content of music and on the methodology of learning and teaching. This reflective attitude has gone along with the actual situation of bringing music to masses of children and young adults; and, although some of the literature seems to the trained philosopher not to be consistently or adequately worked out, the fact remains that significant work has been done in terms of a practical philosophy of music educating. As to the trained philosopher, too often he is talking to an equally well trained elite, rather than to those actually at work in the difficult and often tumultuous arena of music education. His more precise acquaintance with the history of ideas needs embodiment and especially testing in the practical activity of the music classroom or seminar. This does not imply a vulgarization of ideas, nor does it turn philosophy into a serviceable tool for practical activities; yet an astute application and testing of ideas and concepts under the existential conditions of learning and teaching is required. Very often ideas will not survive under such realistic conditions and will then be viewed only as a part of history. Very frequently ideas will emerge from living praxis. Perhaps they should originate here. A good deal of serious music education literature has shown an astuteness in this regard. The professional philosopher should not be above the arena of actual work, nor should he adopt a condescending or patronizing attitude toward those who invade his terrain for insight and ideas. There have been vulgarizations, of course, on the part of educators, musical and otherwise, and here the task of the philosopher becomes apparent. As resource person he can point out false paths, provide cogent criticism, abet the philosophical education process. We base ourselves not on mistakes made by any profession or specialty. Our basis must be principle and that experiential praxis that tests principle. In this we evoke the shades of such American philosophers as Peirce, James, Dewey, and more recently, Suzanne Langer. But it was not only Langer who wrote that pure factual knowledge does not constitute a mental life. Edmund Husserl, the founder of phenomenology, also wrote that "out of facts come only more facts." And though Husserl himself is hardly above critique from several significant contemporary viewpoints, the music educator is inclined to ponder such statements like a philosopher. But he will also attempt to put thought to action in the classroom, and it will become a factor in his developing music curriculum beyond the fact-imparting stage of the classic teacher. This particular insight has in fact brought music education beyond imparting rudimentary facts and skills — as important as that is — along the road to conceptual understanding of music as a process and toward a psychology of music as directly pertinent to music learning and teaching.

1. MUSIC EDUCATION AND PHILOSOPHY

The phrase, "philosophy in action," is offensive to traditional philosophers, for whom thought is a pure mental activity with little or no relationship to the world of sight and hearing, of touching and moving, to the world of social transformations. In short that kind of "mind" is out of touch with the realities of man's bodily and social being, human feeling, and the actual people that go to make up extant society. Such a philosopher of purist inaction is easily identifiable as a classic metaphysician, even though in modern dress. Almost like a recluse of old, he seeks thought and truth in some sort of mentalistic or idealistic Beyond. By contrast, phenomenology looks at concrete things, human and bodily subjectivity, and the relationship between them.

We can wed some of the concepts of Langer's philosophy of music and of mind with phenomenology, if we underscore her insistence on the primacy of feeling. For Langer mind in its most elementary form is not cognitive but esthetic. The key to mind in this case is feeling expressed in artistic form. The philosopher will recognize the classic dualism between the *aisthetón* (that which is felt) and the *noetón* (that which demands thought), as footnoted even in Kant's first *Critique*. Langer puts herself on the side of such thinkers as Nietzsche, a classical scholar and philologist, and Heidegger, the philosopher of Being, in reviving interest in this classic dualism. In writing further of the art object as "imbued with feeling" and seeming even to have a life of its own, one is tempted to say that Langer's thinking runs parallel to that of Husserl. For the art object is no ordinary or utilitarian object, though it may have ritual or even practical use. It has an affective quality that no ordinary object has. But, if it is described as imbued with feeling, whence this feeling? The phenomenologist would want to ask what the relationship is that obtains between the feeling subject and the object imbued with feeling. The relationship is probably identifiable as a primary "intention" (a conative tending-toward) or focusing of the artistic subject on the object of art. In other words, the feeling subject is the agent that imbues the artistic object with feeling, starting with the artist, of course, who through his art and skill so fashions the art object that other subjects can intuit and feel what he himself has intuited and felt in the object he has wrought. Although by cultural conditioning we are more inclined to apply this to the visual arts, as e.g. to a *Guernica*, which visually revives the feeling of cruel massacre, we can also grasp it audially, as e.g. in Beethoven's music to Schiller's *Ode to Joy* in its appeal to the embrace of the millions and masses. In music we do not speak ordinarily of the art object. In a real sense music is a "purer subjectivity" than the art experience, and the composer works with more fluid materials, the recreating of which requires more than stone or canvas but demands interpretative qualities on the part of other human subjects besides the composer himself. The non-composer musician has to enter into the very subjectivity of the composer; he does not merely reflect feeling off a work of stone or canvas.

Similarly, with the current distinction in music education texts between percept and concept. Unlike mentalistic philosophies, phenomenology does not set out to erect a classic conceptual empire, though it does promote understanding and deals with reducible concepts. But its great emphasis, particularly at the hands of Merleau-Ponty, is perception. It goes without saying that perception and understanding are at the heart of musical education today. In phenomenology perception is delivered from the impasse of both mentalistic and empiricist thinking. Percepts were traditionally based on an *idea* of perception, rather than on the thing perceived or the subject perceiving. Perception is the primary opening of the subject onto the object. It inaugurates and even founds knowledge, though not the specific operations of cognitive thinking. Perception is primarily "original" (*originaire*) in that it originates as well as merely receives passively. It is "bodily" rather than merely corporeal, empiricist, or mentalistic. Primary perception thus bridges the metaphysical distinction between bodiless mind and mindless body.

2.   A SEMINAR ON THE EXPERIENCING OF MUSICAL SOUND

At this juncture it might be useful to mention some practical work done with students at primary, college, and graduate levels in the phenomenology of sound. Begun at the college level, this seminar in listening was recently given experimentally also at the primary level (specifically grades, three, six, seven, and eight). At the college level and in graduate courses this seminar was most successful and could be conducted at a relatively high level of thought and discussion. At the primary level the seminar seemed to work best with grades three and six for reasons the writer has still to analyze. Junior High students did not seem amenable to such sessions, and the writer has not yet had a chance to try it out at the High School level. Whatever the case may be, the seminar was basically the same for all levels in its methodology, though obviously it had to be considerably modified to meet varying levels of maturation. Let it suffice for our present purposes simply to describe the phenomenological method used in such a learning-teaching situation.

The general structure of the class follows a definite pattern that is an embodiment of the phenomenological method, in that it begins with perception of music (rather than with mental sets or learned categories) and gradually leads to conceptual understanding through a number of intermediate steps. Consistent with phenomenological method all such concepts are not only achieved but also reduced to concrete content and "eidetic essence." At the very beginning or at primary levels no mention is made of either phenomenology or of such technical terms as reduction, noematic content, etc. Such things may be introduced at the end of an honors course or during a graduate level seminar. They lead from such a musical seminar into a more specialized seminar in phenomenology as such or at least guided readings and research. It is obvious that a teacher employing this method would have had to have basic exposure to phenomenology as such, a task facilitated perhaps by several good introductory seminars in Husserl, Merleau-Ponty, and Scheler.

At the first stage students, preferably sitting in a circle (or at times even holding hands in a circle), listen to given selections of music, often performed by a member of the class or the music teacher. Recordings are most useful, especially if there is good stereophonic sound available. But live performance by one or several people — or even choral performance of some kind by the entire circle — is even better. It is obvious that a circle of people also leads to dance; but that is beyond the present scope of this essay. Everything is based on this listening experience. And the music chosen can be from any era or composer. Once the selection has come to an end (and after a brief pause) the students are free to give expression to what they feel, whether by bodily movement or by verbalization. Here students are asked to give free vent to their impressions and feelings, rather than striving to give learned responses based on knowledge they might have of the particular music just performed. Some students, particularly children, will content themselves with bodily expression — particularly during the music. Most will give their feelings verbal expression of some sort. And here words seem truer to experience, since they no longer tend to be learned formulae. After the verbalizations comes a new stage, viz., analyzing one's impressions and verbalizations. Analysis is seen at this stage not as the logical breaking apart of segments of experience for closer examination, but as a focused reflecting on impressions and feelings, allowing them to fall by themselves into *feeling-structures* and shapes natural to them. But formal analyses may also emerge, and if they are bound to concrete feeling-structures they will now take on meaning they lacked before when they appeared to be merely mental sets, or learned formulae. Many specific "finds" will emerge resulting in questions and problems in music theory and music history, as well as what generally has passed for music esthetics. At this juncture the teacher can introduce general discussions with the help of performers, composers, and other music or philosophy and psychology faculty specially invited to plenary or interdisciplinary sessions. As a result of all this, an understanding of music both in its general and specific concepts is initiated. The concepts are no longer mentalistic, since the entire class began not with mere facts or mental sets but with experience itself. Moreover, the teacher will have also performed reductions on general and specific concepts of music as the seminar proceeded. Mental categories are thus not imposed but emerge from such an experiential situation. And they are "mental" in a different sense since they are born of experience, feeling, and a phenomenological analysis of musical impressions, further enhanced by the expertise of teacher and specialists.

A brief word on "facts" is also in place. In the reality of lived existence nobody deals only with facts, but rather with blocks of reality, like sound impressions, at first global and unanalyzed, later revelatory of patterns and structures. These blocks of reality impressions break down (and do not become mere analyzanda) into fields of sight, sound, feeling and insight. "Facts" are in fact really *hard facts*. And it is precisely this hardening process that precludes intuiting of larger blocks of reality. Facts are creations of narrowly focused and abstract minds. Not only myths but so-called facts keep us ignorant. Hard facts are hardened because of the functional nature they display; thus a narrowing and focusing process is initiated, and unless corrected can lead to total hardening and alienation from the complexity of reality, including musical life.

3. MUSIC IN THE SITUATION OF AMERICAN EDUCATION

Phenomenology, particularly with the dialectical moment restored, is meant to bring people out of their felt isolation and alienation from one another and reality. The state of incapsulation in one's own personal or collective ego is called "solipsism" (from *solus ipse*: me myself alone). Only in feeling dire solipsism is one motivated to overcome it in favor of communal as opposed to individualist identity and action. Husserl called this "intersubjectivity," since the transcended subject is now in touch with other subjects. Of course, in beginning with the individualist subject Husserl betrays the bourgeois origins of his thought. And whether he actually succeeded in overcoming the isolation of the individual subject and made real transit to a truly social subjectivity, the trend of his thinking is in this direction. It seems to this writer that a communal activity, like making music together — and learning to do so from the earliest possible age, whether at home, in school, in the community — is far more apt to get people actually doing what philosophers intend in the abstract.

A chamber ensemble is an excellent example of what can be done by musicians cooperating with one another. Here each performer, who outside the ensemble may be an outstanding soloist, has to accommodate his soloist tendencies and skills to the group. For, a good quartet sound is truly an *ensemble* or "together-sound," quite different from the sound of four soloists who happen to be performing simultaneously. (The writer's only criticism of quartets today is that they do not play only in smaller music rooms, where alone a good quartet sound resonates properly. In a large hall a quartet is more apt to strain to fill the large space, trying, as it were, to be a mini-orchestra, when it is nothing of the kind. This straining for a larger sound leads to considerable distortions, to say the least.) The same applies to a choir, an orchestra, a guitar group, a band, and even team-teaching. For, the players are doing in practice what the philosopher recommends in theory: overcoming individual ego or subjectivity for the same of the ensemble sound. The mistake of the abstract philosopher is not embodying his theory in living practice. Similarly, the musical ensemble would make a tragic mistake not to evolve good musical theory in terms of actual practice. Good theory and good practice must go together. Furthermore, good music theory fleshed out in practice (or emergent from a living musical praxis) is more than just good *music* theory. It also serves as a societal model. A family of four has to do in daily life more or less what a quartet does performing Mozart; only that families of whatever size are only recently beginning to realize that living together calls for considerable skill and insight and not merely good will. In like manner, general society is like a vast orchestra or choir. It needs a good conductor. But the conductor needs a good orchestra as well, and a good personal and musical relationship between them spells the difference between a great ensemble and a failing one. The musical model is applicable to school, to church, to government as well. For, good ensemble sound and all that implies is the very embodiment of intersubjectivity as opposed to isolation, alienation and breakdown. The mistake made by musicians is to feel — even as a good ensemble — that they are only professionals and thus somehow apart from the real world of everyday (except in their private lives), and that what they are doing does not bear on what general society is all about.

The actual situation in American general and musical education falls short, of course, of both the philosophical ideal and the musical model. Especially today there seems to be more breakdown than healthy restructuring in education. Perhaps this is what happens when we are in transit (hopefully) to a better theory and practice in the educational arena. In some of the best schools, for example, there often seems to be a lack of coherence with regard to general and even specific goals, and goals themselves too frequently seem utopian rather than realistic. There is often a precarious mixture of old and new, of static and progressive, with the result that a general and even dangerous drift occurs. And despite individual efforts this can mean low student and faculty morale and consequently less than ideal achievement. This applies also to music schools. Perhaps what is called for is a "phenomenological analysis" of the situation in terms of the very useful musical model just advocated. For, in the overcoming of isolationist and individualistic tendencies on the part of all, a whole new ensemble feeling is made possible; and with it may emerge sooner or later a truer

intersubjectivity of interest and achievement at all levels —
from getting a coherent program and music curriculum
together, to getting ourselves together as people able to
come out of our various forms of solipsism toward a more
palpable communal effort. In this case we have a further
enhanced model of ensemble work to contribute to general
society, viz., an entire music department or school patiently
working together (and willing to call in consultants to abet
the effort) as a going ensemble of people. This model could
provide society at large with an example of what can be
done when individuals become truly socially oriented, first
in terms of the mini-society they represent as a department,
and secondly in terms of being conscious of the societal
import of their emergent intersubjective musical life.

4. RESTORING THE DIALECTICAL MOMENT

Husserl was not amenable to the "dialectical" moment in
the human situation or in philosophy. Despite his slogan,
"back to the things themselves," he overlooked contra-
ductions within things themselves. The name of Hegel, the
modern originator of the dialectical method, can be found in
one stray appendix. Otherwise, Husserl studiously ignored
him. As a result his view of things seems flat and positivistic
compared with the inner dynamic of dialectical thought. In
this Husserl reflected an interbellum consciousness, that
dreaded facing the conflicts of life-struggle going on at a
terrifyingly accelerated tempo all about, a philosophical
consciousness suspended between two violent world wars
brought about by definite social and material causes that
ought to have interested philosophers of ideas. A thinker and
literateur like Max Scheler was far more realistic than his
great mentor, Husserl. Scheler was well aware of the socio-
logical moment of human existence, and his last lecture was a
call for peace. Yet phenomenologists in general neglected
both Scheler's relevance to social reality (with the exception
of someone like Alfred Schutz) as well as dialectical analyses

of reality — including the arts — perhaps because they were so busy "overcoming metaphysics." But dialectical thought has indeed been rescued from its Hegelian metaphysical matrix; and when brought down to earth, or rather, when read *out of* the contexts of social realities and human relationships, dialectics can tell us much about the material conditions of life and about contradictions in individuals and society. Culturally, we are conditioned to regard negation as a threat to our very subjectivity (read: ego), whether as an individual or as a given society. And yet negation is a natural part of growth and development. Pure positivity leads to sterile self-congratulation on the one hand or to dead-end dogmatism and even fanaticism on the other. Yet, if we grow, we have to negate ourselves at every stage ("putting off the things of a child . . ."). If we are to create a musical or social ensemble, we have to "negate" or modify our egos, both individual and societal. This is a creative negation, not the dreaded annihilation of what we have been. What we have been is indeed negated by a new stage of social or musical growth; but the materials of life or music are not merely taken away; their perduring and viable values are taken up into a new stage of growth. (The *taking-away* and the *taking-up* are both contained in the crucial Hegelian word, *aufheben*, which is at the core of the dialectical method.) Thus no new society builds on a vacuum. And, as Stravinsky states in his *Poetics of Music*, new music takes off from the ground of tradition. Those who truly share in the experience of communal growth need not fear to lose what they have or are. Rather, what they had and have been can be transformed and enhanced by a new level of consciousness and development. And, in music history it is not difficult to demonstrate how old materials were transformed and taken up into new choral and instrumental forms, achieving a new existence in a transformed manner. Here again, we have a musical model for society as such. And it can be stated that dialectical *growth* is of the very nature of therapy (*therapeia* = growth, not curing).

The Husserlian reductive process may well be even a

"static" form of the dialectical moment. The phenomenological reduction is meant to get at the concrete essence and
meaning of things, in that it brackets out bias and mental
frameworks in an approach to reality and ideas. In this process the relationship between the living subject and any
object is essentially redefined. So is the relationship between
two living subjects, when solipsistic ego has been reduced
in favor of meaningful social structure, whether it be
marriage, family, nation, or a music department.

Indeed, even the phenomenological reduction might
well be interpreted as the philosopher's typical abstract solution to a live and dynamic problem, and thus it might in fact
be a static form of dialectical process. The reduction itself
seems to begin as a negation of positive phenomena, but it
does not seem to continue beyond a definite point. At best
there is a series of reductions. But a series is not equivalent to
dialectical motion of process. Series proceed unilinearly and
positively, not cyclically as a dualism of positive and negative, of consonant and dissonant, and so forth. What reason is
there to sit around performing reductions on realities, what
motivation, what social context? The musician has a real
context, unlike the abstract thinker. In making music he not
only has to put notes together in ensemble, he also has to
abet the establishment of that interpersonal rapport, without
which a musical ensemble cannot survive as a performing
group, however good individual players might be profession-
ally. The results of a given reduction in phenomenology seem
free-floating, even individualistic in the context of the social
world, apolitical, strangely detached. But viewed dialectically,
the matter is considerably altered. The musico-social motivation is a powerful reason to "reduce" extant reality. What is
laid bare in such a reduction is not a contextless and free-
floating "essence" but the very foundation of personal and
social growth. And in such growth there is motive force,
strategy, and a coherent teleology or purposiveness. The
"life-world" of Husserl seems — as it stands — to be the
underpinning of a subjectivity unrelated to the life-struggle
going on all about. Were it rooted in the natural dialectic of

life-contradictions, the matter would be different.

The working musician in search of theory also contributes to the thinker in search of context and relevance. In the meeting of theory and practice (and in the subtle dialectical interplay between them) a whole new philosophy of music could emerge, no longer isolated from the society that surrounds the music department, but as a dynamic part of it, contributing not only good music to the community but providing also a viable social model of community and an exemplar case of the ensemble of thought and praxis.

Endnotes

1. G. W. F. Hegel, *Wissenschaft der Logik*, I, ed. G. Lasson, Hamburg, 1934/63. Note: It is interesting to note that Hegel speaks of the *rhythm* of the dialectical process (p. 36). He thereby lends a definite musical perspective to dialectics — something never emphasized by philosophers. Rhythm is of the ssence of the dialectical process. And thus, as with Husserl, music provided a viable model for philosophy. (Cf. F. J. Smith, "Musical sound as a model for Husserlian intuition and time-consciousness" in *The Journal of Phenomenological Psychology*, 3, 1973.)
2. Edmund Husserl, *Cartesian Meditations*, transl. D. Cairns, Den Haag, 1960.
3. Suzanne Langer, *Mind, An Essay on Human Understanding*, I, Baltimore, 1967.
4. Maurice Merleau-Ponty, *La phénoménologie de la perception*, Paris, 1945. "La metaphysique dans l'homme" in *Sens et nonsens*, Paris, 1948.
5. Arthur Motycka, "A musical model for an alternative arts in education program in the United States" in *Music and Man*, 1, no. 3, 1974; *Musico-Aesthetic Education: a Phenomenological Proposition*, Jamestown, 1975.
6. Thomas A. Regelski, *Principles and Problems of Music Education*, Engelwood Cliffs, 1975.
7. Bennet Reimer, *A Philosophy of Music Education*, Engelwood Cliffs, 1970.
8. Alfred Schutz, *Collected Papers*, II, *Studies in Social Theory*, cf. p. 159f, "Making music together, a study in social relationship" and p. 179, "Mozart and the philosophers," ed. Brodersen, The Hague, 1964. "Fragments on the phenomenology of music" in

Music and Man, 2, 1976, ed. Fred Kersten.

9.   F. J. Smith, "Toward a phenomenology of musical aesthetics" in
      Aisthesis and Aesthetics, eds. Strauss/Griffiths, Pittsburgh, 1968.
      Note: further bibliography in Motycka's *Musico-Aesthetic Educa-
      tion* (above), p. 34.

Chapter 10

PHENOMENOLOGICAL THEME WITH DIALECTICAL VARIATION

There are two main strains of contemporary philosophy, philosophical analysis and phenomenology, which also gave birth to existentialism. Philosophical analysis studies the import of the conceptuality imbedded in ordinary language and looks to such people as Ludwig Wittgenstein as mentor and guide. Phenomenology, though also involved with conceptuality, is primarily concerned with the flow of consciousness and its various strata. Edmund Husserl researched the relationship between consciousness and phenomena, attempting by means of a reductive process to set aside mentalistic frameworks to get at "the things themselves" and to lay bare the "essence" of phenomena. One of his students, Martin Heidegger, used phenomenology to evolve his own distinctive approach to Being, to what *is*, to what is incorrectly called an "ontology of existence." He thus forces phenomenology into the historical question of Being. Jean Paul Sartre fused this ontology with a rediscovered Hegelian dialectic and gradually came to be called an "existentialist." It is interesting to note that Husserl did not look kindly on Heidegger's efforts, and that Heidegger disavowed any connection with existentialism. However, the students of these various phenomenologists have made use of the insights of their philosophical mentors, and with the aid of psychologists like Merleau-Ponty and social philosophers like Max Scheler have created a body of writings on what can only be styled a "mixed" phenomenology. In addition, phenomenology has been criticized from the viewpoint of both philosophical analysis and of Marxist dialectics. For the present chapter we can only present the more lucid ideas of phenomenology briefly and then present a case for working at a certain level of consciousness in the attempt to descibe some of the import and tasks of akoumenology, i.e. the phenomenology of musical sound.

1. TIME-CONSCIOUSNESS AND AUDIAL PHENOMENA IN HUSSERL

Husserl looked to the example of musical tone and melody for his conception of time-consciousness. Due to his teacher, Carl Stumpf, Husserl was able to begin at a level that had already gone beyond preoccupation with sound as a physical phenomenon (Helmholtz) or as metaphysical speculation. Instead he was able to begin with time as actually experienced in the temporal sequence of a musical composition. From a description of this sequence emerged the patterns of human consciousness of time. Time is now regarded not as merely objective but as "subjective," i.e. as experienced by the human subject and contingent upon it. The experience of musical time embodies a whole network of temporal phenomena in a pattern of thrust and trail, thus according to Husserl, of "protentions" and "retentions." Experience is thus no longer regarded as monolinear but as diffuse and teleological, as a complex, multilinear patterning of human consciousness. Music is, as it were, a comet plumeting through subjective space, leaving a trail of after-echoes, a musical "tail" that is retained in memory. Memory is not, however, merely some sort of electronic storehouse for sense data; rather, it is a part of consciousness as elemental awareness. This memory awareness is a sublevel of consciousness into which the configurations of perceived data temporarily vanish, until such time as they may suddenly emerge on their own or are purposely recalled. Memory data can be recalled without any "mental activity," since awareness is a kind of passivity which knows of spontaneity. Husserl styled this complex process of the interconnection between activity and passivity as "passive synthesis." The forward thrust of musical time builds a horizon of expectations and possibilities for the composer as well as the listener. As the musical tone unfolds in its forward movement or "protension," it leaves in its wake a whole complex of tonal shadows which spread out in ever diminishing diagonal lines behind it. A diagram showing this, demonstrates the multilinear character of subjective time as opposed to the unilinear concept of objective time.

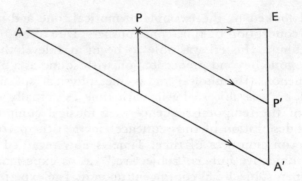

AE = series of "now-points" in musical tone duration
AA′ - evanescing of the sound
EA′ = phase continuum of present and past sounds
PP′ = tracing of one given point (or note)

(Source: F. Husserl, *Zur Phänolenologie des inneren Zeitbewusstseins*, p. 28.)

This diagram emphasizes the forward thrust. It can be further elucidated by ancillary attempts to demonstrate the after-echoes of retention in consciousness (see diagram p. 233).

The point of such diagrams and verbal descriptions as given is to show that musical sound (or any sound) is not limited to linear objectivity, though it obviously has a solid base in it. Rather, we hear globally, synthetically, not as the mind turns actively toward phenomena conceived in linear terms but "passively" as the melody takes shape in audial perception. The implications for analysis of music are

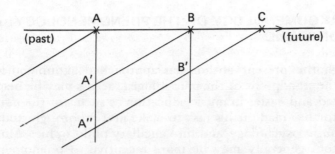

ABC = series of nows in horizontal line
oblique lines = aftershadows of individual now-points
vertical lines = phase continuums

(Source: M. Merleau-Ponty, *La phénoménologie de la perception*, p. 477, his own improvisation on Husserl.)

immediately apparent. Analysis must not be based primarily on objective schemata, actively engaging learned categories of the mind; rather it must become a way of transcribing the global audial phenomena in its passive synthesis. Traditional musical analysis has been almost totally preoccupied with mental activity vis-a-vis musical objectivity; but now we must deal with musical perception and human consciousness or subjectivity and its synesthetic activity. Of this, mental "activity" is but a superstructural stratum of consciousness.

Perception can be obstructed by overreliance on analytical categories, which then function as perceptual depressants, even as suppressants of the natural erotic content of musical sound. What Husserl attempted to break through was the mathematicizing of human consciousness and perception, that had gone on for centuries previously. The phenomenologist is thus not bent on building up a conceptual empire but on describing perceptual content and arriving at the understanding of things (and tones) shorn of their purely mentalistic frameworks.

2.   AKOUMENOLOGY OR THE PHENOMENOLOGY OF SOUND

Though the present author has approached akoumenology from the standpoint of the musicologist, access may be better prepared and easier in music education as such, for the music educator has made it his task to make more thorough studies into music psychology and into ancillary philosophies. Music educators generally may be more receptive to phenomenology than musicologists, whose present horizons seem inordinately restricted to historical and technical questions. Music educators deal with people primarily, and thus the problem of musical perception is faced more directly than by the historians, preoccupied with transcribing old music, often enough without even having firsthand knowledge of the theoretical treatises from which practical transcription rules were gleaned.

Instead of searching for an intellectual grid, whether philosophical or mathematical, through which to filter musical experience, the "akoumenologist" brackets out such mentalistic frameworks in favor of coping with the sound experience *as such*. Let us give a good contemporary example by citing John Cage's composition, *Indeterminacy*. This piece is scored for any and all sounds, including a narrator's voice. To the traditionalist this is no truly musical composition at all, but the work of a court jester or anarchist. According to Cage *all* sounds are material for musical composition, including the sounds of daily life and work. In such an attitude we truly get back "to the things themselves" (Husserl) and cease forcing sound into a historically conditioned mental-audial set, where it qualifies as "music." *Indeterminacy* consists of a series of anecdotes, some amusing, which are consistently interrupted by assorted sounds, produced by a piano, a radio, the tape of a barking dog, noises concocted on an electronic synthesizer, etc. The total effect is to make it quite difficult and sometimes impossible to follow the *meaning* of the words of the narrative. It becomes obvious that this very meaning is being bracketed out by the interference. One is forced to the conclusion that Cage meant only the *sounds as such* to count, whether they be noise, instruments, random sounds, or the human voice narrating whatever. All else, including "meaning" is bracketed (which does not mean destroyed!), and only sound is then thematized in consciousness. Meaning in the traditional sense is at the very least interfered with, pointing to the possibility of its being completely bracketed out in intent. One realizes in a practical sense what Husserl meant by "nóema," the content remaining after primary bracketing takes place. Thus any semantic meaning is at best secondary. What is liberated is the experience of sound as such, to which superstructural experience, such as various audial sets, can be added in a new and meaningful manner. At the everyday level, we often do this ourselves, when we start listening to the quality and intonations of people's *voices* as such, to get at what they are "really" telling us in propositional form.

Husserl addressed himself to the speech phenomenon as well, when he wrote that the phenomenological analyst does not deal merely with judgments based on correctly propositioned sentences, but rather that he attempts to *look directly* at the phenomena which speech conjures up. He looks at — or listens for — the "things themselves," as they begin to appear in the web of words we weave about an experience we have had. Words thus have no other function than to serve as indices for a whole context of experienced phenomena, for a whole world of "noematic" meaning. At this level of consciousness words are and remain *sounds* that indicate *things* in a world context. This might well approach what one philosophical analyst calls "extra-linguistic analysis."

3. THE NOTION OF "PASSIVE SYNTHESIS" EXPANDED

Our traditional conceptuality is captive of any number of dichotomies born of the history of philosophy and metaphysics. One such dualism is that of active vs. passive. Thus, for example, a man is said to be active, while a woman is supposed to be by nature passive. There is no middle ground between these two extremes, and thus a good deal if not most of our ordinary experience, from making love to listening to music, is not adequately covered by such concepts imbedded in ordinary language. What is "passive synthesis," meant to help bridge the dualism of active vs. passive? And how does it bear on the musical experience? According to Husserl, passivity is not merely passive behavior, whether in being made love to, or listening to music. In the latter case the activity of the orchestra or instrumentalist(s) is juxtaposed to the passivity of the audience. Or, a musical composition lies there passively for the active theorist to analyze. But pure awareness of musical sound is not merely a passive process anymore than even sense-perception is mere receptivity for sense data. For perception has its own type of phenomenological "intentionality" (or "active striving"), independent of merely mental activity. It is even a precondition for such activity. Sounds come together, as it were, of themselves, for the listener, independently of his mental activity. The synthetic character of perception has here been thematized, i.e. perception not only receives but "actively" puts data together in human consciousness. And in musical sound the original sound impressions received from whatever instrument(s) acquire a synthetic unity of their own in the temporal process of impression, retention, and protension, as already graphed above. This is done independently of what we traditionally have called conscious activity.

The dovetailing of activity and passivity in ordinary experience leaves its mark on the language we use. This is more immediately obvious in classical languages (Greek) and continental languages (French, German, etc.), though it can certainly be looked for also in English. Thus Husserl states that in this synthetic process a thing builds itself, achieves and constitutes itself in consciousness. One notices these are all reflexive forms. Passive synthesis is thus self-action, the action of human perceptive consciousness on itself, so that the "passivity" of listening to music (or speech) is a shaping up of the music *itself*, of sound contexts *as such*. This notion is also fundamental to an understanding of what Carl Stumpf, a teacher of Husserl, wrote of the amalgamation of musical sounds, come together now not merely in physical (or for the analyst in chordal) fusion, but in human perceptive *consciousness*. Passive synthesis is thus on middle ground between the extremes of the speculative distinction of active vs. passive. But it is on this middle ground rather than at the poles of mentalistic distinctions that most human experience takes place. The student of classical languages knows that the Greeks had a special "middle voice" for this experiential arena of self-action. Modern languages lost this middle voice but retained the middle ground in the reflexive forms of the verb. In the mediation between subjective listener and objective sound the subject is drawn into and becomes a part of the world of music; he is no longer merely a passive spectator, uninvolved in the total process of music itself.

Musical *experience* takes place on the middle ground of passive synthesis. Musical sounds fall together in synthetic patterns in my experiencing of a sonata or symphony. The music is something that "happens" to me, but as a unified and structured happening. I am "passive" as this symphonic happening comes over me. I am affected by the experience, but it happens in a self-structuring consciousness, and thus not merely passively. The sounds of music, whether a symphony or a composition by somebody like John Cage, put themselves together for me in perception and present themselves to my consciousness. The listening process is a self-structuring of my consciousness in "active" response to the sounds that give themselves presentially to me in perception. Tones and colors are, as it were, the materials consciousness works with, even in its "passivity." These tonal data continually constitute themselves, put themselves together (thus: syn-thesis), in a process of temporal becoming. They do not exist merely as objects which *are*; they are continually being shaped in a composition that builds itself gradually and *becomes* a musical composition as such.

Receiving is not an inert or passive matter. To receive a

gift we extend our hand to receive it. The act of receiving is a responsive action. Thus also, in listening to speech or music means "lending one's ears." An animal's ears are even suddenly erected to facilitate this active response of listening. Humans often cup their hand to an ear to catch a sound more fully. Sounds are thus not merely inert data; they are there as *given*, eliciting a response, whether in consciousness or even in bodily action. On this middle ground of the phenomenology of the listening process words or music take shape, constituting themselves in our awareness, making us not inert but creative listeners.

From moment to moment the living subject achieves a higher degree of synthesis in consciousness, as the subject constitutes itself in passive synthesis, which is actually the basis of any superstructural passivity or activity in the ordinary sense. As to music itself, sound perdures from moment to moment and remains synthetically one throughout all such moments. But it remains one not merely in some sort of abstract unilinear sense; while remaining one continuum it builds form, such as, e.g., that of a sonata or symphony. This form-building temporal synthesis comprises the leading edge of temporal movement (the "protention" in Husserl's language) as well as the trail of after-echoes (the "retention" in Husserl), fusing them into one continuously conscious structure. Thus, though the musical experience can be fragmented in its physical unity, or cut apart piece by piece by an analyst, in consciousness it is not a mere series of sounds but retains its essential identity throughout. And even with regard to various musical entries, as, for example, in a fugue, each new musical line joins the others already in progress not as a separate analyzable series of notes (though physically it can be extracted for analysis) but as a line that in fusing with the rest of the music — however disparate its various parts — forms one continuum in musical consciousness as such. Time-consciousness is thus the "primordial place" for the constitution of musical unity and identity, as well as the source of the connective forms of the coexistence and succession of objects (or notes) in consciousness.

Time-consciousness is in reality the origin of what we call form.

The musical analyst is tempted to say that a sonata, as form, simply exists objectively in the musical score or in the physical reproduction of the sound, whether live or on record. Actually, such form is constituted at the pre-analytical stage in the perceptive consciousness of both performers and listeners. It is, of course, a fact that the composers of the classical period, which we now look to for analyzable sonatas and symphonies, did not think at all overtly in terms of the sonata-allegro form so pedantically and meticulously graphed by pedagogues of the nineteenth and twentieth centuries. At the very most, Mozart "thought" in terms of what the classical theorist, C. Koch, called "tripartite division" (Drei-teiligkeit), which referred not to the first movements of sonatas, where sonata-allegro form is characteristically sought and found, but to the entire sonata as a whole. In a letter Mozart even states that he conceived his compositions as a whole, that he heard the entire sonata or symphony within himself, before he ever set it down on paper. This was not an analyst but a composer at work, and the level of conscious-ness of the two is hardly the same. The composer, carried on the stream of creative consciousness, conceives his work as a whole; the analyst regards it as capable of being de-composed into fragments he can subject to categorial treatment. The listener is far closer to the composer in his conscious response to a work, than is the analyst. Both classical composers and theorists thought about music much more phenomeno-logically than subsequent analysts, who try to visualize every-thing, rather than let the audial experience remain dominant in analysis, and who instead of viewing music as a global audial experience regard it either mentalistically as fodder for certain categories or physically as acoustical materials.

Stating that the voices of a fugue or the vocal lines of a medieval composition (e.g. of the *ars antiqua*, best exempli-fied by the Codex Bamberg) fuse with the rest of the voices, does not connote that they lack their individuality, including even "time signatures." Voices of medieval music were often

conceived independently of one another, and yet precisely
such individualistic musical lines are meant to sound together
within the principles of mathematically conceived consonances. This *sounding together* was in fact the exact meaning
of *con-sonantia*. The perceptual process we have been describing was formalized and subsumed under a theory of
consciousness that was metaphysical and mathematical. And
thus despite the fact the voices were often conceived independently, by force of the theory of proportionality they
came together as consonances at key points above a foundation voice or *tenor*. This base voice (called the "holder" or
tenor of the musical edifice) was not a bass voice as in
functional harmony but was the architectural base or foundation of a consonantal column or pillar which the other voices
were expected to help build. These musical columns were not
unlike the cathedral pillars that held up arches and roof. The
model is, at any rate, an architectural and mathematical one.
This was regarded, we might say, as the objective portrayal
of the structure of perceptual consciousness for the medieval
listener. Perception is secondary to the enjoyment of this
mentalistic structure, in itself certainly a great achievement.
Metaphysics, at least outside theology, was indeed regarded
as not beyond reality but firmly imbedded in it. The mistake
was not so much that there existed a metaphysical structure,
but that it supplanted or at least blocked or depressed
perceptuality. The intellect is meant to delight in the interplay of mathematical proportions in music, stated the
medieval theorist Jacques de Liège, but, of course, the ear's
perception was the port of entry to such mathematically
conceived consciousness. For most listeners it was still a fully
musical experience in our sense; the metaphysicians were,
after all, but an elite. In their view the mathematician had
the highest possible musical experience, far better than the
ordinary untutored hearer.

4. THE AMALGAMATION OF MUSICAL SOUNDS

Most students of introductory musicology have heard of Carl Stumpf's theory of the amalgamation or fusion of sounds. Few if any realize that he was a teacher of Husserl and that Husserl took up where his teacher left off on this theory. Briefly, musical tones are not merely physically merged, nor are they simply part of some mathematical schema in the mind, when we speak of a musical composition. Rather, tones fuse in the consciousness of the perceiving subject. A musical interval, as e.g. of a fifth, does not consist merely in the concurrence of two tones. Rather, in sounding together they fuse in consciousness into a new entity. Fusion is given primordially in perception itself, so that the sound, e.g., of a fifth, is essentially different than the sound of each of its components singly or merely concurrently. It is thus not a conscious activity on our part but a fact of musical awareness. Tones enter alert consciousness as *already fused* into the entity we call a fifth. Formal amalgamation of tones is a fact of the primary continuity and unity of perception within a given field of perception. Especially in temporal sequence such fusion consists in the progressive building of compositional unity. Affective fusion has to do with sensations that directly affect consciousness, even though such sense data may never actually attain to being a conscious state. Affective fusion is there as a stratum of musical experience, and active consciousness builds on it with or without direct reference to it. The implications of this for questions of musical form and of esthetics is immediately apparent. The restricting of analysis to mental sets which reduce music to materials to be analyzed is in reality an avoidance of the global spectrum of analyzable musical experience, but also of truer form.

5. CONCLUSION

Akoumenology thus broadens the range of analysis of music

to the inclusion of a phenomenological description of the musical experience as such, musical phenomena not merely as they appear physically on paper or acoustically in audial space but as the "noematic" content of human consciousness. Phenomena are not only those things that are to be found in nature or in physical fact but the bodily essence of things as they manifest themselves to human consciousness in perception. But for this a reductive process is required, which consists in bracketing out purely mental sets and metaphysical conceptuality, so that it becomes indeed possible to get at the "things themselves," liberated from the incrustations of superstructural theory and the weight of learned traditions and techniques. Recovering the "essence" of a thing has little to do with the metaphysician's penchant for peeling off the rings of the onion, to find its "essence" only as he discards the last ring and with it the whole onion. Instead he is like the lover, who takes away one veil after the other from Istar, so that she may be revealed finally in all her bodily presence and allure. Thus in listening to a musical composition, be it one of Mozart's or of Cage's, we are free truly to *listen*, having laid aside prejudices that force a Mozart to be a pedant when he was a classicist, or a Cage to be a traditional composer when he is actually most innovative.

In conclusion, a critique of the phenomenology of subjective perception is useful, not to undo what we have achieved but rather to enhance it. In terms of dialectical thought phenomenology of perception is too individualistic, in that truth is whatever I perceive with clarity. Though the social element is hardly missing from phenomenology and has been greatly enhanced by the efforts of such thinkers as Sartre, Merleau-Ponty, Schutz, and others, the nature of these researched interactions between performer and recipient or hearer seem entirely determined by the subject, almost eliminating the substance of the world we live in as a palpable (and audible) reality. The world as it exists, whether of sound or of social reality, is presupposed — yes, even in existentialism — to remain more or less the same. And over against this opaque sameness the individual subject may perform any number of personally "redeeming" acts, such as the truer listening we have described above. But the concrete nature of the society that still lurks at the periphery of the reductions performed to unveil Istar remains abstract and unanalyzed, in effect if not in intent. Society in its total reality, including the dynamic potential of music-in-society, remains abstract at best, alien at worst. In dialectical philosophy the individual must not only perform a necessary reduction on the theoretical world, in order to liberate his senses for musical and esthetic experiences, he must further reduce his preoccupation with his newly achieved subjectivity, so that he can re-enter the world and its society in terms of social participation. And in the light of his recent internal achievements he is now geared to be an agent of active change in the particular society he is in. For, how can he *not* want to help bring about change in the light of his internal progress? And since, in this view, every aspect of human behavior is understood as mediated through material and social conditions of the actual world we live in, an analysis of the "real world" — along with our analyses of the music that is performed and heard within it — enables the perceptive person to join others in developing alternatives to the frustrating established world we are presently locked into. The final purpose of a phenomenology of sound, to which the internal dialectic of the individual vis-a-vis society has been restored, is not only to enhance one's own individual musical perception, but to see it also in terms of the social order, as one of many paths that has to be taken in bringing about needed changed. The change consists both in the enhancement of the subject's perceptivity and in the co-subjective projecting of a truly more perceptive social order, in which music is not an escape or a mere pleasure, but a crucial and essential part of life.

Endnotes

1. Edmund Husserl, *Zur Phänomenologie des inneren Zeitbewusst-seins*, Husserliana X, (Den Haag, 1966); *Analysen zur passiven Synthesis*, Huss. XI (1966).
2. M. Merleau-Ponty, *La phénoménologie de la perception*, (Paris, 1945).
3. Carl Ratner, "Principles of dialectical psychology," in *Telos*, no. 9, Fall 1971, pp. 83-109.
4. Alfred Scutz, "Fragments on the phenomenology of sound," ed. F. Kersten, in *Music and Man*, vol. 2, Fall 1976.
5. F. J. Smith, "Vers une phénoménologie du son" in *Revue de métaphysique et de morale*, 1968; "Further insights into a pheno-menology of sound" in *The Journal of Value Inquiry*, 1969; "Some notes on the meaning of analysis" in *Philosophy Today*, 1971; "Aesthetic re-education: the experiencing of musical sound," in *Music and Man*, 1973; "Prelude to a phenomenology of sound" in *Main Currents of Modern Thought*, 1973; "Musical sound as a model for Husserlian intuition and time conscious-ness" in *The Journal of Phenomenological Psychology*, 1973; "Music theory and the history of ideas" in *Music and Man*, vol. 2, Fall 1976.

Postscript:

THE "END" OF PHILOSOPHY:
THE MUSER AND MUSIC-MAKER

In a sketch on the "last philosopher" Nietzsche pronounces philosophy since Kant dead. We might say, that not only is God "dead" but also the philosopher. And here we speak of the end of metaphysics in its traditional meaning. Kierkegaard thought along similar lines in his critique of Hegelian philosophy. Both Kierkegaard and Nietzsche stand as prophetic figures at the close of an era, and their spirit rises up again in postwar existentialism. They both called for a return to the concrete, to the flesh-and-blood dimension, to the earth. Is existential philosophy a kind of prophetic last philosophy? Does it lead to another philosophy or does it lead back into life, where philosophy is seen to be but a transitional stage of thinking in the history of human development? Let us attempt to explore the possibility, that philosophy, as such, may be but a temporary stage in the development of thinking, and that philosophy and thought are by no means identical. Just as theology was but a stage out of which we had to grow, perhaps philosophy is also a transitional matter only.

We know that there was a long, long time before anything like "philosophy" existed, and we realize that it is dated as to time and place. The word "philosophy" goes back most likely to Pythagoras and Heraclit, just as the term "first philosophy" goes back to Aristotle. It recurred in Latin Aristotelianism, in the philosophy of Descartes, and that of Edmund Husserl. Obviously this is not the place to discuss the discrepancies of first philosophy from these historic perspectives. But it might be more meaningful to begin to ask about a last philosophy. A definite stage of this "last philosophy" was the first philosophy itself, especially as metaphysics. It is particularly this tradition which Nietzsche criticized and which Heidegger felt must be overcome. Into the hollow shell of metaphysics, cast off by philosophy, have crawled all kinds of "thinkers" who have made a home there, Kierkegaard informs us in somewhat caustic terms. But does "philosophy" go on and on? Or does it, too, like the men who invented it, and outside of whom it has no real existence, live and die? Is it just a question of casting off stages of existence, or is "existence" itself a last stage, which is also cast off — and nothing crawls out of the old burnt out stage? Rather, the last philosophy is succeeded by no new one at all. The last philosopher is simply the last philosopher, who may pass on with an unnoticed sigh or a brief whimper. Even Kierkegaard's "second philosophy" (*Wiederholung*) seems to have passed away. We can hardly agree with L. Richter and J. Wahl that Kierkegaard was more "existential" than Heidegger. After all, Nietzsche's "God is dead" stands between Kierkegaard and Heidegger, to say nothing of Sartre and Merleau-Ponty.

This is a somewhat frightening thought for anyone who wants to (or has to) hold on to philosophy as if it were something everlasting, as if philosophy really had to be *perennis*. Bach was able to sing, "Come sweet Death," but there are few theologians willing to welcome the factual demise of theology and still fewer philosophers ready to admit the end of philosophy. This does not mean the end of concrete "thinking," at least not until the end of man. And the end of man, as man, is something nobody wants to face, especially in an atmosphere of progress, in which things supposedly get better and better and man becomes smarter and smarter. There are various props that hold up such illusions. We need not go into them at present. The end of man, as an individual or as a race, is intimately bound up in the beginning of man, as an individual and as an assortment of races. There was no provable necessity for man's emergence, as man, and there is really no provable necessity for man's continuance as man. There is no reason why he may not turn into something else

— not necessarily a "higher being" — or why for that matter he may simply cease to be at all. If we are incapable of facing this possibility, we are not able to face the life we already have. And with man goes man's thought.

According to Huizinga's *Homo Ludens*, philosophy was born in sacred play, and the whole technique of problem and solution goes back to the man's busying himself with puzzles, especially the puzzle of the universe. Philosophy was born of a kind of "theological" play-mentality. Only gradually did philosophy become "secularized." Only gradually was it split off from theology — as late as the fourteenth century, when it still maintained a relationship with theology. And later, of course, unlike his forebears (Descartes, Spinoza, Leibnitz), Kant challenged the whole theological underpinning of traditional metaphysics. If philosophy is dead since Kant, then it is so because of its theologico-metaphysical basis. Perhaps only in our era, when by bracketing God, as did Husserl, or by coming back to the earth and physis as does Heidegger, or the "bodily" dimension with Merleau-Ponty, do we have a first philosphy free from pseudo-theological implications.

But this very first philosophy of our era might indeed be the last philosophy also, in that it will lead us back into a direct contact with things and realities, and we shall have no felt need for the mediation of philosophical abstractions. Huizinga feels that Nietzsche led philosophy back into the agonal dimension of the Greeks. Heidegger and Nietzsche both tried to regain a genuine understanding of the pre-Platonic world. But this, only after the gods and the metaphysical god of Christianity had been pronounced dead. The Greek gods died of laughter; the metaphysical god was killed by his own theologians, who, now godless, turn upon atheists in order to vent their wrath. But even atheists talk too much about God! It were better perhaps to admit the demise of traditional deities and look at things as they are, rather than as they are imputed to be according to some untenable world cosmogony and theology. Perhaps the demise of theology entails the demise of philosophy also. And what comes afterwards is simply life itself, lived and enjoyed and suffered for what it is, rather than for what it is held to be.

Philosophy is in a transitional period. Some of us feel that especially phenomenology best represents this stage of our existence, but we hasten to say that phenomenology is no eternally true philosophy, all exclusive, well categorized, formulated and institutionalized so as to be able to last a thousand years. It is only one way of approaching matters in our fluid age. It is only preparatory for the future. It itself is but transitional. But does it make transition toward another philosophy, or does it lead us out of the *monde-en-idée* into the world itself, a world which may feel no particular need for philosophizing and is that much better off for it? Perhaps we are making transit not over to a new philosophy — which will keep us academicians well fed for another decade — but simply back into the lived world, where in order to live you may have to do something more creative than rearranging somebody else's thoughts. Perhaps in the new world we shall occupy ourselves with something else than "philosophy." And we may even find that we will be just as nicely fed.

The beginning of a thing is its end also. As soon as we begin to live we begin to die, and this does not mean just physical demise. Death does not have to mean only coming to an end; it may mean simply reaching the high point of life ("being unto the end"), after which just living on or dying off is not very important at all. But there may well be several such "deaths" in life; there may be a whole cycle of them. Perhaps philosophy must die in order to be able to live, and perhaps one day it must die and never again be born, in order to have lived well. There is nothing more pitiful to see than the man who should have died (he may even feel this) fifteen years ago, but is still stalking about, living in a twilight of memories and despairs. Is this not the picture of certain classic philosophers? Only an abstract and willful ideology can mislead us into thinking, that we and our philosophies with us were never meant to die. Death, both as coming to an end and being unto the end, should be a welcomed part of life!

Does the new thinking of philosophy lead us into yet another abstract world alienated and mechanized like the old one we learned to leave? Once we have become established in the bodily dimension — which is neither merely corporeal nor carnal but the full human dimension without the dualism of mind and physical body — will there by any need for a "first" philosophy, which tries to regard life as abstracted from the concrete, flesh-and-blood dimension of our earthly life? A first philosophy leads even with the best and noblest of intentions to a world somewhat or even completely apart from the living world. It was thus Husserl's intention — despite the difficulty of his language — to lead us gradually back into the lived world. What is life? Does it mean a new kind of anti-intellectual existence? Hardly. It simply means that instead of grounding our being in an abstraction we ground it in the "ontological earth" of which our ontological body is a part. We can continue to have fun and games with the abstract intellect, but now we know that intellect is a bodily faculty, i.e. that it is grounded in the living fact of the bodily dimension, as "ontological." Put simply: there is no longer a short-circuit between head, heart and hands. And thinking with the head no longer replaces thinking with our entire body. Rather it has its place, high as that may be, only in the context of and grounded within the fact of the fully human dimension of body and earth.

What is the ontological body? What is ontology? Heidegger writes that traditional metaphysical ontology must be overcome and give place to a true, physis-bound ontology. The overcoming of metaphysics results in a return from the abstract or ontic dimension of being to the living and earthbound dimension of physis. In this, the study of the pre-Socratics, as suggested by Neitzsche and as carried out by Heidegger, is of great help in priming us. In the sketches of a posthumous book, *Visible et Invisible*, Merleau-Ponty himself began to write on physis. Earlier he had written on the logos as cogito. Here we see the close link between the bodily dimension and the treatment of both logos and presumably physis in his work — though it is never adequately spelled out. The opposite is true of Heidegger. While he leaves much to be desired in delineating the importance of body, he does much concerning the treatment of both logos and physis. A dialogue between the bodily dimension as spelled out in Sartre and Merleau-Ponty and the "concept" of physis and logos in Heidegger might be of great assistance to us in understanding the concrete dimension in Heidegger and the bodily in the French phenomenology. And in all this we must reiterate what Husserl has written concerning "bodily selfness" and physis as well. Such a work remains to be written. But the point we want to make here is that it all leads us out of the world of the abstract, i.e. the *monde-en-idée*, into the world of realities, i.e. of flesh-and-blood facts, and of bodily "transcendence," which does not propel us outside ourselves toward another world, but takes place within us as we reach out bodily for the other.

We see that as far as "thinking" is concerned a revolutionary new definition is called for. Thinking will, then, hardly be only abstract intellection or logical reasoning. It will be essentially a reaching out for the other, a reaching out for the living world, and intellection will be but a part of it, sometimes not even the major part. In reaching out for the other, so that I may be in the world and on the earth, abstract philosophizing may or may not be of assistance. In fact it may be our greatest hindrance. Thus it is not sufficient to talk or think about being in the world: we must do it. And we "do it" through body, i.e. as full human beings, acting not only abstractly but concretely, so that being in the world means not just knowing it intellectually, but feeling it in our hands, our hearts, treading on it with our feet, reaching out "sexually" for that contact with other which makes a home and a family and continues the "lived" world in its fullest human dimension. When this stage is arrived at, do we need or want "philosophy"? Obviously this new "first" philosophy is a kind of last philosophy, a kind of end to mere philosophizing. An end to forever thinking about things and merely talking about things. Here begins the language of silence and the full bodily or ontological dimension. The last philosophy lecture must lead directly into the silence of being in and "doing" the world.

What does this "silence" entail? Is not the silent cogito, of which Merleau-Ponty speaks, the coming to an end of intellectual chatter? Especially in the limit-situation, the uselessness and the limitations of traditional thought and talk become evident. We are rendered speechless. Thought and talk come to a sudden halt. We are silent and change over to a new dimension. It is here that the bodily dimension becomes fully engaged — or at least can be. It is here that we begin to "think" with our hands, our feet, our heart, rather than with the "cold light of reason." It is here that ideological considerations prove to be worse than useless. It is here that we are not just abstractly in the world but that we actually "do the world." This doing of the world is no longer "philosophy." But it is bodily thinking, as bodily contact with things. Thinking does not just have a relation to things. Think and thing are one. Only the logico-grammatical fiction of verb and noun keep them apart. And in the limit situation, if that artificial distinction remains absolute, it entails the destruction of personality. The silent or bodily language means breaking out of the straightjacket of abstract thought, which objectifies things. It is the restoration of the true subjectivity (which is not "subjective") of both thinker and thing. Thing in this case is not a material object but a living being. All things are alive — in their own manner, if not according to a narrow human definition.

With regard to "literary" philosophy we are beginning to realize — perhaps fully — why people such as Sartre are only "part-time" philosophers. His plays are frankly much better reading. And seeing his plays is far more rewarding than reading them. But actually hearing his language is what makes these plays living works of art of the highest kind. It is the musical sound of the French language, not its purported intellectual clarity, that makes it one of the most beautiful tongues on earth. Gabriel Marcel, who speaks again and again of a concrete philosophy, also took to writing plays — with considerably less talent and success than Sartre. But in his essays he writes that he is most himself when improvising on a keyboard, and in his latest talk in Frankfurt, where he was awarded the Peace Prize, he states that music is of the essence of philosophy. Though neither Marcel's plays nor his own music can be compared with his essays, his intent is at least in the right direction: toward life, not just abstract philosophy. Perhaps the finest example of all this is Albert Camus. Though dabbling in philosophy (and having read many books half-way, as he admits in *La Chute*) he was — and knew he was — par excellence an essayist. His own life was doubtless more important to him than his essays, a life that came too soon and too young to a sudden end. But it was an end for which he was doubtless ready, an end he had already accepted long before.

There were hundreds of thousands of years before the emergence of what we call "philosophy." And both *philia* and *sophia* were most concrete before the emergence of a *prote philosophia*. The *philosophos* of Heraclit is not an abstract thinker. Philosophy itself arose not out of an abstract "pursuit of truth" but out of the concrete agonal tendency of sacred play, if we are to give credence to such important insights as those of Huizinga, Fink, and others. Even Plato admitted that we must know when to let philosophy alone and tend to more important things. Perhaps philosophy was meant to exist only once: it was a distinctly Greek phenomenon. Perhaps all else is but a shadow of the original, meant to fill the void at the heart of medieval Christianity and our modern world. Perhaps our western philosophy from medieval times until today is but an illusion, an illusory world that has given birth to a series of monsters: ideologies, theories, abstractions, which keep us from life rather than explain its mysteries. If so, the end of philosophy is something ardently to be desired. Perhaps a concrete philosophy means overcoming nor just metaphysics but the very idea of philosophy as such. Though this might possibly be interpreted as anti-intellectual, it might well be the end of mere pseudo-intellectuality with its partial successes and abysmal failures. It might be the rebirth of genuine understanding of life, and understanding that will assign a much more modest role to mere intellection.

With Nietzsche as guide, Heidegger goes back to the time when philosophy and thinking were concrete (if not "bodily"). This does not mean making the pre-Socratics some sort of "golden age." But it might mean using such a dialogue as a primer for a concrete and bodily thinking of our own. The medieval world view cannot be so employed, since it is far too abstract, even as it insists that concepts can be embodied. But we do not want an embodied world. We want a bodily one, because we already are bodily. Our "thinking" is already grounded in body, and body is not just corporality — and certainly not carnality. It is carnality, only, for an ascetic, and sensuality was brought into the world by Christian ascetism (cf. Kierkegaard's *Don Juan*). Neither body-cult nor soul-cult have a place in a bodily or ontological world. And here ontology means not abstract metaphysics but living physis.

Why do we call phenomenology transitional? Because it was never meant to be the last word on anything. Its whole aim, we might say, was to overcome a static tradition in philosophy and science and their questionable "realism." Heidegger makes it very clear in *Sein und Zeit*, in *Ein Gespräch von der Sprache*, and elsewhere, that his ontology is only preparatory, only *one* way of overcoming traditional ontic realism. His is definitely not regarded — least of all by himself — as a final solution or answer to anything. Surely neither Sartre or Merleau-Ponty can be accused of wanting to present their thinking as some sort of eternal verity. From its beginnings phenomenology (in its various branches, whether as ontology, existentialism or as a continuation of Husserlian thought) has sought not to become a new dogmatism. And now we may be able to say that it has reached a dead-end, insofar as it has exhausted the sight-metaphors (*Wesensschau, Sicht*, etc.) that have been a traditonal part of philosophy ever since Aristotle's "*Metaphysics*." As the author has treated elsewhere, sound seems to be the future of phenomenology, whether this be musical sound or the sound of spoken and acted language. The sound of traditional music is already sound that has been filtered through a definite intellectualistic interpretation of art. In as far as musical history bears the marks of musical theory or abstract musical philosophy of number, it, too, needs to come closer to sound, as sound, rather than as sound understood through light-metaphors (thus, music as understood and directed by theoretical "insight" and reason!). But phenomenological musical sound means not just music, that has overcome its own intellectual tradition and its concomitant submission (through *ars musica* and musical theory in general) to sight and light metaphors. It also means the sound of speech. And speech itself is not just lingual speech, but rather the speech of the whole man: his gestures and movements. *Thus musical sound looks to the whole bodily man*, or the *logos mousikos*, rather than just to the logos itself. In this sense a phenomenology of musical sound takes in what we now call music, dance and speech. And we restore a unity that was lost since the Greeks.

Perhaps this is the full bodily dimension we are looking for. And in it we discover far more "art" than philosophy. But this art work is not something objective; it is man, as artist, that is, as a full human being, who lives and dies, who is in the world and on the earth. A phenomenology of the arts lead not to a new philosophy but to art, and not to an art apart from life, but to life itself as *the* art par excellence. Thus, music, dance, and language will be grounded in life, and the "culture" that springs therefrom is neither for mere connoisseurs nor for dilettants — even in the grand style. It is an art or a life style that is the foundation of being truly human in oneself and in reaching out for the other. In this new world there is no need for mere philosophizing, for that will have proven itself needless temporizing or harmful hesitation. Any philosophy of the arts from then on will be not the result of abstract thought combined with art theories. Rather, there will be the *musicus*, who in the full sense of the historical word is not just a musician, but also not only a philosopher. He will be someone who muses and makes music, whether on an instrument or in his life, thus finding both himself and the other in a living dialectic which embraces the spiritual and the material world we actually live in and struggle to build as a decent place for all people to live in and enjoy.

ACKNOWLEDGMENTS

Appreciation and acknowledgment is hereby extended to the following journals and publishers for release of materials used:

Main Currents in Modern Thought, "Prelude to a phenomenology of sound"

The Southern Journal of Philosophy, "Insights leading to a phenomenology of sound"

The Journal of Value Inquiry, "Further insights into a phenomenology of sound"

The Journal of Phenomenological Psychology, "Musical sound as a model for Husserlian intuition and time-consciousness"

Music and Man, an Interdisciplinary Journal of Studies on Music, "Aesthetic re-education: the experiencing of musical sound"

Philosophy Today, "Some notes on the meaning of analysis"

Aisthesis and Aesthetics, Duquesne University Press, eds. Strauss/Griffith, "A phenomonology of musical aesthetics"

Institute of Medieval Music, "Does musicology need a new method?"

Musico-Aesthetic Education, a Phenomenological Proposition, A. Motycka, GAMT Press, "The phenomenology of sound: Akoumenology"

Music Education for Tomorrow's Society, Ed. Motycka, GAMT Press, "Music educating as phenomenologist: an overview"

DATE DUE

DEMCO 38-297